LAST ORDERS

DENZIL MEYRICK

bantam

TRANSWORLD PUBLISHERS

UK | USA | Canada | Ireland | Australia
India | New Zealand | South Africa

Transworld is part of the Penguin Random House group of companies
whose addresses can be found at global.penguinrandomhouse.com.

Penguin Random House UK, One Embassy Gardens,
8 Viaduct Gardens, London SW11 7BW

penguin.co.uk

Penguin
Random House
UK

First published in Great Britain in 2025 by Bantam
an imprint of Transworld Publishers

001

This book is a work of fiction and, except in the case of historical fact,
any resemblance to actual persons, living or dead, is purely coincidental.

The lyrics on p. 103 are from 'Let's Go Out Tonight'
by The Blue Nile, written by Paul Buchanan.

Every effort has been made to obtain the necessary permissions with
reference to copyright material, both illustrative and quoted. We apologize
for any omissions in this respect and will be pleased to make the
appropriate acknowledgements in any future edition.

Typeset in 12.75/16pt Minion Pro by Jouve (UK), Milton Keynes
Printed and bound in Great Britain by Clays Ltd, Elcograf S.p.A.

The authorized representative in the EEA is Penguin Random House Ireland,
Morrison Chambers, 32 Nassau Street, Dublin D02 YH68.

A CIP catalogue record for this book is available from the British Library

ISBN: 978-0-857-50640-5

MIX
Paper | Supporting
responsible forestry
FSC® C018179

LAST ORDERS

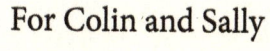

For Colin and Sally

PROLOGUE

The cemetery at Kinloch seemed chilly on the best of days. Cold winds from the sound funnelled out on to the loch, past the island that stood at its head, to tug at black ties, thinning hair, mourning dresses and widows' weeds alike. Still, the community came to say goodbye, a last fond farewell to a man they'd known as intimately as if he were one of their own family. They gathered to mourn the loss of a soul, ready to be cast into eternity by means of a wooden box and a gaping hole in the ground.

This day was no different from so many sad occasions of its kind – or perhaps it was. The corpse in the sleek hearse, adorned with a large wreath rendered in the shape of a fish, had been a firm friend to most. A listening ear in times of trouble and a teller of tales tall enough to pass a long night at the roaring fire of any Kinloch hostelry. Some were in awe of the man, so expansive, warm in his personal dealings, only rarely a note of admonition, of dire warning.

Even the silent voices of the interred at this depository of the dead joined in the lamentation, though only those who had a particular gift could hear their ghostly whispers from beyond death's great chasm. The very fabric of this old cemetery, they said, unlike others, was the thinnest of places, where this world all but touched the next.

They huddled round the grave of one of Kinloch's

legends, found dead in the streets of the town he had graced with his presence for so long. Young, old, man, woman and child alike, had tears brimming in their eyes, as the solemn undertaker and his men removed the coffin from the hearse, and went about the business of preparing it to be lowered down.

One woman, a niece of the deceased, cried out, as the polished wood encasement of eternity was placed above the grave on a pair of stout, wooden sleepers, its occupant now truly hovering betwixt this world and the next.

Tradition dictated that red winding cords attached at equidistant points around the casket be allotted to the selected mourners. Their numbers called out in order of seniority: the deceased's closest relative taking the first, followed by other family members, friends and former colleagues.

The symbolism of each bearing the weight of one so close as he made his final journey, lost on nobody. One day it would be them – perhaps one of the people standing round this very tomb with the tight, red winds of wool would do the same job for them.

'I hate this,' said Brian Scott. 'My faither always cried his eyes oot at funerals. I'm the same.'

'Pull yourself together, Brian,' said Jim Daley, standing tall, barely fitting into the suit trousers he was wearing. 'We're representing Police Scotland, remember. Wouldn't do for you to lose your dignity, would it? Not as though you've ever done that before.' He smiled. 'But I know how you feel. I hate it too.'

'Where's Lizzie? I thought she was coming.'

Daley shrugged his broad shoulders. 'She couldn't face it. Always says she'll be lowered down herself soon enough, without having to take in a rehearsal. It's her usual mantra when she's in bad trim. Her mother's the same.'

'She's still in the doldrums, then?'

'Yup.' Daley's expression was one of resigned acceptance.

The undertaker's voice was a counterpoint to their whispered conversation, as he shouted out each cord number like a rollcall.

'Number four, take your place, please!' His cry echoed from the hills that huddled round the cemetery, watching over, embracing the dead of the town. A piper, standing on a rise, began the heartbreakingly beautiful lament 'Flowers o' the Forest'. To any Scotsman alive, and quite likely many dead, the skirl of this tune induced every soul present to shudder at the pain of loss, the exquisite sadness of final parting – thoughts of their own mortality never far away.

'Number five, please!' The call was slow, precise.

An expectant silence descended over the mourners.

'Cord number five, take your place, please!' The undertaker's white hair was caught on a gust of wind, as his pale eyes searched those assembled. A low murmur overtook the mourners now. After all, number five wouldn't be the first or last to take on the allotted task, only to find it all too overwhelming to bear. Every time this happened, though, the townsfolk looked on the recalcitrant individual with something approaching a mix of sympathy and loathing. Privileged as this task was, all attention belonged to the dead, not the coward unwilling to bear the weight of a solemn undertaking.

'Hang on!' A vision from haute couture's worst nightmares wound his way through the throng. His kilt was too long, one sock flapped at an ankle while the other was raised above the knee, his waistcoat missed two buttons, and the black necktie in place round his neck was skewwhiff. 'I had trouble finding my kilt!' he exclaimed, as he hurried towards the yawning grave, still smoking his pipe.

3

The undertaker cleared his throat.

'Oh aye, sorry aboot this.' Hamish lifted one leg over the other knee and tapped the tobacco out of his pipe on the heel of his shoe. 'Right, Willie, that's me, carry on. Man, you're doing a fine job, so you are. I have my cord.'

Unfortunate incident almost forgotten, and cords now distributed, the minister, his eyes still fixed on Hamish, began to speak.

'Donnie Kerr was a fine man, friend to many, enemy of none. He was a pillar of the town's fishing community. Honest, even-handed – a man to be admired, to look up to.'

'Was he no' a right chancer?' whispered Scott into Daley's ear, only to receive a trademark glare in return.

The minister's voice then droned a hypnotic declaration of faith, his tones sometimes soft, modulated on the breeze, at other times loud, thundering appeals to God.

And so, in the manner and custom of this place, the laying to rest of Donnie Kerr, fish buyer, friend, counsellor, father, brother, son, uncle, husband, grandfather and, foremost of all, Kinlochian to his bootstraps, continued, as the grey skies that hung above the loch broke into silent tears of rain.

1

Glasgow, February 1997

The black BMW raced through the streets of Glasgow, its driver checking the rear-view mirror obsessively. As he turned sharply on to Clyde Street, he breathed a sigh of relief. There was no sign of the police car that had pursued him from the south side of the city.

He wondered where he could dump the car and continue his escape on foot. They knew the vehicle, that was true, but they couldn't identify its driver. He'd made sure that he left only the merest impression on records of the criminal underworld. He could make off calmly, slow his breathing, sit in a pub for a while until the fuss died down. He'd be free of it, problems over.

Even though Glasgow was following other British cities, with deployment of CCTV street cameras growing by the day, most were focused on the road or certain shops favoured by the chief constable or members of the City Council. The places he'd go would leave their trail cold. Run-down old buildings, back streets, the remnants of a rapidly changing world. In with the new, out with the old, the relentless refrain.

People milled about under a leaden sky. The shops were brightly lit, their colours and those of the traffic lights popping like ripe fruit in the gritty city gloom.

Suddenly, though, something in the rear-view mirror caught his eye. The flashing blue light of the police car winked at him from way back in the slow line of vehicles. He cursed his luck.

He put his foot down, manoeuvring quickly through traffic, narrowly avoiding an ambling pedestrian as he went. The roar of the powerful engine filled his ears, punctuated only by car horns and the shouts of protesting road users.

He flew through a red light, narrowly missing a lorry. The split second was like a blur, a moment in time that could so easily have been fatal.

'Shit!' he yelled, as the shock, relief and horror of it all washed over him at once.

'This guy's off his rocker, gaffer! I think we should back off before someone gets hurt,' said the uniformed constable driving Alpha Mike Three.

The detective inspector rubbed his chin with one hand, while holding on for dear life with the other.

'That's a negative, Lambie! If we don't keep him in line of sight, he can skip the motor and we'll never get him. This man needs catching, do you understand?'

'Yes, got it, sir.' Constable Gordon Lambie gripped the steering wheel even more tightly now, as he tried to emulate the movements of the vehicle he was chasing. Mercifully, the red light before him changed to green as he sped after the BMW. Lambie cursed the fact that he was driving a Vauxhall Vectra. In a straight race there was only one winner, and it wasn't going to be the police car.

'Look, he's been boxed in!' shouted the detective.

Lambie squinted ahead, wishing he'd never sat his police driving test, as advised by an older cop on his shift.

'Who wants to be stuck driving a motor when Glasgow's going like a fair? No' me, son. Just stick to Shanks's pony. Take the advice.'

The DI pulled at the wheel, making Lambie start. They mounted the pavement with two wheels.

'In between that green Transit and the Escort, quick!' shouted the DI.

Constable Lambie shut his eyes as he executed the manoeuvre, waiting for the sickening scrape of metal on metal. Thankfully, it didn't come.

As he looked on, he could see the BMW forcing its way past the little huddle of cars that blocked its path, black smoke belching from its tyres as the engine revved. They were within twenty yards of the Beamer now, but they'd have to keep up the pace.

The black car accelerated on to an open stretch of road.

'Come on, man!' roared the detective.

The constable didn't know when he first realized what was going to happen. The scene played out as though in slow motion. As he pulled past the last two cars between them and their quarry, he saw an orange corporation bus emerge in front of the BMW from a side street. The driver tried to swerve to avoid the collision, but he was too late. The BMW caught the bus a glancing blow and reared up like a plane taking to the skies. The vehicle rolled in mid-air over an empty road and pavement mercifully free of people.

As the police officers looked on, the BMW hit the barrier between road and river, somersaulted over it and landed in the Clyde with a crash and a great plume of smoke and water. Pedestrians screamed; one old man, drenched by the displaced river that landed on his head, shook his fist in the direction of the BMW, true to his Glaswegian spirit.

Lambie pulled in to the side of the road. He and the detective exited the police car. They gazed into the Clyde just in time to see the vehicle they'd pursued for almost twenty minutes sink below the brackish water in a flurry of steam, smoke and the acrid stench of burning rubber and spilt fuel, its alarm wailing in protest, gradually dulling due to the immersion. Despite being submerged, flames leapt from the vehicle's engine in flares, illuminating the river with the burning fuel that was resisting the dousing force of the Clyde.

Lambie looked on as the detective beside him stripped off, ready to dive in and rescue the driver. But as he tore at his shirt, there was a low rumble, followed by an ear-splitting explosion. The River Clyde danced with the flames from the stricken car, as the residue of petrol ignited on its brown waters. A tower of black smoke rose in the air in a small mushroom cloud. People screamed, stopped and stared, the morbid fascination of death too compelling to ignore.

'Fuck!' the detective cursed.

'You've nae right racing roon the place chasing folk. Look what you've done!' shouted a young woman with a pram. 'It's a fucking disgrace, so it is! My wean shouldnae be exposed tae this shite!'

Lambie began to shiver. He could hear the distant sirens of the approaching emergency services. He bent double and spewed on to the pavement.

'Not your fault, son,' said DI Jim Daley, consoling the man whom he'd encouraged to chase the BMW. A tyre blew from the submerged vehicle with a great pop, sending a large murmuration of starlings, soaring as one, from under a nearby railway bridge into the grey sky. It was almost as though they flew with the recently departed soul of the driver, now surely embarking on its final journey.

2

The Present

DI Brian Scott was sitting uncomfortably in Jim Daley's lounge. Despite the fabulous view of the loch and the hills and mountain beyond, he focused on the marching headstones of the cemetery across the still waters where they'd been only weeks before. He wasn't sure whether it was this silent presence of death or the argument raging from the kitchen that made him most melancholy. Bit of both, Scott reasoned.

DCI Jim Daley and his wife had never enjoyed the easiest of relationships. The former was as solid as the rock of Gibraltar, a sometime introvert of great depths and fluctuating mood. Liz was the opposite: gregarious, glamorous, witty – often cuttingly acerbic in her assessment of others. She loved holidays, parties, being amongst friends – life – though they both loved their son James junior dearly, and in equal measure.

Scott often wondered what had drawn the pair together. Then again, he reasoned, he and his own wife had many differences in personality. She was organized, determined and resourceful. He took out the bins.

As though someone had turned down the volume, the voices from the kitchen fell silent. Scott heard the heavy tread of his old friend as he made his way up the hall towards the lounge.

'Tea, wasn't it, Brian?' said Daley, his head popping round the door.

'Ach, nae bother, big man. We better get a move on and get to the office. We've that *doom* call from the boss to suffer.'

Daley smiled at Brian Scott's regular interpretation of a Zoom call.

'Yes, you're right. I don't know where the time goes, Bri.' He wandered to the mirror above the fireplace, knotted his tie and ran a hand over his cropped dark hair with a comb.

'Up its own arse, if you ask me, Jimmy.'

'Well put.' Daley smiled weakly. 'I better go and kiss Liz goodbye.'

Scott lowered his voice. 'I'd be careful she doesnae bite your nose off. Man, you were going at it in there.'

'It's the move.' Daley shrugged. 'She doesn't like it. She's been like this for months.'

'But she was the one who never wanted to come down here in the first place.'

'Well, that was before, apparently. She's made friends now. Her photography's selling on that website. She thinks this is a really good place to bring up young James, blah, blah.'

'Aye, I can see that. So, what are you going to do?'

'I'm going up the road myself for a few weeks, try and find a place that'll suit. I know you and Ella will keep an eye on them both. Once she sees a nice new house, things should get better.'

'It's no' going to be easy.'

'You don't need to tell me, Bri. But if you could do me the favour, I'd be grateful.'

'I don't mean difficult for me and Ella. I mean for you and Liz.'

'Right, I see. Yeah, it will.'

'Won't be easy up in Dumbarton, neither. You're the big boss now, my man. Head o' CID across the division.'

'And don't forget, you've got my old job to be getting on with.'

Scott sighed. 'I won't let you down, pal. I know you had to use all your powers o' persuasion to get this one across the line.'

'And then some.'

'Alistair Shaw says you telt them you wouldn't take the job unless I replaced you here. Is that true?'

'Alistair Shaw should learn to keep his mouth shut. He's no saint, as we all know.'

Scott raised his brows. 'None o' us perfect, big man.'

The door swung open, and Liz appeared.

'How you doing, Lizzie?' said Scott, and instantly wished he hadn't.

'I'm just fabulous, Brian. Life's a dream. My husband, who dragged us all down here in the first place, now wants to drag us all back from whence we came. It's great, isn't it? No thought for young James and his friends at school. And as far as I'm concerned, forget it.'

Scott opened his mouth to reply, but on reflection snapped it shut again. He'd seen this movie many times before. And with a tendency to make matters worse rather than better, he followed his wife's long-term advice and said nothing.

'We need to go, Liz.'

'Great! To be continued then,' she replied. 'I'll look forward to it.'

Daley and Scott drove across Kinloch in silence to the office, Daley brooding as he gazed out at the loch sparkling in the morning sunshine.

3

Hamish was weary, very weary. A man who'd spent most of his life rising with the sun, and long before in many cases, he lay in his bed staring at the ceiling, and it was nearly nine o'clock in the morning. He stroked the half-breed wild cat curled up on his chest as he pondered a great flap of paint peeling from above.

'These damned dreams, Hamish,' he said to the cat he'd named after himself. 'I just canna shake them.'

Hamish the cat mewled, almost as though it sympathized with its master's plight.

The old man lay there until the phone at his side on the nightstand burst into life.

'Kinloch two-two-seven-eight, Hamish speaking.' It was a mantra he'd repeated ever since he'd had a phone installed in the late eighties. This, despite the near certainty that the call would be somebody trying to sell him double-glazing or insurance.

'Are you still in your bed?' The voice on the other end was haranguing in tone. 'I can tell by how quickly you answered the phone. It takes you ages when you're in the living room.'

'Aye, and what about it, Ella Scott?' replied Hamish, most definitely on the defensive, but quietly impressed by his interlocutor's observation.

'Well, you'll need to get across here later. It's Tommy Cunningham's birthday. And you know fine he'll want you to be there.'

'Tommy, aye, he can take a fair swallow, right enough. No wonder you're so keen to have a party for him at the County, though I'm no' sure why he bothers going out to get drunk on his birthday. He's out drunk every day of the week. He should stay in with a cup o' tea and make the day special.'

'Full of the joys today again, I hear,' said Ella.

'You'd be the same if you'd no' had a wink o' sleep for nights on end.'

'You should get something from the doctor, Hamish. You cannae go on like this, a man o' your age.'

'Take pills? You know me. Sleep should be achieved naturally or not at all. Before you know it, I'll be hanging about at the surgery corner with a hole in my trousers, fair begging for stronger potions to keep me square. I know where that path leads, an' no mistake. My body's a temple, filled with natural things, like fish.'

'Aye, and they're swimming in whisky.'

'I'll have you know whisky is a cure-all for any kind o' malady. Is it not just three weeks ago a bit of rusty metal got stuck under my fingernail and it got poisoned? The doctor wanted me up the road to have it removed. I just bathed it in a glass of whisky – the cheap stuff, you understand. Before I knew it, the obstruction had gone, and my finger was as fresh as a wean's backside.'

'It's a miracle!' said Ella sarcastically.

'You'd have me on they *dopioids* until I was pissing where I sat. That day might come, Ella, but it's no' here yet.'

'Such a pleasant image.' She sighed and continued. 'I'll expect you tonight. I've not seen you for nearly a whole week. Aye, and there's plenty drams lying behind the bar for you from well-wishers. So, I doubt you'll have to put your hand in those shallow pockets of yours.'

'I'll think on it, Ella. It's kind of you to check in on me.'

'Somebody has to. I'll have Brian come down there and drag you to the County!'

'Man, many a time I've seen the polis drag folk oot o' pubs. I didn't think they performed the whole process in reverse. Now, there's a thing.'

'I'll see you later.' With that, Ella ended the call.

Though Hamish missed her predecessor, Annie, he'd become used to Ella Scott behind the bar at the County Hotel. She was a kind woman, despite her sharp tongue. Mind you, he reasoned, it took a sharp tongue to keep Brian Scott in order.

Hamish ushered the cat from his chest and sat up. He levered himself out of the bed and, in his tattered slippers and frayed tartan pyjamas, padded into the lounge, past the plaster bust of Winston Churchill atop the rough table made from fish boxes, and into his tiny kitchen – or galley, as he liked to think of it. He put the kettle on the gas hob to boil for his tea then sat himself at the kitchen table.

Hamish rubbed the sleep from his eyes and stared at the book before him. It was *London from the Air*, photographed by a gentleman called Joseph Hiscox. He'd bought it at a sale of work held in aid of the church, no more than a month ago. And since then, he'd stared at one image again and again. On pages forty-six and forty-seven, the great River Thames meandered like a huge serpent through the city. He followed its course with the tip of his stubby right index finger. The whole exercise made him shiver, and he felt the same sensation of despair he'd experienced in every dream he'd had for weeks on end.

Hamish banged his fist on the table.

'Damn me! Stop torturing yourself, man.'

Only the insistent whistling of the boiling kettle roused him from these dark thoughts. The old fisherman knew that something was wrong – very wrong. Had it been the loch outside his window that haunted his thoughts, maybe he could have fathomed what was going on. But he had no connection to London, much less the Thames. The troubling nightmares remained a mystery.

Hamish sat back with his strong tea, resisting the temptation to lace it with a dram. Quickly reasoning that it was a bit early, even for him.

'Aye, what's it all about?' he said to himself quietly.

4

Daley and Scott sat in the AV room at Kinloch police office, the huge screen in front of them flickering as Sergeant Alistair Shaw hammered away on a computer console.

'Bugger me, Al, have you no' got the hang o' this yet? It's been here for years, man,' said Scott, regarding the lack of a connection with a jaundiced eye.

'You'll remember what the wifi signal is like here in Kinloch, Brian. It's not as easy as it looks. We'll have to go on to Starlink if I can't get the broadband to work.'

'As long as you beam the boss up before me,' said Scott.

Daley checked his watch. They were due to join the assistant chief constable in two minutes. If they didn't, it would reinforce the theory at HQ that everything in the sub-division was calamitous. He supposed it was no longer his problem. His new role as head of divisional CID would land the responsibility firmly on Scott's shoulders.

Did he think his old friend was up to the challenge? Yes, he did. But such were the shifting sands of regulations governing police officers' lives, he did have a concern that Scott – firmly anchored sometime between the Dark Ages and the eighties in policing terms – might struggle to adapt. Daley decided not to worry about it.

'There we go!' exclaimed Shaw, as the jaggy thistle Police Scotland logo appeared on the screen. 'Can you say something for sound levels, please? One after the other.'

'Testing, testing, one, two, three,' said Daley in a steady voice.

'All cops are bastards!' shouted Scott, repeating the chant often heard on the football terraces.

'I beg your pardon?' said ACC Sam Jordan, his face filling the screen. He was one of the youngest officers to make it to the ranks of assistant chief constable. He was also notoriously difficult. He raised his chin, blue eyes flashing. 'Tell me I didn't hear that!'

'Naw, it's absolutely fine, pal – sir. Me and Jimmy, we was just discussing a case,' said a flustered Scott.

Daley marvelled at the way Brian Scott delivered this lie without hesitation, deviation or a red face.

'DI Scott, I hope you realize it's time to *screw the bobbin*, as I'm sure you say.'

'Aye, sir, definitely. Spot on!'

Daley raised his brow in frustration. At the same time, he knew there was nothing he could do about Scott's propensity to put his foot in it. He also knew there was nobody he'd rather have at his side in times of crisis. Things had a habit of balancing themselves out for the best in the long run. And Scott always seemed to be just on the right side of the balance sheet when the numbers were totted up.

'I take it the handover is going well, DCI Daley?'

'Yes, sir. That is to say, DI Scott is intimately acquainted with the environment and our procedures. This won't be the first time he's taken charge, of course.'

ACC Jordan flashed a youthful smile. 'Yes, I seem to remember a memo that pointed out he had ten officers on one shift and two on another. An odd deployment of personnel, wouldn't you say?'

'Intelligence, sir,' said Scott.

'Really? That's a surprise. I didn't know you had any.' Jordan's turn to raise a brow.

'A tip-off about a squad o' bikers heading this way. You can't be too careful in the rurals, sir. Get it wrong, and you're on your own.' Scott sat back, looking pleased with this explanation.

'The same as threatening to defecate in someone's dinner?'

'No, that was a joke, sir. Taken the wrong way by the humourless bastard concerned.'

'The *humourless bastard* being a frail man in his eighties.'

'I don't think he was anywhere near that age.'

'DI Scott, do you know that you are one of the main topics of conversation at the Senior Officers' Association dinners? Oh yes, how we laugh – and cry.' Jordan leaned into the screen, making his head even larger for those watching in Kinloch. 'No more jokes, Brian. Got it?'

'Yes, sir,' said Scott.

ACC Jordan sat back. 'Now, I have some information to impart. It's come from Special Branch in London.'

'Sir?' said Daley, already intrigued.

'It would appear we've had a security breach. It was so well executed, we didn't notice ourselves. Took the boffins from the Security Service to pick it up. They passed it on to the Met. It would appear as though your records have been compromised, DCI Daley.'

'In what way, sir?'

'Your entire service record was accessed. Every dot and comma of your career. Only *your* records – nobody else is involved.'

'What for?' Daley looked nonplussed.

'No idea, Jim. Though it's fair to say you have rattled a few cages in your time. Both in the underworld and in police circles. We've decided to install a panic button at your domicile in Kinloch, as well as wherever you intend to lay your head when you take up your new post.'

'A panic button? So, my family are in danger? Is that what you're saying, sir?'

'Just a precaution. There's absolutely no intelligence that marks you out as a target of any kind. No internet traffic, either. Dark web included. Probably some spotty teenager in his bedroom trying to prove how smart he isn't. You know the score. At worst, some idiots testing our response. Nothing to do with you, per se.'

'My wife and son will be on their own when I go back up the road, sir. I feel uncomfortable about it now. Panic button or no.'

'They won't be joining you?'

Scott looked at the floor, knowing the prospect of Liz Daley and their son making the move to Dumbarton looked reasonably unlikely.

'It's complicated, sir. Schools, my wife's job, housing – that kind of thing.'

'And yet you told us when you were interviewed that none of this would be an issue.'

Daley bit his lip. The last thing he'd expected was for Liz to be difficult about moving back to *civilization*, as she was wont to call it since their arrival in Kinloch. 'It isn't a problem, sir. Honestly, just taking a little longer than I expected to get the logistics organized.'

'Good. The last thing we need are any domestic setbacks. I need you to help us lower the crime rate in your new job. Bloody Edinburgh is on our back – at the very highest political levels. And if you have any lingering concerns, well, I'm sure the scheduling genius that is DI Scott will be able to spare an officer or two to look after your family before they join you in your new home. Isn't that right, DI Scott?'

'Aye, you've nailed it there, sir. Bang on, chief,' Scott replied with rather too much gusto.

ACC Jordan looked at his desk before addressing his charges in Kinloch once more. 'This will be in your inbox by now, gentlemen. But I thought I'd mention it too. We have a missing person, believed to be heading your way. When I say missing, I should say *absconded*.'

'Who, sir?' said Daley and Scott, almost in unison.

'You probably won't remember him, Jim. It's a long time ago. Gordon Lambie, a former constable from Stewart Street.'

Daley puzzled over the name. It wasn't ringing any bells.

'I remember him,' said Scott. 'Drove you a few times – the Cherwell case, Jimmy. The motor in the Clyde.'

At Scott's prompting, Daley recalled Lambie. He'd been at the wheel of the car when they'd been chasing Anthony Cherwell. The elusive figure who'd brought a huge quantity of high-grade heroin into the city that had killed addicts left, right and centre. It took them weeks to identify him as the man who'd died in the submerged car. He had no previous criminal history; in fact, the reverse. Cherwell had been a high-flying businessman before he discovered an easier way to make money.

'Yes, sir. I remember Lambie now. Highly strung. Blamed himself for the accident and Cherwell's death.'

'Yes, left the job not long after. Drifted into alcoholism and worse. He was sectioned when he tried to kill his wife and son with a carving knife, albeit in a half-hearted manner. Been away ever since. He managed to escape during a private psychiatric appointment out with the State Hospital. He'd been telling other inmates he was going to do it, and head to Kintyre. Your name was never mentioned, Jim. But there's the connection to Cherwell and that car chase. I'm sure you understand.'

'I do, sir,' said Daley.

The rest of the meeting went as planned. When Jordan's face eventually disappeared from the screen, Scott slumped in his seat, found his cigarettes and lit one.

'How many times, Brian? You can't smoke in the office!'

'Ach, who's to know, Jimmy? Are you going to fire me?'

'No, I'm going to throw a bucket of water over you.'

'Lambie, eh? There was an odd one, right enough.'

'I felt sorry for him. He genuinely blamed himself. Couldn't hack it, the lad. I should have done more for him.'

'He wasn't your responsibility, Jimmy. That's why we have Human Resources. Not that they give two fucks.'

'Exactly, Brian.'

'I bumped into him in Glasgow once. Man, he was in some state. Looked like a tramp. I gave him a twenty spot.'

'Which he no doubt used to buy booze.'

Scott shrugged. 'What are you going to do, eh? You're not worried about him, I hope. But they files, that's creepy, don't you reckon?'

'I do. It's just another worry, to be honest.'

'Don't even think about it, pal. You know fine I'll look after Liz and the wean when you're away. Surely you trust me to do that?'

'I do. Without question.' Daley thought for a moment. 'We're planning a break before I go. Just the two of us. You know how she loves a weekend in London.'

'Oh aye. Spends a fortune, if I remember right.'

'Oil on troubled waters. Would you and Ella mind looking after the wee chap?'

'Aye, no bother. I'll be about if she's at work. And I know you've got that child minder. You know we love having the wee fulla.'

'I do. Thanks, Brian.'

'Don't you go worrying about everything. Mountains and molehills. There're some right weirdos on the internet, and as far as Lambie's concerned, just forget him. All is rosy, big man.'

Daley smiled, but it was with a heavy heart that he left Kinloch police office comms room.

5

The old hotel in the Mid Argyll village had seen better days. Paint was peeling everywhere, doors creaked open and shut, the windows were cracked and grubby, and the carpet was sticky enough for guests to believe it was trying to forcefully prolong their stay.

The hotel was isolated, off the main route through the county. Best of all, nobody cared who came and went. The dishevelled man in the grey sweatshirt, jeans and old trainers, his goods and chattels in a large plastic carrier bag, attracted no comment when he arrived brandishing a pre-paid credit card. The staff had seen many stranger sights.

He'd lain low, mostly ordering his meals via room service. His daily routine for the last five days had been to scale the small hill behind the hotel to check the distant road and surrounding landscape, though he was pretty sure nobody would find him here.

Thoughts of living out his life in this place were appealing – until, that was, he remembered the funds that had been paid into his credit card were hardly limitless.

He stared at his reflection in the broken dressing-table mirror. His dirty grey hair, unshaven wrinkly face that sagged with bags, and washed-out eyes. He could easily have passed for a man twenty years older than his actual age.

But none of that mattered now. Gordon Lambie had lost everything – his job, family, dignity, and any sense he had of himself. In short, he was a husk of the younger man who'd once had so much ambition. The bright schoolboy who should have gone to university, until his overbearing father insisted he get a *proper* job and join the police or the military. He'd chosen the former; the lesser of two evils, he'd reasoned at the time.

Lambie reached into the pocket of his jeans, his hand trembling from the lack of the alcohol to which his body had become accustomed. He pulled out a crumpled piece of paper; a young police officer, eyes wide, stared from the newspaper clipping.

The journalist and photographer had caught him by surprise, leaving the front door of Stewart Street police office, ready to walk the beat. Since the chase a few weeks before, he hadn't been permitted to drive police vehicles.

SHOULD THE POLICE BE ALLOWED TO CHASE SUSPECTS TO THEIR DEATHS?

The headline was stark, brutal. He had become the poster boy for injustice; the nuance being that he was also the embodiment of an oppressive police force. A man who cared nothing about chasing down another human being until they died in a flaming, submerged horror.

But Gordon Lambie knew all he'd done wrong was to follow orders from the big, obsessive detective inspector whose face didn't stare from the pages of the newspaper. No, his seniority enabled anonymity.

'I fucking hate you, Daley!' he shouted at the top of his voice. He'd used those words like a mantra for more than twenty years. They slipped off the tongue like the lyrics to an old song or lines from a treasured poem.

It was time to put things right, once and for all.

Lambie picked up the bus timetable the woman at reception had given him. He had to catch the bus to Lochgilphead on the side road near the hotel, then onwards to Kinloch.

Gordon Lambie knew exactly what he was going to do once he got there. He'd gamed it out over and over again in his mind. It would be sweet, sweet revenge.

He lay back on his bed and played the same movie out in his head. It was one he'd seen a thousand times. Then, more quietly this time, 'I fucking hate you, Daley. It's time for you to find out how my life feels.'

Lambie had been studying the hotel and its staff since his arrival. Overall, it was a quiet place, with a few guests here and there, plus a couple of older people who appeared to be long-term residents, likely paid for by the council.

A tall, ruddy-faced man called Shearer was grandly called the head chef, though his actual duties consisted more of knocking up some old standards like fish and chips, tarting up cuts of beef, mince and tatties, cauliflower cheese for vegetarians and some off-the-cuff desserts. Quite often, he heated meals in the microwave. He was assisted by a spotty youth, who said very little and followed his mentor about silently, while constantly checking his phone.

Irene was the receptionist-cum-manager-cum-barmaid. She was a cheery soul who smiled and said all the right things. Uncomplicated, just the way Lambie liked it. These three members of staff, plus the odd chambermaid and regular customers, often sat themselves in the bar at half two every day, just after it closed for the afternoon. They'd pass the time of day over a few drinks or a coffee before the place reopened at six and the kitchen began its business for the evening.

Sure enough, when Gordon Lambie walked into the bar, there they all were – the chef and his assistant, Irene; an old soak he'd seen often who was a resident; and a young woman he marked out as a cleaner, mainly because she was sitting beside a bucket and mop.

'Mr Daley, come in and join us,' said Irene cheerfully. 'You know how we love a wee soiree in the afternoon.'

Lambie knew his alias was a risky one, but it was the first name that had come to mind when the pre-paid card was arranged for him.

'You're fine – but thanks for the offer. I'm a bit knackered, just been up the hill. It's quite hot out there.'

'You should try that bloody kitchen,' said Shearer. 'Totally roasting, man.'

'I don't envy you your job in this weather, Mr Shearer.' Lambie leaned on the sticky Formica counter. 'Could I have a can of Coke for my room, please? I fancy a wee lie down.'

'Sure thing,' said Irene, manoeuvring herself off the high stool. 'Will I just stick it on your bill?'

'Aye, that would be fine, thanks,' Lambie replied.

Irene handed her guest the can of Coke. 'Are you joining us for dinner this evening, Mr Daley?'

'Yes, I'll be down about seven.'

'Fish and chips again, is it, Mr Daley?' the chef asked.

'I do like my fish and chips, Mr Shearer. Can't get enough.' He smiled awkwardly then grabbed the Coke. 'Have a nice afternoon, folks.' He nodded and made his way out of the bar.

'He's such a nice man,' said Irene in an undertone she no doubt thought wouldn't be heard.

'Fucking weirdo, if you ask me,' said Shearer. 'I mean, who has the same meal every night, eh? Plus, all the moping about. No' the full shilling, if you ask me.'

Lambie had lingered at the door and heard every word of this exchange. It didn't bother him in the slightest. After this was over, everyone would know just what kind of man he was.

A long corridor ran from the hotel's front door, past the bar entrance, the toilets, and then to the kitchen at its very end. Lambie held his breath as he looked about before he made his way down it.

The kitchen was a mess. Dirty dishes piled high in two sinks, filthy worktops, shelves, hotplates and cookers. Lambie felt a few moments of revulsion at the thought of having eaten food from this awful place. He swallowed back the retch in his throat and looked around. In a way, it was better for him that such chaos reigned in the hotel kitchen. They wouldn't miss a thing, he reckoned.

Lambie found two knife blocks, with various sizes and shapes of the utensils nestling in little slots. The first block looked new, the hilts of the knives untarnished and clean. The older block was stained and shoved to the back as though no longer in use. When Lambie pulled the largest knife from its slot, though, he was pleased to see that the blade gleamed. It would do. He threaded the knife through his belt under his jumper and stacked up some clean pots in front of the knife block. In this mess, nobody would miss it.

He was about to exit the kitchen when he heard the pad of feet walking down the corridor outside. In his panic, Lambie pinned himself against the wall, knowing that, when the door was opened, he'd be hidden from sight.

The marching feet stopped, and Lambie held his breath,

29

a bead of sweat dripping down his nose. It seemed like hours before he heard the tell-tale squeal from the men's toilet door as it was pushed open on its transom.

Lambie waited a few seconds and edged himself out of the kitchen door. Almost on tiptoes, he crept silently past the toilets, down the corridor and out into the lobby. He took the stairs to the second floor and his room two at a time, being careful not to trip on the threadbare carpet. He breathed a long sigh of relief as he closed the bedroom door behind himself.

Lambie removed the carving knife from his belt and examined it. He ran his index finger down the blade, smiling when his own blood appeared as a crimson line on a fingertip.

'You'll do the job nicely,' he mumbled to himself as he opened the bedside drawer and hid the knife under some brochures. Silently, he played out what he intended to do in his mind and smiled.

6

Hamish was dozing in his old armchair, his feline namesake off on his nightly visits to the hill to chase rabbits and any other creature that moved. Eventually, he'd come back through the improvised cat-flap Hamish had cut in the back door, pad to his master's bed and sleep, his thirst for murder sated for another evening. The old man loved the half-breed wild cat. It was one of the few things from which he took solace these days.

The old wireless was crackling out some big-band standards. They penetrated Hamish's restless sleep and set the fisherman dancing in his dreams with old girlfriends and lost loves. But when Hamish embraced Sandy Hoynes, his former skipper, readying for a waltz, he muttered himself awake.

'Good heavens, Sandy. I loved you dearly, but no' enough to take you for a spin round the floor.' Hamish mashed his dry mouth and contemplated the brewing of yet another cup of tea. Unusually for him, such was the intensity of his nightmares, he'd tried to stay off the whisky; that was just making things worse.

He stared over at the plaster bust of Winston Churchill. 'Aye, Winnie. Just like yourself, I've got a dose o' the black dog, I'm thinking. Though the whisky isn't working for me just as well as it did for yourself. Mind you, I'm no' the civ-ilized world's last hope. I'd have been fair guttered every night if I'd to suffer your responsibilities.'

Just as Hamish was contemplating levering himself from the armchair, an insistent knock sounded at the door.

'Och, bugger it. Who's that at this time o' night?' He shuffled across the living room, switched off the wireless and went out into the small lobby. 'Who's there? I've got a poker in my hand, aye, and I'll fair plant you a dunt on the heid if you've robbery in mind!'

'It's me, you daft old bugger,' said the voice from behind the door.

Hamish struggled with two latches and a mortise key before he could open the door. 'Brian. It's good to see you. Come away in.'

Scott sat himself down on the sofa, sinking as he always did into its oft-used cushions. His eye caught sight of a large, black spider making its way slowly but determinedly along the mantelpiece. It made its way over the man of the house's briar pipe, before disappearing into a crack in the wall.

'Is it a cup of tea you're after, Brian?' said Hamish.

'No, you're fine, thanks. I'm here on a mission.'

'I know fine why you're here, Brian Scott. That wife o' yours has sent you down to pressgang me to Tommy Cun-ningham's party.'

'Aye, that's right. And you know what Ella's like when she gets a bee in her bonnet; cannae wait until it's out flying round the room wae everyone chasing aboot after it.'

'Well, the bee will have to stay where it is, for I'm no' the least inclined for partygoing this night.' Hamish sat on his chair and folded his arms.

'You're looking a bit grey about the gills, old boy, if you don't mind me saying,' Scott observed.

Hamish shook his head and told Scott of his dreams.

'What kind of dreams, Hamish?' asked Scott. In anyone else, he'd have overlooked this problem. But he knew from bitter experience that the workings of this old man's head were to be ignored at risk of some peril.

'Deary me, I was dozing here in front o' the fire, and just about to take the floor with Sandy Hoynes! My heid's all over the place.'

Brian Scott made a face. 'Hoynes? Is that not your old skipper – the man that taught you all you know?'

'Aye, he did that. But the Boston Two-Step wasn't included, I'm here to tell you.'

'We all get bad nights from time to time. I know I've had a few.'

'Aye, wae your noggin filled with a bottle and a half of whisky, I don't doubt it.'

'You're a kind man, Hamish,' said Scott with a curl of his lip.

'It's no' so much the manner o' the dreams. Though they're unsettling enough, no question.'

'What then?'

'It's the location. Every night I'm down in London, down by the Thames. Every damn night.'

Scott's heart missed a beat, but he chose to ignore it. In any case, Hamish couldn't possibly know that the Daleys were about to take a break in the city. 'Is it you and auld Hoynes jigging doon Piccadilly, eh?'

'I might have known you'd be of no help.'

'Hamish, it'll just be some memory of London from a way back.' Scott looked round the room. Remembering Hamish's aversion to television, he altered what he was going to say. 'Maybe something you've heard on the wireless?'

'I was only in London once. Aye, and I couldn't get out of it quick enough. All that noise, people, endless bustle. No' to mention the tiny measures they serve in what passes for pubs. Nothing but a spit in the bottom o' a glass. It's a damn disgrace.'

'How long ago was that?'

Hamish sucked his pipe into life under the flame of a match. 'Let me see. We'd to apply for a special certificate to fish near the new NATO jetty. Man, thon was a pain in the arse, a body from every boat in the fleet all the way down there to fill in a form and be scrutinized. Aye, to keep fishing where we'd done for generations. Vetted, they said. I'd say it was nineteen sixty-nine, from memory. But don't quote me on that. No' that long ago.'

'Your idea of no' long ago and mine are two different things, Hamish. That was the year the Beatles were up on the roof.'

'And they should have stayed there. What a bloody racket. Give me Jimmy Shand anytime. Aye, or the Alexander Brothers. Clean-living lads that could fair hold a tune.' Hamish started humming a song.

'What on earth's that?'

'The one about the orphan. Still brings a tear to my eye to this day.'

'All the fun o' the fair back in the day, eh?'

'Things were better than they are now, Brian. Man, folk could leave their doors open in Kinloch, the planet wasn't setting itself on fire, and you didn't have to remortgage the hoose to buy a decent bottle o' malt whisky.' The old fisherman's face darkened. 'But I tell you this, Brian Scott. There's something dreadful afoot down in London. I've never felt a darkness like it. It's fair sucking the life out of me every night.' Hamish pointed at the detective with the stem of his pipe. 'I know folk think I'm a foolish auld man. But I'm telling you the truth!'

Having failed to persuade his friend to go to the party at the County Hotel, Scott sat with Hamish for a while longer then left. He knew he was in for a tongue-lashing from Ella, but he was used to that.

As he drove on the narrow road between Hamish's tumbledown cottage and Kinloch, a slight haze diffused the view of the town ahead, as if filtered for a perfect picture postcard. The summer had been a blessing so far. But on the west coast of Scotland, that could change so quickly to gales and driving rain.

That weather more reflected Scott's current mood.

The detective had always been a grounded person; it was the way he'd been brought up. There was little room for anything fanciful in Glasgow's old East End, where life was lived on the margins. Men worked if they were lucky enough, they got drunk, and staggered home to clever, resourceful women who made what was left over from the pub and the bookie last until the next pay packet. Lives were short and, in many cases, grim. But it was nothing out of the ordinary.

Scott had seen the evidence of Hamish's prescience with his own eyes. The old man had displayed an extraordinary talent for seeing things before they happened. This most recent bout unsettled him – unsettled him a lot.

7

Daley had strung out the last of the paperwork he had left to do as long as he could. His car had been returned from its service, so he had no excuse not to go home and face the music – the next movement in the symphony, as he often thought of his long-running arguments with Liz. The tone could change in an instant, as could the mood.

The loch looked magnificent in the summer evening sun. It was as still as glass, much to the consternation of those from the local yacht club, desperately trying to race its length and back. They looked to be moving at a glacial pace, the putter of tiny engines aiding their passage.

As he drove up the lane to his house on the hill, Daley was surprised to see a red van parked under the raised decking.

'Shit,' he mumbled to himself. 'They've not wasted any time.'

He'd worked out that the vehicle must belong to the men installing the panic button the ACC had talked about. He'd hoped to break this to Liz before it happened. Clearly, it was too late.

He took to the steps, and on opening the front door heard the tell-tale hammering and drilling associated with such a venture.

'What's this?' said Liz, her hands white with flour, a strand of hair hanging down over one eye. 'Why on earth do we need a panic button?'

'Listen, it's just a precaution. You know, with me going up the road and everything.' Daley shrugged.

James junior appeared from behind his mother; he was equally covered in flour, his face caked with the stuff. It was their weekly baking night. Something Liz and the wee boy enjoyed together.

'Mummy says it's because bad men are coming to hurt us, Daddy.'

Daley fixed Liz with a glare. 'Don't be silly. It's just like an alarm. It's just called a panic button. Hey, have you no homework?'

'Yes, Daddy.' The boy made a face.

'Well, go and get it, and we'll do it together.' Daley looked on as his son went upstairs to find his schoolbag.

'I'm not stupid, Jim. In all the time I've been married to you, we've never needed a panic button. Don't treat me like one of your dim coppers!'

'I've never been in charge of the divisional CID before. Or an acting superintendent, come to that. It's procedure, nothing else.'

'So, if I call Wilma Sloan, she'll tell me she has a panic button, too? After all, her husband's a chief superintendent in charge of the drug squad.'

As often was the case, Daley was wrong-footed by his wife's logic. She'd always been sharper than him when it came to a heated exchange of views. 'But he isn't leaving his family to go and work somewhere else, is he?' It was all he could muster.

Liz shook her head. 'You know, something else crossed my mind.'

'What?'

'Are you just doing this to scare me back up the road with you? We all know you're devious enough.'

'Oh, for fuck's sake, listen to yourself!' His eye caught his son's face peeking through the banister.

'Daddy said another bad word, Mummy,' he cautioned.

'Daddy's good at bad words, James. Just make sure you don't turn out like him, OK.' She smiled at the boy. 'Come on, son. Let's get these cakes finished. You and Daddy can get your homework done later.'

James junior ran down the stairs, leaving his school rucksack on the hall table.

Daley retreated to the lounge, parked himself in his favourite chair and took in the magnificent view from the big picture window. As he tried to relax, a particularly frantic period of hammering broke out in the bedroom above his head, shredding what was left of his frayed nerves. He sat forward, massaging his temples with thumb and forefinger, until he could take no more.

'I'm going to the County for something to eat. I'll see you later,' he shouted on his way down the hall.

Liz poked her head from the kitchen and watched him go. 'Stay in the bloody County, for all I care,' she whispered to herself, as he slammed the door.

8

The coach, in its red-and-cream livery, pulled up at Kinloch's bus stance. A couple of dozen weary travellers stepped out, tired after the long journey from Glasgow. It was just after ten in the evening. Kinloch was a place of long shadows, as the sun sank in the west on the other side of the peninsula.

A small huddle of cars and a couple of taxis waited to pick up loved ones and customers. A teenage student returning from a university trip abroad embraced her parents, while a small man struggled up into an SUV, his face pale following the radiotherapy treatment he'd received in Glasgow.

Passengers almost dispersed, the coach's diesel engine chugged back into life, as it slipped away from the stance, leaving one man with a supermarket bag for life at his feet. He busied himself lighting a self-rolled cigarette.

He took a long puff and looked about at his surroundings. The loch, now dark with shadows, in front of him, the town's leisure centre behind. Carelessly flicking the stub of his smoke away, he picked up his bag, crossed the road and disappeared up a small lane between two buildings.

When he'd first arrived at the County Hotel, Daley had been surprised by the large number of customers on what, after all, was a weeknight. He was also surprised to see his colleague and friend Brian Scott miserably propping up the bar with a ginger beer and lime.

'It's auld Cunningham's birthday bash!' shouted Scott as Daley approached. 'Here, what can I get you?'

'Just a lager shandy please, Brian,' replied Daley. Somehow, since his old friend had forsworn alcohol, he'd felt awkward drinking in his presence, even though Scott didn't seem to mind. Scott reasoned that he'd put enough booze away to cover more than a few lifetimes, and it was everybody else's chance to have a go.

'A trip to London in the offing, I hear,' said Ella Scott as she delivered Daley's shandy. 'Nice. The furthest I get is a deckchair out the back when the sun's out.' This remark was directed at her husband, who raised his eyes by way of a response.

'Thanks for looking after my boy, Ella. You know how grateful I am.'

'Think nothing of it. It means I've got someone intelligent to talk to instead o' listening to this walloper day after day.' Ella smiled.

'I think we'll go through into the coffee lounge. I can't hear myself think,' said Daley.

'These auld boys make a right racket,' said Brian Scott. 'You go through, big man. I'll grab another ginger beer.'

The Scotts looked on as Daley made his way through the birthday guests.

'Bugger me, I've seen happier corpses,' said Ella. 'I thought he'd be in great trim about the promotion.'

'She doesnae want to go. You want to have heard them going at it this morning, doll. It's like World War Four up on that hill.'

'Hey, we've no' had a Three yet.'

Scott shrugged. 'I don't think we'll have long to wait.'

'That's what I've always loved about you, darling.'

'What's that?'

'Fuck all!'

'Charming, I'm sure.'

'Aye, well, toddle off and see if you can charm oor Jimmy into a smile. If his face trips him more than it is, he'll have a nasty accident.'

Scott, half pint of ginger beer in hand, followed Daley. The big detective was sitting in the lounge at the front lobby, a place normally reserved for those participating in coffee and cakes during the day. It was empty now, save for the police officers.

'No joy at home then?' said Scott.

Daley sighed. 'None at all. And to make matters worse, the men were there fitting this bloody panic button when I arrived.'

'What's herself saying to that?'

'She smells a rat.' Daley took a sip of his shandy.

'Looks like you could do with something stronger. If you don't mind me saying, that is.'

'You know I don't like knocking back whisky when you're there like Harry Hound Dog with a soft drink, Brian.'

'I'm no' bothered! How many times? I'm just here to give Ella a hand if things get rowdy.'

'Rowdy? Most of these old blokes can hardly lift their pension.'

'Aye, when they're sober. It's like Superman getting his scants on o'er his tights once they've had a jar or two.'

Daley smiled. 'I'll maybe get a dram next round.'

'Good man.'

Scott adopted a thoughtful expression.

'What's wrong, Brian?'

'Just a passing thought.'

'Spit it out.' Over the years, Daley had become used to his friend's mannerisms. Brian had something to impart – something either worrying or delicate, if he was right.

'Nothing really. Just, I was down at Hamish's a while ago. Ella was trying to get him up here for the party. He's no' been oot the house in o'er a week, so she says.'

'That's not good. What's up with him?'

'Dreams, would you believe?'

Daley looked suddenly weary. 'What kind of dreams?'

'Och, you know him. Nothing specific. Well, he's been dreaming about a place.'

'Is it the County?'

'You're no' taking this seriously, Jimmy.'

'OK, OK. Where's he been dreaming about?'

Scott fixed Daley with his gaze. 'The Thames, big man. Dark, awful dreams, he says. He cannae shake them.'

'What's awful about them?'

'That's just it, he doesnae know. Just that he has a bad feeling.' Scott shrugged.

'Oh wait, I know! You've instantly added two plus two and come up with twenty-seven, Brian?'

'Eh?'

'Liz and I are going to London. Hamish is having bad dreams about the place. Therefore, we should go somewhere else, right?'

'Well, something like that, aye,' said Scott coyly. 'Jimmy, you and me both know that man has something aboot him.'

'I hope you didn't tell him we were going to the Big Smoke.'

'No, I'm no' daft. That would just make him worse.

Though he'll find out. You know that. Cannae keep a secret in this toon.'

'And there you are.'

'There I am what?'

'It makes him worse. Listen, I'm the first to admit that Hamish has had some strange ideas that have come true. But let's face it, there's been a fair few that have been way off the mark.'

'No' so many that I remember,' said Scott.

'What about last Christmas? The party in here, when he went out for a smoke and came back and told us he was dead but not to worry because he'd seen his father.'

'Oh aye, that's right enough. Mind you, he'd a fair cargo aboard.' Scott made a drinking gesture.

'Or the time he saw all those UFOs out in the sound.'

'I remember that too, right enough.'

'Wait, were you not in the boat with him?'

Scott scrunched up his face, trying to remember. 'Man, you're right, Jimmy! I saw them as well!'

'And the green men, I daresay. Don't forget, I talked to the harbour master when you came back in. He'd never seen three men as drunk trying to get off a boat at the pier.'

'Aye, right enough.' Scott nodded sheepishly.

'So, don't worry about Hamish's dreams and fancies. In any case, the only other places Liz will want to go apart from London are Paris and Milan.'

'No' keen on Europe, Jimmy?'

'Not keen on being bankrupt. You've seen my wife in shops. Picture her in Milan!'

'Aye, you're right enough.'

'Hamish will snap out of it, he always does.' Daley took

to his feet. 'Right, what can I get you, Brian? I'm going to get a dram.'

'I'm fine, Jimmy. There's only so much ginger beer a man can shift.'

Daley found himself in absolute agreement with this as he made his way back to the crowded County Hotel bar. But despite himself, Hamish's dreams were unsettling. He decided that he'd enough to fret over as he ordered a large dram of Springbank.

9

As the clock ticked round to eleven thirty, Daley reckoned it was time to go home. He felt as relaxed as he had been for weeks, the whisky's soothing effect working on his troubled mind.

When he stepped out of the County Hotel, there was still an effervescence to the sky through the glare of the streetlights that heralded a short summer night.

The taxi rank, handily positioned outside the front door of the County, was populated by only one cab. Daley knew the driver, so they passed the short journey chatting companionably.

'You'll be missed, Mr Daley,' said Billy the driver.

'You'll have Brian Scott to look after you all,' Daley replied.

Billy hesitated for a moment. 'Aye, there is that, right enough.'

'You don't sound too convinced.'

'He'll be fine as long as he stays off the bottle. It's fair to say that I've had him in this taxi when he's had a good scatter. Aye, and no' just the once, neither.'

'He's on the wagon, you know that. And anyway, this is all confidential police business. Who told you I was moving away?' Daley almost asked the question in jest, knowing what the answer would be.

'You know fine it's Kinloch, Mr Daley. There's no' a body ever kept a secret for long in this place, and that's a fact.'

'True.' Daley nodded in agreement.

'And what about the auld yin?'

'Sorry?'

'Hamish. Man, he's in a right state. I was down at the cottage with some groceries for him yesterday. It must be the lack of company that's getting him down. They tell me he's no' ventured out the door hardly for a fortnight.'

'Perhaps a lack of whisky, Billy.'

'He's no lack o' that. A few tins o' beans, some tatties and a couple o' good malts – that was his shopping.' Billy coughed. 'Mind you, it's none o' my business what he gets up to. But there's hardly a soul in this town he's no' helped over the years. He used to bring my auld faither a bottle up to the hospital when he was on his deathbed.'

'I'll take a look in on him,' said Daley as the car took the steep road to his house on the hill.

'Man, that would be just the thing.'

The taxi stopped just under the steps to the decking and Daley's front door. The big detective paid for the hire and waved as he watched Billy drive off.

Daley stood for a moment, taking in the warm notes of a late-summer evening. The loch lapped at the shore far below, its essence filling his senses. He heard the squawk of some bird of the night and berated himself once more for not having learned to tell one species from another during his time in Kinloch. To his left, the moon was low in the sky, just above the dark looming mass of the island at the head of the loch, which framed it in magnificent silhouette. Another couple of holidaymakers lodging on the island had had to be rescued from the tidal causeway the previous day. It kept the local lifeboat busy. Daley shook his head at the risks some took with their lives against the advancing tide.

He turned swiftly when something rustled in the bushes behind him.

'Hello, is there somebody there?' he said, instantly feeling stupid at asking the question. After all, it was likely some animal or other: a cat, fox – any number of nocturnal creatures. He took to the steps, reckoning himself as bad as Hamish, jumping at every shadow. Nonetheless, even the few drams he'd consumed couldn't quell his instinct that something wasn't right. For once, Jim Daley ignored the feeling at the pit of his stomach.

He turned the key in his front door and tiptoed into the hall. As he'd hoped, Liz had gone to bed. The door to their room swished across the thick carpet as he opened it carefully. There she was, lying in their bed, framed by a shaft of moonlight through the diaphanous curtains billowing at the window to banish the heat of the day.

Daley stood at the end of the bed, admiring his wife as she slept. In the monochrome shadows she looked like an angel, peaceful and quiet. Her high cheekbones were picked out in this light, lips just parted, her breathing soft, the shape of her body marked out under the satin bedsheets.

He bitterly regretted their arguments, as he had done throughout their marriage. They were so different as people he often wondered just how they'd lasted for so long. And despite indiscretions on both sides, he felt his heart swell with love at the sight of this beautiful woman. Despite their many disagreements, he never wanted their relationship to end.

Quietly, stumbling about as he removed his trousers while hopping on one leg, Daley stripped down to a t-shirt and boxer shorts, before slipping between the soft sheets beside the woman he'd loved for so long.

'I can smell whisky,' she murmured, still half asleep.

'I can smell Chanel,' he replied, hushing her gently back to sleep, cuddling into the small of her back.

Jim Daley was asleep the moment his head hit the pillow.

All his life, Daley had been able to come to his senses quickly following sleep. The sudden bright light in his eyes made him sit up in bed with a start, even though he couldn't work out what was happening.

Sometimes, James junior crept into his parents' bed at night if he couldn't settle. But this was becoming less and less common now he was getting older. A bit like his father, James always entered the room as quietly as possible, waking neither his mother nor father if he could help it.

Only when Liz screamed did Daley force his eyes open, as he vaulted from the bed.

'What the fuck is happening?' he roared.

In the harsh glare of the ceiling light, a dishevelled figure was standing at the end of the bed.

'You've put weight on, sir,' said the man, brandishing something in Daley's direction.

'What? Who are you? Get out of my house, you bastard!' shouted Daley, backing off a little when he realized this intruder was wielding a large knife.

The man turned his gaze to Liz. He cocked his head slightly, as a dog would at something it didn't quite understand. 'They said you were pretty. Fuck, they were right,' said the knife-wielder. 'Oh, and you can press that as much as you like. Nobody's coming to help you, be sure of it.'

Daley looked across at his wife. Liz had pulled a bed-sheet up to her neck and was pressing something behind her nightstand over and over again. It dawned on him she was operating the panic button that had been installed earlier that evening.

The intruder turned his attention back to Daley. 'You don't remember me, do you?'

Again, though Daley's thoughts were still dulled by sleep, it didn't take him long to work out who this intruder was. After all, Daley had been told of this man's escape earlier in the day. *Nothing to worry about*, the ACC had said.

He could only see glimpses of the young constable he'd once known. The face that stared defiantly at him did so from underneath filthy salt-and-pepper hair, accompanied by grey stubble and folds of loose skin hanging from a scrawny neck, above a stained, baggy t-shirt.

'Come on, you're supposed to be one of the best detectives there is!'

'Gordon, put the knife down,' said Daley as calmly as he could muster. Despite the setting, he strove to assess the situation with as much professional detachment as possible. Though the policeman knew he wasn't in the best of shape, he reckoned that the emaciated figure of Gordon Lambie wouldn't be able to put up much of a fight once he was disarmed. But that was the tricky part. Daley took a step towards his former colleague.

Lambie rushed away from Daley to Liz's side of the bed. She shrank down under the bedclothes, seemingly too shocked to scream. 'You come any nearer me, and I swear I'll put this knife right through your pretty wife's belly!'

'OK, OK. We do this any way you want, Gordon. I know you've been ill. You're not thinking straight, trust me.

You're a good man.' Daley held up his hands in the meekest gesture of surrender he could muster. Surely he'd hear the wail of sirens soon, though he didn't understand what Lambie had said about the panic button. Underneath his calm demeanour, he was boiling with rage. Daley knew he might yet be the most dangerous person in the room. That he sometimes found it hard to keep his own temper in check was an understatement. He had to subdue these feelings and pray his son slept on in his bedroom down the hall.

Gordon Lambie turned his attention back to Liz, though the knife, its blade glistening in the light, still pointed at the man of the house. 'Do you know what your husband did to me?' he said.

'No!' Liz was sobbing now. 'I just want you to go.'

'I'll be gone when I'm done,' Lambie said menacingly. 'Pull that cover down, I want to see your face. Do you know they used to call you *Helen* at Stewart Street?'

'What?' Liz's response could barely be heard.

'Aye, *Helen. The face that raised a thousand dicks.* Did you know that, Daley?'

Jim Daley was on the edge now. He just wanted to pulverize the man who was making his wife cry with fear. 'Listen, Gordon. I can get you help, right? Get you back home to your family.' As he said it, Daley felt his heart sink. Had the ACC not said something about Lambie being put away because he threatened his family? He cursed his stupidity.

'Show your face!' Lambie demanded again of Liz.

Slowly, her body racked with sobs, Liz pulled the covers from her tear-stained face.

'They weren't joking, eh? Few years ago now, mind. But you've still got it.' Lambie moved towards her.

'I'm warning you, Gordon. Touch her and I'll kill you,' said Daley quietly.

In a flash, Lambie flicked the knife from one hand to the other, then brought it up to Liz's throat. Her squeal was strangled by the presence of the cold steel at her neck. Liz froze, eyes wide with terror.

'Your husband made me kill someone. Did you know that's the kind of man he is?'

'The man was murdering half of Glasgow with pure heroin. In any case, we didn't kill him. He killed himself trying to escape, Gordon. You have it wrong. We were the good guys.'

Lambie caressed Liz's throat with the blade. 'You made me force him off the road. *Faster, faster!* That's all you said. *Faster, faster!*' Lambie's face contorted; his lip curled, and a madness entered his eyes as they widened, the knife still at Liz's throat. 'I want you to know what it's like to be responsible for someone's death. I want you to feel the torment, Jim Daley!'

Daley knew it was now or never. He leapt across the bed in a desperate attempt to subdue Lambie and save his wife's life. But before he could stop the ex-policeman, the knife flashed under the ceiling light once more, and a splatter of blood slathered across the white satin bed covers.

'No!' shouted Jim Daley, watching Liz's eyes glaze over in panic.

Lambie stood still for a fleeting moment, unsteady, swaying on his feet. This, until his eyes rolled back in their sockets, and he fell against the bedroom wall and sank to the floor, blood pumping from the livid gash he'd cut in his own throat slathering down the wall at his back.

Liz screamed and scrambled desperately across the bed into her husband's arms.

Daley held her as tightly as he could without crushing her. 'It's over, Liz, it's over. I love you so, so much.'

He'd been right to sense that something was wrong. He should never have ignored his own instincts. But here she was, safe in his arms. He thanked God for it in a silent prayer.

10

'Here, drink this, Lizzie,' said Brian Scott. 'It'll calm you down.'

'I need something stronger than sweet tea, Brian,' said Liz. She was lying on the sofa in her lounge as Kinloch's small team of forensic officers went to work upstairs in the Daleys' bedroom, photographing, measuring, taking samples of blood – the essence of their trade.

'Worst thing you can do is take alcohol after a shock,' said Scott. 'I'm speaking from experience, trust me.'

Liz smiled. Being married to Jim Daley for so long, she'd known Scott for years. She always thought of them as a pair. Her husband, solid and dependable. Brian Scott, the funny man of the duo, willing to bend the rules to get what he wanted. Despite the evidence of the passing years, Liz Daley placed them in these neat little packages still, knowing full well her husband could bend to suit the occasion, too. But he could never be the tonic Scott was.

'I never liked that bastard Lambie,' said Scott, passing her the beverage. 'He was always cloaking about wae his face tripping him. *Deep depression o'er Cowcaddens*, I used to call him.'

'Last night was the first time I've had the pleasure.' Liz

sighed and took a sip of tea, noticing immediately it was laced with whisky. 'OK, you said the last thing I should do was drink alcohol, Brian.'

Scott put one finger to his lips. 'Don't tell the big man. He'll just moan at me for days.'

Despite everything, she smiled. 'Tell me about it.'

'You relax wae your tea. I need to have a word wae Jimmy, OK?'

'On you go, Brian. I'll finish this and try to get a sleep. Oh, and thanks for taking James up to Ella. I didn't want him around with all this going on. I really do appreciate all you both do, you know.'

'Cannae have the wean getting traumatized with all this. That sounds more like my childhood than his, darling.'

Scott heard Liz giggle as he left the room in search of his old friend. He knew the real shock hadn't hit her yet. She was in for a tough couple of days, that was for sure.

Daley wasn't hard to find. It was a bit like searching for a bear in a phone box. He was standing on the landing, watching over the SOCO team as they went about their business in his bedroom.

'You need to take a break,' said Scott. 'I'm in charge here, remember?'

Daley looked straight ahead, as though he hadn't heard him.

'Why didn't the panic button work, Brian? I mean, what's the point in the damned thing if it doesn't fucking work?' Daley's face was crimson with anger.

'Och, who knows? It was just installed. Likely hasn't been wired up properly yet. You know what it's like nowadays. No such thing as a good tradesman.'

'The engineer said it was good to go when he left. Liz heard him testing it. Lambie told her she'd have no luck pressing it – it wasn't going to do anything. How did he know that?'

'Fuck knows, big man. I have to say, I knew he was a shite driver, I never had him down as an electronics expert.'

'Me neither. There's no way he managed to disable that alarm. I mean, look at the shape he's in.'

Scott made a face. 'No' very bonnie, lying there with his throat cut, right enough.'

'I mean before that. He looked worse than you when you were on the booze, Brian.'

'Well, I'm pleased to hear that. I don't often get compliments, you know.'

Daley turned to his colleague. He was wearing a tartan dressing gown, pulled tightly at his waist by a cord. 'I'm sorry, Bri. It's just the shock, you know.'

'Don't worry. Fuck me, you could have been dead – both of you. The ACC is on his way first thing in the morning. That'll cheer you up.'

'He's getting a piece of my mind, too. Remember he said Lambie was no danger.'

'Aye, I remember. Listen, you need to get some sleep. Get in there wae Lizzie and catch a few winks on that big recliner of yours.'

'I will,' said Daley absently. 'Oh, can you make me a whisky tea, too?'

'Shit! Do you miss nothing?'

Daley nodded to the bedroom. 'When's the ACC due?'

'Division said first thing.'

'Ten o'clock then?'

'Oh aye. He won't be any earlier than that. He's coming down in the chopper.'

'That's the life, eh?'

'Sure is. I'll go and get the kettle on.'

Daley stared at the men in white paper suits as they paraded about his bedroom. They'd covered Lambie's body with some black plastic sheeting, though the detective could still see the slather of dark blood down the white bedroom wall where his attacker had slid to oblivion.

'Something's not right,' Daley muttered to himself, before following Brian Scott downstairs in his dressing gown.

Daley arrived at Kinloch police station at half-past ten. He'd seen the Police Scotland helicopter fly over Kinloch about thirty minutes before, and he was damned if he was going to rush to work just to suit the ACC, certainly not after the night he'd just had. The dark rings round his eyes spoke of the last twelve hours, and the impact they'd had on the detective. Liz, the full horror of what happened now having sunk in, was back to being sullen, wordless. But she'd been like that for months.

He returned his thoughts to the ACC. As always, when a senior officer visited Kinloch, they used the old sub-divisional commander's office as a base. Daley remembered the last incumbent prior to his taking over, the risible Inspector MacLeod. Ever since, Daley had used the glass box in the CID suite as his base of operations.

'Jim!' shouted ACC Jordan as Daley walked past the office door. 'See you in ten minutes or so, eh? Give you a chance to get a coffee, and all that.'

'Yes, sir,' said Daley, walking on without glancing at his superior. He was used to the unctuous behaviour of senior officers when they knew they were in the wrong. He wasn't falling for the charm offensive.

Daley walked through the CID suite to a room full of people with their heads down, immersed in work. He didn't mind. After all, what was there to say to your boss who'd been through what he had the previous night? It was the old west-of-Scotland dread of empathy and what to say to someone who'd been through the mill. He'd done the same thing himself, many times.

Daley kicked open the door to his glass box to find Brian Scott sitting in the visitors' chair at the other side of his big desk.

'There you are, Jimmy. Jordan's been in twice since he arrived to find out where you were.'

'What did you say?'

'I telt him that you might be late on account of being attacked in your bed last night. That seemed to cool his jets.'

'I want you to come in with me, Brian. To speak to Jordan, that is.'

'What, to hold the bastard down while you kick him? Fine wae me. But are you not supposed to have the federation rep wae you?'

'He left, remember?'

'Oh aye, that's right. Simpson – got caught shagging that auld dear.'

'She was fifty-one, Brian.'

'Aye, but he was twenty years younger. What a scandal, man. Imagine getting filmed on a phone in the throes of passion by the folk in the flats across the road. Obviously never heard o' curtains. Worst thing was, he kept his police bunnet on while he was at it.'

'Crime of the century, eh?'

'Dirty bastard, if you ask me. He'd a bonnie-looking girlfriend too.'

'So, in the absence of the fed rep, Standing Orders state that I can take in anyone above the rank of sergeant. You're it.'

'I keep forgetting they promoted me.'

'They've tried to forget it too.'

'Are you going straight in?'

'No, he said I was to have a coffee first. Ten minutes. Let's make it twenty.'

Daley and Scott sat consuming the coffee Scott had brought from the canteen when the phone rang on the desk. Daley gestured to Scott to answer it.

'DCI Daley's office. Inspector Scott speaking.'

'Where on earth has he got to? I said ten minutes; it's been nearly half an hour!'

'He's dealing wae something, sir. I'll give him a nudge when he's free.'

'See that you do, *Inspector.*' The last word was exaggerated for effect.

Scott put the phone down. 'He's a right cheeky bastard, by the way,' said Scott. 'I prefer the likes of John Donald. You know where you are wae a real crook, don't you?'

'John Donald. I've been trying to forget him for the last decade.'

'You'll never forget him, Jimmy.' Scott took to his feet. 'Are you ready?'

'Yes, I suppose.'

The pair left the CID suite and headed back down the corridor. Scott knocked briskly on the door bearing the wooden plaque *Sub-Divisional Commander.*

'Come!' Jordan sounded irritated, even from behind the door.

Daley and Scott entered the room. ACC Jordan seemed to be preoccupied by the latter as he pulled over a spare chair and sat beside his friend.

'What do you think you're doing, Inspector Scott?'

'Following Standing Orders, sir.'

'Which one?'

'I cannae remember the number and that, sir. But it's the one that says, *An officer summoned to a meeting with a senior colleague in rank for anything other than operational reasons is permitted to be accompanied by a federation representative.*'

'You're the federation rep? Good grief, things must be bad in Kinloch. Though I suppose it makes sense as you've been in front of just about every disciplinary apparatus we have.'

'Sir, we currently don't have a fed rep,' Daley explained. 'He left not long ago and hasn't been replaced. Therefore – as per Standing Orders – I can have an officer above the rank of sergeant to accompany me.' Daley shrugged. 'And here he is.'

ACC Jordan gave a resigned shake of the head. 'Whatever, DCI Daley, whatever. Just don't start spouting off, Scott.'

'Yes, sir,' Scott replied.

'Now, first of all, Jim, I – we, Police Scotland – owe you an apology.'

Before the ACC could apologize further, Daley held up his hand.

'I'm not particularly interested in apologies, sir. I want to know why the panic button installed at my domicile on your insistence didn't work.'

'I'm looking into that. Also—'

'Not to stop you, sir, but I would also like to know why Gordon Lambie, who escaped from the State Hospital last week and was known to have threatened me in front of other patients, was able to make his way to Kinloch unhindered, and put a knife to my wife's throat. This, being the man you assured me was *no risk*.'

'Well, that was the intelligence I had to hand,' said Jordan.

'Doesnae sound very intelligent to me,' said Scott.

'I warned you, Inspector!' Jordan pointed a finger in Scott's direction.

'Please, sir, this is far from acceptable.' Daley's face was red now, a sure sign his notorious temper was on the brink of being lost. 'I don't want apologies, I want explanations. I want to know exactly why my records were accessed by person or persons unknown. Why the panic button installed in my house didn't work, despite my wife being assured it had been tested and was fully operational. And why you had faulty intelligence. Until I have satisfactory answers to these questions, I have nothing else to discuss with you, sir.' Daley stood, turned on his heel and left the room, slamming the door behind him.

There followed a rather awkward silence between the men left in the room.

'What on earth's wrong with Daley, Scott? You know him well enough.'

'With respect, sir, I'd say he's right pissed off. And if you pardon the observation, I don't fucking blame him. Thank you, sir.' Scott stood, and for some reason nodded a slight bow at the ACC, then followed Daley from the room.

In the now empty office, Jordan rubbed his tired eyes. He wondered if there was any way to demote Brian Scott from his new responsibilities. The ACC picked up the phone and booked a table at the nice-looking restaurant he'd spotted on the way up the town's Main Street. His next job was to order the helicopter to return for him later that afternoon. After all, he might as well enjoy the away day, he reasoned.

11

Liz Daley sat alone in the family house on the hill, the place she thought she'd breathed her last when the knife was at her throat only a matter of hours ago. She was staring intently at her mobile phone, waiting.

Though many who knew her thought otherwise, Liz Daley did feel guilt, especially when the things she felt most guilty about threatened to come out in the open. Now, she was doing all she could to avoid yet another unwelcome intrusion. She bit her lip and thought back to the party she'd attended at the end of the previous year.

Liz was pleased at how well her photography had been received since she'd applied herself to the craft. Technology made it so much easier than it had been in her teens, when everything had been analogue in the extreme. The whole process of developing her images in a dedicated darkroom, and all that went with it, had put her off professional photography. The red light had a claustrophobic feel, while the smell of the chemicals used to achieve this alchemy made her nauseous.

Now, she simply found the image she wanted, chose the version she felt was best, then manipulated it on her computer until the perfect creation magically appeared on the screen. It was nothing short of a miracle. To make matters even easier, the click of an attached email sent her work anywhere she wished. And, if she was lucky and her image was chosen for some publication or website, the payment for this toil appeared in her bank account.

However, as had so often been the case in Liz's life, hurdles – mainly of her own making – appeared just when she thought she'd cracked it.

In Detail online magazine published the best of landscape photography. She was chuffed when her first image – one of the loch right in front of her home – appeared in its pages a year and a half ago. Ever since, her work had regularly featured in the publication, helping her build quite the reputation for showcasing the beautiful Kintyre Peninsula. The money wasn't bad either, enough to build up a tidy little sum, which made her feel free, independent. No longer did she have to consult the family finances before splashing out on a new dress, a pair of good shoes, a smart handbag or the latest Sony mirrorless camera. In short, she was her own woman; she revelled in the feeling.

When she was invited to the magazine's Christmas party last year in London, Liz dismissed the notion out of hand. But her husband thought she should go. After all, wasn't it a chance for her to meet the team behind *In Detail* – a chance to network and find new opportunities to show off her work? He was right, of course, so she'd agreed.

The event itself was dull, held in a downmarket Soho restaurant with a sticky carpet and very average food. But she'd met some interesting people and made some worthwhile contacts.

Once the meal was over, a few of them decided to break away from the main party and sneak off to a pub – in this case a quiet little hostelry in Marylebone, a favourite of one of her new friends.

They stayed for a while, until one after the other, people drifted away back to their families, hotels, bedsits, guest houses – to their real lives.

Liz had been ready to leave too before Sean had offered her another drink. As always, the call of an illicit liaison appealed to her. She could sense that potential now. After all, Sean was a well-presented, attractive man, younger than her, Liz reckoned.

There were three of them left by this time: Liz, Sean and an older man called Fred, who kept dozing off. By the look of his clothes – striped 'pants', straining at every seam, and a watered-down Sergeant Pepper jacket – he'd struggled to leave the sixties behind, nearly as much as his behind struggled to fit into his trousers.

Eventually, Sean, a well-built forty-something of middle height, persuaded him it might be a good time to take a taxi home. *Time of the year, and all that. Lucky to get a taxi later on with all the office parties in full swing.*

Fred had stumbled off, thanking Sean for his sound advice, leaving only Liz Daley and her fellow photographer to enjoy a nightcap.

Up until a few weeks ago, Liz struggled to remember what Sean looked like. That was, until the large manila envelope had arrived in the post, addressed to her and marked *Private and Confidential*.

On examination, Liz recognized his features amid the tangle of their limbs in the creaky bed of his hotel room. From a photographic standpoint, the images were well executed, leaving the viewer in no doubt regarding the passion on display. But they made Liz's blood run cold. She shuddered at the arc of her back, the pointing of her feet as her tanned legs wrapped round his pale body, pulling him to her.

It turned out that the energetic Sean was a serial blackmailer, liking nothing more than seducing bored, perhaps slightly tipsy middle-aged women for the purposes of extortion.

At first, Liz was inclined to ignore his threats to tell her husband unless she furnished him with three thousand pounds. But when the price started to rise, and he provided the address of Kinloch police station, plus Jim's rank and direct phone extension, she began to worry.

Now, she was anxiously awaiting the call that would end this horror.

Though Liz Daley had limited experience of the art of blackmail, she believed that everyone had their price. That, alongside the threat of what her husband was likely to do to Sean – or whatever his real name was – when he found out. She believed this payoff would be enough to put an end to it all. Liz just hoped she was right.

Just as her nerves, already strained by the attack on their home in the middle of the night, were stretched to breaking point, her mobile rang, the name *Sean* emblazoned across the screen in bold letters.

'You're late,' said Liz, with all the bile she could muster.

'Sorry about that, sweetheart. But I don't care.' Sean's voice was as she remembered, reasonably posh but with more than a hint of estuary. She'd been tempted to think his accent was contrived when she met him. Now, she was convinced.

'I care!' Liz spat the words down the phone.

'Do you have the money?' The question was straight and to the point.

'Yes, I do. But listen, you better remember. My husband will tear you to pieces if he ever finds out about this.'

'Why should he find out? You give me the money and it's over. Simples!'

'If you ever come back for more, I'll tell him myself, got it?'

'Darling, if you were that keen to tell him yourself, you'd save a few quid and spill the beans now. You'll never tell him.'

'Don't push me.' Liz's mind wandered back to the dentist who'd assaulted her during a mutual fling, and what her husband had done to him. She'd have loved to come clean to Jim and unleash the dog of war on this pathetic man. But she knew that their marriage would be the eventual casualty. Liz cursed herself for her brief involvement with Sean. Despite it all, she valued her marriage and she loved her son.

'You've arranged to come to London then? I'm a cash-on-delivery guy, as I said.'

'We'll be there two weeks today.' Liz felt her stomach recoil at the thought.

'Good! Perhaps you can sneak off and I can give you one for the road, eh?'

'Fuck off!'

'Now, now, that's not very ladylike, Elizabeth. Mind you, you aren't much of a lady, are you? Judging by our little dalliance, that is. Quite the filly.' He laughed on the other end of the phone.

'I'll call you in London when I can get away, OK?'

'You do that, darling. But don't make me wait too long.'

'Piss off. I'm going.'

'Hold your horses, Elizabeth. I sent a little present to your email. I hope you appreciate it.'

'What present? What are you on about?' Liz felt panic settle in her chest.

'Let's call it for old times' sake.'

'I want nothing from you. I'll ring when we're in London!'

Liz ended the call, taking deep breaths to calm herself down. In the end, she reached for her handbag, removed a small packet of pills and took a diazepam to do the job.

She swallowed the tablet back with a glug of water from her bottle and sat in her chair, her eyes closed, waiting for the medication to take effect. She must have dozed off, because when she looked at her watch, almost half an hour had passed.

Feeling calmer, her roiling stomach almost banished by the diazepam, Liz picked up her mobile and flicked on the email app. Sure enough, there it was, an email sent half an hour before from Sean.

Hope you enjoy, he'd written. She clicked on the attachment, and shortly, blood rushed to her face. There was the dingy hotel room, the bed she remembered, the dun curtains hanging limp in the fetid air. But the bed was moving. She could hear her own voice: 'Fuck me, please, just fuck me!'

He clambered on top of her, and she heard herself moan at his first thrust.

Liz was roused from the horror of it all when she heard the front door open and her husband's familiar voice.

'Liz, it's me! Just thought I'd come and check you're OK.' His footsteps thudded up the hall.

Liz, her hands trembling, managed to turn off the sound on her phone, before flicking off the footage.

'I'm up here. Give me two secs!' she replied as her heart thudded in her chest.

12

'How's Lizzie?' said Brian Scott, sitting in the driver's seat of his car outside the Daleys' house.

'I don't think I've ever seen her as shaken,' said Daley. 'I thought I'd lost her, I honestly did. I'd never have made it in time before he slit her throat.' Daley punched the car window in front of him. 'I should have charged the bastard the minute he came in!'

'Oh! Steady on, big chap. I've only had this motor for three months. I'm still in the honeymoon phase. It's over; all's well that ends well. I'd call that a result.'

'How long can we keep doing this, Brian?'

'Eh?'

'You know what I mean. How many times have you waved Ella goodbye wondering if it was the last time you'd see her?'

'I live in hope.' Scott shrugged.

'Bollocks! You and her have the tightest marriage I've ever seen.'

'Fuck, she was off to stay with our daughter in New York no' that long ago, Jimmy. Had you forgotten?'

'You were drinking a couple of bottles a day at that time, Brian. Hey, and did she leave?'

'No, she didn't, thankfully. I'd be lost without her. I'll

67

never understand how she works that washing machine. It's alien technology, I'm telling you. Aye, and the kettle's on the skids, too.'

'It's a Bosch, Brian.'

'See, telt you! Don't buy their kettles.'

'The washing machine! Anyway, that's not what I meant. I mean, how many times have we stared down the face of oblivion?'

'Is that the old gaffer from Stewart Street?' Scott laughed. 'Mind, he was that gloomy we called him oblivion.'

'I wish I had your approach to life, I really do.'

'No, you don't. I get up in the morning, and I'm never sure if I'm going to make it through the day without a drink.'

'Still?'

'Still, sparkling – I don't care as long as it's got alcohol in it.'

'I thought you were over that, Bri.'

'Listen. You don't get over it, never. Every guy on the wagon you meet is clinging on by his fingernails. I have strategies for when it gets bad.'

'Strategies?'

'Mind they sent me to that wee lassie. What was she called?'

'A behavioural psychiatrist.'

'Aye, that's it. Nice wee lassie, she was. Bloody good at her job, I'll tell you that for nothing. Anyway, she gave me these coping strategies. You know, for when things were bad, like.'

'Such as?'

Scott shrugged. 'Like when you really want a drink, remember all that you value.'

'Ella, the kids?'

'I usually think o' the Rangers.'

Daley screwed up his face. 'You're kidding, right?'

Scott said nothing for a few moments, his face expressionless. Then he burst out in a fit of laughter. 'You fall for that every time. You, a clever bloke, tae. In any case, who'd want to think about them after last season, eh? I'd be steaming after two minutes of thought aboot it.'

Daley couldn't help smiling. Yet again, as he had done throughout their career, Scott had cheered him up.

'We better get back to the ranch. The new tech officer, or whatever he is, will be here by now.'

'What's his name again?'

'Buggered if I can remember. But it'll stop me having to bite my nails while Shaw tries to get that big screen up every time. They say he's a computer wizard, too. That'll make exactly one o' us in the whole office.' Scott revved the engine and headed off down Daley's narrow driveway to the main road.

When the pair arrived back in Daley's glass box, a young man with short red hair and freckles was sitting on a chair beside the big desk.

'Are you the new boffin?' Daley enquired.

The lad stood. He was just above average height, with a serious expression behind his purple spectacles.

'I'm Duff, sir.'

'Fuck, there's honesty,' Scott observed.

'No, that's my name.' Duff looked anxiously between Daley and Scott.

'He's pulling your leg, son. What's your first name?'

Duff coughed, looking suddenly embarrassed. 'Engelbert, sir.'

'Eh? You're the one pulling our legs now, chief, and nae danger.' Scott looked at the newcomer wide-eyed.

'My grandmother was a big fan, apparently. She named me.' Duff looked apologetic.

'Did you no' wish she'd died before she'd chance to hit you wae that handle?' said Scott.

'She died a month ago, actually. Still a bit raw.'

Daley glared at Scott. 'I'm sorry to hear that – Engelbert,' he said hesitantly.

'Aye, nae offence and all, son. I didnae mean anything by it – Engelbert.' It was Scott's turn to look embarrassed now.

Duff nodded. 'That's OK, no offence taken.' His face broke out into a broad grin and he started to chuckle.

'Wait, are you at the madam, son?' asked Scott.

'I'm afraid so, sir. When you're called Duff, you get used to all the barbs. It's my standard response. I've got that used to biting back. Apologies, Inspector Scott, DCI Daley.'

'So, your granny's sound as a pound, then?'

'Well, no. She died when I was seven.'

'But you're called Engelbert?'

'No, sorry, sir. My name's Bobby. Bobby Duff.'

'Thank fuck for that,' said Scott. 'I don't want to be cutting about calling one of my troops Engelbert.'

'Right, down to business,' said Daley. 'What do you specialize in, Duff?'

'All things tech, sir. Computers, audio-visual, communications, phone forensics, AI, data evaluation, the lot.'

'Phone forensics?' Scott looked puzzled.

'Did you know there's the equivalent of about sixty thousand A4 pages of information on every smartphone?'

'If you say so.' Scott looked unconvinced.

'Aye, and hidden detail too. Folk think they've erased it but nine times out of ten they haven't, sirs.'

'So I've heard,' said Daley. 'You're the very man we need

around here. Welcome to Kinloch, Bobby.' He rubbed his chin. 'Mind you, I'm just about to leave the sub-division. Brian – Inspector Scott – will be your boss.'

'So I understand.'

'Go out and introduce yourself to the rest of the team. They're a good lot. But maybe stay away from the Engelbert routine.'

'Hey, see before you go, son. Do you know anything about kettles?'

'Sorry?'

'Just ignore him, Duff. Off you go. We can have a chat later.'

'Yes, sir.' Bobby Duff nodded to both Daley and Scott, before heading out of the glass box and into the general CID suite, where his new colleagues were quick to make his acquaintance.

'Clever lad,' said Daley.

'Cannae be that smart if he knows fuck all about kettles. Engelbert, indeed.'

'Think about it, Bri. You'll have him drawing up shift rotas, re-rostered rest days, annual leave – all sorts. Before you know it, he'll be a pivotal member of the team.'

'Do you think he'll be able to do all that?'

'Easy, with bells on. He'll have an app for all that kind of stuff. Done in a jiffy, I'm sure.'

'In that case, I don't care what the fuck he's called. Humperdinck has just made my day!'

Daley knew that having the administrative office tasks removed from his shoulders would be an absolute boon for Brian Scott. The art of detection was his forte, not bean counting or making up rosters. The big detective sat on the chair at his expansive desk, feeling somehow melancholy. For all they'd encountered over the years at Kinloch, it had been the happiest time of his career. He'd miss the place, and his old friend Brian Scott.

The phone buzzed on the desk near his hand. 'Daley,' he answered perfunctorily.

'Sir, I've Hamish here. Wants a word with you, if he may,' said Shaw at the front desk.

'Of course, tell him to hang on. I'll be through in a minute. Grab him a cup of tea, Alistair, if you'd be so good.'

On the other end of the phone, Shaw sounded doubtful. He lowered his voice. 'I think he may be refreshed enough, sir. If you know what I mean?'

'What, tea?'

'No, not that.'

Daley heard Hamish's voice sounding thick in the background. 'OK, I get the drift. I'll be through in a minute.' He ended the call.

'What's up?' said Scott.

'It's Hamish at the front desk. And by the sound of things, he's drunk.'

'At least he's oot the house.'

'You're always the man for the stretched logic.'

Daley stood stiffly from his chair, the events of the night before still having their effect. He left the CID suite in search of Hamish.

13

Daley found Hamish in the family room, where Shaw had hidden him in case ACC Jordan was on the prowl. Hamish was on a red sofa that neatly matched his flushed complexion.

'Hey, everything OK?' said Daley, knowing very well it wasn't.

'I hate that expression,' said Hamish slowly but without slurring his words. 'What does it mean, anyway? Aye, and what was wrong with *how do you do*?' Hamish bowed his head slightly while doffing his cap, in the manner of his youth.

Daley took a seat opposite him. With its colourful decor and comfy chairs, the family room was a bit of a haven. He'd often come here to think when things had become particularly difficult during his tenure in Kinloch.

'I heard the very worst news this morning,' said Hamish, fixing Daley with a steely gaze.

'Oh, what? Anything I can do to help?'

'You stay as far away from London as you possibly can. That's what you can do for me, Mr Daley.'

The detective had worked out that the old fisherman had likely heard about his planned long weekend and matched the trip with the bad dreams he'd been having. 'Don't be daft, Hamish. We're staying at a good hotel, just going to see a show, a nice meal or two. Not forgetting Liz's shopping. It's good to get a break – just the two of us.'

Hamish leaned unsteadily forward in his chair. He stared at Daley for a few moments without saying a word.

'Do you feel sick?' said Daley.

'Aye, I do. But not in the way you think. I had a couple o' drams before I arrived up here. Just to steady my nerves, you understand.'

'I see. At the County, by any chance?'

'Aye, at the County. Man, I'm not in the habit o' frequenting other establishments, as you well know.' Hamish hiccoughed just as he said this.

Ella had spilled the beans, that was clear. Unintentionally, of course, but she'd told Hamish about the Daleys' break. It all made sense now.

Daley reached out and held Hamish's hand between his. 'You know how much I value you – all we've been through over the years. But trust me, you've nothing to worry about.' Daley hesitated. 'You know what the problem is, don't you?'

'Don't you dare say the drink, James Daley!'

'No, nothing of the kind. I know how sparing you are with the drams – especially if you're paying for them.'

For this, Daley earned a scowl as his reward, rather than the levity he'd been hoping for.

'The problem is, since you gave up the boat and the lobster creels, you've been at a loose end. Your mind's working overtime.'

'Is that so?' Hamish stared into Daley's eyes. 'I know I'm a fanciful old man, wae much, much more of my life behind me than in front. Very little time left, I shouldna wonder.'

'Don't say that!'

'I say it because it's true. Aye, I'm well aware I haver from time to time. No doubt the product o' too much whisky, and maybe getting carried away in good company. But as you know, when it comes to the important things, I have the right of it more often than not.'

'Come on, Hamish. It's just a trip to London.'

'Aye, that it is. But the feeling I've had in my guts for days now tells me something very different.'

'I'm sure. But it's fine, honestly.'

Hamish ignored Daley's assurances. 'Like you stuck on that wee skerry. Don't tell me you canna mind. Like the day my poor faither breathed his last.' Hamish put his hand to his head and looked at the floor. 'Aye, and like poor wee Annie. I saw them all, Mr Daley. I saw them every bit as plainly as I see your trip to London. I promise you.' When Hamish raised his head, tears filled his eyes.

Daley thought back to the many times Hamish had been right about things to come, in a way he – nobody – could explain. A few people of the *thin places* were notorious for their prescience when it came to events yet to come. It came with the territory, of course. The very name *thin places* derived from the fact the locals, and many others, reckoned they were parts of the world where realms all but collided; where heaven and hell were as close as they could come to the mortal world. The souls of the dead and the Deity alike spoke to those with the sight, whether they liked it or not. And Hamish, sitting drunk and dishevelled in the Kinloch police station family room, was one such person.

Daley thought for a moment. 'Right, I get it.'

'You do?' Hamish looked surprised.

'I'll speak to Liz tonight. We can change our booking – go somewhere else. Will that make you rest easier?'

Hamish nodded sagely. 'You have no idea the weight that would lift off my shoulders.'

'Good! Then it's agreed. It'll not be easy telling Liz, right enough. She loves London, you know.'

'Aye, well, I'm thinking she'd no' have loved it if she'd gone this time, and that's a fact.'

'Happy?'

'I canna tell you how happy I am.'

A broad smile broke out across his face and his eyes looked bright instead of dull and lifeless, as they'd appeared when Daley first entered the room.

'All sorted, excellent stuff!' Daley clapped his hands and stood, towering over the old man. 'I'll get Alistair to bring you a mug of tea and a bite to eat. Then one of the lads can take you home, if you'd like?'

'Indeed not, Mr Daley. I've taken up more than enough of your precious time as it is. I'll enjoy the stroll home. It's a lovely day. At least now, I can appreciate it.'

'Right, I'll show you out.'

'No need at all. Though you could give me a hand off this couch. Man, folk sit so low these days. It's the same as toilets. I feel as though I'm squatting on the ground any time I have the call of nature outside my own hoose.'

Daley pulled Hamish off the sofa with one meaty paw. They stopped in the doorway to the family room.

'I know my way out, as you're aware.' Hamish smiled again. 'And I'm grateful to you, I really am.' The old man turned on his heel, almost bumping into ACC Jordan, who was passing by. 'I beg your pardon, mister,' he said before making his way back along the corridor, using one hand on the wall to steady his passage.

'My goodness, who on earth is that?' said Jordan, watching Hamish on his way.

Daley's face was expressionless, though his eyes would have betrayed guilt to any who knew him well. 'The man who saved my life. That's who he is,' he muttered before leaving ACC Jordan to his business.

14

The days before Daley's break rushed by. He had a world of administrative tasks to take care of, prior to leaving for his new post. All this would pass to Scott on Daley's departure, and the process of getting the new DI into the swing of things proved more difficult than he'd imagined.

'These appraisals, Jimmy,' said Scott, sitting opposite Daley in the glass box, and referring to the annual assessment of the staff in the sub-division. 'What's the point, eh? I've never paid any attention to my appraisals, not once. What does some desk-jockey know about real policing anyway?'

'You mean some desk-jockey like you?'

'Eh?'

'All these people who've done their best to point out the errors of your ways in the last thirty years have been in exactly the same position you're in now.'

'Aye, but half o' them were arseholes.'

Daley shrugged. 'It's up to you how you go about it. But it goes on their records, and you're responsible for their careers. It's serious, Brian.'

'I'd rather show people what I think of them by action rather than words. You know that.'

Quickly, Daley recalled some of Scott's *actions*, and

encouraged his friend to stick to the paper route. 'My advice, take your time, consider. Don't just rush into the office and write an appraisal when your blood's up, OK?'

'I'm beginning to wish you were staying put, big man.'

'That's nice to hear. It really is. But a few weeks of this stuff and it'll be second nature.'

Scott eyed Daley as though he'd just been told he was about to strap himself into a space rocket and head for Mars.

'Who knows you best? Apart from Ella, of course.'

'You do, Jimmy.'

'Correct! And I think you'll do it no problem at all.'

'Ella thinks I'll make a complete arse o' it.' Scott sighed.

'She's only taking the piss.'

'No, she's no.' I've never seen her more certain o' anything.'

'Anyway, Liz will be here any minute. We don't want to miss the plane to Glasgow, Brian.'

'Damn right, you don't. Unless you fancy driving up that road. Come on, I'm sure I'll manage until Monday.'

'And then I'm off the week after, remember.'

'How can I forget, Jimmy?'

Sure enough, Liz, who was always on time when anything she wanted to do was in the offing, was sitting in the car park, young James in the back seat with his bags, ready for a weekend with Auntie Ella and Uncle Brian, or *Muncle*, as the boy insisted on calling him.

They drove the short distance to Brian's house, where Ella was waiting on the doorstep.

'You come with me, son. And we'll let Muncle Brian drive Mummy and Daddy off to the airport,' said Ella while hugging James junior.

The little boy shook his head.

'I want to see the plane,' he said.

Brian Scott shrugged. 'The more the merrier. Get they slippers off and a decent pair o' shoes on, Ella, and we'll get going.'

'Listen to Field Marshal Rommel, o'er here. You're no' in command once you come through this door, mind.' Ella headed towards the house. 'I'll no' be two seconds.'

'Is Field Marshal Rommel a friend of yours, Muncle Brian?' said James junior.

'Nah, more your Auntie Ella's kind o' bloke,' Scott replied.

In a few minutes, with the Daleys packed into the back of Liz's SUV, Ella driving and Scott in the front passenger seat, they made their way out of Kinloch to the airport, only three miles from town.

'You look like a captive elephant the way you're squeezed in there, big man,' said Brian, alluding to Daley's close confinement on the back seat.

'It's what James wanted. Isn't it?' said Liz, her son on her knee.

They drove on to a single-track road, green fields on either side. The land was flat, the bed of an ocean long, long ago. A buzzard, sitting motionlessly on a fence post, stared impassively at the car as it passed by. The sky was an almost flawless blue, the summer's day warm, showing off Kintyre at its best.

'You should be away to the shore, no' off to London,' said Brian Scott as he wound down the window for air.

Ella glared at him from behind the steering wheel, as James junior wondered why they all didn't just head off to the beach instead of his mother and father going away.

'Nae sense, that's your problem,' she said as they turned into the tiny airport's car park.

They all made their way into the terminal building.

'I'll no' need to frisk you pair,' said Alec the security man, smiling at Jim and Liz. 'Just don't get up to any mischief when you're in London, that's all.' The ex-police officer waved them on to the ticket desk, where they were soon checked in for the short flight to Glasgow.

'There she is coming in,' said Scott, pointing to a speck in the blue sky as the fifteen-seater service plane appeared, just a tiny dot in the distance.

'It's really wee!' exclaimed James junior as he followed Scott's pointing finger.

'It's small not *wee*, James,' said Liz, to a raise of eyebrows from Ella.

Daley took Scott aside. 'Remember the whisky festival's on this weekend, Brian. You'll need a double shift tomorrow and Saturday.'

'All in hand, Jimmy. Don't worry. I put Engelbert on it yesterday. And you know the troops are always happy for some overtime.'

'Don't call him Engelbert, Brian. It'll stick.'

'It's his own fault. Mind you, the boy knows what he's doing. He'd our kettle fixed in a jiffy.'

'Tell me you didn't.'

Scott shrugged. 'Aye, just testing him out, you know.'

Daley shook his head, reasoning that very soon what Brian Scott did would be none of his responsibility. Apart from the fact he would still be notionally in charge of his old friend as the boss of divisional CID. Daley winced at the thought.

As the plane was coming in to land, a screech of brakes could be heard from the car park on the other side of the terminal.

Daley and Scott, by force of habit, turned in the direction of the noise.

'Somebody cutting it fine, eh?' said Scott.

As they looked on, a figure almost fell from a local taxi, his cap caught in a sudden gust of wind, flying off across the car park. The driver, young and nimble, managed to retrieve it, replacing it firmly on the head of its owner.

Daley shook his head. 'Tell me this isn't happening too, Brian.'

Scott blew out his cheeks as Hamish made his way from the taxi to the airport, his gait somewhat uncertain. 'Don't worry, big man. I'll cut him off at the pass.' He rushed off to intercept the old man before he could enter the terminal.

'What's up wae you?' said Scott as he caught up with Hamish at the terminal's sliding doors.

'My niece,' Hamish replied curtly. 'She's coming off the plane from Glasgow. Had tae get an ingrowing toenail removed.' He cleared his throat. 'I said I'd get her a taxi. I'm hoping that's no' a criminal offence these days. But mind, I know full well we're heading for a police state, nothing surer.'

Scott looked at the old fisherman doubtfully. 'As long as that's all you're about, Hamish.'

'Am I free to enter the building, Inspector Scott?' Hamish raised his chin in an indignant fashion.

'You are. But I'm warning you, no scenes. Got it? The wee boy's here. And if this is anything to do with oor Jimmy's trip, I'll have your guts for garters.'

'Away and boil your heid,' said Hamish, pushing past Scott.

Daley had been watching their exchange at the door and gave Scott a puzzled look as Hamish made his way across the concourse.

'How are you, young man?' Hamish said, patting James junior's head.

'I'm fine, thanks, Hameby,' said the boy, using his own name for Hamish as he did for Scott.

'Aye, and glad I am to hear it.' He turned to Daley. 'Nice day for a wee jaunt in the plane, Mr Daley.'

'It is, Hamish. We're looking forward to it.'

Hamish removed his pipe from the pocket of his oily dungarees and sucked it, unlit, as was his habit now in places where smoking was prohibited. 'Don't worry, I know when to keep my mouth shut, Mr Daley. Aye, and when I'm beaten, too. But I ask you this, please take care. And don't let that lassie out o' your sight. Do you promise?'

Relieved that Hamish seemed much more sober than he'd appeared when he fell out of the taxi, Daley was mollified. 'Liz has her heart set on London. She has friends there; she likes the shops. What can I say?'

Hamish smiled at Liz and wished her a fine weekend, before shuffling off to sit on a chair in the waiting area.

'Don't blame me, Jimmy,' said Scott, back at Daley's side.

'He was fine, Bri. The old man, you know, no show without Punch.' He laughed.

'Are you OK, darling?' said Liz, aware of her husband's sudden amusement.

'Yeah, I'm fine.' He smiled. 'Looking forward to a break.'

They all watched as the small plane pulled up a few yards from the terminal.

When Daley turned to look for Hamish, the old man was gone, as was his taxi.

The couple headed for the exit, young James waving frantically. Liz stopped in her tracks. She ran back to give her son another hug.

'I love you, James. You be good for Auntie Ella and Muncle Brian, OK.' Tears filled her eyes. She turned to

Brian and handed him a small envelope. 'For emergencies. You don't need to open it, otherwise, OK?'

Scott, assuming it was money in case she and Jim were delayed, shoved it into the depths of his pocket. 'Don't be daft, Lizzie.'

'Just remember it's there, just in case.' She kissed James junior once more on the cheek, thanked Ella again, then ran off to join her husband and board their flight to Glasgow.

15

The flight was glorious; views over the Isle of Arran, and the peak of Goatfell felt almost close enough to touch. They flew across the Ayrshire coast, then north to Glasgow Airport, where their plane landed on a beautiful Paisley afternoon.

Jim Daley was – as always – relieved to leave the confines of a cramped aircraft seat and be able to stretch his large frame as they walked into the clamour of the terminal.

'I've a wee surprise,' he said, grabbing Liz's hand once they'd cleared security and walking her to the first-class BA lounge.

'Wow, Mr Money Bags,' said Liz. 'First class to London, that's not like you.'

'Well, as we're staying at the Rathbone, I thought why not go the whole hog. After all, we're well enough off to treat ourselves now and again.'

The Daleys took their seats in the lounge, with a couple of hours to spare before boarding their next flight to London. Liz gazed at a painting, a grey landscape of Glasgow, after the style of Turner.

'Well, that's depressing,' she said.

'I thought it was quite well done. I mean, obviously it's not by Turner. There's the Hydro,' said Jim.

'It's easy to see you're a top detective,' observed Liz, raising her eyes. 'The brush work is all wrong for a start.'

'I don't have a degree in art history, darling.'

'No, clearly.' Liz looked about. 'I could do with a glass of champagne, Jim. Since we're treating ourselves, that is.'

Daley went off in search of champagne, aware he was treading on eggshells. He'd hoped the excitement of the trip would ease Liz's resolve about moving away from Kinloch, improve her mood. But he could tell she was as determined as ever, and if he were to broach the subject, the whole weekend would rapidly turn into a disaster. Neither he nor his wife had thought he'd get the job in the first place. Though Jim Daley's record of bringing the guilty to justice was second to none, his list of disciplinary misdemeanours was lengthy. More so, his readiness to disobey orders from senior officers was likely to be a distinct disadvantage.

'Better having you in the tent pissing out, Jimmy,' Scott had said, assessing the whole thing with his usual brio. Liz objected to the move there and then, and nothing would shift her. But there was something else he hadn't been able to put his finger on. He was sure of it.

As he collected two flutes of Moët, Daley pondered Liz's change of attitude. When he'd applied last November for the job of the division's head of CID, Liz had celebrated the fact. The things she could do back near the city; old friends; job opportunities. The list of new possibilities seemed endless. But as Christmas passed by, and February brought news that he was now in the next stage of the process, Liz had become less and less enthusiastic.

Now, they were in deadlock and it was beyond infuriating. But for once in his life, Jim was determined that his wife would not have the last say. In the early part of their marriage, her very utterances were as tablets of stone, binding him to her rule. In the last few years, though, things had changed. So much had happened in their lives since they'd moved to Kinloch.

'There we go,' he said, handing her the drink.

'What is it? Not Moët, I hope.'

Daley toyed with the idea of telling a white lie based on the fact his wife knew as much about champagne as he did, her taste being purely based on what she'd read, seen and what her friends claimed to enjoy. However, the prospect of being uncovered drove him to take the only real option he had – to tell the truth.

'Bloody hell, Jim. It gives me a headache!'

Daley could recall numerous occasions when his wife had happily quaffed bottles of the stuff without suffering a hangover. 'It's all they had,' he said sheepishly.

They sat in silence for a while, Liz people-watching, her husband checking his phone in case some calamity had befallen Brian Scott in the short time since they parted.

'I have to pop out when we get there,' said Liz.

'Eh? What about dinner?' said Daley, disappointed at the possibility of missing some of the fine food at the Rathbone.

'It's fine! I'll be back for dinner.' She looked about guiltily. 'It's Perdita. She wants to speak to me – probably needs some money.'

'Why on earth do you bother with her, Liz? She's the most bizarre person I think I've ever met.'

'I know. She's had a rough time, remember. First with Callum, then that swine Burgess – it's not been easy for her. Especially with the kids.'

'Why did she have kids in the first place? I mean, it's not as if she didn't know what hapless bastards she got in tow with.' Daley tried to drink his champagne. As always, his nose interfered with the glass, and he found himself tossing his head back to take a sip. 'And if it's money she's after, don't give her a fortune! Shit, I feel as though I'm bringing up her kids too.'

Liz shrugged. She kept her expression neutral, despite knowing the risk of what she was about to do. 'Don't worry, Scrooge. I have money of my own, and she is my best friend. But you're welcome to come and hold my hand, if you want. Make sure I don't do anything reckless with your precious money.' Liz's throat was dry now, despite the Moët.

'Go and see Perdita? Are you out of your mind? I'm going to London to enjoy myself, not hang about with mad women on the take. The pleasure's all yours, darling.'

Liz's smile was genuine. 'I thought not. Listen, I'll be an hour at the very most. I'm meeting her in a bar on Tottenham Court Road, so it's not far from the hotel. I'll taxi there and back. It'll be fine. Then you can get your precious dinner.'

'I suppose so.' Daley folded his arms. 'Some of your friends are hard work. You're too loyal to them.'

Liz cleared her throat dramatically. 'Excuse me! This coming from *oor* Brian's best friend. Have you forgotten that he's got you in more scrapes than I can remember?'

'Huh, maybe. But you're quite happy to leave him in charge of our son.'

'Hang on. My son is in the charge of Ella. Do you really think I'd have Brian look after him? He'd come back in a Rangers top, drinking whisky and swearing like a trooper.'

Just like Scott, Liz made her husband laugh, as she'd always managed to throughout their marriage. He believed that, despite everything, it was what had kept them together.

*

Brian Scott left work early, to find his wife and James Daley junior ensconced in a game of Snakes and Ladders in their lounge.

'Can I get a drink please, Auntie Ella?' the boy enquired, just as Brian was going about the difficult business of removing his shoes and putting on his slippers.

'You know where the fridge is, son. Just you help yourself. I've got some cans o' Tango, your favourite,' said Ella, watching her young charge rush off.

'Here, I hope you bought the diet, caffeine-free, juice-free stuff, Ella. You know what Liz is like with the wean. It's a wonder she didn't want the standard tour of inspection before she left,' said Scott.

'Nah, I'm no' spending money on that muck. Anyway, it's full o' chemicals and they numbers. Nothing wrong wae good old sugar, if you ask me.'

'He'll be running about all night.'

'If that's the effect it has, maybe you should try some. Listen, dear, you do what you always did when we were bringing up our own children.'

'I cannae mind. What was that again?'

'Bugger all, Brian!' Ella made a face.

'Aye, some things never change. Anyway, I had my work.'

'And the Press Bar, the Legion and the football, if I remember correctly.'

'You're forgetting the bowls, Ella.'

'My goodness, how could I possibly forget that? What a joy it was seeing you fall in the door with a wee plastic trophy as drunk as a lord.'

'Here, I was good at the bowls before my back went.'

'Before you started drinking that much you couldn't bend down for your shot, you mean.'

'I won plenty trophies.'

'And I wanted to stick every one of them up your—'

'I found the Tango, Auntie Ella,' said James, running back into the room with the can.

'That's good, son. We'll need to get on with our game, eh?'

'What were you saying to Muncle Brian?'

'Och, I was just telling him what a special person he was. Wasn't I, Brian?'

'Something like that, dearest,' said Scott, looking at his watch. 'Time flies. Your mummy and daddy will near be in London now.'

Ella cast a malicious glance in his direction.

Young James looked puzzled. 'That was quick. Every time we drive to Glasgow it takes ages.' He lowered his head. 'I miss Mummy and Daddy already.'

'Och, son. Come and give Auntie Ella a big cuddle.'

James ran and jumped on to her knee.

'Don't you worry. We'll have a great time while they're away, son.' Behind James's back, she lifted one hand and raised one finger in the direction of her husband.

'We'll go to the beach if it's a nice day tomorrow,' said Scott by way of mitigation. 'I hope you've got your trunks.'

'Trunks?' said James.

'You know, to go in the sea with. Like shorts, son.'

'Oh, is that like a swimming costume?'

'Aye, that's right,' said Ella. 'If we're lucky, we'll see Muncle Brian get his swimming costume on too.'

'Yay! You can take me swimming in the sea, Muncle Brian.'

'Well, your uncle isn't too good in the sea, son,' said Brian.

'He keeps falling out of boats,' said Ella.

'Like your Auntie Ella's up the creek without a paddle, son.'

Scott, his slippers now securely on his feet, grabbed the newspaper, as Ella and James continued their game of Snakes and Ladders, any trouble from the young boy's reference to his parents' absence seemingly avoided.

16

Liz and Jim arrived at the Rathbone, an expensive guilty secret ever since they'd stayed there on their first wedding anniversary. Its quirky but well-appointed rooms, excellent staff, odd little nooks and crannies and fabulous food had appealed initially to Liz. But now Jim Daley, with his rather more reserved tastes and inclinations, enjoyed it all just as much – despite the expense. His reasoning for this change of heart was sound. After all, it wasn't as though they lived the high life in Kinloch; he had worked hard and made a living of which his parents could never have hoped.

In their room, attractively decorated with some original paintings on the walls and a big, deep bath, Liz unpacked with her habitually neat efficiency. Meanwhile, Daley poked about in his bag for his charger and the book he'd brought with him, which he began reading as soon as he discovered it.

'Great, this promises to be a fabulous weekend if you're going to sit with your head in a book,' said Liz.

'You're going to meet Perdita, remember? So, it doesn't really matter what I do, does it?'

Liz shook her head, though she was glad her husband had taken the news with little of his usual fuss. She knew that the merest mention of Perdita would be enough to put him off accompanying her.

'I've changed into this now just so I can go straight for dinner when I come back, Jim.' Liz stood in a short, black leather jacket and an equally short approximation of a red tartan kilt, with black ankle boots at the end of her tanned legs.

'You look like a million dollars,' said Daley, meaning it.

Liz checked her bag; she had everything she needed. 'OK, I'll be back in about an hour. I'll flag down a cab in the street.' She planted a kiss on her husband's forehead.

'You're better just calling. There aren't as many black cabs as there used to be. Not since Covid and Uber. Don't get into a private hire, Liz – not here.'

'Once a policeman, eh?'

He shrugged.

'Can I remind you I used to live here before I was married to a cop?'

'No need, I remember. Just be careful. We're not in Kinloch.'

'I promise. Just read your book. I'll be back before you know it.'

Liz left their room as though she hadn't a care in the world, looking forward to meeting an old friend. The truth was, she felt as though she was lugging around a ton in weight. Though she assured herself this would be the last time she'd be having any dealings with the risible, grasping Sean.

Despite the feeling of dread, being on her own on a London street took her back to the carefree days she'd spent in the city as a student. The place was just as busy as always. Shoppers, tourists and sharp-suited business-people thronged the thoroughfares. A warm evening sun beat down on a hot pavement as she passed shops, little cafes and offices. Somehow, it was strange to see young people sitting smoking or vaping on the stairs of older office buildings, men with open-necked shirts, women in fashionable skirts, jeans or dresses. Liz was old enough to remember when the office used to be a much more formal place.

She caught the scent of strawberry from a woman vaping as she passed by – another change. Liz reckoned that the aroma was much more to her liking than the acrid stench of cigarette smoke, which always made her feel nauseous. Even the roads, where traffic inched along at a snail's pace – no change there – appeared less malodorous. No doubt the positive impact of electric vehicles, as opposed to their gas-guzzling counterparts.

There was no question that the city had changed. But these changes were – to Liz at least – on the periphery of her experience. The place still had an engaging, invigorating vibe that made her feel young and energetic again, at the heart of something alive and exciting.

Then she remembered Sean.

Liz had arranged to meet him in a place she knew would be busy and noisy. She'd lied to her husband about grabbing a taxi. The red-painted lounge bar, a haunt for the young and carefree, was just the place to maintain her anonymity for such a folly. Nobody would take any notice of her and the man who'd made her last few months a misery. On a positive note, it would soon be over once and for all.

As predicted, the bar was packed. In the past, Liz would have enjoyed the clamour and buzz. Now, she just felt older than she'd expected to and put out by the whole experience, finding it too loud and claustrophobic.

She sat at one of the few empty tables on a couch covered in red faux leather. The colour, she mused, matched the nature of her indiscretion, one of many during her married life. This time, it had cost her, not to mention the accompanying feeling of guilt, to which she was unaccustomed. During her life of risky promiscuity, she'd been the user, not the reverse.

Liz checked her watch, glad to be early, as intended. It would give her time to calm down, to treat this as a business transaction, nothing more. She'd arranged the place and time by texting Sean when her husband was off in search of champagne at Glasgow Airport.

So far, so good, she thought, as she caught the attention of a waiter and ordered a large gin with plentiful accompaniment.

Back at the Rathbone, Daley was lying on the king-size bed feeling drowsy. He'd had to give up on his book as his eyes were heavy. Travelling always made him tired.

Daley contemplated a snooze, though he knew he'd end up drifting into a deep sleep, which was bound to ruin his appetite and make him feel dozy and disconnected for the rest of the evening. His eyes alighted on something that resembled a small kettle on a table by the chest of drawers.

On closer inspection, the kettle turned out to be a new-fangled coffee maker, complete with little plastic pods to be inserted somewhere within the machine. It took the big policeman a few moments to figure out how all this worked, before the coffee of his choice – an Americano – began to pour slowly into his mug.

He sat back on the bed with the beverage, hoping to banish his weariness before Liz returned. This was no time to incur her disapproval. He had a mission to achieve here in the Big Smoke.

As he stared into space, Daley's mind worked overtime

on what was left to be done back in Kinloch to ease Brian Scott's progress to becoming sub-divisional commander. He ticked things off one by one in his mind. Only when he got to Scott's official authorization to sign documents, both on paper and electronically, did he remember the email sent to him by Police Scotland's Human Resources earlier that day. With all the excitement of heading away for the weekend, he'd forgotten to pass it on to Scott, and the damned thing had to be sent back on Monday morning, before his return to Kinloch.

'Bugger!' Daley exclaimed, as he brought up the email app on his phone and tried to forward the email to Scott with a short explanation. Unfortunately, the message wouldn't send. This was down to some security protocol inhibiting the sharing of a document like this by such means.

It was then he remembered the instructions to upload the document into Police Scotland's cloud account and make it available for Scott that way.

'What was wrong with paper?' Daley muttered. The only way to complete the task now would be to access his official cloud account, and that meant a laptop, which he hadn't brought along for this weekend away.

He remembered Liz had packed her MacBook Air. And even though he didn't know her password, he was sure he'd be able to figure it out so that he could access his work accounts from the computer. Liz was notoriously lax when it came to password settings. She used only the most obvious methods, like birthdays and family names, to secure her tech. In any case, she would have penned a little *aide memoire* somewhere to remind herself, should all else fail.

Sure enough, in her bag, at the bottom of the wardrobe, he found the MacBook in its soft case. He pulled it out, setting the machine on his lap as he stretched out on the bed.

Daley opened the computer and tried his best to work out the password. First James's name and date of birth, then his own. Neither were correct. Then, he worried that if he tried again and failed, both he and Liz would be locked out for the weekend, and that wouldn't improve her mood. He was sure something like that had happened to him before, and he'd had to seek the advice of a boffin in Glasgow. So far, there was absolutely no sign of the list of passwords he'd hoped for.

Thinking further on the matter, Daley thought about calling Liz on her mobile. But he reckoned the likelihood of her answering was remote. His wife always carried her phone at the bottom of her tote bag, and the chances of it attracting her attention in some pub or other while listening to Perdita's woes seemed unlikely.

Daley had all but given up when he spotted a small credit card wallet lurking at the bottom of Liz's computer case. Sure enough, inside the little wallet was a scrap of paper displaying her handwriting.

Mac: Barricade)&&89*, was penned in tiny writing.

Marvelling at his wife's new-found attention to digital security, Daley typed the password into her Mac. He was in!

17

Sitting in the bar, chewing on a thin slice of lemon from her gin, Liz was beginning to become restless. Sean was late, and that annoyed her. She reached into the bottom of her bag and searched blindly for her mobile.

'Another drink?' said one of the casually dressed waiters, noticing her large glass of gin was in need of replenishment.

'Why not,' said Liz, fiddling with the screen on her phone. 'Same again, please.'

The young man fought his way back through the crowds to fetch the drink, while Liz found Sean's number and placed the mobile to her ear.

'*Your call cannot be answered right now. Please leave a message or send a text,*' she just about made out, despite the hubbub.

'Bastard,' Liz whispered, as she hammered out a text with both thumbs.

Where are you? If you want what you asked for, I'll give you another ten minutes, then I have to go.

Liz clutched the phone, looking about yet again to see if there was any sign of her blackmailer. She jumped when the device vibrated in her hand.

Don't sweat it, lover. I'll be with you in five. Don't you have traffic in Scotland?

The response was dismissive, typical of the man she now despised. Once more, Liz grimaced and damned herself for being so stupid. Deep down, she feared that this monster of a man might not hold true to his word, and just ask for more and more until she couldn't pay. She longed for her husband to mete out natural justice, as he had with the man who had so mercilessly raped her. Though Jim would find it all too much to take, the threat might give Sean pause for thought. Liz resolved to force this point home, to ensure that her tormentor was as good as his word and, once paid off, stayed that way.

'Anyone sitting here?'

The question startled Liz for a moment. She looked up to see a middle-aged woman, dressed in a plain-looking floral dress, a cheap handbag strung across her torso. She was overweight and frumpy, her mousy hair short and ill-kempt.

'I'm so sorry, I'm waiting for someone.' Liz smiled apologetically.

Despite this, the woman took a seat across the table from her.

'Listen, I'm sorry but I told you I'm waiting for somebody.' Liz was really flustered now, first by Sean, now by this ignorant newcomer.

The woman stared Liz straight in the face for a moment. 'You're as pretty as they said.'

'I beg your pardon? Just who are *they*? Are you something to do with Sean?'

'Sean's not coming, love.' She said this in a monotone, with an expressionless face.

'What? Who the fuck are you?' Liz felt as though her head was going to burst.

'Right, before we continue our little conversation, remember to make it look as if you and I are old pals having a chat. I have the video. You know what I'm talking about. You're quite the girl, eh? Put your heart and soul into a good shag, at any rate. Most of us ain't got that enthusiasm no more.'

Liz recoiled from this frumpy woman and her heavy estuary accent. 'Don't be disgusting!'

'Me, disgusting? You're the disgusting one, m'lady, not me. Listen to it.' She shook her head with a smile. 'You can call me Martha, if you like. That, or you can call me whatever the fuck you want. Just don't make a fuss or I press *send*.' Martha produced a mobile from her handbag.

'You're just bluffing.'

'So, how do I know about your little fling then, love?'

'Don't call me *love*.'

'I'll call you anything I like, *love*. In any case, I don't think you can say much about it.'

The waiter arrived with Liz's gin, which he placed on the table while staring at Martha.

'A tap of your credit card, please?' he said to Liz, then to Martha, 'Can I get you something, madam?'

'Sorry, you'll have to speak up. Isn't half a racket in here.'

'Can I get you something to drink!' said the waiter, almost shouting.

'Nah, you're all right, lad. But thanks for the offer, though.'

Liz waved her credit card over the machine in the waiter's hand. As soon as he left, Martha grabbed the large gin and took a slurp of it through a red straw sticking proud of the glass.

'That's mine! Buy your own drink if you want one.'

'Now, now, remember what we said. Friends, having a drink, yeah?'

'If you're after more money, you can forget it.'

'I don't want more money, as it happens.' Martha pulled a dirty hankie from her handbag and blew her nose pro-digiously. 'Bloody summer – it's my hay fever. Right bastard, it is.'

'I'm glad,' said Liz, folding her arms.

'Charming, I'm sure. Anyhow, I'm not after your money, love.'

'What?'

'I said, I'm not after your money! Honestly, the bloody noise in here.'

'What about Sean?'

'Sean who? He doesn't exist.' Martha paused. 'Well, of course, he's real enough as you know, having had it away with him. But he's not called Sean, and you needn't think another thing about him, got it? Just concentrate on what I have to say, there's a good gal.'

Liz felt her heart miss a beat. Now, she was really out of her depth.

'I need you to bring your husband somewhere.'

'What?'

'That lovely husband of yours, that's what.' Liz made to speak but Martha hushed her. 'Just listen to me for a while. Sometime tomorrow, I want you to bring your husband to a place, got it?' Martha took another slurp of Liz's gin.

'What place? What on earth are you talking about?'

'All will be revealed to you in a text tomorrow morning. Somebody wants to meet him, that's all.' Martha wiped her mouth on her sleeve.

'I don't know what's wrong with you. I'm not taking my husband anywhere.'

'Treat it as a surprise, something you've done for him you want to keep secret. I mean, we all know how good you are at secrets, love.' Martha sent Liz a knowing look.

'It's not happening.'

'I can promise you'll really regret it if you don't do as I say.'

'In what way?'

'You don't want to know, trust me.'

Liz Daley snapped. 'I've had enough of this. Of you and *Sean*, whoever he is. My husband's forgiven me for affairs before, he will do again. Fuck you!' Liz got to her feet and made her way out of the bar, through the throng of drinkers, her heart thumping as she did.

Martha grabbed the gin and looked on, her expression almost sad. 'Oh well, done my best with you, love. Such a pity, really. Yeah, a real bloody shame. Some folk just don't know when they've got it easy.' She took a final deep draw of the gin before she too left the bar.

Jim Daley was all at sea with his wife's laptop. The Apple operating system wasn't generally used in the office. And as hard as he tried, he couldn't figure out how to sign into his work account, never mind retrieve and send Scott the information required.

'Bastard!' he said under his breath as he tried to navigate the seemingly labyrinthine laptop.

The room was warm, so Daley decided to seek out the air conditioning unit. He found it attached to the wall near the door. It, too, seemed as complicated as Liz's MacBook. Eventually, after more cursing, he felt the room's temperature dip to what he found more acceptable. Of course, it would be another matter when his wife returned. Liz felt the cold, so inevitably, she'd want the temperature restored to her liking.

Daley, heartily sick of confrontation and problems at work, sat back on the bed and retrieved the MacBook. He resolved to give it one last go before contacting Scott. He'd have to get something done from Kinloch. Daley hated how his life had become, governed by red tape, accessed on these infernal machines.

He decided to sign into his email account on Liz's computer. That way, he might be able to download the message and send it the old-fashioned way, which had proved impossible from his phone. He clicked on the email app, and Liz's list of emails appeared on the screen.

As Daley searched for the icon that would enable him to sign into his own Gmail account, he couldn't help noticing a few recent messages sent to Liz, marked simply *Sean*.

He wondered for a moment who this man might be. Of course, Liz communicated with a whole host of people since her photography business had taken off, though he couldn't remember her talking about anyone by that name.

Jim Daley had reached this agony of indecision many times. He'd been told by friends and colleagues that once a partner had been unfaithful, it's almost impossible to truly trust them again. And though he'd tried his level best to wipe the slate clean, other dalliances had sent his confidence in the sanctity of their marriage tumbling out of control.

He'd even resorted to infidelity himself with the tragic Mary Dunn. For a second her face passed before his mind's eye, as he heard her favourite song in his head.

Where the cars go by, all the day and night . . .

The big man banished these thoughts. But though his lover had been dead for many years, he still found himself thinking of her from time to time, especially when things at home became difficult. For a fleeting second, he tried to imagine what life with her would have been like. This lasted until he felt the familiar ache of loss in his heart that brought him back to the here and now.

Daley knew all too well that when it came to Liz, ignorance was, more often than not, bliss. Did he love his wife? Yes, despite everything, he did. He'd been caught up and captivated by her since they'd met.

His every instinct told him to leave well alone. He had no right to invade her privacy. It was yet another act of cowardice perpetrated by a cuckold, almost a guilty obsession, from which he and men like him throughout time had been unable to free themselves. He realized he'd no choice.

Daley's mouth was dry as the cursor hovered above the email from *Sean*. He pressed the trackpad.

Liz knew she had to calm down before she got back to the hotel. In a little coffee shop, only a few hundred yards from the Rathbone, she sat nursing a cup of herbal tea, as she gathered her thoughts.

Idly, Liz watched the bustle of people and traffic from her perch on a stool at the big picture window, registering not one face. Those passing only a few feet from her were a mere blur in the sunshine. All she could see was Sean, and the face of the woman who'd arrived in his stead.

Her head hurt thinking about it all as she sipped at the camomile tea, hoping the hot drink would act as a salve on her frayed nerves.

Liz took another sip and retrieved her phone from the little shelf beside her. Quickly, she typed a message to her husband.

On my way back in the taxi. Perdita a pain as usual. See you very soon. Love xxx.

She studied the screen. As always, Jim picked up the message quickly, and the flashing dots appeared underneath her message to indicate he was typing his reply.

No probs. See you soon. I'm starving! Xx

Liz felt some kind of tortured relief. She wasn't sure what she'd expected; maybe that they'd already been in touch with her husband, and everything was about to become as awful as she'd been fearing for months. She smiled at the fact Jim's stomach was yet again ruling his head. He'd loved his food since the day she'd met him.

Liz, feeling more like herself, and praying the encounter with the frumpy *Martha* was just an attempted extortion gone wrong, levered herself off the stool and left the coffee shop, stepping back into the crowds under the warm summer sunshine. As she strode out towards the hotel, she assured herself that her would-be extorters had taken fright at her husband's job.

Very soon, she was back at the Rathbone.

18

Ella Scott appeared back in the lounge, finger to her mouth in a hushing gesture, startling her husband.

'Hey, did you float doon they stairs?' he exclaimed. 'They're the creakiest stairs in Scotland. I'm always waiting to fall through the bastards. How come you managed to get here without making a sound?'

'With great difficulty, Brian,' said Ella, sitting heavily on the couch.

'You've been up there for near three hours.'

'I know where I've been and for how long, Brian. Poor wee lad just wanted me to keep reading to him. Missing his mammy, so he is.'

'Jimmy's a terrible man for no' sleeping, as you know. The boy likely takes after him.' Scott put down the heavy tome he'd been reading. 'Spends half his time on thon recliner looking across the loch at that graveyard.' Scott shook his head at the thought. 'He can be a right miserable bastard when he's in the mood.'

'Poor man. He should have followed your method of catching some sleep.'

'What method?'

'Getting walloped into a couple of bottles of whisky and sparking oot in front of the telly.'

'Thank you, dearest. As you know, those days are in the past.'

'Huh, and the band played "Believe It If You like".' Ella glanced at the coffee table and the large book her husband had been reading. 'Firstly, can I say I'm shocked to see you reading a book – though I might have known you'd start wae the biggest one you could find.'

'It's Force Standing Orders, Ella. Never mind the whisky, this'll put you to sleep in two minutes. They tell me you can read them on a tablet. But I canna work the bloody things.'

'Is this you getting ready to be the boss?'

'Aye, what do you think?'

'I'd have thought you'd know all this stuff by now. After all, it's no' as though you joined up last Friday.'

'Ach, they're always changing the damn things. And in any case, I'm a *need tae know* kinda guy. Carrying all that guff in your heid canna be good for anyone.'

'You're a *needing a kick up the arse* kinda guy. I bet oor Jimmy knows every dot and comma in there.'

'Likely. But has it made him a happier man?'

'No, just better at his job. And that job's just about to be yours. So, buck up!'

'It's those few kind words that keep me going, my dear.'

Ella picked up a magazine, scanning the pages for something of interest. 'See the blonde lassie from that band oor Will likes assaulted some poor woman in a bar.'

'What, in Kinloch?'

'No, stupid. In Los Angeles!'

'Right.'

'Imagine that, eh? Going oot for a couple o' drinks and getting walloped by a celebrity.'

'Happened to my Uncle Jonny.'

'Your arse! He couldn't remember if he'd been hit by a

lorry, the state he used to get himself into wae the drink. What celebrity is supposed to have hit him?'

'Hauld your horses. Anyway, he went for a pint in the Bruce Arms. He was standing at the urinal when he got battered on the heid from behind. Didnae stand a chance, poor Jonny.'

'And who did that battering?' Ella's expression was sceptical.

'You'll no' believe me.'

'That's a fair assessment.'

'Big Sean Connery – James Bond himself.'

Ella eyed her husband for a few moments without saying a word.

'What!?'

'You've come out wae some shite over the years. But that takes the biscuit.'

'He swore by it until his dying day. Poor bastard came to lying in all the pish and they wee smelly cube things. He looks up, and there's big Connery glowering doon at him.'

'Big Sean Connery. Who'd have thought he drank in the Bruce Arms in Paisley, eh?' Ella raised a brow.

'Just shows you. I never could take to the big man after that. I just thought aboot it every time I watched one o' his films. Mind you, that one in the submarine where he wore the wig was quite good.'

Ella stared, wide-eyed. 'You know, I've been married to you all these years, and you can still surprise me with anything you say.'

Scott shrugged.

'Listen, I'll have an early start with young James in the morning, getting him tae school. Mind, you promised him you'd take him to the beach when he comes back.'

'Oh aye, so I did. I'll likely get a flyer in the afternoon.

When the boss is away, and all that, Ella.' He winked at his wife.

'Brian, you are the boss, remember?' She got to her feet, yawned and made her way quietly to bed.

Scott eyed the brick of a book that was the Force Standing Orders. 'I should have got that on a tablet like Engelbert said,' he muttered to himself, before following Ella in a yawn, and deciding it was indeed time for bed.

As usual, it took Brian Scott very little time to get to sleep. His head was full of the Standing Orders, his takeover of the sub-division, and the many, many things he'd have to get right once Daley left. He fell into a parade of mixed dreams, culminating in standing before the promotions board with no clothes on.

Scott woke with a start, the dream lingering into his semi-wakeful state.

Ella nudged him in the back. 'Shut that damn thing up before it wakes wee James,' she said in a loud whisper.

Turning over, Scott realized his mobile was steadily vibrating itself off his nightstand. He fumbled the phone into his hands, grabbed his reading glasses from the table and squinted at it. He noted it was after two in the morning, and Daley's name shone brightly from the screen.

Brian Scott answered the call. 'Hey, big man. Everything OK? Do you know what time it is?' For a moment Scott thought there was nobody on the other end of the call, and he was ready to put it down to a misdial. But then he heard Daley's voice. He was breathing heavily and sounded stressed.

'She's dead, Brian. I couldn't take it any more – I killed her. You have to help.'

'Eh? What are you slavering aboot, Jimmy? Are you

pished?' Scott waited for a reply, but the line was dead. He sat up in the bed, blinking the sleep from his eyes. He dialled Daley's number back twice but there was no reply. 'Fuck!' Scott swore to himself while making a third attempt to contact his old friend.

Ella switched her bedside lamp on. 'What's going on, Brian? I told you, you'll wake that poor wean.'

Scott was sitting upright in bed, his face a mask of confusion. 'It was oor Jimmy, Ella. He says he's killed Liz.' Scott gazed at his wife in disbelief.

19

George Chambers, huddled in the doorway under a filthy blanket, was only forty-five, though he could easily have passed for someone twenty years older. The homeless man's face was bloated and great bags had morphed his eyes into mere slits. His nose, twisted from more than one break, squatted above an almost toothless mouth.

Still, Chambers blessed the summer and its mild nights, the better weather. At least he'd be relatively warm and, given this location in London's newly gentrified East End, reasonably safe. His bed for the night was a recessed step in front of a wicket door on the building beside Oliver's Wharf, an old warehouse that now housed luxury flats for the wealthy. Chambers had tried to bed down in the city centre when he first was forced to sleep rough, but it was too dangerous. Young thugs with knives roamed the streets, ready to rob the homeless of what few possessions they owned, or simply use them for some twisted entertainment, a blood sport where the prey was humanity. He had taken a blade across his right cheek for the crime of being down and out. There was little mercy on the streets of the nation's capital in the twenty-first century. Maybe there never had been.

Chambers stared out over the lane that led to the steps

down to the Thames. On each bank of the river, light spilled from expensive flats and business properties. But only yards away were dark nooks and crannies, harking back to another time by the great waterway. He was dozing, half remembering his days in the army that now seemed so long ago. Other cities, different rivers – another life. Back then he'd stood proud and tall. The days before alcohol and drugs had taken his dignity, his occupation and his life, leaving behind a withered shell of a man, penniless, broken and cowed.

But at least here he was safe. The security man – son of an old army colleague – let him bed down in this sheltered doorway, on the understanding he left before the city decided to get moving. Chambers was as good as his word, spending the long days in search of food and alternative shelter. More often than not, he managed to beg a few quid, grab a morsel to eat, and some cheap, nasty wine to get him through the night. It was a relentless task, a daily grind that – judging by his racking cough and the colour of his spit – would come to an end sooner than even he hoped.

Chambers was roused from this dwam by the thud of heavy footsteps. Sensing danger, something to which he'd become more than accustomed, he withdrew further into the shadows of the deep doorway, making himself as small as possible, guarded by the invisibility of the unfortunate, to whom few gave a thought.

The lane was narrow, unlit, the only light spilling from the nearby streets and buildings. Chambers crouched as far into the doorway as he could, sure his presence would go unnoticed.

The man was big, both tall and broad, shadowed in black. Over his shoulder, he carried something in dark refuse sacks. His was the purposeful stride of a man on a mission, determined, focused.

Chambers had learned to read people by the way they walked. The light tread of the reveller, the slow shuffle of the wretched for whom life dragged on miserably, just like their gait. He studied them all from the dark recesses of his life.

The man stepped into a pool of thin light for a moment. Chambers was sure he caught a flash of red plaid from a gap in the plastic refuse sack. It was there and gone. He could feel his heart thudding in his chest, his hands shaking. There was the right thing to do; Chambers wasn't sure he still possessed the strength of virtue.

Reflected light from the Thames silhouetted this animal of a man for a moment, as he stood at the head of Wapping Old Stairs, one of London's last remaining sets of steps down to the river. He grunted as he hefted his burden higher up on his shoulder. In a moment he was out of sight, disappearing down the steps.

George Chambers held his breath, his eyes even more tightly shut behind his swollen face. Still, a fat tear managed to slip from the slits of his eyes as he waited. He sensed danger, the presence of evil, almost.

It wasn't long before the great hulk of a man returned, though this time he carried nothing. No sign of the refuse sacks. Chambers reasoned this man was a fly-tipper, dumping unwanted goods into the river, as so many others did. His instinct, however, told him otherwise, and he began to shake almost uncontrollably. So much so, some of the old newspapers he'd placed on the cold step to offer a tiny modicum of insulation rustled at the movement of his emaciated body. With his last fumes of resolve, he managed to take hold of himself, steadying his trembling frame, silencing the sound.

As though by dint of some base instinct, the man, now back under the pale lick of light from high above, stopped and sniffed the air like a wild animal. He scanned his environment as would a predator, eyes sucking at the darkness like an invisible torch.

His face was, for a second, revealed. It imprinted itself on the homeless man's brain like a sizzling brand on a farm animal.

Part of George Chambers wanted to cry, bemoan his lot. He prayed this monster would go away. Another, more distant facet of his character, buried deep, long ago, urged him to stand up and be the man he once was.

As the shadowy bulk of the stranger passed by his hiding place, Chambers took not one breath.

The footsteps passed. But even then, the homeless man waited for what seemed like an eternity before he dared step out from the darkness into the gloom of the lane. He looked back the way the man had gone and saw nothing. Common sense told him not to get involved. However, deep within him again, the tiny voice that had once been his dignity called out.

As guilt all but overwhelmed him, Chambers shuffled off in search of redemption. The steps were only a few yards away. Even that short distance made him puff. He desperately wanted to cough up the mucus from his lungs but it was still too dangerous. Sound travelled in strange ways in and around water.

Like a child hiding under the blankets, picking up the courage to stare into a dark bedroom, George Chambers edged his gaze down the bank and into the obscure waters of the Thames. At first, he saw very little other than the relentless flow of water fighting to leave the city and head for the sea. But as he stared, the lights from the embankment hit upon a flash of red. Plaid, he thought, like that worn by the Scottish regiments he'd been with on formal parades in the army.

Chambers caught his breath, as a tiny eruption in the river disturbed the focus of his attention and revealed a deathly white face. In a grotesque parody of life, the body rolled in the fast-moving water, flinging one arm up in the air, as though this remnant of flesh and bone was bidding a cruel world one regretful farewell.

Chambers shrank back from the sight, his stomach churning. He had felt the evil the stranger exuded. Its palpable results were before him now.

He whined to himself, a pitiful noise, born out of self-loathing. With his last vestige of decency, ignoring the urgent voice in his head, Chambers turned on his heel and made for the nearest police station on the Thames.

20

Brian Scott's next few hours were filled with nagging worry that verged on panic, coupled with a sense of unreality. He'd called the Rathbone, only to be told, after announcing that he was a police officer and the matter was urgent, that Mr and Mrs Daley had not returned to the hotel after leaving for the evening. Calls to Daley's mobile simply rang out, while Liz's phone was switched off.

It was almost five in the morning, with Brian and Ella drinking yet more tea in their lounge, when Scott's own mobile burst into life. The detective squinted at the phone.

'No number, Ella. Might be oor Jimmy.'

'I hope so,' she replied, her own nerves frayed.

'Hello.' Scott's voice wavered as he answered the call.

'Inspector Scott?' The voice was abrupt and unfamiliar.

'Yes, who's this?' The detective felt his stomach sink.

'It's Superintendent Turner in Glasgow. I think we have a problem, Inspector.'

'Is it Jimmy – DCI Daley, sir?'

'Yes, it is. Listen, I want you to get back to the office. I want to speak to you securely, face to face.'

'Surely you can give me an idea of what's going on, sir?'

'I don't want to go into details on an open line, Brian.

Suffice it to say, things aren't good, not good at all. How soon can you be back at the office?'

'Can you give me fifteen minutes, sir?'

'Yes. I'll speak to you then.' The call ended as abruptly as it had begun.

'What's happening?' said Ella, leaning forward on the sofa.

'It's one of the bosses, the nightshift superintendent from up the road, honey. Wants me in, PDQ.'

'I cannae believe this. Do you really think Jimmy's – well, done what he said he did?'

'Nah, no way. Come on, Ella, you know the big fulla near as well as me. Do you think he could do something like that?'

'She can be an irritating bastard when she wants to be.'

'So can you! Doesnae mean I'm going to pan your heid in, does it?'

'But that temper o' his. When he snaps, he snaps.'

'No, I'm no' having it!' Scott picked up his phone and searched for *Engelbert* in his list of contacts.

'Hello?' Duff's speech was slurred as if he'd just woken from sleep.

'It's Inspector Scott, son. Get yourself into the office. I mean right now! You've ten minutes.'

Ella lit a cigarette, her hands shaking. 'What am I going to say to that poor wee boy?'

'Don't tell him anything – don't say a word to anybody. In any case, we don't know anything.'

'I'm not stupid, Brian. But what if something *has* happened?'

'We just have to take this as it comes.'

Scott arrived at Kinloch police office to find DC Duff at the front door. Scott waved him over to his vehicle, and the pair drove to the building's rear car park. It was already getting light, the birds singing in the trees behind the office, a bright blue sky forcing its way through the retreating velvet darkness.

'Now's your big moment, young man. I'll need you to get that screen sorted. I'm just about to speak to Glasgow.' Scott pressed the security code into the door from the car park into the building.

'No bother,' said Duff, shrugging his shoulders. 'I hope I get overtime for this?'

'You'll get a rapid toe up the arse, if you're not careful.' Scott stopped in his tracks. 'And listen. You're going to hear a lot of shite in a while, OK? It goes in your lugs and stays in your heid, got it?'

'Yes, sir,' said Duff, looking puzzled as Scott took off at a canter.

As with most police stations at night, the place was quiet, the corridors illuminated by low light. When Scott burst into the CID suite with Duff in tow, two nightshift detectives looked up from their screens.

'You two. Get a hold of the nightshift. I want men on the front door and the gate. They stay on duty until I say they can go home, got it?'

'Yes, sir!' The reply was almost in unison.

'Can I ask what's going on, sir?' said DC Singh, putting down her mug of coffee.

'You'll know when you need to know. Until then, it's gobs shut.' Scott rushed into Daley's glass box, sat behind the big desk and unlocked one drawer with a key from his breast pocket. He searched about until he found a small, red notebook.

'Do you have the access codes in there, sir?' said Duff.

'Aye. Jimmy can remember them. I've no idea how he

does it.' Scott was thankful that he was ready to take over the sub-division, otherwise much of this protocol would have been beyond him.

'Impressive.'

The pair left the glass box and headed for the AV suite. Scott switched on the light as they entered. The UV bulbs flashed into life with clicks and pings as Duff took his place behind the computer.

The younger man tapped away on the keyboard. 'We have an email. Video call scheduled for five minutes' time, sir.'

'OK. Quick work, Engelbert. I hope you'll no' be all fingers and thumbs the way Shaw is with that bloody thing.'

'It's fine, sir. Really simple, if you know what you're doing.'

'That's the problem. None of us have a fucking clue.' As Scott said this, the jaggy thistle, Police Scotland's emblem, filled the screen. A digital readout at the bottom right-hand corner counted down the time until the video meeting was scheduled to begin.

Scott took his place in the chair normally used by Daley, facing his interlocutor straight-on.

'Ready to roll, sir. We just have to wait for the host,' said Duff.

'Right. Fuck, I never wanted to be on telly.' Scott turned in his chair to face the young detective. 'I want you to stay here, because as sure as shit is shit, the minute you leave the room, that bloody thing will stop working. Be prepared to hear some *real* bollocks, like I told you, son.'

After this, the pair sat in silence, the only noise in the soundproofed room being Scott's fingers drumming impatiently on the arm of his chair, and a slight hum from the lights overhead. Just as Scott sighed deeply, the image of a uniformed superintendent appeared larger than life on the screen. Behind him was a well-appointed office, with wooden filing cabinets, and a rubber plant just caught in frame. Scott, who was terrible with names, recognized Turner from his time as an inspector at Stewart Street. Both he and Daley had worked with the man for a short time. This reassured Scott slightly. Even more so, when his Christian name came to mind.

'Brian, good to see you again. It's a pity we have to meet under these circumstances.'

'Good to see you too, Paul. I didnae recognize your voice on the phone. It's been a while, eh? Where's Jordan, in his bed or taking over at a reasonable hour?'

'Taken time off. Something to do with his father – I don't know.'

'Typical. Bosses on the run when there's trouble afoot.'

'Whatever you think, I'm sure. But down to business. Listen, I've no time for you to come the old soldier with me now, Brian. I know you've been on the phone to the Rathbone Hotel. So, DCI Daley's been in touch, right?'

'Aye, kind of.'

'Cards on the table here. It's the only way. You know as well as I do, these PIRC bastards will be all over this soon. I don't want you getting rolled up in it too. Tell me what you know, and tell me everything, OK?' Turner glared at Scott through the screen.

'I got a call.'

'From Jim Daley?'

'Aye, from the big man.' Scott's mouth was dry. He dearly wished he'd brought a mug of tea into the meeting.

'What time?'

'Just after two, sir.'

'What did he say? I want it word for word, Brian.'

'Ach, you know what it's like, sir. I was half asleep when the phone went.'

'Brian, I'm warning you.' Turner shook his head at the screen wearily.

'Right, got it. The call was brief. He just told me he was in trouble. That something had happened between him and Liz.' Scott shrugged. 'Then the line went dead. I tried to phone him back but it just rang out. Been trying ever since. Also, the hotel, as you said.'

'*Something had happened.* Was that all he said?'

'Aye, just that, sir.'

'Have you anyone with you, Brian – in the room, I mean?'

'Just Engle – one of our detectives, sir.'

'Ask him to leave.'

Scott nodded to Duff, who left the room, closing the door gently behind him. His attention returned to the screen, where he could see Turner speaking to someone out of shot.

'Brian, I'm going to show you something. I know you're not going to like it, so be prepared.'

Scott felt his stomach turn over. He'd not been honest about Daley's call. Instinct told him to dread what he was about to see.

'This CCTV footage is from a lane in the East End, Brian. It was sent to a detective at the Met about an hour ago.' In a flash, Turner's face was removed from the screen, and an urban image replaced it. The lane was narrow but well lit. Buildings sprouted on either side of the lane, itself broad enough to let one vehicle pass. He saw two skips, one red, one green, on the far side of the narrow roadway. A small blue van – a Ford, Scott reckoned – was parked at the far end. As he leaned forward on his chair, the camera zoomed in on two figures entering the lane from the top right of the image. Though they appeared to be in a pool of darkness, these individuals were lit intermittently by lights from traffic on the other side of the buildings, the main thoroughfare, Scott assumed. The figures were still too far away from the camera to be identified.

Scott was surprised by the quality of the image. As the pair walked nearer to the camera, clearly positioned high up on a wall, it became obvious they were a man and a woman. Judging by their body language, they were in the middle of an argument. The woman tried to pull away from her partner, a much larger man. She appeared to turn on her heel, in an attempt to walk away from him. The burly man caught her by the arm and pulled her back, dragging her down the lane towards the camera.

Scott's heart sank to his boots when he saw the woman being pushed into a recessed doorway. The bile rose in his throat as he watched the man aim kick after kick at the woman, now out of shot.

The assault lasted for more than a minute, Scott feeling more and more disgusted as he looked at the huge screen. This was something he'd much rather have viewed on a laptop. The detail here was sickening, and this was no movie; certainly not one he wanted to watch.

The man in the lane stepped back, dragging his right sleeve across his face, as though admiring his handiwork. Then he looked about and made for one of the skips across the lane, where he levered himself up and appeared to be looking for something. Having not found what he wanted, the large figure walked to the second skip and repeated the process.

Again, the camera zoomed in, making the image slightly grainier but still good enough to make out exactly what was going on.

He pulled something from the skip, as Scott squinted at

the screen, wondering what it was he was dragging from it. He realized that the length of black material was likely builders' film. The only explanation being he had killed the woman and was now trying to find something with which to either conceal or remove her body.

It only took a few more seconds for Brian Scott's world to be turned upside down. The man, happy with his find, finished pulling the builders' film from the skip. He walked back towards the doorway and more clearly into Scott's vision. In an agonizing split second, he raised his gaze and stared almost directly into the camera.

Grainy though the footage was, there was no doubting the identity of the face that stared at Brian Scott from the screen. He'd just watched Jim Daley, the man he'd known and respected for so long, kick his wife Liz to death.

21

Scott sat back, bewildered, unwilling to believe his eyes. Mercifully, the screen switched back to Turner. 'Sorry to subject you to that, Brian. As you can see, it's all pretty awful. We still don't know who the source is. They're looking into it.'

Scott wasn't sure what to say. He couldn't reconcile what he'd just seen with Daley, though there was a spark of doubt. His friend had severely beaten the man who'd raped Liz only a couple of years before, getting away with it on a technicality of procedure. Police officers who'd no time for rapists and were loyal to one of their colleagues had been careless with the mechanics of their case.

But that wasn't going to happen this time.

'Where's Jimmy now?' he asked Turner.

'At large. The Met are trying to piece together their movements before this happened, though it appears that cameras near the lane you saw were disabled by some kind of power cut or other. They're still on the job.'

'Needle in a haystack, sir?'

'These days? Not at all. They've got face recognition technology, the lot. They'll find him.'

'And the lassie in the picture. Is it definitely Lizzie?'

'We don't know.'

Scott felt his stomach turn again. 'Don't tell me she was that bad they couldnae identify her!'

'No, she wasn't there by the time officers arrived. But they think there was enough forensic evidence to make an identification soon.'

'Shit.' Scott leaned forward, his head in his hands. 'I'm confused by one thing.'

'Just the one? I'm surprised.'

'Aye, obviously I'm shocked about that footage. But how come they got it so quickly – the Met, I mean?'

'Good point. We're trying to get a handle on that, too. I suppose we'll hear something tomorrow.'

'From PIRC?'

'The very same.'

'What next then, Paul?'

'We have to wait for formal identification of who was in that doorway. And wait for them to find Daley and his wife.'

Scott swallowed hard. The very question he was about to ask made him feel sick. 'Do you think she's dead?'

Turner sighed, rubbing his temples, looking as weary as Scott felt. 'What do you think? It's too early to draw informed conclusions, that's true. But we've been here before, Brian, you and me. How many times have you attended murder scenes like this?'

'Too many.'

'Exactly. We just have to sit and wait.'

Scott was deep in thought. 'I'm no' having it, sir.'

'What?'

'That Jimmy did this. You said yourself, we've all seen this before. There's no' a cop in the world that hasn't seen shit like this. It's the same old story, I know. But I *know* that man. I trust him with my life. He didnae do this!'

'You're a good friend, Brian. But if you had this case handed to you, what would you do?'

Scott looked at the ceiling for inspiration. 'PIRC will take things over from this end, right?'

Turner looked at his watch. 'As soon as the cock crows, Brian.'

'Right, you know me, Paul, you agree?'

'I do, Brian.'

'As my senior officer, I want to ask you a favour. I want you to sign me off duty, sir. This is all too much – I'm depressed. My mental health is a priority. I've been reading FSO. I know my rights.'

Despite the circumstances, Turner smiled. 'You know Force Standing Orders? That's the biggest shock of the night.'

'I'm no' kidding, sir.'

Turner leaned back in his chair. 'OK. In that case, I'll tell you what I'd tell any officer in such circumstances.'

'Which is?'

'Seek medical help and go through the procedure.'

'I'll do that.'

'And between you and me, Brian, make sure that you seek the best professional help there is. Some very good specialists in London, they tell me. Do you get my drift?'

'I do, Paul. Thank you for the sound advice, sir.'

'Good luck, Brian. I'm not sure even *you* can pull this off, mind you.'

'You know I have to try.'

'I do.'

With that, the video call to headquarters ended. Brian Scott was left alone in Kinloch's AV suite, his world turned upside down.

22

The man woke on a bench in a small oasis of grass over-shadowed by tall buildings. He shivered and pulled his jacket tight about himself for warmth.

He sat up and craned his neck up to where the towering roofs of London's financial district at Canary Wharf met the sky. He had to turn away, the early-morning summer sun too much for his eyes to bear.

Just beyond his bench, London's traffic was beginning to build, and already people were walking to and fro, all with a determined tread. Vaguely, he remembered a passage by Robert Louis Stevenson about the footfall of unseen passers-by, and how he could discern what they were doing by footsteps alone. Though the passage wouldn't spring properly to mind, he reckoned that these pedestrians had a unified purpose: the pursuit of money.

He looked down at his clothes, crumpled and stained, as though he hadn't changed for a fortnight. On his left trouser leg, he discovered a dried-in stain so deep that it had stiffened the material. Whatever this substance was, it left a dark residue under the nail of his right forefinger when he scratched at it. Tomato ketchup, he assumed.

The man closed his eyes and tried to remember what had happened the previous evening. Somehow, his memory had chosen not to work. He mashed his dry mouth; the not-unfamiliar feeling of a heavy hangover, its sensations of dislocation, thirst, nausea and paranoia, lay weightily on him. But something wasn't right. He knew he wasn't functioning as he should. He longed to banish the taste of stale whisky on his tongue.

Though the man instantly recognized his surroundings, he couldn't work out why he was here, much less how he'd arrived at this place. But in the pit of his stomach something unpleasant brewed like an undiscovered dread. This made him feel melancholy, especially as he couldn't work out its cause.

All this aside, the basic human need for food and water usurped his conscious mind. He was ravenous, so dry he could barely swallow.

'You're too old for this shit,' he mumbled to himself as he struggled, somewhat unsteadily, to his feet.

This place reminded him of a bad dream, a dystopia. Everything looked so antiseptic and benign, but also contrived, unnatural. Trees were small, and neatly trimmed into geometric shapes. Everything appeared sculpted, artificial. Man's heavy hand on nature, crushing it. He saw no birds in the sky and felt not a hint of breeze on his face. Only the swish of traffic and the steady stream of unseeing pedestrians assured him that he wasn't the last man alive.

'Is there a decent cafe about here?' he asked a man walking past. This young chap was dressed in an expensive suit designed to look cheap and cheerful, but not quite managing it.

Expensive suit man eyed him on his way by. 'Fuck off, you low-life prick,' he muttered.

In no mood for another encounter like this, he sighed and decided to take a walk.

It was only now he felt the mobile phone against his thigh. He pulled it out of his pocket. The screen was black, and when he tried to switch it on, nothing happened.

'Bloody batteries,' he grumbled, before placing it back in his pocket.

As he strode off, he realized that it already seemed too warm for this time of the morning. For the first time, he checked his watch – just after six. Whatever happened today, it was going to be a scorcher. The last thing he needed with such a thumping head.

The man turned a corner on to a street of steel and glass, briefly catching his reflection in the mirrored window of a building. He'd tried to avoid doing this all his life. As far as he was concerned, there were few things more depressing in life than reflections and photographs, suddenly thrust upon you without warning. He found the image he held of himself in his head rarely matched up with the stark reality. He walked on, pausing only to let three cars and a van pass before he could cross the road.

Just along the street, he could see a couple of little tables positioned on the street. This could be what he was looking for.

When he reached it – a cafe of sorts – he couldn't resist the smell of coffee, so, despite the austere look of the place, he decided to enter.

He stood at the counter for a while, as the guy behind it, sporting a long beard tied at its length with a little red bow, poured noisy coffee from a hulking machine. It was rendered in aluminium, and festooned with gauges and levers, steam shooting out hither and thon across its bulk.

'Just take a seat, mate. I'll be with you in two ticks,' said the coffee man, his pouring job now done, the machine almost silent, save for an exasperated sigh of discharged steam here and there.

He did as he was told, taking a chair at a table as far away as possible from the other three customers in the small-ish space. One young woman was checking her phone through scarlet spectacles that matched her vivid lipstick.

At the table next to her sat a man almost identical to the guy who'd been rude to him in the little park. His hair was perfectly cut; a side parting as straight as a gun barrel revealed the white line of his scalp. Somehow, his square jaw and small mouth looked too perfect. He was reading a book, its title too far away to make out.

The only other customer was a painfully thin young man. His suit, uncontrived, was undoubtably cheap, no expensive confection. He wore white socks; his Adam's apple was prominent, as though he was in the process of swallowing a tennis ball.

The space itself was antiseptic and depressing, like the area. More steel and glass, angles, the absence of warmth. Even the chairs were made of cold steel, straight backs making them uncomfortable. Still, it was a means to an end, nothing more.

'What can I get you, mate?' said the waiter, complete with red-bowed beard, who'd appeared by his table.

'The works, please. A full English.'

'Right, so we don't do fry-ups. But how does Parma ham, poached eggs and guacamole on sourdough sound? That's our *full works*.'

He stared at the waiter for a moment or two. 'I know you have coffee, yeah?'

'Oh yes, what's your poison?'

'Coffee.'

'Mocha, Americano, frappe?'

'Just black coffee, please. And plenty of it. I'll take two of your sourdough breads and all the trimmings too, please. Oh, and a large glass of water.'

'Out of the tap?'

'Out of the first place you find it, son.'

The waiter hurried off. He was light on his feet and pleasant, which was, at least, encouraging.

He must have dozed off for a second, because he woke with a start, the thin young man staring at him. 'You OK?' he said, rather put off by this spotty youth's gaze.

The lad turned his head away to face the window.

'Right,' said the waiter. 'Straight black coffee and a glass of tap water. Just let me know when you need a refill – of either. Your food won't be long.'

He thanked his host and gulped down half the glass of water. It felt good; better cool water than the finest wine for a thirsty man, he reasoned. He was surprised to note his hand trembling as he picked up the white enamel coffee mug. He put this down to alcohol, nothing more.

As he sipped at the beverage, his attention was taken by a kerfuffle outside. Three cars pulled up in the street beyond with a screech of brakes. Doors were pushed open and men tumbled out of the vehicles, just before a police van, a Met crest on its side, roared to a halt, double parking right outside the cafe.

Some bastard is about to get it, he mused – then, to his surprise, in moments the cafe door was pushed open, and the officers poured in.

It was only then that a fleeting memory from the night before crossed his mind, the flash of her face, her features screwed up in a vison of spite, hatred. He tried again to clear his mind, to make sense of what had happened the previous night.

A tall man with flaxen hair stood at his table. He reached inside the pocket of his jacket and produced his ID.

'James Daley, my name is Inspector Thomas Bright. You are under arrest for the murder of Elizabeth Daley. You do not have to say anything, but it may harm your defence if you do not mention when questioned something which you later rely on in court. Anything you do say may be given in evidence. You got all that, *Chief Inspector*?' The rank was an afterthought, more of a taunt than a sign of respect.

Daley's mind was doing somersaults now. He felt the flat of her hand across his face, her words cutting to the core, almost spat out, designed to belittle him.

'*At least I came! I can't remember the last time you could do that for me!*' The words crowded in on his mind from nowhere. Daley felt sheer panic rise in his chest.

He was grabbed roughly by two plain-clothed officers. They pulled him up from his chair, knocking his table. The glass of water spilled. His mug clanged to the floor, making the girl in the scarlet glasses shriek. A dark brown pool of coffee spread across the floor.

'She called an Uber. Liz went to stay with a friend. What do you mean, *murdered*?' His thoughts were tumbling now, as he pulled at the men who held him tight by each arm.

DI Bright leaned into him. 'Do me a favour, mate. You know the score here. Come with us and we can talk about this down the station. Remember, we're all *job*, right? Let me help you.'

Jim Daley looked at the men on either side of him, and those beyond, now crowding the tiny coffee shop. He noticed that the lad with the spots and the Adam's apple was gone, the remaining customers and the bearded waiter staring at him open-mouthed.

'You coming then?' said Bright.

'Yeah, I'm coming,' Daley replied.

'OK, we'll do without the cuffs. But behave, mate. I'm sure you'd do me the same courtesy.'

Daley nodded.

The big Scottish detective was bundled out of the cafe, surrounded by his colleagues from the Met. The back doors of the van were opened, and he was pushed inside a metal cage, almost too small for his large frame.

Bright appeared beyond the mesh grille, making sure Daley was secure inside. 'OK. We don't have far to go, right. I was going to say, stay where you are. But you don't got much choice.' He smiled.

The back door slammed in Daley's face, leaving him confined in a low gloom.

He closed his eyes tightly, hoping, praying this was all a bad dream.

'Liz!' he yelled at the top of his voice, as the police van moved off slowly into the London traffic.

23

'I need to go, Ella. I don't have a choice,' said Brian Scott as he piled clothes into a holdall.

'Right, I get it. But let me pack your bag, at least. You'll be away with all the wrong stuff. You've never packed a bag in all the years I've known you.'

'Aye, good idea. My auld mother was great at the packing, so she was. Then it was you. Mind and put in my good slippers and my jogging bottoms. I don't want to be sitting round the hotel in my scants.'

'I'm sure nobody wants you doing that, dear,' Ella replied.

'You want to have seen that video, Ella. Horrific, man.'

'And you're sure it was Jim? I mean, it sounds a bit dark to be so certain.'

'Aye, it was him. How many years have I known the man? No mistaking the big bastard.' Scott sat on a bedroom chair and held his head in his hands. 'I cannae believe it, Ella. Honest, I cannae.'

She bit her lip.

'What do you want to say, darling?'

'I mean, if you're sure it was him – absolutely sure. What do you think you can do?'

Scott sighed. 'I don't know. Try and work out what

happened, maybe? Anything I can think of doing. I owe the big man this, at least.'

'And what do you owe Lizzie, eh? I mean, you've known her nearly as long as him. Both of us have.'

'Fucked if I know. After all, I don't even know if it *was* Lizzie. Aye, I recognized him. But I didn't identify her.'

'Ah well, that's OK then. I mean, if it's just some other lassie he's booted to death, we're all right behind that.' Ella raised her eyes.

'Don't. That's the last thing I need right now. I need to catch the wee plane at ten, then the London flight at half one, OK.'

Both of them were distracted when the bedroom door was pushed open.

'Son, are you all right?' said Ella, as James junior's face appeared round the corner of the door.

'I woke up. You and Muncle Brian were shouting.'

'Och, you know your Muncle Brian. He shouts all the time.'

'Why?' James cocked his head to one side.

'It's so that folk know he's coming and can run away before he gets there, James.'

'Don't you listen to her,' said Brian.

'Anyway, it's time you were up. Away and get washed and Auntie Ella will come in and get you sorted. I've just to pack this bag.'

'Who's the bag for?' said James.

'Me. I'm needing to go away for a wee while for work, Jamie.'

Ella nudged her husband with her elbow. 'You know his mother hates you calling him that.' Realizing what she'd just said, she looked away and rubbed a tear from her eye.

'But you said we were going to the beach, Muncle Brian.'

'Don't worry, your Auntie Ella will take you. We can go another time.'

'Just you go and get washed, son. Aye, and don't forget to clean your teeth. Your toilet bag's on the sink, and your clothes are all ready for you at the end of the bed.'

'OK.'

The bedroom door closed. Ella and Brian Scott looked at each other.

'Should I send him to school?' Ella asked.

'Aye, why not?'

'You know fine what this place is like. They'll likely know all about it. Aye, and you know how cruel kids are.' She lowered her voice. 'I don't want him hearing that his daddy's just murdered his mummy, do I? Though I don't know how I'm going to tell him.'

Brian Scott stared into space for a moment. He shook his head. 'I don't know what's going to happen, Ella. Honest, I don't. But there's no way folk here can know anything. He goes to school. What else can you do?' Ella gave him a tearful nod, and the pair held each other.

'I know you'll always do the right thing, Brian,' she whispered in his ear.

Their embrace was cut short when the phone pinged in Brian's pocket. He pulled away from his wife to look at the message. Ella could see his face fall as he searched the screen with his eyes.

Scott threw the phone on the bed and sat down heavily on the chair.

'What now?'

'It's a text from the boss. They've just arrested the big man in London.'

'Oh no!'

Scott shrugged. 'These days, who knows what passes for

evidence? Shit, maybe that video will be enough. I don't know what to say or feel.'

'This is such a mess. I mean, I knew things were bad between them, but nobody expected this!'

The bedroom door was pushed open again. 'I'm ready. I cleaned my teeth, and everything.' James Daley junior smiled broadly, showing off his handiwork.

'OK, just coming, James.' Ella lightened her tone for the boy's benefit. Turning to her husband, she said, 'Don't forget your phone charger. Are you taking a laptop?'

'Aye, I suppose. It might come in handy – if I can work the damned thing.'

Ella Scott reached out and cupped her husband's face in her hands. 'I downloaded a few old war films on it. Just in case you need to take your mind off all this.' She smiled. 'I do love you, Brian.'

'I love you too, darling. I'll miss you.'

'Just do something. Anything you can.' She kissed him on the forehead.

He watched her leave the room to organize James.

'What the fuck have you done, Jimmy?' he muttered to himself.

Only then did he remember the little envelope Liz had slipped into his pocket at Kinloch Airport.

In case of emergencies.

That's what she'd said, he was sure.

Scott stepped over to the wardrobe. The suit he'd been wearing yesterday was hanging there. He fished into one of the trouser pockets then the other – there it was. Scott opened the letter.

Dear Brian. If you're reading this, something isn't right. Probably Jim has left me. I'm being blackmailed. I've left the details of it all on my iPad. It's sitting on the dressing table in our room. The password is Jameso986. Please help me if you can or want to. Liz

Scott checked his watch. It was almost twenty past eight. He had time.

He grabbed his mobile. The phone rang in his ear a couple of times.

'Hello, sir.'

'Engelbert. I need you up at my house pronto. I mean now!'

'Yes, sir. On my way.' The line went dead.

'Blackmail? What the fuck!'

The whole thing was becoming more and more bizarre by the minute.

Scott grabbed his bag, flung on his jacket and hurried downstairs.

24

Almost inevitably, it was a man walking his dog that spotted her. A red tartan skirt caught up in a clump of detritus close to the bank, held tight by some jettisoned chain-link fencing, a rusting shopping trolley, a tangle of low-hanging tree branches and a small bank of putrid mud.

Now, a unit from the Met's diving team were on the scene carefully removing the remains by means of a tiny crane and a body bag.

Inspector Jill Unwin looked on as the morning sun's golden light made the scene look like something from a diffused Turner painting. The river was her beat, and it was ever-changing. Though it was rare to be called to inspect anything that culminated happily, Unwin herself was always happy down by the water. She hated the city streets and their relentless bustle. This was the place to be. Only one thing hampered her enjoyment of the job: the dead people who kept appearing in whole or part along the great river's length. Here was another one.

'Do you think it's her, then?' she said to Sergeant John Parks, who headed up the diving team.

'Only got a glimpse. But it fits the description from the Rathbone. You know, dark hair, leather jacket, short kilt. She's taken a battering, by the looks of things.'

'Lovely, just what I wanted to hear before breakfast.'

'On the bright side, she's not been in the river long enough to get knocked about much by the water. The formals should be quite easy.'

'They arrested the suspect earlier. He's kicking his heels at Bethnal Green, as we speak.'

'Fuck, that was quick.'

'Yeah, that's what I thought.' Unwin leaned into Park. 'He's in the job. Her old man, apparently.'

'Anyone we know?'

'Nah, a DCI from out in the sticks up in Scotland, so I hear. It's that little bastard Bright who's got the case.'

'That twat.'

'You know him, then?'

'Do I ever. Worked on a case with him four years ago when he was a DS. Cut and dried cigarette smuggling. Geezers from Holland, sailing up the Thames and leaving the cigs in dry bags to be picked up when the time was right.'

Unwin shrugged. 'Doesn't sound too hard to crack.'

'Shouldn't have been. Me and the boys spent a whole shift fishing them all out. Bloody January, into the bargain. Honestly, my hands were so cold I thought they'd come off.'

'How'd it end up, then?'

'Bright only makes a mistake with the paperwork. They all got off on a technicality. Steam was coming out our ears, I can tell you.'

Unwin gazed at the river, brown and unappealing, as it washed by in little waves and eddies. 'He tried it on with me at a party once, did Bright. Wasn't taking no for an answer, neither.'

'So, not for a polite no, then?'

'Nah, sadly not. I kicked him in the nuts and threatened to tell his missus. Scarpered like the coward he is. Don't have much time for him, I have to say.'

'But he's the type what'll make it all the way, Jill.'

'No doubt. Thankfully, by the time he's got there, me and Dan will be in our little place in Spain.'

'Quite right. That's the only way to think when you come across these pricks.'

They looked across as the body bag was placed into a hard shell, then into the back of a mortuary van. The noise of the city was the only backdrop.

'That looks like us.'

'OK, Johnny boy. I'll be seeing you. Thanks for the help, and all that.'

'Don't suppose it'll be too long until our paths cross again, ma'am.'

'*Ma'am*, listen to it. Go and get some breakfast with the lads.'

'That's the plan, Jill. See you anon.'

Unwin watched her colleague as he strolled away across the tumble of rough grass tuffets, bricks and old rubbish. The Thames had always been a place to get rid, to end things. In that respect, nothing had changed, though the city that had grown around it was beginning to look like something from a sci-fi comic, tall buildings of increasingly odd shapes and designs springing up along the length of the waterway. To Jill Unwin they looked ugly and out of place. But she'd been born down near the Thames and took it personally. Her grandfather had piloted one of the old refuse barges that ploughed the waterway, in the never-ending task of keeping the great city clean. This dirty old river was her life.

She looked on as the mortuary van pulled away from the

riverbank. For too many others, this place meant death. Then she thought of DI Bright, the little prick who would, no doubt, soon be a borough commander.

Once again, she counted every day of the two years and seven months that would pass until she retired.

25

Jim Daley was in a small cell at Bethnal Green police station. They'd offered him food and water. He'd accepted the latter only. His hunger had been banished utterly by what he'd been told by the chirpy inspector with the blond hair.

But unpleasant things were flashing across his memory.

He'd decided not to confront Liz about what he'd found on her computer, even though it almost broke any resolve he had about saving their marriage. He remembered feeling as cooped up in the Rathbone as he felt now in the cell. They'd opted to have drinks elsewhere then head for something to eat, depending on how they felt.

Through his thudding head, Daley could still remember the effort it had been to bottle up his temper. He'd never loathed Liz – despite her many affairs. His overwhelming emotion was one of despairing sorrow. Liz had broken all of the many promises she'd made about changing her ways. But he'd been unfaithful with Mary Dunn. Since then, their lives had been governed by a kind of détente, an exercise in mutual mistrust. All that was holding them together was their young son.

He remembered when she told him she was pregnant. Daley hadn't believed himself to be the father until a DNA test ended all speculation. Since then, they'd just carried on. Some good times, some bad. But always, from his perspective at least, a cloying mistrust.

But surely they'd got it wrong. She wasn't dead, he was certain. He knew he hadn't killed her, despite the fact he could recall so little from the night before. He'd learned that they didn't have a body, and that any evidence against him came from a CCTV recording.

Of course, they'd made a mistake. It was the only explanation. She'd come bounding in to end this mess, wouldn't she?

He tried and tried to remember how he and his wife had become separated the previous evening. But nothing came, just flashes of her face, distorted with anger.

Had he confronted her about the video of her and this other man? Had drink loosened his tongue, released his true feelings? He couldn't remember.

There was movement outside his cell. A key turned in the lock, and the door swung open. Two impossibly young men in uniform called him forth.

You know you're getting old when policemen start to look young.

Daley was given another bottle of water and taken to an interview room. Like all such places, it was stark, unwelcoming, bare of any comfort. It was a place where – one way or the other – the truth would be extracted. He'd done this a thousand times, using all his knowledge and guile to break an individual into confessing.

But how could one confess to something one couldn't remember, couldn't contemplate doing – not ever?

The interview room door was opened by a young woman in a black trouser suit, a briefcase in her right hand. Her hair was neatly bobbed. Though Daley placed her in her late twenties, she had dark rings round her eyes, the tell-tale signs of too much work, too many late nights, a surfeit of dedication. He knew the feeling well.

Behind her appeared DI Bright, a large grin spread across his face. He was carrying an iPad under one arm.

'Now then, DCI Daley. How's the hangover?'

Daley said nothing.

'You've refused legal counsel, I hear,' said Bright.

'I have.'

'OK. Well, since you're *job*, I want to do you a favour.'

'I don't want any favours from you, Inspector.'

'You will after you've seen and heard what I have here, mate.'

'DCI Daley, I'm DS Kenton, prisoner welfare rep,' said the woman. 'I do think you should reconsider legal rep-resentation. Especially given the evidence we now have in our possession. DI Bright is trying to help you here. We're not required to reveal this evidence until we question you. We just wanted to give you another chance.'

'I don't care what evidence you have. I'm not guilty of any murder. My wife will be holed up at some friend or other's. She has plenty to choose from here in London. We had an argument, nothing more.' Daley sat back in his chair and folded his arms. 'Do yourselves a favour and release me before it's too late.'

The Met detectives glanced at each other. DS Kenton looked sympathetic, DI Bright did not.

'OK, OK. You've been warned. James Daley, I must cau-tion you again before I reveal the evidence we have.' Bright repeated the caution he'd given Daley on arrest. The *in connection with the murder of Elizabeth Daley* part made the big Scot flinch. Despite being convinced that he could never harm a hair on Liz's head, he still couldn't remember what had happened the previous evening, and that worried him. His mind felt altered, as though somebody had tried to erase his memories.

'James Daley,' DS Kenton said, looking up from her paperwork, 'I must inform you that a body was found in the River Thames earlier this morning that matches the description of your wife. Do you understand?'

Daley remained outwardly impassive, though a gaping hole was already appearing in his world. 'Say it again with the tape on,' he said.

Bright shrugged. 'If that's what you want. But remember, the minute I make this an official interview, you're being questioned without a brief. I want to remind you of that.'

Daley nodded.

'It's 10.02 a.m., on June 15. This is DI Bright. I'm accompanied by DS Kenton. We're interviewing James Daley, currently of the Rathbone Hotel, London. He's been cautioned on arrest about the suspected murder of his wife, Elizabeth Daley. For the tape, he has refused the statutory services of a legal representative.'

'Mr Daley,' said Kenton, 'you have been informed that a body matching the description of your wife was found in the River Thames earlier this morning. Can you acknowledge that for the tape, please?'

'Yes,' said Daley weakly.

'Mr Daley, I want to draw this to your attention. For the tape, I'm showing the accused CCTV images captured yesterday evening at Broddings Lane in the East End of London.' Bright slid the large iPad across the table to Daley.

Though the screen was black, Daley could see a countdown timer in the top corner. He swallowed hard and waited for the recording to appear. Soon, he was looking at a gloomy scene, where a couple appeared at the far end of a narrow lane.

As he gazed on, Daley felt a revulsion so powerful it made him tremble from head to foot. Though the figures remained slightly blurred in the poor-quality video, the woman did have Liz's bearing, her walk. When he saw the man push her into the doorway, he began to feel sick, as again and again the male figure aimed kick after kick into the now unseen woman in the doorway.

He watched as the man searched skips, dragged something from the second one he'd looked in, then made his way back down the lane. Suddenly, as light passed across his face, the image froze, and so did Daley's heart. Being closer to the camera, the man's features were instantly recognizable.

'James Daley, can you confirm that is an image of you?'

Daley didn't know what to say. Of course he recognized his own face, but he could do nothing but gaze at the screen in astonishment, as though this was all some bad dream, a nightmare from which he couldn't free himself.

'Can you identify the man you see in that image, please, Mr Daley?' said Bright for a second time.

'No, it's not me!' Daley shouted with frustration and banged the table with a fist, startling DS Kenton.

'Come on. You're caught bang to rights here! We have what we believe to be your wife's body, and there's no denying this, is there?' Bright leaned forward and grabbed the iPad from in front of Daley, holding it up before the accused man. 'Look at the face. It's you, just as I can see you now. You and your wife went out last night, and for some reason, you took her here and killed her.'

'It's not me!' Daley's expression blazed, his eyes brimming with tears.

'Admit it. You and your wife were arguing. You lost your temper with her – couldn't stand it no more. You pushed her into a doorway and you kicked her to death!' Bright was on his feet now, his teeth bared, a strand of his blond hair straggling over one eye. 'You killed your own wife, plain and simple!' Bright pointed an accusing finger at Daley to emphasize his point.

Jim Daley pushed himself up from the chair, and in one fluid motion swung his large fist at his interrogator. The blow connected with Bright's chin, sending him flying backwards on to the floor.

In a flash, the interview room door was flung open and three uniformed constables rushed in.

The DCI swung another punch, which this time connected with the shoulder of one of the constables, making him yell in pain. But despite his size and strength, Daley was wrestled face down on to the floor. As he was held there, he yelled, 'It's not fucking me!'

DS Kenton rushed from her side of the desk. In seconds, she leaned on Daley's legs as her colleagues continued the struggle and handcuffed the Scottish detective.

'Lie still!' she shouted. 'They'll taser you if you don't!'

Through his horror, rage, fear and sorrow, her words made sense. Daley let his body go limp. In any case, he was finding it hard to breathe with four police officers on top of him.

'Get him to his feet,' ordered Bright, managing to push himself off the floor, blood pouring from a cut on his chin. 'You're going down! Job or no fucking job, you're never going to see your little bit of Scotland no more!' he yelled. 'Take him to the cells!'

26

It had been odd being in Daley's home with neither him nor Liz there. Brian Scott found the iPad he'd been looking for. It was now tucked into his hand luggage as he sat in the service plane en route from Kinloch to Glasgow.

Scott stared out of the window, not looking at anything in particular, though a small yacht pushing through a moderately heavy sea did catch his eye. The white flush of its bow wave against the dark water made him think of the struggle he now faced in order to save his friend.

Scott was a straight thinker, normally unhindered by the burden of nuance or etiquette. To him, it was all black and white, good and bad. Good people were on the right side, bad on the other. A bit like the cowboy films he'd watched as a kid. The bad guy always wore the black hat. In his experience, those who appeared to be model citizens, suddenly gone wrong for no apparent reason, often held dark secrets in their past. It was all quite simple. He'd seen it time and time again.

Then, he thought of those who acted in extremis. The ordinary men and women who could take no more and lashed out against oppression and cruelty. He'd heard too many of Jim and Liz's arguments. And though Jim Daley always tried to hold his own, he often lost out to his wife's quick, acerbic tongue. She had no problem saying things in the heat of the moment that would cut his friend deep. And they had.

Part of him wished that the pair could have resolved their differences long ago. The other side mourned the loss of Mary Dunn. Her and Daley's affair would have removed the big man from the toxic relationship he had with his wife, once and for all. It wasn't to be. So paper-thin was the Daleys' relationship, the tiniest thing was likely to cast it asunder.

He knew that Daley's decision to leave Kinloch had been enough to do just that, though he wondered why Liz had changed her mind about leaving. Maybe the answer was on her iPad. He'd check when he was closeted in his hotel room, not far from Euston Station. Cheap, cheerful and close to everything, he hoped, though as long as he had somewhere to lay his head, he wasn't really bothered. The Paul Young song played in his head.

The landscape spread out beneath him, as he puzzled on what to do. After all, he wasn't investigating this case. He was a civilian, a member of the public. But he did have one advantage. He'd attend to that later.

Below, the sea disappeared, to be replaced by more familiar territory. He could see the spires of Paisley as they made a rather bumpy landing at Glasgow Airport. The plane was small enough that the cockpit was obscured from view only by a curtain. Once the aircraft came to a halt, Scott undid his safety belt.

The pilot was making his way down the aisle, bidding his passengers a safe onward journey.

'I hope you enjoyed the flight?' he said to Scott in passing.

'I'll tell you when my breakfast settles back doon. It was like a washing machine in here when you were landing. Hey, maybe you need more time on thon stimulator. Take off they rough edges, pal. Practice makes perfect, and all that.'

The pilot smiled. 'I'll see if they have any *stimulators* handy. Have a nice day.' He continued his huddling passage down the rest of the aircraft with a mirthless grin.

'Aye, cheerio, Top Gun,' said Scott as he retrieved his hand luggage.

Once he'd taken the short steps down on to the tarmac, Scott remembered to switch his mobile back on. As he leaned against the rail on the bus taking them to the terminal, he checked the device. A message from Superintendent Turner stood out.

Body removed from the Thames matching the description of L Daley. Don't do anything stupid.

Scott stared at this message blankly. He couldn't take in the meaning of the few words on the screen. He read them over and over again.

'Sir, that's us at the terminal, you can disembark now.' The flight attendant smiled at him through her caked makeup.

'Eh? Oh aye, thanks, doll.' Scott hadn't realized the bus had stopped. In a state of near trance, he made his way off the airport transport and into the terminal.

The flight attendant raised her eyes at her colleague. 'Would you listen to that. Last of the dinosaurs. Can you remember the last time you were called *doll*, Emma?'

'Never. But my granny likely got it a few times.'

'Maybe your great-granny.'

The attendants followed Brian Scott into the bustle of Glasgow Airport.

*

151

Ella Scott was back behind the bar at the County Hotel. Already, she'd served a few people coffee. These were mainly women out to meet friends for a natter before continuing their shopping. They sat in the hotel vestibule, on green leather chairs, at tables covered with studded brass.

Only one customer sat at the bar. He was a man in his late thirties, his puffy face, distended belly and bloodshot eyes testament to a life spent too long in places like this. He was a regular, never any trouble. At least he gave her something to do, though she couldn't help but feel sorry for a man of his age, seemingly intent on killing himself with booze before he was fifty.

Ella worried about her husband as she polished a pint glass with a white tea towel. Though she'd tried her best to encourage him in his attempt to get to the bottom of whatever was going on in London, he had a definite knack of getting himself into trouble. What could he do if Daley had done as he'd suggested in his phone call? Precious little, Ella reckoned, though she knew he had to try. Her husband had many qualities, and foremost amongst them was loyalty. He'd proven this time and time again during their marriage.

As Ella placed the polished glass neatly on a shelf beside others, she wondered what would happen to James junior. How would any child be able to come to terms with something like this, if what they'd heard was true? The only thing she could do was put it all to the back of her mind until she heard from Brian. And that wasn't going to be easy.

Ella heard the hotel's front door swing open on its squeaky transom and remembered that she needed to have it fixed. She was just jotting this little task down in her notebook when she was aware of someone standing in front of her at the bar.

'I'll be with you in a second,' she said without raising her head.

'I wouldna worry, Ella. I think it's too late anyway.'

Ella Scott looked up to see Hamish standing before her. The lines on his old face seemed deeper, more pronounced than usual, his eyes downcast. She knew she couldn't let her thoughts show in front of Hamish. He had an unerring knack of perception to go with his fabled second sight, of which she was sceptical.

'Hello, Hamish. Did you drop a fiver and find ten bob?' she said as cheerfully as she could muster.

'Ach, no. In any case, money's of no use where I'm going, and that's a fact.'

'Right. Just like this shift's going to fly by wae your miserable face for company.'

'I'll no' trouble you for long. Just a couple o' drams before I head back doon that road and try for some sleep. For I'm here to tell you, I slept not a wink last night.'

'And why on earth was that?' said Ella, feeling her stomach turn.

'Death, that's why. Just so. I feel it heavy on me yet, and my dream's long over.'

'You need to find a hobby. You've been a sad bastard since you retired.' She placed a dram on the counter before the old man.

'That's as maybe. But at least I'm still here, breathing God's good, clean air.'

'Funny, I thought it was quite stuffy in here when I came in.'

'You know full well that I didn't mean in *here*, rather on this earth.' Hamish eyed her as he took a sip of whisky from the small glass.

'And you'll be breathing it for many more years to come, I'm sure. Aye, and many more drams into the bargain.'

'Mind you, some folk aren't so lucky.' Hamish pushed his greasy old Breton cap to the back of his head, still staring at Ella.

'Och, would you just spit it out, if you've got something to say!' This sounded more strident than Ella intended. But her nerves were frayed enough without having to play mind games with her wily old customer.

'You can maybe tell me why your husband was rushing across the esplanade to the Daley house earlier this morning. Aye, and why he dashed from there to the Glasgow plane, right afterwards? All the while, him bearing a look that could chill the soul, too.'

'How do you hear about these things?'

'Because I've a mind to, that's why.' Hamish removed a briar pipe from the pocket of his shabby dungarees and began to suck at it unlit.

'My husband is going about his business as a police officer, as you well know. And that business is none of my affair, and certainly none of yours.'

'Thanks. I'll see you tomorrow,' said the younger man at the counter. He drank up and left the bar with a smile.

'See, you're driving away my customers!'

'Young Hughie needs to go easy on the drink, anyway. Man, his grandfather was just the same. He'd a fair swallow until the day he died.'

'And what age was he?'

'Just a lad, really – seventy-six. Many-a-time I bumped into him in port on Islay or Arran. Aye, and him as drunk as a lord. They said his boat could sail itself, for none o' the crew were ever capable enough to take the wheel.'

'Doesnae say much for health and safety, does it?'

'I don't know about that. They tell me they have cars that drive themselves these days. Well, they were beaten to it by

Alec Thomson's boat fifty years ago, and no lie. We used to see the vessel making fine headway down the sound and be sure to give him plenty o' sea room.'

'It all sounds bloody careless, if you ask me,' said Ella.

'Och, you're from the city. You canna be expected to understand such things.' Hamish took another sip at his dram. 'So, you're no' for telling me where Brian's gone?'

'I am not.'

Hamish sat wearily on a bar stool. 'I'm an old man. I don't have too many folk left I'd care to call close, these days. There's that niece o' mine in Firdale, mind. But her heid's too full of new carpets, curtains and the like – soft furnishings, they call them. Aye, and her son's violin lessons. According to her he's going to be the next Yehudi McEwan, or whatever his name was. I must say, I was forced to listen to the boy for ten minutes a while ago, and all I could think of was getting myself oot o' that room before I went stone deaf.'

'You've got plenty of friends. Don't give me that old tosh.'

Hamish carried on, as though she hadn't spoken. 'They say that once you've saved a man's life, you're responsible for it for the rest o' time.'

'Is that no' from *Game of Thrones*? The big boy wae the burnt face?'

'I'm no' acquainted with such a thing. Though it seems fair enough to me.'

'Will you get to the point, Hamish!'

'Jim Daley, that's my point. I saved that man's life. Now, I'm sure it's in danger all over again.'

Ella was about to open her mouth in reply when the hotel phone rang. 'I'll need to get that.' She dashed off to answer the call in the little office behind the bar.

The old fisherman leaned on the bar from his stool. 'A

fortuitous telephone call, right enough, Ella Scott. Saved by the bell. But I'll no' stop until I've got to the bottom o' all this. Though I'm feart of what I'll find.' Hamish took another sip of his whisky and sucked his unlit pipe with little enthusiasm and a heavy heart.

27

Scott was deposited by the taxi across the road from his hotel. That it was slightly off the tourist map didn't matter. To Scott, it looked perfectly acceptable from outside. His temporary residence was a red-brick building sporting a neon sign that should have read *The Plymouth Inn*. Unfortunately, some of the letters were dead, so it appeared more like the *mouth n*. It stood next to a patch of wasteground; across the road, a few terraced houses huddled together, likely once part of a much longer street. They looked badly in need of refurbishment, by Scott's measure of such things. In short, this wasn't somewhere visitors from all round the world wanted to see. It was a side street, a sidenote. He reckoned it was like parts of Glasgow in that regard. Hidden places, secret lives.

Scott strode up the front steps and into reception, in reality a small table at the end of the hall on which perched a broad register, open at an empty page.

'Hello!' shouted Scott, anxious to get into his room and find out what Liz had left on her tablet.

'You fill in the book. I be with you soon!' The voice was distant, the words in broken English.

Scott studied the register. His name, address and mobile

phone number were required. He leaned over the table, ready to fill in these sections. But when he checked in his pockets, it quickly became clear he had no pen. 'I need a pen!' he called into space.

'Why do people have no pens these days!' The distant voice now had an admonishing tone. 'When I first come here to England, everyone had pen!'

'Well, I've no' got one!' Scott replied indignantly. He heard a door close, then the shuffle of feet coming somewhere from his left. A small Asian man appeared. He was bald, wearing steel-framed glasses too big for his face, and a blue dressing gown that covered his rotund body from neck to tartan slippers.

'Here is pen.' The hotelier produced the writing implement from his dressing-gown pocket. 'You not steal it, neither.' The little man shook his head and wagged one finger at his new guest.

'Cool your jets, wee man,' said Scott as he went about the business of filling in the register. 'I've had a long day, and it's no' finished yet.'

The hotelier screwed up his face. 'I cannot understand a word you say. Are you bloody foreigner?'

'Me? No, I'm from Scotland,' he said, whispering, 'You cheeky bastard,' under his breath.

'It rain there lots. I know, my niece lives in Edinburg.'

'Edinburgh,' Scott corrected.

'You make no sense. What is your name? My name is Suraj.' He held out his chubby hand for Scott to shake.

'Pleased to meet you, I'm Brian Scott.' He shook his new landlord's hand.

'You already tell me you Scottish.'

'No, that's my name, Brian *Scott*.'

'That's like me being called Suraj Pakistan. It is stupid, no?'

'Well, whatever you think, buddy. Each to their own, you know. I just want to get to my room. I have to go back out in a couple of hours.'

'Wait!' Suraj commanded. 'You listen to rules of hotel first.'

'Aye, OK. But make it quick.' Scott sighed in surrender.

'There will be no smoking.'

'No bother. That's the usual now, eh?'

'No prostitutes.'

'Steady on, wee man!'

'No racists neither. I hate fucking racists. You understand?'

'Don't worry, I'm no racist, Suraj.'

'This is good. You give me racist, I boot you out!'

'Listen, see where I come from, we see everybody the same. We're all Jock Tamson's bairns, right.'

'Who is this Jock?'

'No, it's just a saying. It means we're all the same. Everybody is the same.'

'I not the same as the fucking racists!' Suraj raised his finger of admonishment once more.

'No, not you. You're OK. Now, can I go to my room, please?'

'You can.' Suraj reached into the pocket of his dressing gown once more, and produced a large mortise key that looked very much as though it came from another century. 'Room fourteen. You go upstair to third floor, OK?'

'Aye, fine. Thank you.' Scott took his room key.

'And one more thing,' said Suraj, grabbing Scott's arm in an effort to whisper into his ear.

'What's that?'

'You no' piss in the sink, got it!?'

On his way upstairs to his room, Brian Scott mentally compared the Rathbone, where the ill-fated Daleys had booked in last night, to this hotel. *Character*, he told him-self. *The place has loads of character.*

The big key was stiff in the lock. Eventually, he managed to turn it. The door squealed open, to reveal a small room containing a double bed with a beige duvet matching the carpet. The walls were yellow – two different shades, one mustard, the other verging on orange. The obligatory wardrobe and chest of drawers stood together against the wall opposite the bed. Both were old but functional, with the merest touch of woodworm.

Scott made his way over to the window. The view was obscured by stained net curtains. When he pushed them aside, he looked straight on to the roof. Across the way sat a factory unit, its walls covered in moss, the odd tuft of grass poking out here and there from gutters. Scott closed the net curtains, rapidly concluding he wasn't here for the view. He threw his bag on the bed and sat beside it.

'I've never liked London,' he muttered to himself.

'Aye, but the question is, what do you like, eh?' The bath-room door swung open. A short man with greying red hair was framed in the doorway.

'What the fuck!?' said Scott, jumping to his feet, eyes wide.

The pair stared at each other for a moment or two before bursting into mutual laughter.

'Brian Scott. Fuck me, it must be twenty years since I last saw you, eh? At my mother's funeral, if I remember correctly.'

'You're right enough, Eddie. Sad day that. Your mother fed half the street when we were weans.'

'She was a good-hearted old soul, I'll say that. She'd a mean right hook, mind.'

Scott laughed. 'I remember that too. I always called her Mrs Beattie, but she wisnae having it.'

'Even we called her Helen. She wouldnae have Mum or Mother, neither.'

'A fine woman.' Scott shook his head at the memories. 'Hey, how did you manage to get in here?'

'You told me this was where you were staying. Don't you remember?'

'Of course I do. But I still want to know how you got in.'

'Wee Suraj is an old friend of mine. I was a DS round here. He's a cracking bloke. When I told him you were one of my pals, he told me he'd make sure you got the best room.'

Scott looked about. 'Man, I'd hate to see the others. He's a wee bit odd, is he no'?'

'I'm telling you, he's smart as a tack, Bri. Heart of gold, too. He's helped a lot of folk in this community. Fills the place with homeless on the worst night of the winter. Aye, he's brave, too. Saw him face off a gang of BNP skinheads once. He's a good man, trust me.'

Scott was surprised, though he'd long since learned not to make hasty judgements about anyone, but guessed he just had. 'No great shakes at running a hotel, though.'

'Come on, Brian. Me and you have stayed in worse.'

'You're no' joking. Who'd have thought we'd have ended up as polis?'

'You were the brave one. I fucked off to the Met. You stayed in Glasgow. No' easy, considering our old pals fae the street, I'll bet.'

'You'll have heard Frank MacDougall died.'

'I did. Frank was just a fool to himself. JayMac was the evil bastard.'

'Deid too.'

'Not before he shot you, right?'

'You heard that?'

'Of course. Machie's reach was long. We nearly had him not long before you did. How the bastard got away, I'll never know.'

'He would have killed me if it wisnae for big Jimmy.'

Beattie looked at the floor. 'He's in the shite right up to his neck, Brian. It's odd, too.'

'I thought as much. How come odd? They found a body. I heard on the way doon.'

'They did. Her parents are on the way to identify her.'

'Fuck's sake. I just cannae believe all this.'

'Then there's the video.'

'Saw it. Made me feel sick.'

'Something's no' right, Brian. It's open house for rumours down here, normally. Not heard one word about the bloody CCTV footage being AI, not heard lots of things.'

'How dae you mean?'

'Too neat. Too quick. Too easy. Do you know, they've left it to the local DI. MIT aren't involved; the order came from the top. By the way, who's ACC Jordan?'

'A boy-king fae up the road. You know, accelerated promotion, letters after his name. Why do you ask?'

'Was head and ears into us about some data breach, then it went quiet.'

'Something up wae his faither. It'll be some other ambitious senior officer wae notions of being your commissioner who'll take over. Anyway, how do you know all this, Eddie?'

'Perks of being a detective superintendent.' He smiled broadly.

'Eddie Beattie a detective superintendent. I cannae believe it!'

'You've just been made an inspector. I'd say that's much more unbelievable.'

'Cheeky bastard! But I'm glad you think there's something afoot.'

'No' just me. An old pal o' mine was in charge o' finding the body. Jill Unwin – she's a good copper. I spoke to her this morning when I found out she was involved. You see, we've a wee problem – a couple of wee problems, as it goes.'

'Which are?'

'The IO is a right little bastard from Bethnal Green nick.'

'The inspector you mentioned?'

'Aye, the very man. His name is Bright, though by name only.'

'Not by nature.'

'Most definitely not. But he's dangerous. It'd be much better if Jill ran the case. After all, she found the body, so to speak.'

'Doable?'

'Not sure. There's another complication, by the way.'

'Which is?'

'Your man Jimmy lamped Bright earlier. Caught him a belter on the chin, by all accounts.'

Scott sighed and sat back down on the bed. 'See Jimmy and that temper. He's like a rocket.'

'Not doing himself any favours.'

'The body, you got any inkling if it's actually her?'

'She took a battering. But I've seen the mortuary images. Compared to the picture I saw of her from the records, it looks like it to me.'

'Bastard. Poor Lizzie. They were only supposed to be having a weekend away to help keep their marriage going. There's still a chance it's no' her. I'll cling to that.'

'Up to you. But what you've told me doesn't sound good, either. Mutual antipathy already established, if they're trying to save their marriage.'

'Where the fuck did you learn a word like *antipathy*?'

'Along the way, Brian. Along the way. We're no' in the East End of Glasgow any more.'

'Don't worry, I'm no' wearing my ruby slippers, neither.'

'Do you think he did it?' Beattie looked suddenly serious, as though Scott himself was being questioned.

'You saw the video.'

'Videos these days.' He shrugged.

'They've been fighting like cat and dog for years. But I don't think he could ever harm a hair on her head. The big man will be devastated if that's her in the river.'

'Listen, can you think of anything odd that happened to them recently?'

'Like somebody hacking Jimmy's profile from the Police Scotland database? Or a guy committing suicide in their bedroom?'

'Really?'

'Aye, *really*.'

'Right, that is interesting.'

'Is there much you can do, Eddie?'

Beattie tapped his nose. 'You know me, Scooty.'

'Fuck, here we go wae the Scooty again.'

'Long time ago.'

'Machie called me that too. Just before he shot me.'

'Ooft, nae luck. But you're still here.'

'By the skin o' my haw maws, Eddie.'

'OK, first things first. We need to get you in to speak to Daley.'

'You can do that?'

'Brian, I can do anything. And anyway, one of the custody officers at Bethnal Green owes me a favour. Likes a good sauna, if you know what I mean. Aye, and a massage afterwards.' He winked. 'Of course, when we raided the place, I never saw him leave with a towel wrapped round his arse.'

The old friends laughed together once more. But Brian Scott still had a boulder at the pit of his stomach that he couldn't shift.

'Listen, Eddie. Liz left me a note – you know, just when they were leaving. There's something on this iPad she wanted me to see if things went wrong.'

'*Went wrong?* So, you reckon she was expecting something?'

'We're about to find out.' Scott removed the iPad from his bag and opened it using the password Liz had left him in the note. He clicked on files, opening the one entitled *For Brian Scott.*

'Impressive IT skills. To think, you couldn't write until you were seven.'

'Haha! Anyway, the boy at the office showed me what to do. No' that difficult when you know.'

A document appeared on the screen. There was a close-up image of a man's face, and another – the same picture – showing him full-length. By the background, he was standing in a bar. They began to read the text.

Brian. I dread to think what's happened if you're reading this. In case I don't get the chance again, I want to tell you and Ella how much I love and admire you. Please look after Jim and James for me, if the worst comes to the worst. After the other night, who really knows what the future holds.

The images are of a man called 'Sean'. I had a fling with him at that photography course I went on last winter. I'm sorry, but it just happened. If it's any consolation, I've hated myself ever since. He's been blackmailing me. I've paid him money, but he wants more, I just know it.

If things get bad, please try and find this man. I'm only leaving this because I'm worried.

Thank you, my old friend. And I'm sorry, I really am.

Liz

Scott had a tear in his eye when he turned to Eddie Beattie. 'Shit, it's as though she knew!'

'You ever seen this guy, Brian?'

'Nah. The course she's talking about was here – in London.'

'OK. I'll need a screenshot of these images.' Beattie nodded to Scott.

'Why are you looking at me? I don't have a clue how to do that.'

'Give it here.' Beattie began working on the iPad, and soon his own phone pinged in his pocket. 'OK, that's it. I'll run this through the computer, quiet like. Best we don't show anyone this until we know more.'

'Aye, sure thing.'

'They have as long as ninety-six hours to hold your pal without charge. They'll get an extension no bother under these circumstances.'

'A race against time, as well as everything else. Poor Jimmy.'

'Then there's the possibility he did it. You need to get your head round that just in case. If it is Liz, he could have snapped.'

'I know. But I also know he didn't do it!'

Beattie handed Scott a card. 'Be here in a couple of hours, OK? We'll have a bite to eat. By that time, I'll have spoken to Bethnal Green. I'll know when my man's on the custody desk.'

'OK. Thanks, pal.'

'Good to see you, Brian. I better get on my toes.'

In a few moments, Scott was left alone, with only cares and woes for company.

28

Ella Scott arrived at James junior's primary school just as the children were spilling out into the playground. The girl taking over at the County Hotel had turned up late. Ella was glad that she was in time for young James. She stepped out of her car, and soon spotted him running in her direction with a big smile spread across his face. He was carrying a large piece of paper that flapped about as he ran.

'Did you have a good day at school, James?'

'Yes, Auntie Ella. I painted a picture of us at the beach, look!' The little boy handed his painting to Ella. There were five people standing on yellow ground. One of these people was very tall, another small.

'That's lovely, James. And who's in the picture?' asked Ella, suspecting she knew only too well the identity of the painted images.

'We're at the beach. Look, there's the yellow sand.'

'Oh, that's clever.'

'And that's you, Auntie Ella.' James pointed to a woman with brown hair, and lipstick plastered across her face.

'Lovely.'

'There's Muncle Brian beside Daddy.'

'Is that a bottle of juice Muncle Brian has in his hand?' said Ella with one eyebrow raised.

'No, it's whisky. Mummy says Muncle Brian loves whisky more than anything.'

Ella made a face, then felt guilty about it.

'And that's me and Mummy at the end.' The child had painted himself in his mother's arms, a strand of her dark hair falling over her face. It was well observed – Liz's hair was often like this.

Ella swallowed away the huge lump in her throat. As they walked to the car, she wiped tears from her eyes, unseen by James, who plodded on ahead, humming a tune to himself.

'OK, we'll go to the beach for a wee while, since Muncle Brian promised you. I've got your stuff in a bag on the back seat.'

'Yay!' squealed James. For most young children in Kintyre, the summer meant sea and sand, right on their doorstep.

Ella drove out of Kinloch, and was soon heading into the country, the radio blaring, as requested by James. The sky was a bright blue, not a cloud to be seen. Cows grazed lazily in fields and birds tumbled on the light breeze from tree to tree. It was as though all was right with the world. Ella turned up the air conditioning and breathed the welcome cool draught, knowing that everything was far from well.

'Me and Mummy always have the radio on when we're out in the car,' James shouted over the racket.

'I know, son. Mummy likes her music, eh?' Once again, Ella felt a lump in her throat. This time, she found it harder to banish.

Suddenly, James let out a yell.

'What's the matter, James?' said Ella, stepping on the brakes.

'That's Mummy's favourite song!' exclaimed the child, clapping his hands to the music, as Simple Minds' 'Don't You Forget About Me' blared out of the car's speakers. 'Remind me to tell Mummy when she gets home, Auntie Ella.'

'I will, James.' This time, Ella had to banish her tears in order to see the road ahead. Her heart was breaking for the wee boy, but there was nothing she could do. She knew that James was young enough to almost start again, that memories of his mother would fade as time went by, but she prayed that he didn't have to, that her husband would arrive back home with Jim and Liz, that all of it was some horrible mistake. But the emptiness she felt in her heart told Ella Scott otherwise. She'd felt it when her own mother had died. Now, that pain was just as real.

They passed the signpost for Blaan. Ella drove through the village, passing the hotel, cottages and the little shop and restaurant that served up some of the best cakes she'd ever tasted. Normally, she'd have asked James if he wanted a cake, but she couldn't bear the thought of him sitting there asking questions about when Mummy and Daddy would be back. At the beach, she knew he'd be occupied, either playing in the sand or hunting in rock pools. She could try and switch off, put things to the back of her mind.

They arrived at the little layby above the beach. It didn't take James long to pile out of the car. She gave him the bag that had his swimming trunks and sunscreen, along with his bucket and spade. She pulled a travelling rug from the boot of the car, and the bag of juice and sandwiches she'd made for the trip.

She and James tramped down the small hill, across the narrow machair and on to the sand. James pulled Ella along until they were at the part of the beach where he and his mother usually sat. She spread out the rug, helped James into his trunks while covered by a towel, then liberally applied his sunscreen.

'There, that's you good to go,' said Ella, satisfied she'd covered every exposed part of the child. She remembered a lecture that Liz had given her about making sure that James didn't get burned. Though Ella had resented it at the time, she wished with all her heart that the woman she'd known for so long was there to irritate her again.

'I'm going to dig a sandcastle on this bit of wet sand,' shouted James, from a few yards away. She watched the little boy digging for a few minutes. He was almost a perfect cross between his father and mother. Only a fleeting expression here and there saw him resemble one parent over the other. Satisfied he was content, she removed a paperback from her bag, donned her reading glasses and read back into the story that was helping to distract her.

On finishing a particularly tense chapter, Ella returned to the real world. But when she looked round, there was no sign of James. Her heart sank.

Ella rushed to her feet. She called his name desperately. 'James! Where are you? James!' There were few folk on the beach. Though primary school had finished for the weekend, a lot of people were still at work. She could see a couple about fifty yards down the sand and resolved to ask them if they'd seen James.

Panic was beginning to rise in Ella's chest now. This

was her worst nightmare come true. It had happened to her many years before. After Ella had been busy squeezing loaves in a supermarket to find the freshest, she could see no sign of her four-year-old daughter. The relief she'd felt when she found the little girl sitting at a checkout being fed sweets by a member of staff was beyond description.

But there were no kindly supermarket staff on this beach to save the day.

Ella was frantic now. She looked up to the old ruin of a hotel on the hillside, its crumbling white facade the echo of another time. Right along the sand in both directions, she spotted three children, none of them her young charge.

'James! James!' Ella's calls were panicked now.

She was just about to set off to speak to the couple further down the beach when she heard a noise from behind, feet on the sand.

'Excuse me. Does this child belong to you?' The man was wearing a Hawaiian shirt and chinos. The breeze tugged at his dark hair, above a pair of expensive sunglasses. He had James by the hand.

'Where did you go!?' Ella asked James urgently. The relief she felt at seeing the little boy was now tempered by a flush of anger that he'd clearly wandered off.

'It's my fault. He must have followed our dog up the dunes.'

Ella shook her head in exasperation. 'How many times have you been told not to go anywhere by yourself?'

'Sorry, Auntie Ella.' The little boy began to sob.

'No harm done. All safe and sound,' said the man.

'Thank you so much,' said Ella, meaning it. 'So, so kind of you.'

'Not at all. Enjoy the rest of your day. Bye bye, James.' He waved at the little boy before making his way back up the dunes. He was soon engulfed by them.

'Here, you,' said Ella. 'Sit there until I put some more sunscreen on you.'

'Are you still angry, Auntie Ella?'

'No, I was worried. You must never do that again.' She rubbed some cream into the boy's shoulders. 'It's good that you told the man your name. Did you show him where I was?'

'No.'

'No, what?'

'I didn't tell him my name, Auntie Ella. And he took me back here without me telling him.'

'But he called you James. You must have told him.'

James turned to face Ella; a glimmer of anger crossed his face, making him look so like his mother. 'I didn't tell him my name, Auntie Ella!'

Suddenly, Ella Scott felt very vulnerable. She hugged James close, tears spilling on to his back.

'What's wrong?' said James.

'Nothing, son. Just ignore me. You dig the sand beside me here. Then we'll have some sandwiches and juice, OK?'

'What kind of sandwiches?'

'Cheese, ham and tomato. Your favourites.'

'Yes, I love them!'

Ella watched James as he puttered about in the sand. It had all happened so quickly. She wondered about the man who'd returned him to her knowing his name, soon dismissing it. The little boy must have told him.

Ella's mobile phone rang in the pocket of her jeans, making her jump. She noticed Brian's name on the screen.

'Hello, honey,' she said hopefully.

'Where are you, Ella?' Brian Scott's voice was subdued.

'On the beach at Blaan with James. Remember you said you'd take him?'

'Can he hear you?'

Ella stood up, walking a few feet away from James. She turned to keep him in sight as soon as she was sure he was far enough away not to hear the contents of Brian's call. 'He can't hear me now. What's happening, Brian?'

'Bad news. I've been speaking to Eddie.'

'Eddie Beattie?'

'Aye. They found a body in the Thames early this morning, doll. Liz's parents are coming to identify it – if it's her. Mind, we don't know anything for sure yet.'

Ella put her hand to her mouth, wanting to scream, but knowing she couldn't.

'Are you there?'

'Yes,' replied Ella in a tiny voice.

'Just try and keep calm, darling. I know, it's bloody terrible. We have to think of the wee man, OK?'

'OK.' Ella toyed with the idea of telling her husband about James disappearing, about the man on the beach who'd brought him back. In the end, she decided that he had enough to worry about, so said nothing.

'I'll keep you posted, OK.'

'What about Jimmy?' Ella whispered this into the mobile.

'Fuck knows. But he'll need to dae his best Houdini if he wants out o' this one. Honestly, I don't know what's going to happen. Anyway, I'm settled in the hotel. I've seen Eddie, and we're going to where they're holding him, just to see how the land lies. Listen, I better go. Is everything OK with you and wee Jamie?'

Again, it crossed Ella's mind to tell her husband about the stranger. Again, she decided not to. 'We're fine. Just you do your best. And look after yourself.'

'Good to hear. And do your best to keep calm, Ella. See you later.'

'OK, I'll try. I love you, Brian.' Ella waited for a reply, but the line was already dead.

29

Bethnal Green police station was, as usual, busy. Two young men were standing handcuffed at the charge bar. One looked miserable, the other defiant, staring the custody officer square in the eye, his chin raised.

'There's no point you trying to withhold your address, son. We'll find out where you live.' The custody officer, a balding man of middle years, looked harassed. He had a growing queue of miscreants to be processed, and he didn't have time for some arrogant lad playing stupid games.

A young DC passed by with an armful of files. She tripped over a carelessly discarded bag. The files scattered across the custody suite. Various police officers and clerical staff came to her aid.

'You give me your address!' the custody officer shouted at the lad in cuffs. 'It's bloody bedlam in here today.'

A large constable loomed behind him.

'Here, Tony. You want a hand? Bright says you'll need to check the custody cells soon. I'm happy to help.'

'Ricky, my boy. You are an angel in disguise. Heavy disguise, as it goes.'

They laughed.

'Everything you need is on that keyring. You know how to present the fobs to these fancy new locks, yeah?'

'Yeah, no problem. Do you want me to give CCTV a once-over while I'm at it?'

'Yeah, good lad. You know the score, eh? Belts and braces, mate.'

'Certainly do. You owe me a couple of pints at the Dog and Whatsit.'

'You're on!' Tony returned his attention to the recalcitrant youth who refused to supply his address, while Ricky punched a code into the small safe and removed a keyring, filled with a mix of old-fashioned keys and new-fangled fobs. He made his way to the cells.

'Everything OK?' said a large constable, standing in the corridor beside the CCTV room.

'Couldn't be better, Tel. Tony's up to his arse in new arrivals.'

'Good for him. Right, let's get this done. You know what the boss said. We have him at our backs if – well, you know.'

Tel took the keys from Ricky and entered the small CCTV room. He was only in there for a couple of minutes before returning with the keys and a wink. 'First part of the mission accomplished, mate.'

'Now for part two, eh?'

'My favourite bit.'

The pair made their way to the cells.

Daley was sitting on the end of the blue mattress in his cell. Though he was dog tired, he knew he'd get no sleep on the bed that was carved into the wall.

Try as he might, he couldn't banish the images he'd seen in the lane. The memory of his own face appearing on the iPad screen would stay with him for ever.

But he knew that the man who had pushed the woman into a doorway, before kicking her mercilessly, wasn't him.

Now, though, his heart ached at the possibility that Liz was the woman being attacked.

He tried and tried to make sense of it all, until his brain hurt. It was like some horrific dream. Daley remembered watching a film once in which the main character was having a nightmare. Each time he thought he'd woken up, the dream continued, though worse than before. Daley remembered it ended with the character impaled on a long spear, hanging there, unable to scream.

He gazed up at the frosted glass of a tiny window, the shadow of the bars that protected it picked out by the summer sun.

It was then he heard a buzz, and a key was turned in the lock of his cell door.

Daley looked up to see two tall young constables in their shirtsleeves.

'What now?' he asked.

'Just here to see how you're doing, *sir*,' said the taller of the two.

'I'm fine. Tell your boss I want to see him.'

'You what?' said the other cop.

Daley sighed. 'Please tell Inspector Bright I'd like to speak to him, thank you.'

'You'll be lucky. He's down the hospital getting his jaw X-rayed. Seems you caught him with a haymaker. That's not on. Is it, Ricky?'

'It certainly isn't, mate.'

Daley looked tired. 'Listen, forget the amateur dramatics. If you think I'm going to be intimidated by this shit, think again.'

'See me,' said Ricky, 'I fucking hate the *jocks*, I do. I mean, what are you for, eh?'

'What are you on about, son?' said Daley.

'What I say. I hate the Scots. Bunch of parasites, if you ask me.'

'Just grow up, will you. I've more to worry about than your pathetic racism.' Daley put his head in his hands, trying to keep his temper.

'Is that right, *sir*?'

Daley looked up just in time to see the bunched fist coming his way, but too late to do much about it. He saw stars when the blow landed; the constable was young and strong. Daley tried to force his way off the cell bed, but he was held fast by blow after blow raining down on his head and shoulders.

'You had enough then, Jocko?' said one of the men.

Daley had rolled himself into a ball on the floor. All he could see were two pairs of feet. He gritted his teeth. 'Get fucked! I'll see you both inside over this.'

'What do you think of that, Tel?' Without warning, Ricky aimed a vicious kick at Daley's head. It connected with his protecting hands, sending him sprawling.

Ricky leaned over the stricken detective. 'That was from Inspector Bright, you fucking murdering scum!'

Daley tried to get up, to face down his attackers. Soon, though, he gave up. He had neither the strength nor the will to fight back. If Liz was dead, he couldn't carry on. Part of him hoped they'd keep going, batter him to death.

He heard the cell door shut tight. Jim Daley was left nursing his cuts and bruises. He could stand that – it wasn't the first time he'd taken a beating – though the pain in his head, shoulders and stomach couldn't hide the real agony in his heart.

30

Brian Scott saw his old friend Eddie Beattie sitting by the window of the restaurant. The Kinloch detective had managed to make his way across London by careful study of the Underground map. Secretly, despite it all, he was quite pleased with himself.

He entered the eatery, to find a place bedecked in orange, with chairs, banquettes and lampshades all rendered in that colour. It gave the restaurant a vibrant feel. Not only that but the food on offer also smelled enticing, to say the least.

'You made it,' said Beattie. 'I could have sent a car.'

'I daresay you could. You're doing enough as it is, without having me chauffeur driven across London, pal.'

'Anything for an old friend. You must be starving. My man doesn't start his shift until after seven at Bethnal Green nick. So, we've got a couple of hours to kill.'

'I'm ravenous. It's already been a long day.'

'Get ready for some more of those.'

'Aye, no doubt.'

'Here's the menu, Brian. They do a cracking steak in here, so fill your boots. I'll get the drinks in. The usual bucket of whisky for you, is it?'

'Nah, just a ginger beer and lime for me, buddy.'

Beattie eyed his old friend, a playful smile on his lips.

'Aye, right. The day I see you drinking ginger beer, there'll be green snow and yellow hailstones, Scooty.'

'Times change. I'm on the wagon. Have been for a while.'

'Fuck. Mind you, it's hardly a surprise. Man, you could shift the booze.'

'Aye, and Ella was going to shift hooses and leave me where I was.'

'That bad, eh? How is blondie, anyway?'

'No' as blonde as she used to be. Getting older and carnaptious like the rest o' us.'

'I remember you going out with her. You, strolling down the street with Ella on your arm. Wasn't long before I joined the Met. You encouraged me.'

'Long time ago. Too long, maybe.'

'Thinking of chucking it?'

'Maybe. Though I've just been promoted. Jim's off to head up the divisional CID in Dumbarton. Well, that was the idea. I'm the boss of the sub-division, whatever happens.'

'What, like sub-divisional commander?'

'Yes. And don't look so amazed. I can do it nae bother.'

Beattie laughed. 'I've no doubt about that, Brian. But there's no chance you'll do things the way the bosses want them done.'

The waiter arrived at a click of Beattie's fingers. He ordered himself a pint of bitter and a ginger beer and lime for Scott. They placed their food orders.

'What's the latest? You heard anything?'

'Only that the victim is to be identified officially first thing in the morning.'

'Her folks?'

'Yes. I think they're on their way down on the sleeper.'

'They've no time for oor Jimmy. Never liked him, not fae the start,' said Scott with a tut.

181

'I'm told they've done the lab work, Brian. Inconclusive until they find her dental records from up the road.'

Scott leaned back in his chair and passed his hands across his forehead. 'Fingers crossed, then.'

'Yes, all you can do. I realize you've known Jimmy and her for years.'

'I have that. Och, me and Lizzie were often at daggers drawn. I didnae like the way she treated the big fulla sometimes. But it wasn't my business, and we tolerated each other. Aye, and she's a fine lassie, in many ways. Then there's the wee boy – he adores her.' Scott sighed.

'What do you really think about Jimmy? He's got some record of misconduct – violence, into the bargain.'

'He's good at his job, Eddie. That's why he's still around. You know the score.'

Beattie shifted uncomfortably in his seat.

'Ants in your pants or piles?'

'Neither. That screenshot I took from Liz's iPad.'

'Aye, how did you get on?'

'That's the problem. I didn't get on.'

'Eh?' Scott looked puzzled.

'I ran it through everything we have – even our face recognition tech. Nothing, absolutely nothing. It's as though this guy doesn't exist.'

'What the fuck does that mean?'

'Few things, maybe. It could be an AI image, in which case your Lizzie is leading us a merry dance.'

'No way. What would be the point? She told me about the bloody iPad. Doesnae make sense she'd draw it to my attention, just for it to be a fake.'

'True, it doesn't sound likely. But you know people, Brian. You must have come across all sorts.'

'What's the other option?'

'This face ID stuff is good but it's not infallible. It would be better if the politicians would let us take the brakes off.'

'Tut-tut, Eddie. We cannae live in a polis state.'

'Do you know how many times you've been photographed since you arrived here? Hundreds already. This city has more surveillance than anywhere else on earth. I include China in that. This ID software would just help us make sense of all the data, that's all.'

'Fair enough, Big Brother. I'll remember that when they stick the electrodes to my bollocks.' Scott looked about for the waiter to return with his drink. Not only was he hungry, he was thirsty too. London in the summer dehydrated the soul as well as the body, he thought. 'You said there were a couple o' alternatives?'

'The fact we don't have this bastard on file is the most likely. But there is another.'

'Fuck, don't leave me in suspense!'

'Our friend – Liz Daley's paramour – could be, you know . . .' Beattie shrugged, screwing up his face.

'What does *you know* mean?'

'I didn't think I'd have to spell it out, Brian. He could be from the intelligence community.'

'Oh no. Me and the big man have had plenty o' run-ins wae that mob over the years.'

'Such as?'

'Long story. I'll fill you in when we get oor dinner.' Scott looked round hopefully. 'Why would they want to kill Lizzie? That doesnae make sense. I mean, dae they really get up to that stuff or is it just in the movies?'

'I'm not suggesting they would. That's why I'm confused. But we're checking other things. Like what happened when the Daleys arrived in the city. I've a small team tracing their movements.'

It was Scott's turn to look confused. 'I'm really grateful and all that. But how come you can divert resources to this case? I mean, you're no' the MIT.'

'That's just it, Brian. You'll be aware that we've had some high-profile problems in the last few years here in the Met?'

'You'd have tae be a blind and deaf man buried in the Arctic no' to know. All due respect, and that.'

Superintendent Eddie Beattie shifted in his seat again. 'No offence taken. You see, I've been moved to a new unit that investigates that kind of stuff.'

'What, Complaints and Discipline? Away tae fuck!'

'A wee bit like that. Remember, we've got PACE down here.'

'We're no slouches off the mark up the road, Eddie.'

'You know what I mean.'

'Don't tell me. You're investigating Jimmy for being a bent copper. Is that it?' The sudden revelation banished Scott's hunger. 'I've no' only left the henhoose door open. I've taken the fox doon in my motor and telt him to help himself!'

'Why would I be investigating Daley? Think about it.' Beattie lowered his voice. 'But I *am* investigating someone.'

'Shit, is it me?'

'You should go back on the drink, Scooty. You're getting paranoid. When did you sign on as a Met detective?'

'Trust me, I was much worse than this when I was drinking. They wee Mexicans at the end o' the bed every morning.'

'What?'

'One o' they mariachi bands. You know, wae the big guitars and the sombreros. If I'd had a bucket, I'd wake up to them at the bottom of the bed.'

'You are kidding, right?'

'That's no' the worst bit, neither.'

'Fuck me!' Beattie's jaw dropped.

'They were only three feet tall.' Scott folded his arms, revelation complete.

'Let's just draw a veil over that, eh?'

'Aye, that's for the best, Eddie.'

'It's true, we are investigating someone who's involved in this case.'

'Who?'

'DI Bright, that's who.'

At this, their meals and drinks arrived. Scott polished off most of the ginger beer in a few gulps. He found his appetite had returned and set knife and fork to a well-done steak. It was clear that nothing was as it seemed. But he was grateful for Beattie's help. Thoughts of Liz, he banished to the back of his mind. But there, he found Ella and young James. 'This is all a real nightmare, you know, pal.'

'I'm beginning to get a sense of that,' said Scott's old friend.

31

Ella Scott wasn't a person taken by fits of fanciful paranoia. She'd lived on the edge with her husband far too long to take to looking over her shoulder for things that weren't there. However, since the helpful stranger had brought young James back on the beach, something was nagging at her. How had he known the boy's name? That was a major concern.

As it was a Friday night with no school the next day, the pair had played a few games of Snakes and Ladders. Because his mother never allowed James to play computer games, he'd become a shark at draughts, Ludo, Jenga and all manner of board games. It was almost as though the boy came from another age. When he'd sent Ella down many snakes and up a few ladders, she decided to let him watch some of his favourite TV programmes, while she fretted. Even making dinner was no distraction, though Ella knew she couldn't let James see this.

'There you go, son. You eat that up. Daddy tells me it's your favourite.'

She put the plate in front of him on the table. James gave her a knowing look.

'It's only my daddy that gives me a baked potato with beans and sausages. He always tells me not to tell Mummy.'

'You can trust me. Beans and sausages won't do you any harm.'

The boy smiled. 'Just don't tell Mummy when she comes back.'

'That's a good idea, son.' Ella's heart was breaking more and more as the time passed. She imagined Liz coming through her front door, her glorious smile. It wasn't going to happen, she feared. She found herself wishing the pair had stayed in Kinloch. Why had they gone to London? But there was no point in ifs and maybes.

Young James and Ella ate their meal in front of a cartoon, James gawping at it when he wasn't laughing, while Ella failed to understand what was going on. A sensation she was becoming accustomed to, she felt.

Ella took the plates through to the kitchen, glad the boy had eaten almost all his dinner. As she set the dishes in the sink, she gazed idly out of the kitchen window over their small back garden, and across the car park they shared with the other residents. A little rectangle of houses that she now thought of as home.

Ella's gaze alighted on a large black saloon with smoked-out windows. Having a good memory, as well as a more than passing interest in what was going on in the neighbourhood, she knew all the neighbours and their vehicles; this car certainly wasn't one of them.

Telling herself she was becoming utterly paranoid, Ella decided to ignore the car and get on with the washing up. But when she'd completed her task and looked up, there it was, still sitting a few yards from her house, looking alien, menacing, out of place.

Ella bit her lip. She remembered that she hadn't brought in her bin. Collection day was on a Friday, and the task had slipped her mind after her trip to the seaside. It would be a perfect excuse to go out to the car park where the refuse collectors left the neighbourhood bins.

'You stay where you are, James. I've just got to bring the bin back into the garden.'

'OK!' James called from the lounge.

'And don't go missing again!'

'I won't!'

Perhaps it was her paranoia or just natural caution that made Ella check her front door was locked and bolted. She made sure the front door was on the snib and the back door was locked behind her.

Ella put her keys in her pocket and made her way towards the bin. It was large, green and marked *P/H*, the letters standing for Police House. As usual, her bin was the last not to have been retrieved by its owner. To date, a Tuesday had been the longest period the Scotts' bin had stood in splendid isolation prior to being reclaimed. And even then, it had taken a call from the nosy Mrs Campbell at number three, asking after her health, and less than subtly reminding Ella of her refuse regime, to make her do the decent thing.

Ella made sure her route to the bin took her right past the black car. As she neared the vehicle, through the smoked glass she spotted a person in the driver's seat.

All the time, she was trying to work out what Brian would have done under such circumstances. Undoubtedly, he would have been as curious as her to discover why the car was sitting there. He wouldn't have hesitated to chap the door and speak to the driver. Ella also reasoned that her husband was a police officer, and therefore had a ready excuse to do so. She decided that she might catch a glimpse of the driver's face on the way back. If it was the man from the beach, she would call Kinloch police office without hesitation.

As Ella grabbed the handle of the bin, she heard a noise and swung round to face it. The driver's door had been pushed open but there was no sign of the occupant.

Ella cleared her throat and, pulling the bin behind her, marched off, again past the black car. The need to know who was in the vehicle was now replaced by concerns over her own safety.

Her heart almost stopped when she was halfway to her garden gate.

'Mrs Scott!'

She carried on walking, her whole body beginning to tremble.

'Ella!' The voice sounded again, though this time slightly louder.

Nailing her courage to the mast, Ella swung round. It was better to face her fears than run away. She had her mobile phone in the pocket of her jeans and wouldn't hesitate to use it if things took a turn for the worse. Screaming at the top of her voice was also an option.

Heart in her mouth, Ella looked across to the car.

A man struggled from the vehicle. 'Aye, sorry, I dropped my mints on the floor. Didna see you. Tell me, what do you make o' this?' said McMurchy, a newly retired farmer who'd moved into the house two doors down from Ella and Brian a few months before.

'Oh, that's a lovely car, Mr McMurchy. Quite big, eh?'

'Aye, she's big – meant to be. The wife's no' so keen. She canna get into it just as easily – wanted one o' they SUVs. Och, but they're just glorified Land Rovers, and I've been driving them for decades. I've fancied a big BMW like this since I was a boy. But it would have got ruined going up and doon thon farm track of ours. That's no' a problem now, so I went out and bought her. And if Margaret canna get in the damned thing, well, it's just bad luck. Aye, and I wasted a pile o' money on they yoga classes she went to for years. In any event, she's a hellish back seat driver. All's well that ends well.'

'Lovely,' said Ella, clearing her dry throat.

'I was taking a seat in her there to try and work out all that computer stuff on the dashboard. Man, I'll need tae get one o' they whizz kids to give me a hand. It's all double Dutch to me.'

'I'm sure you'll get to grips with it.'

'I just thought I better tell you what I was up to after auld Marion Cook chapped the window to see if I was deid. It's no' like the farm. Right nosey bastards in this place, and that's a fact.'

'You're right there,' said Ella. 'I better get back in. See you later. Enjoy your new car!'

Ella turned on her heel and pulled the bin into their garden. Despite the false alarm, her heart was still beating ten to the dozen. She left the bin in the corner by the drainpipe, hauled out her keys and opened the back door. Once it was closed behind her, Ella leaned on the door, wiping the sweat from her brow to calm herself.

In a few moments, she'd regained her composure, and walked back through to the lounge. But, although the television was still blaring out a cartoon, there was no sign of James.

She dashed into the hall, intent on running upstairs, but to her horror, the front door was ajar. 'James!' she shouted as she stepped outside. The only sound was her own voice echoing round the other houses.

32

Eddie Beattie walked confidently to the front desk at Bethnal Green police station and flashed his ID.

'I'm Superintendent Beattie, this is DI Scott. We're here to see Sergeant Osman. He's on custody duty tonight, I believe.'

The officer examined Beattie's warrant card closely. Knowing that Beattie was the head of the new team in charge of implementing PACE, he smiled and buzzed the pair through into the main office.

'Custody is along that corridor on your right, sir.'

'Thank you, son,' said Beattie. He made his way down the corridor, Scott in tow.

'That's a relief,' said Scott. 'I thought for sure he'd ask for my card.'

'Bloody well should have done. You've no idea how long we've spent telling this lot to examine visitors properly. Falls on deaf ears, of course. As you've just seen.'

'Just as well.'

The internal door to the custody suite was open. They walked through.

'Taj, me old pal. How are you doing?' shouted Beattie across two cops with a young man handcuffed between them.

'Hello, sir.' Osman smiled broadly. 'I'll be with you in two shakes. Just about done here.'

Beattie and Scott looked on as the prisoner signed a document and was subsequently taken to the cells by the officers.

'You've hit it lucky tonight. It's quiet, boss,' said Osman.

'Walk in the park here, compared to your days on the squad with me, eh, Taj?'

'Needed a rest. I don't know how you keep going. I really don't.'

'Drink and a good wife. It's all there is, my friend.'

'I agree on the wife. Not so sure about the drink. You know me. A good coffee is what keeps me going.'

'Whatever, pal. Now, that little favour I asked you about.' Beattie lowered his voice. 'All good?'

'Lot of interest round the prisoner, I hear. He's job, isn't he?'

'Aye, sort of. Up in Scotland, though. That doesn't count.' Beattie laughed, nudging Scott with his elbow. 'Hey, and listen. I sign the book, OK. Nobody can land this at your door if things go pear-shaped. Not as though you can refuse me, not these days. But still and all, I'd like to keep this as quiet as we can.'

Scott noticed that his old friend's accent had changed. When it had been just the two of them, Beattie had sounded just the way he'd remembered him back in Glasgow. In this environment, his vowels had taken on a soft, English tone, with even a touch of estuary to accompany it.

'I'll take a look. Make sure there's nobody about,' said Osman. He walked over to a bank of CCTV screens. 'That's funny. Your man's camera's off. I'll have a word with the comms room. Bloody things are always breaking down. Nothing lasts these days.'

Though the custody sergeant seemed unperturbed by this turn of events, Brian Scott felt his hackles rise.

Osman spoke up. 'I've got a little diversion planned. You know, just in case anyone wants to run interference.'

'Clever. I taught you well, my boy. What's the score?'

'Long time since we had a proper fire drill round here. You get yourselves down there. Then I'll press the button. Should be perfect.'

'Fabulous! How do we get there?'

'Take this fob. That'll gain you entry. Cell eighteen. You can't miss it. Through that door, straight along the corridor, down a short flight of stairs. Here. You better get your IDs in these.' Osman handed them two accreditation lanyards, each with a clear pouch in which to slip a warrant card.

Scott fumbled his in, making sure the card was lying back to front on his chest. He looked on as Osman handed the entry fob to Beattie. Then Osman buzzed them through, and they were on their way to the cells.

Beattie and Scott followed their instructions and found themselves in a long corridor, lined with cell doors. They marched to the far end of the space. As arranged, the fire alarm sounded. It was a squealing buzz that made Scott want to put his fingers in his ears.

They reached the door to cell eighteen. Beattie presented the fob to the entry plate, and the lock buzzed. The pair pushed their way inside.

Despite the subdued light, Scott noticed Daley's body lying curled on the floor, a pool of blood near his head.

'What the fuck!' he shouted, rushing to his friend's side.

The floor was slick with Daley's blood. Scott knelt beside the stricken man and placed two fingers on the pulse point on his neck. 'His heart's beating, Eddie. But he'll need an ambulance fast.'

'You stay here, Brian. I'll go and get Osman to call one. See if you can get a response out of him!'

'Big man, it's me.' Scott spoke gently into Daley's ear. His face was a mess, eyes swollen, nose apparently broken, and that was all Scott could see with him lying in the foetal position.

Daley's lips moved. 'Brian,' he croaked.

'Don't worry, Jimmy. Help's on its way. Who did this to you?'

'Two cops,' Daley whispered.

'This DI Bright bastard?'

'Nah, two uniforms. Randoms.'

Scott grasped Daley's hand. 'Hang in there. No' the first time you've taken a kicking, eh?' Scott felt Daley's grip tighten.

Daley tried to lick his bloodied lips. 'Listen, Bri. I need you to tell me the truth. Is Liz dead?'

Scott swallowed back the lump in his throat. His vision blurred with tears. 'You don't need to worry about that just now.'

Daley tried to lift his head, but the effort was too painful. 'Tell me, Brian!' The urgency in his voice was unmistakable.

'OK. Last thing I heard, they found a body – in the river. Still not been officially identified.'

'I know that!' Daley mashed at his broken mouth. 'Tell me the truth.'

Scott wiped the tears from his eyes. 'You know me, Jimmy. I'll always tell you as it is. There's been no identification. Whatever happens, though, I'll keep you right. You should know that by now.'

Scott held Daley as his broken body convulsed in sobs. He let out an almost silent scream. Scott knew the pain behind it was worse than any beating his pal had taken.

It was a cry of despair from Daley's very soul.

33

Ella Scott was frantic now. She rushed into her small front garden, searching for any sign of James Daley junior.

'James!' The yell made her vision blur. Ella thought she might faint away, such was the anguish she felt.

'Ella!'

The voice that came from behind was strangely familiar.

Ella swung round on her heel so quickly, she thought she might fall over. There, in the doorway of her home, stood Hamish, replete with his old dungarees and greasy Breton cap. James's head poked out from behind the old man's legs.

'Auntie Ella, Hameby tapped on the window. So, I let him in. He was desperate to use the toilet. He said he was going to fair pish himself if he didn't get to go. I got a chair and unlocked the door and showed him where the lavatory was.'

'I'll show him where to go, just in two minutes,' Ella growled.

'I'm sorry, Ella. Fair desperate I was. Man, I thought I might have to pee in your lovely flower beds there,' said Hamish.

It took Ella Scott a few moments to process what had

happened. She was still furious about the boy's second disappearance of the day.

'I'll wrap the toilet round your fucking heid!'

'Now, Ella,' said Hamish, holding his hands out to protect himself from her wrath. 'That's no way to speak in front o' the boy. Man, you sound like a navvy, and that's a fact.'

'You did say a very bad word,' said James, nodding from behind Hamish's legs.

'Get in there, the pair of you.' Ella shooed them indoors like a farmer's wife herding hens.

Hamish ended up sitting on the couch, looking rather sorry for himself, while James opted to stay in front of the din of the TV.

'Aye, that's the last thing I expected, I must admit. You fair raging at me on the doorstep.'

'Raging? What do you expect?' Though Ella still wore a furious expression, the flood of relief she was experiencing made her feel a little ashamed of swearing at the old man.

'You're no yourself, I can see that. It's amazing how no' having a man about the place affects some women, though I didna have you down for one of the *canna cope* brigade.'

'James, you stay right where you are. Do not move one inch!'

'Yes, Auntie Ella,' said the little boy sheepishly.

'You, come with me.' Ella hurried Hamish through into the kitchen. 'Just sit down there, I'll get you a cup of tea.'

'Tea, is it? I must say, I'd have preferred a dram, if I'm honest,' said Hamish.

Ella glared at him.

'Mind you, there's much to be said for the healing power of the leaf when things look bleak.'

'Right answer,' said Ella as she poured water into the kettle from the kitchen tap.

Tea made, she sat in front of Hamish, still feeling rather ashamed of her outburst. 'You might be right about Liz. They found a body. Not identified yet, mind.' Ella had a tear in her eye.

'I knew it,' Hamish wailed. 'I telt Mr Daley no' to go.'

'I know you did.'

Hamish sniffed back his tears. 'Such a bonnie lassie – kind, too. The trouble is she didna let folk see that side of her enough. Always too concerned with what impression she was making on others wae her fine clothes and pretty face.' He took a slurp of tea. 'Tell me, was this body found in the water?'

'I don't know. All I've heard is that her parents are going down to identify a body.' When the old man broke down, she hurried to his side and hugged him. 'There was nothing you could have done, Hamish. If it's her, we just have to cope. For Jimmy and the wee boy's sake. Though please keep this to yourself. Nobody knows better what Kinloch's like than you.'

'You can be assured o' that.' Hamish removed a grey-looking hankie from a pocket of his dungarees and blew his nose loudly. 'The evil that exists in the world, there's no end to it.'

'It's the boy I'm worried about – and Jimmy, of course.'

'Himself will be on his way back up the road, eh?' Hamish cocked his head almost slyly. 'Wait, why on earth are her parents going to identify the body when Mr Daley's there?'

For a few moments, Ella considered telling Hamish the whole sorry tale. But on second thoughts, she decided to stay quiet on the matter. It would come out soon enough, in all its horror. She dreaded it.

'Things aren't as straightforward as you think. That's why Brian's away to sort it all out.'

'Loyalty is a commendable thing. But I'd expect nothing more from you. Whatever is happening, if I can be of help, all you have to do is ask. I hope you know that.'

'I do.'

Hamish sat back in his chair, looking as though he'd aged ten years. His face was ashen and his eyes had somehow lost their sheen. 'I hate the things I can see, Ella. Aye, I've made light of it over the years. Turned myself into a laughing stock, I daresay. But that was just an attempt to look normal. They tell me my grandfaither was the same. He saw things that drove him half mad – certainly turned him to the drink. At least I managed to avoid that curse.'

Ella couldn't help the doubtful look that crossed her face. 'I don't think we really know anything about the world, Hamish. You've been right too many times for people to ignore you. You know folk, though. We all think we've cracked it wae our mobile phones, AI and the likes. But we're all as daft as when we first stood up straight, if you ask me.'

'You're a philosopher right enough. I saw my own faither die, you know,' said Hamish.

'That must have been horrible.'

'I wasna there, you understand. I was at home wae my mother. I'd taken a right dose o' pleurisy. Man, it was sore. He'd drunk our wee boat away by that time. So, he was skippering for Willie Duncan at Firdale, who had a broken leg after falling doon the stairs drunk at a wedding. Norrie Meenan's, I think.'

'Oh,' said Ella, vaguely hoping Hamish would get to the point soon.

'Anyhow, I was in my bed. My dear old mother had

made me a mug of cocoa to see if I'd be able to get a sleep. She was great at the cocoa, you know.'

Ella nodded.

'I must have dropped off right enough, for I was in the wheelhouse with my faither. As real as though I was standing there in life.' Hamish drained his cup of tea. 'Man, he was as grey as the sky just before dawn. Great bags under his eyes. They'd a yellow tinge to them I'll never forget.'

'His eyes?'

'Just that. The whites o' his eyes had turned yellow. Och, my mother blamed his smoking. But I knew fine his organs were fighting a losing battle wae the drink.'

'That's terrible, Hamish.' For a moment, Ella thought of her husband's battle with booze.

'There was a quarter bottle of whisky sitting on the wee ledge at the wheelhouse window. I remember him reaching for it in my dream. I was shouting and shouting at the top of my voice for him to stop, to leave the bloody bottle where it was. But he couldna hear me. He placed the damned thing to his lips and took a fair glug at it, let me tell you.'

'What happened then?'

'He staggered a bit, almost as though he was fighting a gale, though it was a flat calm day. He grabbed at the wheel to steady himself, but his strength had gone. He tumbled to the floor, and that's where he died.'

'And you saw all this in your dream?'

'I did. In any event, I told my mother. She had none o' the sight herself, but she respected it. We headed doon the quay. They were due back for the fish buyer at six. But we were there by four.' Hamish sighed. 'Just before five, one o' the lads shouted that the *English Lass* – that was the boat – had appeared roon the island and was heading up the loch.

They landed at the quay wae my faither deid in the wheel-house. He'd died just as I'd seen it.'

'Poor you. How did you and your mother take it?'

'I passed clean oot. I shouldna have been out of my bed, on account o' the pleurisy. But later, after he was in his grave, my mother made me promise never to tell the tale o' this dream again. I kept that promise for years, until she passed on herself – which I foresaw too, right enough. It's a curse, I tell you. Nothing but a curse. Those who long to see what's in front o' them should have a good, hard think. It's better no' tae know.'

'I'm so sorry. That's so sad. I had no idea you'd suffered like this.'

'When I saw poor Mrs Daley in that water, I knew she was away. I tried to stop them going. Ach, but you can't fight fate. It's solid as a rock for each and every one of us.'

Feeling even more emotional than she'd already been, Ella left Hamish to his thoughts for a moment and went to check on James. He was still at the TV, laughing at a cartoon he was watching.

'You poor wee boy,' she whispered to herself.

34

DI Bright had been discharged from hospital. Though there was no sign of a fracture to his jaw, it was badly bruised, and he found eating anything absolute agony. He sat nursing a coffee at a table in a run-down bar not far from Canary Wharf. In truth, he'd have much rather been at home, where he knew his wife would pamper him.

Bright looked at his watch. The man he was going to meet was late. It was the story of his life. He wondered how much of his time he'd spent just waiting for pointless people with no manners to turn up.

The barman was busy giving the tables a cursory wipe with a dirty dishcloth. When he'd finished with Bright's table, streaks of food and detergent were slathered from one end to the other. It made the inspector's stomach churn. This meeting place wasn't his idea. He sipped his coffee again, wondering if any of this was worth it. At least the big Scotsman had been put in his place. He intended to have a dram or two of whisky that night to celebrate. It seemed appropriate somehow.

Bright was about to text his contact when the door swung open. A man, wearing a most incongruous red baseball cap with a dark grey suit, appeared in the bar.

Though the police officer, to his almost certain knowledge, had never seen him before, this could only be *his* man.

Baseball-cap man looked about, fixed his gaze on Bright's table, ambled over and took the seat opposite the inspector.

'Are you trying to look inconspicuous? 'Cos, let me tell you now, it's not working,' said Bright. He attempted a dismissive sneer, before thinking better of it as a sharp pain shot up his jaw.

'You don't speak, got it?' The new arrival's face was hidden by the brim of his baseball cap. He kept his head down purposefully. 'You've fucked up, haven't you, eh?'

'Sorry?' Bright was beginning to feel uncomfortable.

'You know what I mean.'

'No, what do you mean?'

'You had our man beaten in the cells. We didn't ask you to do that. What have we said about improvisation? Why?'

'It's none of your fucking business!'

'Keep your voice down. I'm here to pass on a message. As far as you're concerned, this job's over, got it?'

'What?'

'You heard. You'll get the money for what you've done, but it's finished.'

'No way! I need that money.'

The barman cocked his head. 'Everything all right, gents?'

Bright glared at him. 'Instead of listening to your punters' conversations, you'd be better off cleaning those tables again. They're disgusting.' He smiled to himself. He'd put the slovenly prick in his place.

'You can't help it, can you?' said baseball-cap man.

'Help what?'

'Being a cocky little shit, that's what.'

'Enough of this. I want my money, got it?'

'That's why I'm here. I want you to listen carefully.'

'All ears, mate.'

'You get out of here. Stand by the bus stop across the road. In a bit, you'll see a white taxi heading towards you. The driver will flash his lights. Step on to the pavement. He'll pay you.'

'Fuck, it's like a spy novel.'

'You don't speak to him, you don't ask questions, and you don't get smart. We might be able to use you again. But you only do what we say next time. Nothing more, nothing less, right?'

Bright blew out his cheeks. 'Yeah, whatever. You know how to get a hold of me.'

'Yeah, I know how to do that.' Baseball-cap man got to his feet. 'Give me a couple of minutes, then you come out.'

'What, as in literally a couple of minutes?'

'What did I say?' The man turned away and left the bar.

Bright glanced at his Rolex, took another painful slug of tea, then searched in his pocket for some money. He placed a crisp twenty-pound note on the table. 'Hey, you!'

The barman looked up. 'You what?'

'I've left the money on here. Keep the change. You'll need it when they sack you for being shit.' Bright grinned to himself once more.

'Arsehole,' said the barman as he carried on cleaning glasses.

Just as DI Bright was about to leave, he heard a sharp shower batter the bar's windows. A flash of lightning cracked across the sky outside, followed by a deep, per-cussive roll of boiling thunder. Bright checked his watch once more.

'I'd hang on until that blows over, mate,' said the barman.

'I'm not interested in what you think,' said Bright, before turning up the collar of his jacket and leaving the premises.

'Fucking wanker,' muttered the barman as he walked from behind the counter and collected the banknote. He looked on with satisfaction as he spotted his erstwhile customer leaning into the torrential rain as he raced across the road outside, the collar of his suit jacket held tight at his neck. The sky was dark under the lowering thundercloud now. 'I hope you get hit by lightning, arsehole,' he said before making his way back behind the bar.

Now at the bus stop, Bright squinted into the horizontal downpour, searching for the white taxi. The battering rain was so heavy it had hurt his jaw. In moments, he spotted a white taxi making its way up the road towards him.

When the vehicle flashed its lights, Bright stepped away from the bus stop on to the pavement. He heard the squeal of rubber tyres on the wet road.

His vison was now filled by the white taxi, only feet away.

Thomas Bright's first notion was to dive back into the bus stop. It would be the last thought he would ever have.

The white taxi mounted the pavement and caught him head on, forcing his body up and over its roof. Bright landed in a muddy puddle of rainwater in the middle of the road. A blue Transit van, travelling too fast behind the taxi, ran over the dying man, the impact a sickening thud. Car brakes squealed, red lights flashed, lightning lit up the sky and thunder roared, all punctuated by the harsh counterpoint of car horns. The white taxi disappeared into the gloom.

The Transit skidded to a halt. Its driver dashed from behind the wheel, a look of shock on his face.

'Did you see that!?' he stammered to the barman, who'd

left his place of work unattended. 'He came out of nowhere. I had no chance of stopping!'

'I saw it all, don't worry. He was run down by a taxi before you hit him. He was only in my gaff a couple of minutes ago.'

Soon, drivers and pedestrians hurried to see what had happened. Blood dripped from the lips of the man lying dead in the street. It was being washed away along the road by the cascading rain. Thomas Bright's eyes stared into the dark thunder cloud, unblinking, unseeing, dull.

Nobody noticed the man in the red baseball cap as he hurried away from the scene. He still had work to do. There was a taxi to set on fire.

35

Ella had read to James until the little boy's eyelids had grown heavy and he'd fallen fast asleep. She brushed a strand of hair from his face, and marvelled yet again how like his mother he looked.

Ella tramped back downstairs and did a quick tidy round. She lifted the small glass and a bottle of whisky from the coffee table, before taking them through to the kitchen. Hamish had stayed for a couple of hours. And apart from his unfortunate arrival, she'd been glad of the company. She liked the old man, though she found his ability to sense things before they happened deeply unsettling. She'd toyed with the idea of asking if he'd had any dreams about Brian but stopped herself in the nick of time. Sometimes, it was better not to know.

Ella felt weary as she hauled herself upstairs. She had a bad taste in her mouth, so she retrieved a barley sugar from her pocket and went to work on it, carelessly flicking the wrapper to the bottom of the bed. Brian had sent her a simple text saying goodnight and that he loved her. Again, it was a case of ignorance being bliss. Even so, she couldn't help worrying about him, about everything.

She decided to pick up her book. The pages, though,

seemed endless and the words began to jump about on the page. Ella managed a chapter before deciding it was best to switch off the light and try to get some sleep.

Once she'd slipped over, her dreams were troubled. At first, she was running along a beach, calling desperately after her own children, who were nowhere to be seen. The tide was rising quickly, water already lapping at her feet. She raced on, more and more desperate, until she heard a child call out.

Ella then found herself in the ruins of an old castle on a rise above the machair. When she looked up, its ancient walls teetered under a sheltering sky, giving the feeling of motion, travelling through time. She called out, but the child's voice was gone.

She woke with a start, her heart thumping, sweat on her brow. 'Fuck,' she whispered to herself, before taking a sip of water from the bottle on the nightstand. She turned over in bed and tried to get back to sleep.

Ella was now in the storeroom of a shop. It looked and smelled like the grocer's in which she'd worked part-time as a schoolgirl, a heady mix of rotting veg, detergent and damp cardboard. A ramshackle door swung creakily open on its hinge. Brian angled his head round it. He had a bottle of whisky in his hand.

'This way, doll!' he shouted, then disappeared.

Ella was angry; she wanted to ask him why on earth he was drinking again. She followed him, ready for an argument, only to find herself in a huge room, a disused warehouse, amid towering stacks empty of goods or chattels. In the distance, her husband was standing in a pool of light beside an old couch. Ella walked closer, her footsteps percussive, anxious, marching to the beat of her own sense of urgency.

As she got closer, she noticed a figure silently reclining on the couch. 'Liz!' she called out in amazement.

The woman she'd known for so long looked up at her. Her dark hair fell over her brow on to a deathly pale face, lipstick as red as blood, matching the figure-hugging dress she was wearing. Liz appeared untroubled – happy, even. She pointed a long finger towards Brian, who was taking a slug of whisky from the bottle in his left hand.

'He's going to kill me,' said Liz, her voice matter of fact.

'No, he's not,' Ella replied. 'You can rely on that.'

'Nah, you're wrong, doll,' said Brian with a smile and another gulp of whisky. 'I am!' Without preamble, he swung the bottle high in the air and brought it right down, over and over, on Liz's head.

'Stop!' Ella shouted helplessly, as she tried to get near enough to her husband to end this brutal act, but she couldn't move. It was as though she was frozen, held fast by invisible hands. Her only purpose here in this place, it seemed, was to view Brian Scott's murderous brutality.

'Wait, give me a moment,' said Liz, holding out her hand for Scott to stop, as though the sickening injuries he was inflicting on her were as nothing. Blood poured from a livid gash in her head, trickling down her white cheek and over the red lipstick. Her brain could be seen, pulsing grey under her cracked skull. Scott did as he was told, though he kept the bottle poised over Liz's head. They both gazed at Ella, unmoved. Brian Scott laughed when, with a distinct pop, Liz's right eye sprang from its socket, and hung on a gory thread of nerve and sinew over her bloodied cheek. Liz looked surprised for a moment before joining him in a belly laugh.

The laughter stopped. 'We have something to tell you,' they said in unison.

'Eh?' Ella felt furious about her husband's behaviour. 'Brian Scott, I told you this would happen if you kept drinking.'

'Tell her, Brian!' Liz demanded.

'Tell me what?' said Ella.

Scott cocked his head to one side, the mannerism one of the first things she'd noticed about him when they first met. She remembered it as being cute, loveable. Now it made a travesty of the emotion. From nowhere, a cigarette appeared in Scott's hand. He gestured towards Liz with it. 'Me and her have been having an affair. I telt her no' to say anything to you.' Scott shrugged. 'That's why I'm beating her to death. Get it? She can't keep a secret.' Scott smiled and waved to her, before recommencing the battering of Liz's head with the whisky bottle, again and again.

'He's good,' said Liz through the blows. 'So good. Again, Brian, harder!' She angled her head back as though in the throes of passion, her blood spattering Scott's face.

Ella felt herself being dragged away from this horrific scene. She was back in her bed, breathing heavily, the taste of bile in her mouth. She lay still in the dark, trying to make sense of these dreams, trying to breathe.

Suddenly, the ceiling light came on above her head.

'It was just Auntie Ella having a bad dream, James. I'm sorry I woke you up, son.' Ella was still staring at the ceiling, too tired and unsettled to force her head off the pillow.

'Don't be sorry.' The man's voice was flat, no emotion.

Ella shot up in the bed. Before her was the man who'd brought James back on the beach. Now in his arms, the little boy was pale-faced and limp in his blue pyjamas.

Ella looked round frantically, as though trying to find help, desperately hoping this too was a dream, a nightmare from which she could emerge. 'I know I'm dreaming,' she said.

'It's no dream, Ella. This is the here and now. I want you to listen.' His voice sounded measured, neither sad nor happy, passive rather than threatening. As detached as if they were strangers striking up a casual conversation.

Ella spotted the sweet wrapper at the bottom of the bed. He was right, this was no dream, no nightmare. Now, she was sure of it. 'What have you done to him?' she said, recoiling from the man, pushing herself up the bed, as far away from the intruder as she could get.

'Bit of chloroform, nothing more. He'll be right as rain in a couple of hours, don't worry.'

'Put him down and get out of my house, you bastard!' Ella jumped out of her bed, confronting the intruder with nothing more than her Winnie-the-Pooh pyjamas.

'Well, well, you're game, eh?'

'I'm mair than that! Put the boy doon!' Ella had no idea what she was going to do but she just knew she had to do something. To her surprise, he laid James ever so gently at the bottom of the bed. Ella rushed forward and took the little boy in her arms.

'Now, I'll leave you be. Though you must admit, today must have been a lesson, yes?'

'What?' Ella was crying now, tears spilling down her face as she stroked James's hair.

'He's back with you now, safe and sound. The next time will be very different.'

Ella felt as though she might pass out. What was happening seemed so unreal, as mad as the nightmares she'd been having, and every bit as unsettling. The intruder's voice also freaked her out. How could he stay so calm?

'Listen carefully. You tell no one of this. You stay in this house. You don't go to work. Both of your phones are being monitored, the house is being watched. We'll hear everything you have to say, see every move you make. You have one chance to save this *precious* little boy.'

'Which is?' Ella's voice was wavering.

'You call your husband first thing in the morning. You tell him to come home.'

'Oh aye, simple as that, is it?'

The intruder smiled. 'You can do that; I know you can. Make sure your husband is on his way home soon – tomorrow. He has nothing more to do with the Daley case, OK?' He glanced at the child in Ella's arms. 'Such a young boy to be without his mother. But still so much life ahead of him – maybe.' With that, he turned on his heel and was gone.

Ella sat on the edge of the bed shaking, hugging her friend's son, not knowing what to do. She felt utterly defeated.

36

Brian Scott waited anxiously in the Royal London Hospital corridor. Daley had been taken into A&E almost immediately to be assessed by the staff. Not long after, Beattie had been called away on urgent police business. So, he was on his own, save for the two uniformed cops guarding the murder suspect.

He tried to puzzle his way through what was happening. Liz Daley dead, her husband the only suspect. Who could hold such a grudge against a man that they were willing to kill his wife? It made no sense. Or was Daley nothing more than a handy patsy? Could the people who'd been extorting Liz be to blame? It was a mess.

The only thing he could do was work his way through the usual suspects. But to cover the long list of criminals he and Daley had brought to justice, he'd need all the information at his fingertips. He'd also have to try to discover more about the man on Liz's iPad – that was proving difficult.

James Machie was dead, as were those who may have carried his torch – maybe. When he was alive, would he have been capable of what had happened to Liz? Yes, without doubt. In fact, the case had all the hallmarks of the madman who had been so much part of his and Daley's lives for so long.

Absently, Scott rubbed his shoulder. The scar of the bullet that Machie had sent his way was still there, as it always would be. The man he'd grown up with had nearly killed him on two occasions. But it was ridiculous, he thought, to entertain the notion Machie could be responsible for Daley's current predicament. That had already happened, the disciples were gone. It was in the past, he hoped.

Scott thought deeply, drawing on his training and experience. What was it Daley always said? Something about the most obvious theory often being the right one.

But how on earth did this fit in with what had happened since? It seemed like no time at all since he, Ella and young James had waved Jim and Liz off at the airport.

Brian thought about his wife. He knew how upset she'd be about what had happened to Liz and was still happening to Jim Daley. They'd known each other for so long. In a job that rarely encouraged friendships, the Daleys and the Scotts were bosom buddies. The road had not always been smooth, but it was what it was – the way it had always been.

He recalled Liz's infidelity. What really left her scared enough to leave him the note? Surely not the proof of another unfaithful episode. That had happened too often. The more Brian Scott thought about it, the more he was convinced that this was the point from which everything sprang.

'You can go in and see your colleague now,' said a nurse, making Scott jump. 'Just for a short time. And please, try not to upset him.'

'Right, of course. How is the big man, anyhow?'

The nurse smiled flatly, her eyes showing little emotion. Scott recognized the carapace. There could be many reasons for this. Not least, his state of mind. Also, that Daley might well be in a bad way, worse than even Scott himself expected. He decided not to overthink it. Anyway, it wasn't his style.

'He's doing well. Broken ribs, fingers, nose – perhaps a fractured cheekbone. He'll have to go for a brain scan soon. We're waiting for a machine to become available.'

'He could have a brain injury, you mean?' Scott's worried expression spoke volumes.

'A precaution. We do this with anyone who's been – well, injured in this manner.'

Scott noted the hesitation. He got to his feet.

'This way. I presume you visiting is fine with your colleagues?' The nurse eyed the two officers guarding the door to Daley's room.

'As long as one of us comes with you, Inspector,' said one.

Scott looked at the constable. He was tall, well built, with red hair. 'If you fancy putting me in beside Jimmy, like your colleagues did, think again. I didn't learn how to fight down the rugby club. D'you know what I mean, pal?'

The constable looked at him and shrugged his shoulders. 'I'm just here to do a job, sir. I'm sure you know how that feels, having done it yourself.'

Scott felt rather ashamed of himself for the outburst, though he guessed it had taken more than one assailant to overcome Daley and leave him bleeding and broken on a holding cell floor. He remained unapologetic.

'A few minutes only, OK?' said the nurse.

'Aye, got it,' replied Scott. He opened the door to Daley's room as quietly as he could.

Inside, the lights were subdued. Wired to various machines that clicked and beeped lay the broken figure of Jim Daley. He had a large bandage wrapped round his head, covered in a blue cap. His nose had been set, and a cast placed over it to make sure it remained so. Daley's right eye was so swollen, it was hard to recognize him. The rest of his body was hidden under hospital blankets, though one of his arms was held up out of the bed on a support.

'Jimmy, it's me,' said Scott.

'I know, I can see you,' Daley replied in little more than a whisper.

'Ah, right. I wisnae sure if you were awake, big man.'

'You try sleeping like this, Bri.'

'Aye, right enough, good point.' Scott grimaced at his own bedside manner. 'Anyway, how are you feeling?'

Daley blinked one eye, whether through tiredness or disbelief, Scott wasn't sure.

'I'm fine and dandy, Brian. I've been beaten to fuck, my wife's dead, and if that wasn't bad enough, everybody is blaming me for it. Apart from that, I'm tip-top.'

'You know sarcasm is the lowest form of wit, eh? You tell me that all the time.'

Daley did his best to smile, the right corner of his mouth curling.

'Are you sure she's gone, Bri? I mean a hundred per cent sure.'

'You know I cannae tell you that until she's been iden-tified, Jimmy.' Scott lowered his head. 'Not for sure.'

One tear slipped down Daley's cheek from his good eye. He swallowed hard. 'That's good enough for me.'

'Right, Jimmy.' Scott knew he had to pick Daley's brain,

regardless of the circumstances. 'Listen, I need you to think. I know it'll be the hardest thing you've ever done but try.'

'Think about who did this, you mean?'

'Yes, any ideas? I don't mind if you're havering. Just fire something at me.'

Daley closed his eye and took a deep breath. 'She had another affair, Brian. Find the guy and you might have the bastard who did this.'

'You know about that?' Scott's surprise was obvious.

'So do you, by the sound of things. Why the fuck didn't you tell me, Brian?'

'I only just found out. Liz left me a note.' Scott chose not to elaborate on the means. It would only make things more complex.

'That was nice of her.'

'Fuck me, Jimmy. You cannae still be angry wae her. No matter what's passed between you.'

'Why not? I mean, it's not the first time she put herself in danger for a shag, is it?'

'You're upset. It isnae a good time to go into this. But you know better than most folk. They have to charge you to hold you. They'll get the ninety-six hours' extension, but the clock's ticking, buddy.'

'I know exactly what's happening. Why do you think they put me in here? It's to make defending myself harder, that's why.' Daley had to stop. He pressed the little morphine clicker in his right hand.

'Sore, eh?'

'No, just a bit of thumb exercise,' Daley muttered.

'Aye, stupid thing to say – again.'

'Find the guy she was messing about with, and we're

halfway there. But to be honest, I don't really care if I go down for this. I mean, what else is there, eh?' Daley turned his head away on the pillow.

'C'mon, man. This isnae like you. You've had the worst shock possible, you're no' yourself. But you have to remember, the wee man will need you more than ever now. Do you know what I mean?'

'What am I going to say to him?' Daley wailed.

'Listen, we have tae take one thing at a time. We find out who did it, we nail the bastard!' Scott's teeth were clenched.

'The affair, Brian. That's the key. Find that guy.'

'I've tried that. Nobody can identify him. He always comes up as unknown. Eddie Beattie's on the case. You've met him, he's a good guy.'

'Yeah, he's been your pal for a long time.'

'He has – aye, and a good one, at that. Any other bright ideas?'

'Lambie. Take a look at that bastard. That's all I can think of. How did he escape? Where did he get money? You know the score.'

Scott felt his heart sink. Daley obviously wasn't thinking properly. Probably the morphine, he reckoned. 'He's deid, Jimmy. Mind, he topped himself in your bedroom.'

Daley made to get out of the bed, but apart from being wired to monitors, he was too weak. 'I didn't mean him personally, Brian. He must have had support. To go on the run like that, stay in that hotel, travel. Where did the funds come from?' Daley mashed at his dry mouth.

'But he did what he came to do. The poor guy was mad as fuck. You know that. He probably stole the money. That's the most likely thing.'

'He had a credit card, Brian.'

'Any stupid prick and his friend can get one o' they pre-paid credit cards these days. Ella's got one.'

'OK, OK. But listen, you're all I've got. Work the problem. You don't need to come and see me. You're every bit as good a detective as I am. I'll be in here for a while, anyway. Just concentrate on getting who did this.' He reached out for Scott's hand. His old friend grabbed it. 'You'll get there, Brian. I know you will.' Tears were spilling down Daley's face.

Behind them, the red-haired constable's mobile started to ring. He apologized as he took the call.

'The guard, I take it?'

'Aye.'

'Fuck!' the constable swore, which attracted Scott's attention.

'Oh! Watch the bad language o'er there. Can't you see my pal's suffering? He doesnae need to hear that, you fucking moron!'

'Sorry, sir – sirs. Just had some shocking news.'

'You too? Lot o' it going aboot,' Scott opined.

'DI Bright – you know him, yeah? He's copped it – stone dead. Hit and run, apparently. Can I trust you both for two seconds while I tell me mate?'

'Aye, we're polis, of course you can trust us,' said Scott. The Kinloch detectives looked on as Daley's police guard left the room.

'Right, Jimmy. Come on, unplug all this shite, and we'll go for the window. No time like the present!'

Daley smiled weakly again. 'Do you know, if I was fit enough I'd take you up on that, Brian.'

'Wish we could, big man. We're only aboot twelve floors up.'

'Knotted bedsheets.'

The door opened once more. The constable entered looking rather subdued. 'Can I have a word, Inspector Scott?'

'You can have as many words as you like, as long as you tell me you've made an arse of it, and Jimmy's a free man.' Scott ambled over to the uniformed man, who whispered something in his ear.

'Right, son. Thanks for that.'

'This guy getting killed, Brian. He's an arsehole, but it'll put even more heat on me.' Daley recalled the venal DI Bright.

'Wait a minute, Jimmy. I've something to tell you.'

Daley's uninjured eye widened. 'It's about Liz, isn't it?'

'Aye, it is. She's definitely gone, Jimmy. Her mother did the ID. Took it bad, by the sounds o' things. Fainted away when she saw Lizzie's body.'

From what could be seen of Daley's face, his expression seemed blank.

'What am I going to say to the wee man, Brian?'

Scott grabbed Daley's hand once more. 'I'll be with you, Jimmy. We'll work it out. We always do.'

'Work it out? Even if we find out who's behind it, my wife – his mother – won't be coming back.'

Scott could feel Daley's sadness, his hopelessness. The task ahead of him appeared impossible. But all he could do was try. There remained one question to ask.

'Jimmy, do you remember calling me in the wee small hours?'

'What?'

'You phoned me at half two in the morning – to my mobile. You know, on the night . . . on the night Liz died.'

'Brian, you've lost it. I've not spoken to you since we were at the airport back home.' Even though Daley's voice was nothing but a harsh whisper, his anger was more than apparent. 'What did I say during this *call*?'

'Just forget about it, Jimmy.'

Daley grabbed Scott's arm. 'What did I say?'

Scott shook his head. 'You telt me you couldn't take any more. That you were sorry.'

'And?'

Brian Scott swallowed hard. 'You telt me you killed Liz!'

37

Jill Unwin was at her desk at six in the morning. As the river didn't stop, neither did she. Last night, officers had taken a human trafficker into custody as he tried to smuggle sixteen women into the city using an old cabin cruiser. They'd been abducted in Eastern Europe and were destined for London's illegal sex trade.

As Unwin read the statements made by some of the women, her stomach churned. Almost unbelievable tales of cruelty and inhumanity jumped out from every page. She looked forward to breaking this man, seeing him sent down. Jill Unwin would have done her job free of charge for the pleasure of seeing such individuals in receipt of the justice they so richly deserved. But it came too infrequently; quite often, the sentence did not match the crime.

The door to her office swung open. The nightshift sergeant popped his head round into the room. 'You attended the body in the river at Wapping yesterday, didn't you?'

'Yeah, I did. Poor woman. I see she was officially identified late on yesterday. Wife of a Scottish DCI, would you believe. They've got him over at Bethnal Green. DI Bright's case.'

'Not now it isn't.'

'What?'

'It's not Bright's case no more, Jill. He'd dead. Hit and run last night. Didn't you hear?'

'Duh! Obviously not, Eric!'

'Wasn't keen on the bloke. Feel sorry for his missus and the kids, mind you.'

'How many did he have?'

'Two, neither of them in school yet, poor little things.'

Unwin sighed. It always seemed it was those most vulnerable who suffered the most. Though she was shocked by Bright's death, she couldn't find it in herself to mourn him for long. Some people you just didn't like. It was sad but true.

'Why did you want to know about me and the body yesterday, Eric? I was just there for form's sake, really.'

'I have an eyewitness. Close to one, anyhow.'

'Who?'

'A street guy called Chambers. When he turned up in the early hours of yesterday morning to report someone dumping a body in the river, they locked him up for drunk and incapable, would you believe?'

'After all these years in this job, I believe anything.'

'Anyhow, he says he saw this bloke at the Wapping Old Stairs. Got a good look at him, too.'

'Brilliant! Where is he?'

'Downstairs. Sober as a judge now, and still swears by what he says. I thought you'd like a word before we chuck him in the system. It being a murder inquiry, and all.'

'Absolutely! Wheel him up, Eric. Good work!'

Unwin tapped a pen against her front teeth. If there was one thing she hated in life, it was a bent cop. But she also worried about Bright's processes. Having seen Bright in action, she suspected the newly departed DI was no stranger to corruption. For a second, she chastised herself for the thought. In her part of the East End, it didn't do to think ill of the dead. But her revulsion for Bright and his ilk soon took over. If this man could definitively identify the DCI from Scotland, all the better. He would meet the justice he richly deserved. On the other hand, if he was innocent, this Daley had already paid a heavy price.

She thought about Bright, then his wife and children. What Jill Unwin really needed was retirement to happen today, not the endless days she had left in the job between then and now, more bodies, more misery, more death.

Unwin logged on to her computer and searched for the case in which she'd already played a small part. Soon, the face of DCI James Daley filled her screen. Middle aged, slightly sagging features, like so many cops of his vintage – including her – though there was something about his high forehead and his sharpness of eye that made her think him an intelligent man. And judging by his record, he was no shrinking violet. What could possibly turn a man who had devoted so much of his life to law and order into a wife murderer?

She was reading through the dive team's report when Eric delivered the witness. The sergeant sat Chambers on the chair at the other end of Unwin's desk and handed her the drunk and incapable charge sheet from the previous evening. She was shocked by his age. The man before her looked to be in his sixties, not forties. On reflection, she'd seen so many unfortunates the world had chewed up and spat out. Many, ravaged by drink and drugs, were old before their time. The river attracted these unfortunates like flies. Jill Unwin could feel nothing but compassion for such people. It only took a tragedy, moments of weakness, some wicked chance, to send anyone into a spiral that could end beside the Thames, seeking scant succour from a bottle of cheap spirits. She shuddered at the thought.

'Mr Chambers, I'm Inspector Jill Unwin. I'm so sorry for what happened to you last night. It was a misunderstanding. I do apologize.'

Chambers regarded her through sad, world-weary eyes.

'No surprise, to be honest. State I'm in, any decent person could be forgiven for thinking the same as your constables. I'm ashamed of myself, and not afraid to admit it.'

Unwin heard Chambers' voice as a rasping whisper, vocal cords ruined by strong alcohol and exposure to every kind of weather. His words were often lisped through missing teeth. His hair was wet, slicked back. She reckoned he'd been offered a shower and a change of clothes. Each station had a bank of garments left behind in various circumstances. As a uniform sergeant, she used to pick up homeless people regularly, just to make sure they had a bed for the night, some hot food in their stomach and a change of clothes. It was the least an ungrateful city could do for its unwanted, in her opinion.

'They were wrong, Mr Chambers, end of story. We need to admit to our shortcomings, not run away from them. That's already happened far too often, as you are no doubt aware.'

'Very honest, I must say. Thank you, Inspector.' Chambers nodded.

'Says here, you were in the army, Mr Chambers.'

'I was. Fifteen years, as it goes. Made me realize how shit things are, mainly.' He sniffed at his own observation, as though underlining it.

'I hear you, mate. This job does the exact same thing.'

'Though you're not about to spend tonight in a doorway, eh?'

'No, that's very true.'

'You want to know what I saw last night, don't you?'

'Yes, please.'

Chambers related, word for word, the feelings of fear, sadness and revulsion he'd experienced near the Wapping Old Stairs. He also related to Unwin how ashamed he was of doing nothing to stop the huge man with his burden. 'I know he dumped the body of a gal in the river. Saw her tartan skirt, didn't I.'

'Yes, we think you're right. She was found not far away downstream.'

Chambers looked surprised.

'Didn't anyone tell you we'd found a body?'

'First I heard. When I saw it was, you know, a person, like – well, I knew I should tell the Old Bill, right. Fuck me, I've seen the day I'd have sorted him myself – despite his size.'

'Big, was he?' Unwin asked, noting Daley was well over six feet.

'I should say so. Huge lump of a thing, tall and broad with it. He frightened me, I'll tell you that for nothing.'

'You saw his face on the way back, yes?'

'That's right. It's what scared me most, to be honest with you.'

Chambers was suddenly enveloped by a paroxysm of coughing. To Unwin, his chest sounded like an old washing machine churning jeans with coins left in the pockets.

'Here, drink this.' Unwin handed the witness a bottle of water from her handbag.

Chambers drew deeply on it, smacking his lips when he was done. 'That's done the trick, thanks.' He made to hand the water back, but Unwin waved it away. 'Not easy to find good clean water on the streets, you know.'

'I can imagine.' Unwin glanced at the nightshift's notes. 'You said that he stopped, and his face was lit up. Is that right, Mr Chambers?'

'Yeah, that's it. He was all lit up by a light across the way. He just stood there, sniffing the air like a dog. I'm telling you, it was as though he knew where I was. I nearly shat myself. Sorry to be so crude.'

'And you got a good look at him?'

'I should say so. Stood about for at least a couple of minutes. His head was like a lighthouse, you know, peering all about, like.'

Unwin smiled at the allusion. 'So, you reckon you might recognize him if you saw him again, yeah?'

'Too right I would. You tend to remember the folks that want to kill you. It was the same as in the army. Still see the bastards to this day.'

Jill Unwin reached for her laptop. She pulled up the headshot of James Daley, provided by Police Scotland. She turned the computer to face Chambers. 'Is this the man, then?'

Chambers sat forward on his chair, his eyes screwed up as he squinted at the image. 'No, that's not him. Yeah, this guy's got dark hair, and he's big, like. Maybe even round about the right age, I dunno. But this isn't the man I saw. No way. The face is all wrong.'

'You're sure, Mr Chambers?'

'Couldn't be surer. The guy with the body was foreign. Like a Russian or a Slav, that type of look. Saw plenty of them in the Balkans. I know people these days think it's racist, like, but folk around the world look different, don't they? Stands to reason, if you ask me. The man I saw was Slavic, and that's the truth.'

Unwin felt a tingle on the back of her neck. Though

she'd read about the damning CCTV footage, she hadn't seen it. She recalled a week-long course she'd been on, all about the way video images could be manipulated. It seemed easy to do, especially if the person chosen to mimic another was of a similar height, age, hair colour and the like. Unwin had laughed when they'd manipulated footage of one of the other cops on the course to look as though he was dancing on *Strictly*. She'd been amazed at what could be done.

'Everything OK, Inspector? I hope you believe me. I'm telling you the truth, honest.'

Unwin thought of DI Bright. A hit and run, they'd said. She needed to know more. Now, not only was the back of her neck tingling, but there was also a lump at the pit of her stomach. 'Oh, I believe you, Mr Chambers. Tell me, how would you like to stay in a nice little hostel in Bromley for a while? Clean, no riffraff, drugs and all that. It's run by a friend of mine.'

Chambers narrowed his eyes. 'What's the catch?'

'If you're needed, you give evidence when required. Just what you've told me, nothing more. Right?'

Chambers shrugged. 'I'm in. Not been down to Kent for a long time. Used to have a lady friend down there when I first joined the army. Wonder what she's up to.' Chambers flashed a toothless grin.

'Excellent!' Unwin leaned across the desk at her new witness. 'But keep this to yourself, OK. Don't tell a soul, not even people at the hostel, right?'

'My lips are sealed, Inspector. That's a promise.'

Unwin made a call to the witness liaison sergeant. He was to take Chambers to the canteen and make sure he was well fed.

When Chambers left, Unwin called her friend the hostel

manager in Bromley. As expected, she was happy to make a place available. It was a favour long overdue.

Call over, Unwin gazed at the face on the laptop screen once more. 'Well now, James Daley. If I'm not mistaken, somebody doesn't like you.' She closed the computer and left the office in search of CCTV footage.

38

Brian Scott woke with a jolt in a strange bed. Then, he remembered he was in a cheap hotel in London, and all that had happened in the previous couple of days began to crowd in on him. He'd slept well, despite the noisy trains and the unfamiliar night-time bustle of the city. He supposed he'd spent so long in the peace and quiet of Kinloch, it had become second nature.

Scott tumbled out of bed and gathered his thoughts in front of the mirror on the wall.

'Shit, I look like my faither,' he muttered, remembering the ruined man who had helped give him life. If he'd ever entertained the idea of drinking whisky again, the face that stared at him now was enough to banish the thought for ever.

Scott had set Duff, the new DC in Kinloch, on the footage of Daley's apparent crime. The young man had seemed utterly unsurprised at the thought that what was apparently real was, in fact, nothing of the kind.

'You can do this stuff on your phone these days, sir,' he'd said brightly.

For Scott, switching the bloody thing on was challenge enough.

The thought that they might be able to cast doubt over

this damning piece of evidence raised his spirits. He showered and dressed. It wouldn't do to become maudlin. He had to do what Daley had asked and focus everything on shedding light on what had really happened to Liz.

When his phone buzzed on the old table that served as his nightstand, he remembered Daley calling him in the middle of the night to confess to his heinous crime. He didn't recognize the number on the screen but decided to answer anyway. After all, this could be one of his many bosses from Scotland, interested to know what he was doing in London, away from Kinloch and well and truly out of his jurisdiction.

'Hello,' he said.

There was silence on the other end of the line for a few moments. Scott heard a crackle, like someone trying to fill an old coin box, like the phone boxes of his youth.

'Hey, who is this? If you don't speak, you can fuck off.'

'You are very abrupt, Inspector Scott. I know you come with a reputation, but I expected more from you somehow.' The accent was upper-class English, polished tones, redolent of the public school system, perhaps.

'You've phoned to tell me I'm dog-rough? Thanks!' said Scott, already irritated by the call.

'I want to make sure you're aware of something, that's all.'

'Eh? See, if you're trying tae sell me loft insulation, I promise, I'll find you and kill you.'

'Good grief, how the police service has changed! Used to be, all you'd get was a damned good thrashing in a cell. Now it's the promise of violent death. Progress of a sort, I'm sure.'

'Right, you've had your fun. Cheeri-fucking-oh.' Scott made to end the call.

'So, you aren't worried about your wife and little James, eh?'

Scott sat on the bed. Suddenly his knees felt weak. 'Right, I want you to tell me who you are. No messing this time!'

'That would be rather short-sighted, don't you think? Anyway, here's some advice instead. Feel free to take it or not.'

'Who are you?'

The posh man on the other end of the phone ignored the question again. 'I want you to agree to leave the Daley case alone. Book a plane back to Scotland and enjoy your promotion. There's a good chap.'

'Aye, right!'

'What about Ella? Don't you care what happens to her? Maybe you should give her a call. See if you think she sounds herself.'

'I'll have you know that every call to this phone is recorded and logged. We will find you, whoever you are. You got it, arsehole? Hello?' Scott pressed a random button on his mobile, for no reason other than he felt he should do something. But no matter what he tried, the man with the mocking tone had gone.

Scott bit his lip, trying to work out what to do. He thought about calling Kinloch police office, but that was too complicated. He'd have to speak to his temporary replacement. When Daley had decided to tilt at windmills – something he did often – Scott was his faithful and more than capable replacement. The deputy enjoyed no such luxury. He decided to call Ella and see what her reaction was, find out if she'd been contacted by the man with the posh voice. He scrolled to her name.

'Hello.'

To Scott, Ella's voice already sounded strange. 'You OK, honey?'

Ella cleared her throat on the other end of the line. 'Yes, I'm fine, Brian.'

'What's wae the Sunday voice, doll?'

'I don't know what you mean, darling.'

Scott felt he was talking to a stranger. The way she was speaking sounded odd, robotic almost. Most certainly not like the woman he'd known so long. He decided to change tack. 'I sank a good few drams last night, Ella. I know you'll wish you were there with me.'

Ella hesitated. 'Oh aye, Brian. You know how much I enjoy being with you and a bottle of whisky.'

And there it was. The mention of his drinking whisky, he knew, would have normally outraged his wife. She was trying to get a message to him without saying it outright on the phone. She'd been got at. Scott tried to work out what he might say to help her along. 'How's the wee man?'

'Oh, Jamie's fine, Brian. You know what a wee gem he is.'

Jamie. They both knew only too well not to call the Daleys' son *Jamie.* Liz hated it, insisting he was called James and nothing else. 'Wee Jamie, eh. Hope he's no' been picking his nose, Ella?'

'Eh?' Ella's reply was instantaneous.

'Och, you know how he likes a good root aboot up there. Has to know what's lurking about – up his nose, I mean.' Scott grimaced at this awkward exchange.

'Oh aye.' Ella finally cottoned on. 'No doubt there's something lurking about up there that he can't get out.'

Can't get out. Did that mean neither she nor James could escape? Scott knew he had to think up something else that would sound normal to anyone listening in. He furrowed his brow. 'Here, I had that dream last night, doll.'

'What dream?' Ella sounded slightly unsure.

'The one wae me and you on the mountain top.' Scott made his best attempt to make his voice sound sexy. 'You'll remember all the stuff we did up there, babes?'

'No!' Ella's reply was emphatic.

'Aye you do. Remember you said we couldn't – you know – in case somebody else was listening, turned up on the summit, sort o' thing.' He forced a laugh.

'All I know is that you're going too far, Brian Scott.'

Scott could hear the reluctance in his wife's voice, but he had to press on.

'I remember the time we got stuck in the lift at Marks and Spencer's in Sauchiehall Street, if that's what you mean,' said Ella.

Scott strained to remember what she was talking about. Trust his wife to use a real memory.

'You remember, Brian. You wanted to take the *wee man* out, but you couldn't because the engineers arrived.'

A memory sparked in Scott's mind, and he blushed instantly. 'Oh aye. We didn't know there was a camera in the lift, neither.'

'That's right, you've got it now, sweetheart. Nearly got arrested, if I remember. The first flush o' true love. Gosh, such happy memories.'

Scott heard the words *sweetheart* and *gosh*, recognizing them as things Ella would never say. And also recalled that Ella had been so furious, she'd abandoned their brand-new marital home and stayed at her mother's for nearly a week. 'Right, I better go, *munchkin*.' Scott thought he'd add his own little abnormality, just to let Ella know he understood.

'For fuck's sake,' she muttered. 'We need you home, Brian. As quickly as possible, please.'

'Aye, no bother. In any case, I've done all I can here. I'll be back later. Hope to make the plane back to Kinloch this evening.'

'How nice! I hope you're bringing a surprise, Brian.'

'Oh aye, there's a big surprise waiting. See you later, doll. Love you.'

When Scott ended the call, he puzzled at what she meant by *surprise*. As bizarre as the conversation had been, he was now sure she was under some kind of threat, scrutiny. He had to work out something to do, and quickly. He called Duff at Kinloch. He was to keep an eye on the house as unobtrusively as possible. 'Aye, and take a camera with you. If you spot anything or anyone unusual, take a picture o' it. You young folk will take a snap o' anything these days.'

'A snap?' Duff sounded confused.

Scott ended the call. He had work to do, and that must entail a visit to DI Unwin, the woman who'd uncovered Liz's body. He'd hoped Beattie would be able to join him. However, he'd just sent a text message to say he was tied up and would see him later. Scott knew he'd have to wing it, though Beattie had said he'd left word with the inspector to expect him.

Keys, phone, ID, cigarettes and bank cards. Scott made the mental check before leaving his room. As it had been when he arrived, the hotel lobby seemed deserted. He toyed with the idea of shouting to Suraj to tell him he was going out, but decided there was no real reason to do that, so carried on out of the front door.

He rushed down the front steps and on to the pavement, vaguely aware of a figure to his left hurrying along the street. This was London – everyone was in a hurry. The place was just one rush to be somewhere else. That aside, the street appeared devoid of life. It was odd to think he was in one of the biggest cities in the world.

Just as Scott turned on his heel, he heard the footsteps come closer. He had taken only two steps towards the main road when he was hit by a sharp blow from behind. Something collided with his right shoulder, and he cried out in pain, almost falling on to the pavement. As he struggled against a tumble, a brawny arm snaked around his throat, tightening into a headlock, leaving Scott helpless.

'You were warned,' said the voice. It was rough, gritty. Scott was sure the accent was of the north of England. Though he struggled, the hold his attacker had over him became tighter and tighter. In no time, the Scottish detective was struggling for breath.

'I'm a police officer,' Scott managed to croak against the hold.

'I know who you are.'

Scott's vision began to blur. On the verge of passing out, he was sure he heard raised voices, and the stranglehold he'd been held in so tightly loosened. He crashed to the floor, landing on his right elbow, which made him yell in pain. Scott struggled to his feet.

'You bloody racist! This is what happens to people like you!' Suraj the hotel owner was laying into Scott's assailant with a huge nightstick, crashing it down on the man's head, over and over again. 'You take your bloody medicine, you absolute rascal!'

'Here, leave this to me. You go and call the cops, Suraj.' Scott pushed the big man to the floor, face down, and straddled his back. The man growled and roared in protest, trying to grab Scott with flailing arms.

'I told you about these absolute bastards, Mr Scotland.

You have to be ready, oh yes.' Suraj wore a broad grin as he tightened the cord of his dressing gown.

'Just call the police,' shouted Scott, while still wrestling with his barely subdued attacker. 'And hide that nightstick or you'll be in big trouble, my man.'

'It's OK. I know the constables round here. We have understanding, you get me?'

Just as the rotund hotelier made to hurry back into the hotel, a siren sounded at the end of the street. A police van sped to the pavement. It squealed to a halt, and two police constables hurried to Scott's aid.

'My goodness,' said Suraj. 'People in this country always down on the police. But look at this! They arrive before we make call. Arrest this racist bastard!' He bounced on tiptoes, thoroughly enjoying the spectacle of the constables dragging Scott's assailant to his feet and handcuffing him.

As one officer piled the man into the back of the van, the other spoke to Scott.

'Right, what happened here?' He took out his notebook.

'You don't mess about. Just passing by, eh?' said Scott.

'Yeah, something like that. Lucky, wasn't it? We're up to our ears here. I want your name and address, and we'll be back to take statements.'

'You serious?' said Scott. He noticed that the young officer hadn't shaved, boasting a dark stubble on his chin.

'Your address, please, sir.' The constable looked irritated as he eyed Scott.

'The hotel behind me, son. That's my address.'

'That'll do. We'll be back in half an hour or so. Stay here, OK?'

Scott watched the officer hurry off and reached for his mobile.

'What is it you are doing?' said Suraj.

'Calling the real polis.'

'You are so hard to understand, Mr Scotland.'

'Those men aren't police, Suraj. For a start, how did they know what was happening?'

'The instinct of the good old British bobby.' Suraj smiled broadly.

'If that's the case, these boys are Mystic Meg.' Scott typed the registration number of the police van into his phone so he wouldn't forget it.

'You are very strange man. Very strange indeed.' Suraj shook his head in bewilderment.

Scott dialled 999 and put his phone to his ear.

39

Jill Unwin gazed at the dark waters of the Thames once more. She was at the very spot where Liz Daley's remains had been dragged from the river by police divers. It was busier now, a group of kids playing on the bank, just as she had done as a child. A couple were out for a walk, pushing a buggy with a happily chortling baby inside. A sleek cabin cruiser passed her at a stately pace, a young woman out on deck, sunning herself, all tanned limbs and over-the-top hair-do. It wasn't oligarch level, but it would have done for Jill Unwin.

She was depressed. Her husband had called to say they'd all been sent home from the office. The company for whom he'd worked for thirty years was in administration. Worse still, they'd been using the pension fund to try to bail themselves out. Employees would be lucky to get a penny. Her dream of a place in Spain was receding rapidly.

It all felt like a kick in the head.

She turned her attention back to the river. There was nothing at all here to mark the fact that this place had been intended as the grave of a murdered woman. Unwin threw a single red rose she'd bought from a local florist on to the water. While she was no stranger to bodies turning up in the river, something had touched her about this case. Maybe it was the death of such a beautiful woman – perhaps the fact her husband was a copper like Unwin herself. Ultimately, it was a gesture, nothing more. But at least she'd done her best to mark the place. Surely any decent person deserved that. Though she was aware of Elizabeth Daley, she knew precious little about her as a person.

Unwin hated the way things had become. She'd been taught to fear and respect the police in equal measure. Even the former was preferable to the casual indifference facing so many of her colleagues now.

'*Don't look at me as though I'm nothing to worry about.*'

She remembered the line from an American gangster show she'd watched over and over again. Yes, there had been violence, but there was also wit and philosophy. These were attributes every police officer needed in abundance. These days, though, those clambering through the ranks were, in her opinion, like a legion of clones, heads stuck in phones, more interested in TikTok than career building. Nobody lived to work any more; in fact, the opposite was true. Perhaps it always should have been.

As Unwin watched the river flow by, she recalled having to break the bad news to a young probationer that he hadn't made the grade, and his police career was at an end, over before it started. She'd felt sorry for the youngster, whom she'd found pleasant and personable. It would surely be a blow to find one's ambitions dashed at the first hurdle, never mind the imminent prosect of unemployment. Her husband's face passed before her mind's eye again – broken, lost.

'I'm sorry,' she'd said to the young man across the desk.

'That's OK. It was my dad that wanted me to join up in the first place. He never passed the entrance exam, you see. I did, with ninety per cent. I can hold that over his head for a while, at least.'

When she asked him what he'd do next, he'd shrugged. It seemed his ultimate ambition was either modelling or to become a DJ on Ibiza. It was another thing that worried her about the next generation. For all their knowledge about the world, answers to any question available from the mobile phone in their hand, they seemed so naive. Unwin's grandparents hadn't known much beyond the river, and the streets where they grew up. Their world view was almost non-existent. However, they knew the value of a quid, and the reality of life. More broken dreams, sadness, depression and crime. That was all she could envisage.

Unwin watched the man as he made his way along the bank. Short, for a policeman, red hair, fading to copper and grey. But a confident walk, head high, an air of superiority. A man you wouldn't look at as though he was nothing.

'Jill! Thanks for taking the time to see me,' shouted Eddie Beattie, still a good ten yards away.

While she liked him, she knew that to get where he had took more than smiles and glad-handing. They'd met at a training seminar at Henley years ago. She was a solid copper – so was he. But Jill Unwin lacked the ruthlessness to climb to the top. She valued people too much, unwilling to use anyone as an unsuspecting crutch.

'You're looking good, Jill. What's the secret?' said Beattie, his Scottish burr still apparent after decades in London.

'Huh, I can tell you that for nothing, sir. No sleep, shit food, very little time off and an ulcer.'

'Ah, without such sacrifice us police officers would be as nothing, kid. Then where would everyone else be?'

'How's the new unit, Eddie? I know you've got everyone running scared. I hope you didn't want me to sprint off to safety. A swift hobble is all you'll get, I'm warning you.'

They hugged, just like the old friends they were.

'It's been too long. The last thing I want is for you to go dashing off.' Beattie sniffed the air. 'Why here, by the way?'

'This is where we found your Liz Daley.'

'Mine?'

'I heard you was friends with his oppo. DI Scott, is that right?'

'I should have known you'd be on it, Jill.'

'They have interesting files, he and Daley. More pages than the Argos catalogue.'

'Let's walk.'

Unwin followed Beattie along the narrow path on the riverbank, until they came to a wooden bench that had seen much better days, the graffiti fighting for space with dried bird droppings and green moss. The pair sat together in silence for a while, merely taking in the scene: gentrified old warehouses, young people dressing down to dress up, the buzz of rich, indifferent up-and-comers stamped on a place where once poverty and community had reigned supreme.

'I need a favour, Jill. I hope you can help.'

'If it's money you're after, think again.' This came from the heart.

'Nah, not that. I need to speak to somebody.'

'*Somebody* I know that you don't? *Somebody* that matters? I wouldn't bet too heavy on that, Eddie.'

'You might be surprised.' Beattie crossed his legs and cleared his throat, as though delaying what he wanted to say.

'Come on, then.'

'The man you interviewed about Liz Daley – the tramp. I need to speak to him too.'

'*Street person*, Eddie. Thought you'd know all them woke terms by now.'

'OK, *street person*, whatever. He's interesting. I know you'll think it's an old pals' thing, but me and DI Scott, we go way back, even before we were cops. We grew up together, for a while, at least.'

'Oh yeah, the dark heart of bonnie Glasgow. Is that it?'

'Something like that. He's a good lad, and so's this Daley. If Brian doesn't think he did it . . . well, I owe it to my instincts as a copper to get to the truth.'

'How do you know about Chambers?'

'You logged it in, didn't you?'

'Like a good little gal? Yes, I did.'

'I read the statement.'

'Gosh, I didn't think anyone cared.'

'Everyone cares. The problem is, it's mainly about themselves. You put him somewhere safe. And you did that for a reason.'

'You'll have heard about Bright, Eddie?'

'Of course. I've got people on it as we speak.'

'So, you don't think it was just a hit and run?'

'I don't know yet. I will soon.'

'You think this Daley thing is a fit-up. They killed her to get at him. You'll have heard the story about the ex-cop killing himself in this Daley's bedroom a couple of weeks ago?'

'Yeah, I read that. Odd, I must admit.'

'Related?'

'Who knows? But she had secrets, lots of them too.'

'Don't tell me. She was having an affair.'

'Not just the one. Lots of little dalliances over the years, so I believe.'

'So does my sister. It hasn't left her dead in the river yet.'

'No, you're right.' Beattie shook his head. 'As far as Bright is concerned, it was all too neat. He met someone just before he died. They had words; so says the boss of this bar. He walks out and gets killed by a taxi travelling at almost ninety. Does that sound like coincidence to you?'

'No. You find the taxi?'

'Burnt out in Staines.'

'Nasty.'

'What, Staines or getting burnt out?'

'Both.'

'But really. How does that relate to Daley? Yeah, I get that he arrested him – maybe even sent his friends to give him a going-over in the cells. But is Bright really going to get killed for that?'

'I always thought the little shit was as bent as Yuri's spoons.'

'Forks – he bends forks.'

'Oh dear, I am sorry.'

'I've always thought that too, Eddie. But that doesn't mean to say he has anything to do with framing Daley.' She paused and stared at her superior. 'That's what we're talking about, isn't it?'

Beattie shrugged. 'What else? How better to get back at someone who's done you wrong than killing his wife and making sure he gets the blame?'

'And he'd have put away all sorts, this Daley, right?'

'You remember James Machie?'

'Do I ever. Ran a sword through one of our own. I cheered when I heard he was dead.'

'Guess who despatched him? Happened on a beach on the west coast of Scotland.'

'Daley? You are kidding me!'

'No, absolutely true. A few years ago, as you know.'

Unwin thought for a moment. 'He can't have any influence now, Eddie. You know what they say – when you're dead, you're dead. No criminal I know has that kind of loyalty.'

'Plenty of nutters about willing to worship at the shrine of some evil prick.'

'Possible, I suppose.'

'So, where have you stashed him away, Jill? This Chambers, I mean.'

'He's with a friend of a friend of a friend. I'll get you the address as quick as I can.'

'Today, yeah?'

'How about tomorrow morning? I've a few things to get on with first.'

'No later than tomorrow morning, OK?'

'I promise.'

Eddie Beattie took to his feet in one fluid motion. No sign of worn knees or a bad back. 'You got time for some late lunch then? My treat.'

Unwin looked at her watch. 'Sorry, Eddie. I'm in court in an hour. Next time, yeah?'

'I'll hold you to that. Once we get Daley out, how about that?'

'It's a deal.'

They said their goodbyes on the riverbank. Jill Unwin remained seated, while Eddie Beattie strode off in search of his car. She pondered what she'd just heard. The name James Machie brought fear to the heart of every good copper who'd crossed his path. If anyone was truly evil, it was him. She was quietly impressed that this Daley had taken his life. It was a sin to wish another dead, she knew that. But longing for the death of James Machie could be no such thing. It was like wishing for an end to poverty and hunger.

She reached into her pocket and pulled out her mobile phone.

'It's me again. I'm sorry to be a pain, but I really need another favour, if you can help?'

Overhead, a grey gull circled the spot where Liz Daley's body had been found, tangled in tree branches.

40

Hamish had spent so much time in Kinloch, he knew every inch of the place. He also recognized when things were wrong. He had this feeling as he walked towards the small estate where Ella and Brian Scott had their home.

In Kinloch not only did you *know* a person, a true local could also make a decent stab at the names, occupations and characters of their grandparents. Once Hamish's age was attained, his family history could well extend to great-grandparents and beyond. A proper Kinlochian would recognize the car before the driver – Hamish even knew the names and owners of the local dogs he regularly encountered on his walks.

For this reason, the man in the expensive saloon car, doing his level best to look inconspicuous at the top of the road that led to the Scotts' home, stood out like a sore thumb. He was pretending to read a broadsheet newspaper. The old man had seen this before in the many films he'd watched at the town's cinema. Nobody could read a paper and stare over the top of it at the same time. And what was the point when there was very little to look at?

Hamish remembered his dream: the dread of London,

the flash of red tartan in fetid water. Though he didn't know all of the details, he knew enough. Liz Daley was dead, and someone was to blame. If he could find who had done this terrible thing, he'd have strangled them with his bare hands. And though he had never been a man of violence, sometimes, he reasoned, it was justified. He was an Old Testament man, more in favour of an eye for an eye than turning the other cheek.

Hamish stopped a few yards from the vehicle. He turned into a tiny park, its gardens complete with tall trees and benches. He took a seat, making sure he could still see the unfamiliar car and its furtive driver. Hamish remembered the worried look on Ella's face, and took it for what it really was, well-disguised fear.

He removed his pipe and tobacco from the bib pocket of his dungarees and tamped down a full bowl. At times like this, a body needed the power of a good smoke to aid the thought process.

As puffs of blue smoke appeared in clouds above his head, the old man decided it was time for action rather than prevarication. He took his ancient mobile phone from the same pocket that contained his baccy.

'How are you doing, Duncan?' he said when the call connected.

'It's yourself, Hamish. Aye, I'm no' too bad. Just working away. What else is there to do at my age?'

Background noise was enough to inform Hamish that his old first mate was at the pier. He'd been listening to the throaty screams of gulls, the crash of fish boxes and the patter of fishermen all his life.

'Are you calling from that defunct mobile, Hamish?'

'Man, there's nothing defunct about it. I dial a number and invariably someone answers. Unless I'm calling the surgery, where you've fair got to go and beg to see a doctor these days. What else do you want from a damned phone? Aye, and remember, I'm no' looking for Tock-Tock nor thon book o' faces carry-on. If I want to talk to somebody, I damn well head for the pub they drink in and speak to them face to face.'

'My Stuart says when you call a taxi fae that phone, a horse and carriage turns up to take you home.'

'Your Stuart has been too smart for his own good since he was a toddler.' Hamish frowned at the hilarity on the other end of the call. He was fond of Duncan McLatchie, whom he'd taken on as ship's boy when Sandy Hoynes, his own mentor, handed him command of the *Girl Maggie* on retirement. Duncan had proven to be a bright lad, and soon became the fishing boat's fully fledged first mate. He'd married a bonnie lassie from Blaan, and they'd had five sons in short order, all of whom now toiled away at the fishing like their father before them. Duncan and his sons owned three boats, including the *Girl Maggie IV*, the sight of which regularly brought a tear to Hamish's eye as he watched it sail in and out of the loch.

They were fine men, one and all, but they – and their own sons – carried on Duncan's famous wit, sometimes of the harsh, mocking variety.

'I'll give him horse and carriage right enough,' said Hamish.

'Och, you know they all adore you – my grandsons too, come to that.'

'I do, and I'm most grateful.' Hamish lowered his voice. 'I have a favour to ask you, Duncan. Please say no if you're so inclined. I'll no' think the worse of you in any way.'

'Whatever it is, just ask. You know better than to think I'd no' help you, my old friend.'

'I know fine. Mind, you might need one or two of that army of boys you have.'

'Aye, and they'll be there wae bells on too, as you know.'

'Just like the old days, we make a fine team.' Hamish lowered his voice. 'Now, here's what I need you to do for me.'

Hamish's plan didn't take long from inception to practice. In half an hour he heard the distinctive chug of McLatchie's tractor, usually deployed at the pier for hauling the fruits of the sea, fish boxes and the like. He waved at Stuart McLatchie behind the wheel to the return of a loud *halloo* from the cab. Stuart proceeded to execute a complex turn of tractor and trailer in the middle of the road, much to the interest of the man behind the wheel of the BMW.

The driver cast aside his newspaper, as McLatchie manoeuvred his charge in front of the car, reversing until the trailer was almost bumper to bumper with the expensive saloon. Fearing that the driver was going to collide with his car, BMW man jumped out of the vehicle to confront Stuart McLatchie. He ran towards the tractor and knocked sharply on the window.

'What the bloody hell do you think you're doing, man?' His voice was strident and not of Kinloch.

McLatchie wound down the window of the tractor cab.

'Am I getting too close? Damn me! I've told my father we should have a reversing camera on the back of the trailer. Of course, he'll no' listen, being the tightest bastard this side of Tarbert. I'll pull her forward a bit.' Stuart McLatchie stared at the console before him. 'You'll excuse me, but this is a new vehicle. I'm no' just acquainted with her as I should be.'

'Be careful, man! If you damage my car, you'll regret it!'

'You're just flustering me! A man never does his best work under pressure, and that's a fact. Just give me peace a second while I get this tractor out of reverse.'

'What on earth is that reek?' The driver of the BMW screwed up his nose, groped in his pocket and found a hankie with which he covered his nose.

'Mainly fish heids, if that means anything to you, at all? That, and intestines. I'm booked in at the dump at two. I thought I'd park here until then and have my lunch.' McLatchie reached over to the dashboard. 'Here, would you like a sandwich? They're tuna and onion. My wife makes a lovely job o' them, so she does.' He watched his interlocutor's face turn green.

'Pull this stinking heap away from my car right now!'

'Fuck me, who died and made you boss o' the world?' McLatchie left his packet of sandwiches on the dashboard. Stroking his chin, deep in thought, he pushed a lever beside the gear stick, engendering the sound of an electric motor and the squealing of metal on metal.

'What on earth is happening?'

'I canna hear you! But don't worry. I'll find somewhere else to park!' McLatchie pushed the lever further forward. He looked mystified when the tractor stayed exactly where it was.

From his seat on the bench, Hamish couldn't conceal his mirth as the trailer angled into the air, its tailgate opened, and piles of rotting fish heads and entrails tumbled out on to the bonnet of the BMW.

'No! Stop this right now!' shouted the driver.

Stuart McLatchie cupped his ear. 'I canna hear you! You'll have to gie me a moment to work out why this bloody tractor isn't moving.'

Hamish tapped the used tobacco from his pipe, placed

it back into the bib of his dungarees and got up stiffly from the park bench. He passed the BMW, noting with great pleasure that the vehicle was half submerged in pelagic detritus, its driver still shouting at McLatchie.

'Aye, that'll do fine,' he muttered to himself as he took the road to see Ella Scott.

It only took him a few minutes to reach the police house. He chapped the door with one grizzled fist.

'Hamish, it's you,' said Ella. She looked flustered.

'Aye, me again. Just thought I'd pop in for a mug o' tae. And don't worry, I'm no' looking for a dram at this time o' day.'

Ella sighed. 'OK, you better come in.' She held the door open. Hamish went through the lounge, where James junior was busy at the TV watching a noisy cartoon. So engrossed was he, he didn't notice the new visitor. Ella led Hamish into the kitchen, where she turned on the radio. 'You canna stay, Hamish.'

'A fine welcome, I must say.'

'I'll explain later. Please take my word for it. Things aren't as they should be.'

'Anything to do with the man at the end of the road in the big car pretending to read the newspaper?'

'What?'

'Tall, well dressed, wae light brown hair and a posh accent. Has an earpiece in one ear into the bargain.'

'How do you know him, Hamish?'

'I thought as much. He's the man from the beach. I reckon he's fair keeping you under surveillance, Ella.'

Ella Scott gestured round the room and held one finger up to her lips.

'There's no need to worry. He's busy dealing with a wee accident at the moment.'

252

'What are you talking about, Hamish?'

'Man, I've lived in this toon long enough to know when a stranger's up to no good. But we have to be quick. We can get you out of here while he's distracted. Come on, we'll take your car down the Castle Road. That way, he'll no' see you.'

'I don't know how you do it, Hamish, but you're a lifesaver!' She kissed the old man on the cheek.

'I've been called much worse. Now, come on. We'll get down to mine. Nobody will find you there.'

41

Brian Scott was glad to be back in a normal police station. He hadn't enjoyed his sojourn at Bethnal Green. Especially when they'd found Jim Daley broken on the cell floor.

He was sitting at Jill Unwin's desk, waiting for her arrival. That she'd agreed to see him so readily was a surprise. But when he'd phoned, Unwin had asked him to come to her office as quickly as possible.

He looked out of the window, which perfectly framed the Thames, on its journey through the East End of London. Thoughts of Liz, Jim, Ella and young James tumbled over each other in his mind. He longed to be able to resolve his friend's issues, but he knew that the attack on him outside the hotel signalled malign intent. Scott wanted to tell Unwin what had happened, but he didn't know who to trust. He decided to gauge her as a person before saying anything. She was already late, and that only served to make him even more unsettled.

The door burst open, revealing a woman of middle age. She was slightly plump, with a grey, careworn expression. Scott recognized her for an overworked detective straight away.

'Good afternoon, Inspector Scott. Sorry to keep you

waiting. I've just been dealing with a domestic on a narrowboat.'

'No need tae apologize. If I'd a penny for every domestic dispute I've attended, I wouldn't be sitting here.'

'Let me guess, you'd be somewhere sunny, sipping on a negroni, yeah?'

'Aye, something like that.'

'I've got just over two years to go. I can't wait.'

Scott nodded, slightly envious, until he remembered he could have retired some time ago. Ella hadn't liked the idea of a little pub on one of the Costas. Now he was sober, he agreed with her.

'Right, down to business, Inspector Scott. Your friend is still in hospital, right?'

'Aye, they busted him up quite badly, the bastards.'

'If it's any consolation, I think justice may well have been done on that front.'

'DI Bright, you mean?'

'You know about that? Good.' Unwin looked a little surprised.

'One of the cops they put in the hospital told me. A wee bastard, right?'

'Not a pleasant man, our DI Bright. Not that I wished what happened to him.'

'No. But as an old boss o' mine used to say, once you sup wae the devil, don't expect to finish your dinner.'

Unwin studied Scott for a second. 'Eh?'

'Wait, that might no' be right. But it was something like that.'

'I see.' Unwin fetched a file from a drawer and began reading. 'How well do you know Commander Beattie, DI Scott?'

'Eddie? Known him since he was a boy. He's a bit younger than me. We grew up on the same street.'

'You grew up with some interesting people.'

'You could say that.'

'James Machie, for one.'

'You knew him?'

'I did. What police officer our age in the UK didn't know him? Evil bastard, if you ask me.'

'He was such a nice wee boy, tae.'

'He was?'

'No, he was a psycho. But you know what folk are like looking back. Where I lived, we produced doctors, junkies, gangsters, footballers, polis, professors, businessmen – you name it. That's the way the East End of Glasgow was in those days.'

'Sounds a bit like round here.'

'I daresay. What did you want to know about Beattie for?'

'I notice you never talked about politicians in your long list of careers.'

'Very few o' them came from oor bit, right enough. Folk I grew up with are too decent for that caper.'

'Well, Beattie's one.'

'What dae you mean?'

'Trust me. You don't get to where he is by just being a copper. You've got to shake hands and kiss babies to get to commander level down here.'

'Huh! Up the road, you've just got to be shite at your job. Eventually they'll promote you oot the way.'

Jill Unwin leaned back in her chair. 'Someone doesn't like your boss.'

'Jimmy? I'm glad you've noticed that.'

'And now things are starting to go wrong.'

'He didn't kill her, if that's what you mean.' Scott was emphatic.

'No, I'm beginning to agree with you.'

'Beginning?'

'But you have to be careful who you trust, yeah?'

'Eddie, you mean?'

'I know he's your friend. But he's just been promoted, he has to consolidate his new role. The next step could be one of the very top jobs. It's likely, in fact. If Daley gets in the way – well, that could be a problem.'

'Nah, Eddie's no' like that.' Scott shook his head.

'How long ago is it since you and him were kicking a ball down the streets of the East End of Glasgow? People change, DI Scott. And nothing changes them more than success.'

'I was at his wedding!'

'When was that?'

'I dunno – ten years ago?'

'Nineteen ninety-seven.'

'Really? Where does the time go? I'd never have thought it was that long ago.'

'Just be careful, that's all I'm saying.'

'He did rush off last night, mind you. Said something came up.'

'Yeah, found your pal beaten up on the floor, that's what came up, I bet.'

'And what about this Bright? An accident, surely?'

'I doubt it. He ran with a bad crowd, if you know what I mean.'

'On the take?'

'Probably.'

Scott held his head in his hands. 'This isnae good. If I canna trust Eddie, I'm snookered wae all this.'

'I have a witness.'

'You do?'

'Not to the murder itself. But the guy who dumped the body bears a remarkable similarity to your friend Daley. Big, broad, tall, dark-haired.'

'Right enough?' Scott's expression changed to one of resigned defeat. 'I canna say you're cheering me up any.'

'The good part is that our witness is convinced it isn't him. Says the man he saw was likely Eastern European. Judging by his features, at least.'

'Ya dancer!' Scott clapped his hands. 'That's the first ray of light we've had.'

'There are caveats.'

'He was wearing a tie? What's that got to do with it?'

'Caveats, as in qualifying conditions.'

'Right, and they are?'

'Our witness is a street person.'

'A jakey? Shit, that's not good.'

'Ex-army. You can still see that. When he's sober, at least.'

'Poor bastard. No respect for anyone in this country now. You're out on your ear and on the street, no matter what you've done for folk.'

'But his evidence is convincing. He's a sincere guy, despite his circumstances.'

'That's good then. What else are you worried about?'

'Now, he's a big problem for those who want to frame your friend. If indeed that's what's happening.'

'You don't believe any of this, do you?'

'I have to keep an open mind, DI Scott.'

'Brian, just call me Brian. It's the best it gets for me, usually.'

'And I'm Jill.' She shuffled some papers on her desk. 'Just now, I moved him from where we placed him originally.'

'What for?'

'A senior officer was showing an unhealthy interest in the bloke.' She nodded with a knowing smile.

'Who?' said Scott, his head too full of more pressing concerns to be bothered playing a game of cat and mouse with the woman on the other side of the desk.

'Your pal Eddie.'

'He's likely just interested because it's me and Jimmy.'

'Do you want to take the chance?'

Scott gazed out at the Thames for a few moments. Like the old river, the hustle never stopped. Always someone trying to get something over on someone else, regardless of whether it was crime, business, relationships, religion – everything. People were complicated. He'd realized that a long time ago. But he had something going in his favour. Scott always trusted his instincts, just like Jim Daley. He liked this straight-talking detective. 'So, what do I do about Eddie, then?'

'By all means, let him help where he can. But be careful. And don't let on about our witness and his where-abouts. Yes?'

Scott nodded. 'OK. We have a deal.'

'If we can cast doubt over the CCTV footage, there's a chance we can have him released. But that's another hurdle.'

'I've got someone on it.'

'You have, Brian?'

'Young whizz kid from up the road – a DC. What he doesnae know aboot computers isn't worth knowing. Boy's a star.'

'Good. We'll need as many stars as we can muster if we're to help your friend.'

Scott sat back in his chair. He'd take a little more light over darkness any time. And things did look brighter. Then he remembered Eddie Beattie.

42

'Where on earth did you get this?' said Ella, regarding the battered VW Golf with a jaundiced eye. It was – or had been – beige in colour, though now most of the bodywork was patched up and in various states of decay due to rust. There was moss growing along the perished rubber on the passenger window, and the whole vehicle exuded an overwhelming stink of fish.

'Aye, she's perfect for the job, right enough. Just blend into the background, so she will. You and James jump in quickly.'

'I feel sick, Auntie Ella,' said James when Hamish opened the door to the back seat. 'And there's a lobster on the floor.' The small boy's eyes were wide.

'Do they teach you nothing at school, these days?' said Hamish. 'That's no lobster, it's a deid prawn. It'll no' dae you any harm.'

'Yes, get in the back, son. Just ignore it,' said Ella, as she hefted the last of their bags into the boot, beside an old creel and some oilskins. She walked round to the passenger seat and pulled at the door.

'Hang on! What are you at?'

'I'm getting in, what does it look like?'

'No, no. You don't have the right of it at all. You'll

have to drive. My friend left it here for our use. I cannae drive.'

'Why not?'

'Och, I'd a wee smash a while ago. They took my licence off me and never gave it back.'

'How long ago?'

Hamish stroked his chin. 'It was auld Sheriff MacNeil. Man, he's been deid for a good few years now. Let me think.'

'Hamish, we're meant to be making a speedy getaway, have you forgotten?'

'Well, what are you waiting for? Jump in and fire her up!'

Ella shook her head, ran round to the driver's side and jumped in behind the wheel. All this while James Daley junior was making exaggerated boaking noises on the back seat.

'Now, that's us ready to go. Hit the gas, Ella!' said Hamish.

'*Hit the gas?* We're in an ancient, knackered Volkswagen, no' a Formula One car.'

'It's what the Americans say before they set off any-where. I saw it on the television in the Douglas Arms once.'

'Aye, in nineteen seventy-two.'

'That's it! That's when I lost my licence – nineteen seventy-two. Well, I say *lost*. I never really had one in the first place. It's a long story.'

'Save it for the journey, Hamish.' Ella turned a key with a broken fob that was in the ignition. Nothing happened. She tried again. With a judder, a pop and an indistinct whine, the VW came alive. The diesel engine was ridicu-lously loud.

'Fine engineers, the Germans,' Hamish shouted above the din.

'I'm sure,' Ella replied. 'They'd burst into tears if they

could see the fruits of their labours now!' She managed to get the car into first gear. It pulled away slowly, the whine getting louder.

'It's no' as though we're going far,' said Hamish.

'I'm going to be sick, Auntie Ella,' shouted James from the back seat.

Ella turned out of the car park and was soon on her way, turning left on to the hill that led down to the town's main street. Though they were passing the usual shops, the County Hotel, familiar faces, many now friends, Ella felt a sense of unreality. Here she was, running away from her own home, with the son of the woman she'd known for so many years now lying dead on a London mortuary slab. At least she'd be able to speak to Brian properly on another phone, without the scrutiny of the man who'd broken into her house the previous evening.

'It was young Angela Mitchell,' Hamish announced, apropos of nothing at all.

'Eh?'

'I was working on the *Girl Maggie* – a lick of paint, if I remember right.'

'Oh, is this the long-awaited story of you losing your licence?'

'Just that, aye.' Hamish went for his pipe until Ella's scowl made him think again.

'You're no' polluting that boy's lungs wae that. The car is bad enough.'

'I like the smell of Hameby's pipe!' protested James.

'Away and play with your lobster,' said Ella with a smile.

'She worked in the fishery office doon on the quay. Right pregnant she was, wee Angela. A belly like a whale, and no mistake.'

Ella raised her eyes to the heavens.

'Her man was away oot on a boat, and the quay was just aboot deserted. They'd spied a fine shoal just off the Cock o' Arran, and the fleet hurried out en masse to take advantage.'

'But not the *Girl Maggie*?'

'We were waiting on a part. Sandy had been right tardy ordering the bloody thing. Mind you, he was like that.'

'Right, just carry on with it. We'll be at your house in a few minutes.'

'She comes running up tae me shouting aboot broken waters or something. In any event, it didna sound too bonnie, and it was clear the hospital beckoned. I spotted Willie Henderson's auld van. He'd bought it second hand from the Post Office and tried to paint it white, the same colour as the wheelhouse on his boat. It turned oot pink, which was a shame but what can you do, eh? Anyhow, he'd left the keys. It was way back then, you know.'

'No' much different nowadays, Hamish,' said Ella.

'I daresay.' Hamish nodded. 'I was no driver, as you can imagine. But I'd driven the forklift in the fish sheds a few times.'

'You hadn't passed a test, then?'

'I hadn't sat one to pass. But there comes a time in a man's life when he has to step forward and do what's best. I ushered Angela into the front seat and dashed behind the wheel. A bit like you, just there, Ella.'

'It would be in better nick than this heap, I'm sure.'

'Och, I canna remember. Anyhow, we set off for the cottage hospital, poor wee Angie fair roaring in pain by this time.'

'Did you make it?'

'Oh aye, we made it. But we had a few bumps on the way, right enough. I think I hit Sergeant McConnachie's car first, then I knocked Mrs Hughes the dentist's wife off her bike. She was a hardy soul, mind you. And I saw her get back to her feet in the mirror, none the worse.'

'Are you being serious?'

'You'll understand my steering wasna just so, what wae Angela bawling beside me, and me none too sure o' how to drive in the first place. It was damnably difficult.'

'No wonder you lost your licence.'

'That wasn't the end of it, neither. In those days, the cottage hospital had a long, winding driveway up from the road.'

'Oh no!'

'I got halfway up, and I couldna get the thing to turn the last bend. Sadly, auld Morris Leckie had had a heart attack just a while before, and when the ambulance appeared at my back, well, there was nothing to be done. They couldn't get past, and I was stuck fast. In the end, they'd to cart Morris up through the shrubbery on a stretcher, Angela too. It turned out that he'd just got indigestion – he was a greedy bugger anyway. Ate more fish suppers than any man has the right to. Angela's wee boy appeared less than half an hour later, and he was just grand.' Hamish smiled beatifically at the end of his tale.

Ella sat open-mouthed. 'Did you get the jail?'

'No, the authorities were sensible back then. The sheriff made me promise never to do it again or apply for a full driving licence. And that was that.'

Ella slowed down at the very thought of it all.

'Nearly there,' said Hamish, as they drove along the side of the loch. 'You can pull into the wee drive thonder, Ella.'

'You're sure they'll not find us here?'

'You're as safe as can be. Wae the hoose tucked behind these bushes, hardly anybody knows it's here.'

And looking at Hamish's home as she drove into the

gravel drive, she supposed he was right. Only a couple of windows showed to the front of the property, so Hamish could gaze out at the loch from his lounge and bedroom. And to be honest, the place was so run-down, it looked derelict.

She parked the car and they made their way inside.

Young James looked about wide-eyed when he walked into the living room.

'Why have you got someone's head on the table, Hameby?' he said without guile, staring at the plaster bust of Winston Churchill.

'He was a fine, fine man, James. And anyway, it's no' his real heid.'

Ella too looked about agog. 'It's a unique style, Hamish. I'll give you that.'

'It suits me. I canna be fussed wae these fancy homes. Everything looks white, soulless. That niece o' mine's hoose at Firdale is like walking into a laboratory. A home should reflect the owner's personality, their wee foibles and suchlike.'

'Are these your wee foibles?' said James, holding a large pair of string underpants that may once have been green but were now distinctly grey.

'Put those down at once!' shouted Ella. 'Hamish has been very kind to let us stay here for a while. I want you to thank him.'

'OK. Where's the TV, Hameby?'

'I don't have such a thing. I tried one once, but damn me, every time I switched the thing on, it was the same programme.'

'What was that?' Ella asked.

'*Coronation Street*. I couldna stand thon Sharples woman. She reminded me of my great-aunt Morag. My, she was up there with Joe Stalin when it came tae despotism. No doubt he'd have shrunk away back to Georgia if she'd chosen Moscow as home.'

'That bad?'

'Worse. Anyhow, I took the television straight back to Grant's, the shop I rented it from. I missed the moon landing, but och, I was never sure they went there at all.'

'You've no' had a TV since the sixties?' Ella found this more incredible than the state of the house.

'No, and I'm missing nothing. I catch a glimpse o' it now and again in the County and other places. Seems to me there's nothing on but football and tired old crime dramas. Who needs another one of them?'

'It's true, right enough. We've enough crime drama to last us a lifetime, as it is. You can watch your stuff on my phone, James. It'll be fine for a wee while.' But as she looked round and spotted the table clearly made from fish boxes, and a huge spider emerging from an even larger web up in the corner of the room, Ella had her doubts. She hoped beyond hope Brian would get home as quickly as he could.

43

George Chambers reflected on his luck, and how doing a good turn was not the albatross round the neck some maintained. He'd been moved from the hostel to a little hotel in the Kent countryside. Though Chambers had no idea why, he was more than happy with his new accommodation. His room was small and neatly arranged, with a view of a kiln-shaped oast house across a village cricket pitch, surrounded by trees. Here, the world was soft, easy on the eye. So unlike the streets of London's East End.

He eyed himself in the dressing-table mirror. Though the ravages of drugs, alcohol and homelessness were with him for ever, the benefits of a good lunch, comfortable bed and freedom from constant fear were already beginning to show. There was renewed colour to his cheeks and his forehead was less lined, his eyes noticeably brighter. Ultimately, for the first time in a really long while, he felt at peace. Able to enjoy the world.

Chambers made himself another cup of tea and indulged in a biscuit. Even this seemed like luxury. He knew others would take these simple acts for granted. He didn't.

Stretched out on the bed, Chambers vowed to change his life. He knew there were places that could help those in his predicament. He might never end up in the leafy surroundings he was currently enjoying, but he would be happy if he had as little as a bed and a roof over his head, and the security of a locked door behind which he could hide away from a cruel world.

He remembered the face that had brought him here. Heavy brows above almost feline eyes, sharp and unforgiving. The purposeful walk to the river with the body of a murdered woman. How do such people live with themselves, he wondered. He hoped the inspector could bring the monster to justice. The very memory made him restless. Maybe because he was used to spending time out in the open, he began to feel trapped, the prospect of facing the man across a courtroom somehow overwhelming.

Chambers was pleased he could leave his room, go for a walk and return. This was again a novelty. He took to his feet, slipped on the summer jacket the police had given him and opened the door. Before leaving he turned, taking in the pleasant, airy room. He smiled at its perfection.

As he stepped out of the hotel, Chambers said a cheery hello to the man attending to the flower beds, taking his advice on a route through the woods, round the cricket pitch and out on to some even better vistas. He thanked the gardener and, following his directions, made for a gap in the trees.

The world here smelled of cut grass and honeysuckle; the sun beat down on the back of his neck before he walked under the canopy of the little thicket of oak and shrubs. Chambers breathed deeply. There was a slight chill in the air now, a more earthy aroma. He heard a crack from behind, swung round and looked on as a rabbit raced out of the woods, its bobbing tail flashing in the diffused light.

He walked on, spotting some flowers he recognized but could not name, and a large species of fungus clinging to a tree trunk, resembling a horse's hoof. A small flock of birds scattered with a chorus of calls and flapping wings, as he picked his way along a narrow path, likely worn by generations of people.

He took a step, but instead of moving forward, Chambers felt himself being dragged backwards through a chaos of tree branches, sunlight flitting on to his face from gaps in the canopy above. He'd been so relaxed the paralysing sensation of fear took longer than usual to set in. Chambers felt a powerful arm tighten round his throat, as he was pushed to his knees. He could hear his captor grunt with the effort, feel his breath on the back of his head through his thinning hair. He closed his eyes as something bright and shiny flashed across his vision.

Then, there was a feeling of fleeting pressure on his throat. In a split second, he could no longer breathe. His body felt too heavy to kneel upright. George Chambers fell face down into the rush of rough grass, his last memory.

44

Brian Scott was back in his hotel room, feeling more optimistic following his meeting with Inspector Unwin. However, the thought that he could no longer trust his old friend Eddie Beattie was a burdensome one.

He'd been developing an idea, something that would require help from his superiors in Scotland. But as he was here unofficially, with no investigative remit, it was hard to know just how to play it. He'd always considered the Metropolitan Police to be a nest of vipers: some officers on the take, others blinded by ambition, willing to compromise their morals for advancement, success at any price.

Then he thought of Unwin, in many ways his opposite number in all this. A hard-working cog in the wheel; no frills, no flashes of insight, just the tough grind of investigation, using the old rules as a guide. Scott knew that people thought him a stranger to the rule book. He used intuition and resourcefulness to be effective. It was a matter of choice, really.

On a notepad, Scott had formulated a plan of attack. He'd put together a case for slamming the brakes on the investigation of Daley. After all, when Scott had first approached the problem, even he was beginning to be convinced of his friend's guilt. He had never given this notion voice. It just hung there in his mind like the proverbial elephant in the room.

For no reason, he began to ponder the differences between the ears of African and Indian elephants, quickly deciding his mind was wandering, and that he must try to stay focused.

Armed with aspects of his chat with Unwin, doubts over the digital evidence – even the presence of a Daley doppelganger dumping Liz's body – he could put together a document sound enough to move those connected with the case at the highest levels to intervene. Otherwise, he feared, the notion of Daley's guilt was being taken as read. No longer did the public expect to encounter a genial, well-doing bobby, who'd be there to help keep them safe.

His phone rang. It was the call he was expecting: DC Duff from Kinloch with news about the incriminating footage of Daley.

'Right, son. Where are we at?'

'You got a laptop handy, gaffer?'

Scott eyed the laptop lying on the nightstand beside his bed. 'Aye, what about it?'

'I need you to fire it up. I've sent you something. You'll need to open it up in that app we installed a couple of weeks ago, remember?'

'No, not at all. What *app*?'

'The one where you can access encrypted video, sir.'

'Aye, aye, got you now, son.' Scott lifted the laptop on to his knee, desperately hoping that the little icon thing would jolt his memory into recognition.

'You need to go to email first.'

'Fuck me, make up your mind, son. It's either this map affair or it's the emails. One thing at a time!'

'App!'

'Eh?'

'You said *map*, sir.'

'Oh, come on! App, map, what's the difference?' Silence was deafening on the other side of the call. Scott clicked rather uncertainly on to his emails and, to his great relief, spotted a new one from Duff at the top. 'Aye, got it.'

'OK, open it up, then click on the link I've put in.'

Scott was peering through the reading glasses now balanced on his nose. 'I don't know how folk can be bothered with this bollocks,' he muttered to himself. 'Right, what now? I've clicked on the link.'

'Has it taken you to the new app?'

'How should I know? You're the expert, son. Oh, and while I'm on, what's happening with Ella, and why aren't you there?'

'There's a uniform on it. It's quiet here today, and your deputy is off back to Mid Argyll for a break. The only thing that's happened out of the ordinary was some twat getting a load of fish guts spilled on to the bonnet of his fancy Beamer. Oh aye, and that old boy is visiting again.'

'What old boy?'

'The one with the pipe and the dungarees.'

'Hamish, aye right. Good stuff.'

'You could have competition there, gaffer.'

'Eh, what are you talking aboot?'

'Some women like older men – just saying.'

'Can you take reminder notes on this thing?'

'Yes, of course. Just go into the calendar and set a date and reminder.'

'Good, that means I'll no' forget to boot you right up the arse when I get back. What do I do now?'

'Press *play* on the screen. The arrowhead icon.'

'Fuck me, *arrow icons, apps*. The world's gone mad.' Scott

pressed what he considered to be the arrowhead icon on the black screen. Almost instantly, it started, revealing the gloom of the alleyway and the figure of Daley rummaging in a skip. 'No way. I'm no' going through this again. I've seen too much of it already, son. Makes me feel sick.'

'It's after, you know, what happens to Mrs Daley. Just keep watching. I want to hear your reaction.'

Scott sighed and kept his eyes on the screen. The very sight of the video was enough to jangle his nerves. His stomach churned, and the face of Liz Daley crossed his mind's eye.

'What's he doing now?' said Duff.

'Just pulling that builders' film from the skip. Just like he's done every fucking time I've watched this bloody awful thing!'

'Good, you're nearly there.'

Scott took a deep breath as he watched his old pal remove what he wanted from the skip. He knew the video off by heart, so he was ready for the point where Daley stepped forward and angled his head towards the CCTV camera. But something was different. 'What the actual fuck is that?'

'Can you see it?'

'Aye, I can see it.' As Scott said the words, the screen paused. Though, this time, the man looking at the camera wasn't Jim Daley, it was himself. Scott rubbed his eyes and gazed at the frozen image, just as he had when he'd first set eyes on the disgusting footage. There, plain as day, was his face, staring defiantly at the camera. Scott recognized his worn features, the arch of his eyebrows that so reminded him of his late father. There was no doubt, it was him.

'What do you think, sir?'

Scott's first response was anger. 'So, this is what you do wae your time! I've lost a good friend and my best pal is facing a murder charge, and you're fucking about wae computers. You wait until I get back. You'll be back on the beat in some really shitty place before you know it, son!'

'You're missing the point, sir.'

'I'll no' miss your jaw wae a right hook!'

'Listen, if I can do that with the software available to me, anyone can do it. You've found a witness to say another man dumped the body and he was DCI Daley's size and shape. It's so easy to replace the features now. Especially when there is a close physical resemblance. I just used an AI program today to get this. Took me a couple of hours.'

The penny dropped. Scott punched one fist in the air. 'I knew it couldnae be Jimmy – that some bugger had changed what we thought we were seeing. I never reckoned it was so easy to do.' For Brian Scott, the world was changing at a terrifyingly rapid pace.

45

Liz smiled as she walked towards him across the sand. She was wearing a red bikini, her tanned skin making the colour pop. She lay beside him on the rug, the sun warming their bodies, as they embraced under the blue sky.

'Do you still love me?' she said, looking up at him with her cornflower-blue eyes.

'Why do you ask me that over and over again? You must know the answer.'

'It's a yes, then?'

'Of course it's a yes!'

'So, why have things ended up the way they have?'

'I don't know what you mean, Liz.' He shook his head in bewilderment.

'You do. You know what you did.'

He looked up, just as the blue sky was obscured by a dark, lowering cloud. Suddenly, he could feel the wind tear at his naked torso. It was as though, in an instant, he had been transported from a beautifully warm beach to the Arctic. He shivered, holding himself against the cold.

'You did this. You're to blame.'

He looked at Liz. The red bikini was faded now, hanging off her wasted body. Her skin was grey, turning black on her cheeks, above which her eyes bulged. There were livid gashes all over her skin; a flap of her forehead had been torn and hung over her right brow.

'You killed me, and you've left our son an orphan!'

'How can he be an orphan?' Jim Daley asked. 'I'm still here for him.'

'Not for much longer!' She spat out the words. 'Look!' She pointed one bony finger at his midriff.

He looked down just as the tail of a rat disappeared through a bloody hole into his stomach. He felt it wriggle inside him. Jim Daley screamed at the top of his voice.

'It's OK, you're having a nightmare.'

Daley could feel a hand on one shoulder, though he was only half awake. His scream still echoed inside his head like a distant memory. 'It's Liz, she's alive!' he muttered.

'Don't worry, just lie back.' The nurse was mopping his brow with a warm flannel. 'It's a dream, nothing more.'

Daley began to wake properly. He smiled at the nurse, though her words, to him at least, were empty. There was no way out of this nightmare, he feared. And it was so very real. Not the bad dream of his sleeping state but the horror of reality that tortured him every waking moment. He caught the nurse's arm. 'I didn't kill her, I promise.'

'Listen, try not to worry,' she said, neatly avoiding the subject.

'Thank you,' he said, his breathing beginning to get back to normal.

'You can't control what you do, can you? With that scalpel, I mean.'

'What!?' Daley was bewildered.

She stood, revealing a livid red stain that was spreading across her white uniform, turning it crimson. 'You've killed me too,' said the nurse, her voice flat, without emotion.

Daley looked at a blood-stained scalpel in his hand.

Despite the pain from his injuries, Jim Daley pushed himself upright in the bed, tearing some of the monitors from his skin and setting alarms pinging.

'Nurse!' The constable rushed from Daley's room. 'You better come quickly, it's Mr Daley!'

The nurse dashed down the corridor, a man in a suit following in her wake.

'Wait here, please, sir.'

As directed, the man stopped in his tracks and watched the nurse as she entered the private room. As he listened, the screaming coming from inside abated. He could hear the nurse's soft voice as she spoke to her patient.

He sat on a chair and waited, the constable gazing at him.

'You lost your tongue, lad?'

'Excuse me, sir. Who are you, and what are you doing here?'

Wearily, he pulled a small leather case from inside his jacket, opening it to reveal his ID. 'If you want to go and have a break, you can. As long as you bring me back a flat white, no sugar, OK?'

The constable gulped. 'Yes, sir. I'm sorry . . .'

'Don't be sorry. It's not your fault. How long have you been in the job for, son?'

'Fourteen months, sir.' The young lad stood to attention, as though he was on parade.

'Relax! I'll no' tell anyone, if you don't. Get yourself a cup of coffee in that wee canteen. Calm down!'

'Yes, sir. Just going.'

For Beattie, it was like a cuckoo clock. As he watched the police constable head back down the corridor, the nurse appeared from Daley's room.

'Is he OK?'

277

'I've calmed him down. He keeps having these really bad nightmares. It's partly to do with the painkillers. But that can't be the only reason. We have to be careful with him, he has heart problems, you know.'

'He does? Did you discover them recently?'

'No, he was diagnosed a couple of years ago.' She shook her head. 'Listen to me, discussing a patient. You can go through for a while. I know you're a friend but please go easy.'

'Aye, we've met a few times. Friend of a friend would be more apt.'

'Good, might help him calm down. He's really worked up.'

'He has every reason to be.'

Eddie Beattie smiled at her then entered Daley's room. The big man was wired to a number of machines but was no longer being fed by any drips. He was deathly pale. 'Remember me, Jimmy?'

'Of course, Eddie.' Daley moved awkwardly in the bed, his body aching.

'Bad dreams, eh?'

'Yes. I can't shake the bloody things.'

'No wonder. I'd be the exact same. Where's Robin?'

'Who?'

'As in Batman and Robin.'

'Brian, you mean. He's away, trying to make sense of all this.'

'He's a sound bloke, is Brian. Always was, even back in Glasgow when we were kids. He knew right from wrong, basically.'

'Basically,' said Daley with the shadow of a smile.

Beattie grabbed a chair by the bed and sat himself down on it. He brushed some lint from his trousers and regarded

Daley. 'You'll have worked out by now that somebody wishes you harm.'

'Not as much harm as they wished Liz.'

'I'm sorry, I really am. You have my sincere condolences.'

'She was mixed up with some guy, you know.'

'Brian showed me.'

'Showed you?'

'Lot for you to take in, once we get this mess sorted, Jimmy. Things you won't like. But I don't think they were after Liz. They were coming for you. She – and please forgive me for saying this – was just a means to an end.'

'What have I done to warrant all this?'

'You've taken down some heavy hitters in your time. Put a couple of bullets in James Machie, for a start. Aye, and you brought a few rotten apples to book into the bargain. Real shite.'

'Bent cops. Nothing worse.'

'And the irony is everyone thinks *you're* a wrong 'un now, Jimmy.'

'They're wrong!' Daley was emphatic.

'Listen, I'm going to say something to you now. I want you to take it in, process it, right?'

'What now?' Daley sounded instantly defeated.

'They found a witness to the disposal of your wife's body.'

'Shit.'

'Of course it is, Jimmy. But like everything, it had a silver lining.'

'Had?'

'They hid him away. You know, a safe house where nobody could get to him. The guy was basically a home-less drunk. But he was sharp enough – ex-army.'

'You keep using the past tense.'

'Found him earlier. Turns out that the safe house wasn't safe enough. Some bastard cut his throat.'

'Fuck.' Daley stared at the ceiling. 'I can't believe this.'

'I don't blame you.' Beattie bit his lip. 'I have a proposal.'

'Which is?'

'First, how do you feel? Do you think you can walk, for instance?'

'I'm sore. But they let me walk to the toilet for the first time yesterday. It'll get easier.'

'Nasty, eh?'

'I'm not up to sprinting. Put it like that.'

'We need to break you out of here, Jimmy.'

'Ha! You've been talking to Brian too much.'

'I'm not kidding. The way it looks, this goes high up, even here in the Met.'

'Are you serious?'

'I am. And we need to be quick about it too.'

'What does Brian say?' Daley was suddenly bewildered.

'Brian doesn't know. And that's the way it should stay. The truth is, him, you – yours – everyone is in danger.'

'Not James!'

'Your boy?'

'Yes. Please tell me he's safe.'

'He is – for now. But we need to spring you. I don't know any other way.'

'But what about your job? They'll crucify you.'

'No' if I crucify them first, don't worry. We go for it, tonight.' Beattie stared at Daley. 'You have to trust me, Jimmy, or you'll no' live to see the inside of a court. Do you understand?'

Jim Daley nodded slowly. Tears appeared in his eyes. 'If

I'd known this was the price I'd pay for this job, I'd have resigned years ago.'

'The price has been high for you. Don't let it become any higher. We have to discuss the plan before that young copper gets back. And promise me, you don't tell Brian – don't tell him anything.'

Jim Daley nodded slowly by way of a reply.

46

Jill Unwin was sitting in a pub in the East End, but there was no sign of men in flat caps singing round a piano these days. The male of the species here was tall, slim – dressed up in clothes worn by their grandfathers. Long but well-manicured beards, little waistcoats, tattoos, expensive brogue boots.

Unwin considered how bizarre this all was. In a way, they aped the dress of the working class in the early twentieth century. But these men were well-groomed, preening echoes of what had once been. Hipsters that weren't hip, she reasoned.

The women were fresh-faced, a minimum of makeup on their clear complexions. Their dresses were beautifully patterned, pricey. Some wore jeans with turn-ups like the ones she'd worn in the eighties. Though these were the best selvedge denim, Japanese.

In her mind, Jill Unwin played her life back briefly. A middling student at a less than middling school; average result at the police college. All to the shock of her family and friends, who never expected to see one of their own in such a place. She earned more than most of her peers who plied their trade behind bars, in factories, call centres, in the gig economy, but she wanted more from life than them.

Finished with this introspection, Unwin went back to scrolling down the Spanish property page on her phone. She'd found a little villa in the very north of the country. Great weather but not too hot. Fecund; green trees, and greener grass. For her, this was a slice of heaven, a billion miles away from the grey river under greyer skies.

Unwin heard the little bell tinkle as the pub door opened. DI Brian Scott was scanning the room. She waved to get his attention. Scott, she thought, looked strangely out of place in his cheap suit, open-neck shirt and loosened tie and dirty shoes, in amongst these beautiful people.

'Fuck me, why's everyone so tall roon here, eh? It's like the land o' the giants,' he said, taking a seat opposite Unwin.

She shrugged. 'Rich mummies and daddies, Brian. Going back a long way, too. No poverty to sully their genes, mate.'

'And they're all wearing them, too.'

Unwin smiled to herself. There was something attractive about this man. No hint of guile, a kind of rough readiness that she couldn't explain. But there was also sadness in those blue eyes. Tough background, she reckoned. As she was well aware, that stayed with you.

'I've got some good news,' said Scott. 'A wee bit o' hope, anyway.'

'Good! What is it?'

'My tech guy up the road reckons that the CCTV footage is fake. Hey, coupled with your witness, we're quids-in.'

Unwin smiled weakly. 'I'll have a gin, since you didn't ask.'

'Oh aye, sorry. My heid's full o' helping Jimmy.' Scott

made his way to the bar. He came back quickly, winding his way through the forest of tall hipsters, a flamboyant gin for Unwin in one hand, a pint of Coke with a slice of orange for himself in the other.

'You're not a drinker. Unusual for a Scotsman, isn't it?'

'Jimmy would call that a racial stereotype.'

'He'd be right.'

'Hey, I've done my bit for the survival o' the whisky industry over the years. As my wife would tell you, I did it just aboot single-handed.'

'You've sunk a few, then?'

'About as many as Nelson. Aye, and near sunk myself into the bargain.'

'I've got some bad news for you on the witness front, I'm sad to say.'

'Cold feet?'

'Cold everything. He had his throat cut earlier today.'

Scott looked at her in disbelief. 'You had him somewhere safe, you said.'

'Clearly not. We still have his statement. But as you know, that doesn't go far without the witness. And him being a drunk, homeless man with PTSD doesn't help.'

Scott cursed. 'But we've still got the footage. My man is confident he can take it back to the original.'

'Really?' Unwin looked surprised.

'Something to do with pixie memory. Don't ask me.'

'Could it be *pixel* memory?'

'Aye, that's the boy! On yerself, Jill. But losing the witness is a blow, right? Poor guy. I'm not going to tell the big man anything about this.'

Unwin bit her lip. 'I've a message for you.'

'Fae where?'

Unwin pointed to the ceiling with one finger. 'The higher-ups, Brian.'

'Braid, you mean?'

'That's the one.'

'I didn't think they'd know I existed.'

'You've got an important pal. Everybody wants to know what he's up to, trust me.'

'Eddie? I can't believe it. Me and him have been pals since we were boys.'

'Tell me, does he know about your wife – you know, with Daley's son?'

A cold hand gripped Scott's heart. 'Aye, he does. Well, most of it.'

'OK. Just wondered.' She looked about, as though searching for the words.

'What dae you mean?'

'Honestly? I'm not sure how safe they are. Not after what happened today. I mean, you know the score, right? The bosses are worried, too.'

'A wee boy? What the fuck can he do, apart fae miss his mammy?'

'It's another way to get to Daley.'

Scott considered this and nodded his head in agreement. 'You're saying after Liz, and your witness, anything could happen, right?'

'I dunno, Brian. What do you think? Better to be safe than sorry, I reckon.'

Just as he was about to reply, Brian Scott's phone pinged with a text alert in his pocket. 'You don't mind if I read this?'

'Sure, go ahead.' Unwin sipped at her gin.

Scott noticed the message was from Duff. He opened it.

Remember I told you about the guy who got the bonnet of his car covered in fish guts? The plate has bounced back registered but unavailable. I guess you know what that means.

'Everything OK?' Unwin asked.

'No' sure, to be honest.' Scott thought for a few moments. 'Do you know anything about spooks?'

'As in?'

'Having anything to do with this thing wae Jimmy. Eddie mentioned it, that's all.'

'I think we have to be really careful with what's happening up there. Would it help if I could send some of our Special Branch? You know, just to make sure all is as you want it?'

'You think that's necessary?' Scott looked shocked.

'Listen. We have no idea who is trying to do this or why. As for the Security Service, you *never* know what they're up to. Haven't you read le Carré?'

'Nah. Can't speak French, doll.'

'No! As in John le Carré. The thriller writer.'

'Has his stuff been on the telly?'

'Yeah, just a bit!'

'Why do you ask?'

'They move in mysterious ways, that's all.'

'Not taking folk out, surely?'

Unwin shrugged.

'Fuck! I don't know what to do.' Scott ran his hand over his short salt-and-pepper hair in desperation.

'Let me know where they are and I'll engineer something with SB.'

'I should tell my boss up the road. Your lads have to go all the way up to Scotland.'

'Do you trust him? Your boss, I mean.'

Brian Scott thought back on his long association with senior police officers. 'No, no' really.'

'OK. Leave it with me, then. And don't worry. You don't think our lads are only parked up in London, do you? They can get there quite quickly.'

'Doon that road? Tell them tae bring a helicopter.'

'Don't worry. I'm sure we'll be in time.'

'You're scaring me!' Scott looked worried.

'I'm sorry. The last thing I want to do is worry you, Brian. I'll be happier when we know our lads are on it. It's a precaution, nothing else. But at times like this, it's for the best.'

Scott reasoned it all out in his mind. He liked Unwin, trusted her. Saw himself in her manner and dedication – maybe also in her lack of respect for her bosses.

'She's already had problems. Ella, I mean.'

'What kind of problems?'

Scott told Unwin about the man on the beach, who turned up in Ella's bedroom with threats and menaces.

'Shit! How was she able to tell you this?'

'They did a runner. She's with a friend of mine. At his place, you know.'

'OK, tell me exactly where it is.' Jill Unwin pulled her mobile phone from her handbag. 'You should have told me before.'

'They'll be safe as houses with him. I'm sure o' it.' Despite his protestations, Scott was beginning to lose faith in his own reasoning.

'I wish I could tell you that was true. Honestly, I do.' With that, her call was answered. With no little urgency, Unwin walked out of the pub to organize protection for Ella and young James.

Scott was left staring at his Coke and withered slice of

orange, wishing it was a large dram. 'Fuck,' he swore under his breath. Jim Daley had already lost his wife. Brian Scott didn't want the same thing happening to his wife, or the boy. He stared at the ceiling. There was a key to all this, and he had to find it.

47

In Kinloch, the shadows of the long day were lengthening across the loch, as the sun began to set. Hamish stood in his small patch of garden, puffing at his pipe. He'd decided not to smoke in front of the child. Well, in all honesty, Ella had argued, reasonably forcibly, that it was a bad idea.

Hamish gazed at the island, as it slowly turned into a dark silhouette before his very eyes. Soon, the short summer night would descend upon the town. He hoped that Ella would be able to settle young James, who up until now had made it his mission to wander round Hamish's home, lip curled in disgust, asking about the various peculiarities of the place. But though the old man wasn't accustomed to children, he was still fond of them. His heart broke for the lad, still unaware he'd lost his mother.

'Fretting gets you nowhere,' said Hamish to himself, as he tapped out the used tobacco from the pipe against his heel. He took one long draw at the night air, before spotting Hamish the cat disappearing through the shrubbery up the hill behind the house, where he'd undoubtedly spend the rest of the night on his nocturnal meanderings.

Hamish stepped back inside. He could hear Ella reading James a story, still in the process of getting him off to sleep.

They were sharing Hamish's bed, while he was happy to sleep in the rocking chair in front of the fire, as he'd done on many a late night. He took a seat there, and poured himself a modest dram from the bottle he kept on the table beside him.

After a few minutes, Ella appeared in the room. The flickering storm lanterns atop the mantelpiece were just about holding sway against the fading light.

'Did you get him over, Ella?' said Hamish.

Ella hushed him, one finger to her lips. 'Quieten doon, Hamish. He wakes up with the grass growing, that one,' she whispered.

'Just like his father, I'll bet.'

'No doubt. Though, I wonder just how well he'll be sleeping now.'

'Aye, the soul. Here, would you like a dram?'

'I'll have one. And no' a great bumper, neither. I'm bloody tired after all the excitement.'

'I daresay,' said Hamish, pouring Ella what he considered a splash in a glass and handing it to her.

'That's near half a bottle!' she said, taking a sip.

'Och, isn't that just typical of a woman, eh? Fair exaggerating everything oot o' all proportion. Just get it doon your neck. You'll feel the better o' it directly. Man, where'd we be without the water o' life?'

'My Brian would be much better off.'

'Have you heard from him?'

'Just a quick call. He says he's hopeful but can't say too much. Told us to take care, Hamish.'

'Och, the man that had his eyes on you is keener on cleaning up his expensive car to worry aboot us. We're safe as hooses here.'

'Aye, likely we are,' said Ella, the warmth of the dram already calming her jangled soul.

The pair passed a convivial hour, talking about their lives and myriad other subjects. Anything to keep their minds from the horror of what was happening.

Soon, Ella felt the tiredness wash over her like a wave. 'Well, that's me,' she announced. 'Wake me around seven, if you don't mind. Young James is an early riser.'

'I'd have expected nothing less. I hope you sleep well, Ella.'

He watched her pad out of the living room and pondered a while on how lucky Brian Scott had been in his choice of wife. Ella was smart, sensible, grounded. She was an excellent foil for the sometimes-erratic detective. At the same time, he lamented the absence of a spouse of his own. But the time had never been right. And despite some youthful dalliances, the right woman had come along once, only to be lost to another.

Memories of his life swirled round Hamish's mind until he drifted off to sleep in the rocking chair.

He woke with a start, cold without a blanket, even on such a balmy night as this.

The big storm lanterns still flickered away over the dying embers of the fire. Stars twinkled through a gap in the curtains from the velvet sky beyond the dirty living room window. But Hamish could tell something wasn't right.

He sat up in his chair, sniffing the air like a dog. At first, straight from sleep, he couldn't work out what didn't fit. The house was quiet, no footsteps in the hall, not a creak of a floorboard in the bedroom.

Hamish got stiffly to his feet, his intention to pay a visit to the toilet. But as he did, the realization of what was out of place struck him like a sudden change of the wind at sea. He grabbed the big brass poker from the fireplace and rushed out into the lobby.

'Ella, quickly, get up!' he roared. He heard her mumble from the bedroom, and dashed through to where she and young James were bedded down.

'What's wrong, Hameby?' said the child, his tiny voice sleepy.

'Ella! Will you damn well wake up!' Hamish shook the recumbent figure in the bed.

'It's surely no' seven in the morning yet, Hamish?'

'We need to get out of the house, Ella. The roof's on fire. There's smoke billowing oot the hatch to the loft.'

Ella, always quick to come to her senses, grabbed James and pulled him out of the bed.

'Follow me!' shouted Hamish, as he raced off for the front door.

'What about teddy? I can't find him, Auntie Ella,' protested James.

'Never mind that, son. We have to go now!' She dragged the boy from the bed, as he began to wail at the absence of his stuffed toy.

Ella met Hamish on his way back up the short lobby. 'Where on earth are you going?' she shouted, noting the old man was heading away from the front door.

'Take a look for yourself. Someone's set a fire at the door. I can see the flames outside. If we open that, we'll be incinerated. Through to the kitchen!'

Ella Scott needed no convincing. Her eyes were watering now, and she was coughing loudly. By her side, young James coughed and cried in equal measure.

Though the kitchen was pitch black, smoke adding to

the dark of night, Ella could still make out the figure of Hamish before her. She felt the cool rush of air on her face as he opened the back door. But something in the doorway was obstructing his passage. It took Ella a few seconds to realize that a shadowy figure appeared to be trying to stop them reaching safety.

Ella began to panic. The heat of the fire from above grew stronger. James was screaming with the full force of his small lungs, but she kept a tight hold of his hand in case he tried to break free and run.

'Gargle on that, you bastard!' bellowed Hamish as he brought the poker down on the dark figure's shoulder.

Ella saw a shadowy object swing through the air again, illuminated by the pale moonlight from the garden. A man yelled in pain, and the object swung through an arc in the night once more.

'Come on, Ella! Have you got the boy?' Hamish shouted.

In moments, they were outside. Ella could breathe again, though James was still coughing and wailing for all he was worth.

'This way!' yelled Hamish. 'Hold on to the back of my dungarees, so we don't lose each other.'

For Ella, it was easier to see Hamish now than it had been in the smoke, darkness and chaos of his flaming home, which now helped light their way. Nonetheless, she grabbed at his bib and braces, as they made their way through tall shrubs and began to climb the hill at the back of the house, under the gibbous moon, high in the sky.

They trailed through bushes that clawed at them like tiny needles. Nettles stung bare skin, while large ferns brushed against their faces, no more than a gentle caress. Underfoot, the ground was stony, rough with tiny boulders; a path of sorts.

Hamish forged ahead, as though it was a bright, sunny day. Not only did he know the waters around Kinloch like the back of his hand, but he was also as sure-footed as a mountain goat on the hills above his home.

They drove on, the sounds and smells of the hill somehow exaggerated on the night air, all seemingly more robust than in the hours of daylight. But the air was tainted by the bitter smell of fire, as Hamish's home burned below.

They splashed across a stream, the cool water lapping at their ankles. Hamish turned to Ella and grabbed her hand. 'This way, we'll be out of sight. But be careful, the path ends here.' His breathing was heavy, a mixture of exertion and fear.

Cautiously, they pushed through thickets of tall grass and heather, until Hamish stopped. The moon was out of sight, hidden by tall bushes and the tilt of the cliff. He delved into the front bib pocket of his dungarees and produced a Zippo lighter. Though he shaded the flame with one hand, lest it be spotted by any likely pursuers, it illuminated the scene sufficiently for Ella to be able to spot a slit in the rock.

'In here!' Hamish's voice was a hoarse whisper.

The entrance wasn't the tight squeeze Ella expected. The cave opening was angled in such a way that it faced sideways on, looking out over the loch. The dark shadow of the island loomed over the quicksilver waters, as illuminated by the moon, which in turn dulled the stars. Far below, flames leapt from Hamish's house, now like a Viking bonfire under the great expanse of the velvet sky.

'Please, James. We need to keep quiet.' Ella held the boy tight to her, stifling the sobs that racked his small frame.

'Aye, quiet as a moose. Everything's going to be fine. Just listen to your Auntie Ella. Nod your head if you understand.'

James Daley junior nodded his head, his face tear stained. 'I understand, Hameby.'

'What now? They'll be looking for us, for sure,' said Ella.

'This is the cave they used in the last war – aye, and many wars before that. Man, did clansmen not hole up here in this very spot, and signal if they saw war galleys out in the sound.'

'That's all very well but they'll still find us, no matter what your clansmen used to get up to.' Ella's voice was shaking with cold and fear.

'I'd agree with you, except for one thing.'

'And that is?'

'Look below. The house is burning like a beacon. Half of Kinloch will know about it by now.' He leaned into Ella, quieting his voice. 'They hoped to catch us asleep, Ella. Burn us alive,' he whispered. 'They canna think that help won't be on its way.'

Ella Scott knew all about Hamish's powers of prediction. And as though by the old man's command, she heard the distant wail of sirens on the air, lifting the weight of fear from her shoulders.

'Where can we go now, Hamish? You've lost your home.'

'Och, that niece o' mine has been wanting me to move into the retirement home down on the esplanade for years, now. It looks like she may well have her wish granted. And anyhow, what's important is flesh and bones, no' bricks and mortar. We'll huddle here for a while until we see the blue lights down at the house. As for finding a place you can go next, I'm thinking that will be a job for the police.'

'I wish I knew what was happening,' said Ella. 'I wish Brian was here, too.'

'I daresay he feels the same.' Hamish hugged Ella and young James, looking on dolefully as all he'd ever owned went up in flames in the bonfire of his home.

48

Blissfully unaware of what was happening in Kinloch, Brian Scott was studying the documents sent to him by Duff. These mostly concerned the incident that had happened so long ago on the Clydeside in Glasgow, plus some notes on the late Gordon Lambie, his family, and more behind the reason for Lambie's and Daley's hot pursuit of a BMW through the streets of Glasgow that far-off day.

Lambie, it turned out, after years of suffering depression, had eventually been admitted to a hospital, where treatment for his poor mental health had proven to be elusive.

Scott, however, wasn't as interested in Lambie as he was in his family. If his theory was right, Daley's ordering him to pursue a car through the Glasgow traffic back then had unimaginable consequences. Lambie had taken his own life in front of the Daleys only weeks before, proving the incident had stayed with him for decades, festering until he could no longer cope with the guilt and pain.

Scott peered through his glasses at the background research DC Duff had produced in his absence. Almost inevitably, Lambie and his wife Claire had separated then divorced. She remarried a silversmith in Aberdeenshire, taking Lambie's son and daughter with her to settle in the county.

All, it seemed, had been well. The marriage thrived, until Claire's second husband had died three years ago. She now lived a quiet life in a suburb of Aberdeen, her children long since left home for lives of their own.

Fraser, Gordon and Claire's son, had studied biology at Aberdeen University, then taken himself to the south of England to work for a research company. As far as Duff's report detailed, he was happily married with a young son of his own. An ordinary man, in an ordinary world. Duff had also discovered that he and his father hadn't seen or spoken to each other for many years. So, Scott reasoned, Fraser Lambie was unlikely to be the cause of Jim Daley's acute predicament.

As for Amanda Lambie, Gordon and Claire's daughter, things were very different. Duff had tracked her down to a hostel in the East End of Glasgow. She was addicted to drugs and spent a lot of time in and out of hospital. Duff's report detailed that, lately, she'd begun work in a fast-food shop, cleaning dishes and sweeping up. She'd been smart enough at school, but mixed with the wrong characters, who'd led her down a ruinous path.

Scott took a moment to picture her existence. Poor, addicted, haunted by yearning for drugs, what chance did she stand? She and her mother were seemingly estranged, leaving Amanda with no family to guard her from the sharp edges of the world. In Scott's opinion, it was most unlikely she had anything to do with the Daley case.

His mobile rang. He looked at the screen and quickly realized that Eddie Beattie was on the other end. As he had done three times already that day, Scott ignored the call. He still found it hard to believe his old pal was corrupt, but he trusted Jill Unwin to such an extent he'd no choice other than to believe her.

One thing seemed certain: any thought that the Lambie

family had anything to do with the elaborate plot against Jim Daley that had cost Liz her life could now be completely ruled out.

Scott sat back in his chair and stared as a cockroach made its way across the ceiling above. The creature took its time, feeling its way along, slowly but surely. Scott didn't feel at all disgusted by its presence; if anything, he knew how the cockroach felt, taking slow steps, forward progress stilted, its direction uncertain.

A noisy family had moved into the room next to his. Through the thin walls of the hotel, he could hear loud music and a child crying even at this late hour. Why people couldn't show respect for others had often puzzled him in the past. His time in the police had taught Scott that too many people simply didn't care. It was merely their natural way of being.

Scott picked up the tablet again and began to plough through the rest of Duff's impressive notes. This time, they concerned the driver forced into the Clyde during the chase with Lambie and Daley.

It appeared that Lee Mackin was a petty criminal from Merseyside. His job had been to help distribute one of the most dangerous consignments of heroin Glasgow had ever seen. Hence Daley's determination to catch him. The heroin was much more potent than that normally found on the streets of Scottish cities. Addicts were dying in large numbers, and the police had been under massive pressure to stop the supply.

Scott remembered those days, being called out to investigate the deaths of junkies all over Glasgow. These poor souls were keeling over in the streets. There was a public outcry; after all, junkies should die quietly in a squalid flat or doss house, shouldn't they?

For Scott, each death was a tragedy, each prematurely ended life a warning that this could happen to anyone. He hated those who shrugged their shoulders at these deaths – the *one less to worry about* brigade.

He was about to read further into Mackin's details when the music in the next room became so loud, he could barely think. Scott dragged himself wearily from his chair and banged on the wall with his fist.

'Shut up! I'm no' here to listen to your shit!' he shouted, hoping to be heard over the din.

Almost instantly, the music stopped. Scott made his way back to his notes, mumbling expletives under his breath.

Just as he was about to resume his reading, there was a loud knock at his door. Hoping it wasn't more bad news, and remembering that Beattie had just called, he shot up to answer it.

Before him stood a man, likely in his early forties, behind him a youth, perhaps in his mid-teens. They were both overweight, the man sporting a vest depicting a bulldog with a baseball bat in its mouth, the teenager a tracksuit and a tattooed neck.

'What the fuck do you think you're doing knocking on the wall, you prick.' The man's breath stank of alcohol and he spat as he spoke. The boy stood behind him, a sneer spread across his face.

'Eh? Are you being serious? You're in a hotel, man. You don't make that racket. Keep it doon!'

'Oh-oh,' said the man, turning to the teenager. 'I fink we've got ourselves a Scotch one, here.' He returned his gaze to Scott. 'Take this as a warning, Jocko. The next time you knock on the wall, I'll kick in this door and knock your fucking head off, yeah?'

Brian Scott had lived through some difficult times in his life. The last few days numbered amongst the worst. Consequently, his patience was worn paper-thin. In a flash, he took one step forward and planted his forehead on the nose of his grubby interlocutor, and watched him fall to the floor, screaming and holding his nose.

'Just thought I'd kiss you goodnight, you plank,' said Scott.

The teenage boy took one look at what had happened and dashed off to the safety of his room.

'Don't bleed all over the floor, you ugly bastard. Fuck off!' Scott stepped back into his room and slammed the door. He heard the shrill voice of a woman, followed by another squeal of pain outside in the corridor.

'Serves you right. I've been telling you something like this would happen for years. People ain't frightened of you no more, got it!'

At last, peace reigned. Scott decided to lie on his bed. He knew he should be asleep, but it just wouldn't come. The horror of the last few days had seen him lie in the dark, night after night, staring at the ceiling, as the world crowded in.

At least he knew that Duff had done an excellent job on background checks of the Lambie family. Despite turning up nothing, Scott hoped that something about the long-deceased Lee Mackin would shed light on what was happening to Daley. Or maybe they were just running out of options. There was no doubt that they'd focused on Lambie, following his death in Kinloch. Had they been wrong?

His mobile rang again. Scott groaned, thinking it could only be Eddie Beattie. He decided to answer, to make something up about being unwell, maybe tell the old friend he now mistrusted he'd decided to go back home, utterly defeated.

The name *Jimmy* speared across the screen had Scott rushing to answer the call.

'Jimmy, what's up, big man?'

'It's complicated, Bri. But I wanted you to know there's nothing to worry about.' Daley's voice sounded weak, even over the phone.

'What? Have they found something – your health?'

'No, nothing like that. I just got a good kicking. It's Eddie, he's worried that I'm a sitting duck here. Somebody in the Met is helping whoever it is that's targeted me.'

'Eddie? Listen, Jimmy, Eddie might not be the best man to trust.'

'He's your friend, Brian! The great white hope, remember?'

'Aye, I know. But things might have changed.'

'Changed how?'

'You'll need to trust me on that one, big man. I've heard a few things, that's all.'

'Well, all I'm hearing is that I'm fucked. Evidence is being fabricated against me, they're back-pedalling on clean evidence, and someone in the Met is pulling strings.'

'How do you know it's no' Eddie?'

There was a silence on the end of the phone.

'Jimmy, you still there?'

'Yes, I am. You're not making sense, Brian. Listen, I trust Eddie, even if you don't. Remember Bright? Someone took him out, got him out of the way. I need to listen to Eddie Beattie. This is his job. He's cleaning things up, corruption and the like. I *need* to do something, Brian.'

'Just give me time to get there, Jimmy. OK?'

Daley sighed. 'Yeah, OK, OK, Brian.' The call ended.

Scott rushed to his feet. He'd seen a couple of

brochures and a couple of cards in a drawer, left by taxi companies for the use of guests. After a couple of attempts, he found them.

As Brian Scott waited for his call to be answered, he shook his head and cursed his luck. Should he say something to Unwin? But what had he to tell?

Eventually, his call was answered and he ordered a taxi right away.

49

'**R**ight, Maybury, take a break,' said Commander Eddie Beattie to the constable reading the evening newspaper in the corridor outside Daley's room in the hospital. He was carting a net bag bulging with oranges. 'I'll keep an eye on things here, pal. Our man needs his fruit, eh?'

The cop laughed. He knew who Beattie was, having met his superior earlier the previous day.

Beattie handed the young police officer a twenty-pound note. 'Get me a coffee, while you're at it. Milk and two sugars. Aye, and take your time. I remember doing this kind of shite when I was your age. Messes with your head, so it does.'

'You sure, sir?'

'Aye, I'm sure, Maybury. On you go, before I change my mind.'

The constable happily took off, desperate for a cup of tea and a break from the unrelenting boredom of guarding the room.

Beattie knocked gently on Daley's door, entering before he'd heard a reply.

Daley turned his head to face his new visitor. 'Where've you been, Eddie? I thought you'd taken cold feet.'

'Took longer to get things organized than I thought. We need to be careful, Jimmy. Don't want some nurse rushing in 'cos your bell's gone off.' He nodded to the machine monitoring Daley's heart.

'I suppose you're right.'

'I am, trust me. One of my boys is coming along with a wheelchair. You think you can get into it? I have to say, Jim, no' a lot of choice here.' He handed Daley the bag of oranges. 'For appearances' sake, you know?'

The door swung open. A man in a nurse's uniform appeared in Daley's room. He was tall, brawny, and looked somehow out of place in the blue kit.

'He'll need a hand, Tipton. Help him up, eh?'

'You mean, we're going now?' said Daley, remembering what Scott had said about Beattie.

'You wanting to hang on for a discharge note?'

'No, just something Brian said.'

'I've been trying to get hold of that arsehole all day. What's up with him?'

'He's worried you might be part of all this.'

'All what? Killing Liz, you mean?'

Daley shrugged.

'Somebody's got to him. I should have known. Hey, you don't think he's been – you know.' Beattie mimed a drinking motion at his mouth with his left hand.

'Don't think so. He got a fright the last time.'

'You can never trust a drunk, Jimmy. You should know that. Life can just get too much. It's no' as though things are exactly moonlight and roses for him just now, is it?'

'I know, he's worried – devastated about Liz.'

Beattie held his hands up in a gesture of surrender. 'Not

as devastated as you, and you're still functioning. Hey, if you've changed your mind, it's no skin off my nose.'

'It's OK, I've made up my mind.' Daley nodded his head to Beattie.

'Right, Tipton, give me that doodah.'

Tipton searched in the pockets of his uniform and produced a small black box, no larger than a phone charger, which he handed over.

The commander made his way over to the machine monitoring Daley's heart. He pressed two buttons, waited until he heard a ping, and removed the probes taped on to Daley's arm, connecting them instead to the little box. He waited for a few moments before leaving it carefully on Daley's nightstand.

Tipton and Eddie Beattie loomed over the big policeman, took an arm each and hauled him on to the side of the bed.

Jim Daley gasped for breath, as his bare feet planted on the cold vinyl flooring.

'How do you feel?'

'Shit.'

'Just the usual, then? Good.'

Daley nodded.

'Catch your breath. We get you into the wheelchair first then down in the lift and out.'

'I hope you're right, Eddie.'

'I am. You're a bit of a godsend, you know, Jim Daley. Just what we needed to help to get rid of the last pieces of shit in this police force.'

'Heavy price, Eddie – too heavy.'

'Sorry about that. Just talking my usual empty-headed nonsense out loud.'

'OK, are we ready for stage two?' said Daley.

'Sure are. Get his arm round your shoulder, Tipton.'

Now in the taxi, Brian Scott was conflicted. He knew he should call Unwin. But it was late, and he had no idea what he'd say. After all, Daley hadn't really said anything about Beattie's intentions. But still Scott fretted that he was doing the wrong thing.

'How long, bud?' he said to the taxi driver.

'How long is a piece of string, mate? This time of night, they close roads left, right and centre for repairs, gas, internet – all kinds of things. The satnav says another forty minutes. But that don't mean nothing.'

'Here, I'm no' some daft tourist.' Scott produced his warrant card and flashed it so the driver could see in his rear-view mirror. 'I'm no' wanting a spin aboot the beauty spots before we get there so you can bump up the fare, right!'

'Steady on! I'm doing this as fast as I can. There might be some bastards what will take advantage of people who don't know the city, but not going to a hospital. Old Bill, I don't know. You never change.' He shook his head.

Scott sat back in his seat. He felt guilty now. His mobile phone was hot in his hand. He looked on as they passed a row of shops, mainly chicken takeaways, bookmaker's, cut-price stores and a newsagent's, punctuated by boarded-up premises slathered with graffiti. The place was run-down, untidy, with litter in the streets and a general feeling of decay. In short, as far away from the sparkling tourist promo videos of the nation's capital as it was likely to get. Scott found himself longing for the clean, open spaces of Kintyre. Cities, it seemed, were no longer for him.

Still unsure whether or not to raise Unwin, and feeling helpless in the taxi, he decided to call Daley. That way, at least he'd be able to talk his best friend down from whatever it was that Beattie had suggested.

The screen flashed in front of him, but Daley did not reply.

For Scott, calling Beattie seemed like the only other option. He dialled his number, and the same thing happened: no reply.

'Do me a favour, buddy. I don't care what you have to do, just get me to this hospital as quick as you can, OK? There's an extra twenty in it for you.'

'Do me best, mate!' the taxi driver shouted in reply. Then, under his breath he muttered, 'Last of the big spenders. It's true what they say about the Scots.'

Sitting in the back seat of the taxi, in his mind's eye, all Brian Scott could see was the grainy footage from the alleyway. Liz being pushed into the recessed doorway, the man kicking mercilessly at her hidden body.

He picked up his phone again. 'Jill, I'm sorry to call you so late – or early – whatever you want tae call it. Something's happening with Jimmy. Beattie's with him, I think. Big Jimmy was coy with me. That's how I know.'

'You what?' Jill Unwin had come to, quickly. 'Beattie is with him now. Is that what you're saying?'

'I'm not sure. It was just something Jimmy said. I don't know what to do.'

'You leave it with me, Brian. Got it? Just you stay put.'

'Aye, got it. Nae bother.' Scott ended the call, still wondering if he'd done the right thing.

'Fuck!' the driver swore forcefully.

'What now?'

'I told you. They've closed this road. We'll have to go

another way. It'll add another ten minutes on to the journey. Just warning you now.'

'I'm just warning *you*. If we pass Buckingham Palace twice on the way there, you're getting it.'

They both laughed, ploughing on into the London night.

50

Constable Maybury drained the last of his second cup of tea in the hospital canteen. He'd met a few senior officers in his short time as a police officer. None were as companionable as Beattie – or as generous.

He patted his belly, hunger sated by a tuna sandwich and a Danish pastry. He'd sat at a table near the serving counter. There were only three other customers, a group of doctors, discussing what sounded like a matter of great import at a table towards the back of the big room. The only member of staff on duty was a looker, of that there was no doubt. Maybury smiled at her.

'Quiet in here, isn't it?'

'Now it is. In a couple of hours, it'll be rammed for breakfast.' The young woman behind the counter, with her blonde hair in a ponytail, rolled her eyes. 'But the cavalry comes in at half-five. I don't mind working nights.'

'Can I have a large flat white, please?' said Maybury.

'You're thirsty, eh? Two cups of tea, now a coffee.'

'It's for my boss. I better get back up there. Been here for nearly an hour. I don't want to take the piss.'

'Thought your gaffer told you to take your time?'

'He did. But this is stretching it.'

'Pity.' She smiled at him. 'Nice to have company.'

'Yeah.' Maybury thought for a second. 'I'm not just good company in here, you know. Available for the cinema, a nice meal out – a drink, even.'

'You're a chancer!' She giggled. 'Here, take this.' The waitress scribbled her number down on a paper napkin and handed it to the constable. 'You busy tomorrow night?'

'I'm off, as it goes.' He grinned. 'Here, what's your name?'

'Deborah. But you can call me Debbie.'

'I'm Dez.' He rose from his table to shake her hand, when his radio crackled into life.

'E-4672, go ahead.'

'Why aren't you sitting at that door?'

'Hello?' Maybury didn't instantly recognize the voice.

'It's Inspector Unwin. Get back up them stairs right now! And whatever Commander Beattie has told you, forget it, right. I want to hear from you in the next few minutes!'

'Sorry, better go,' said Maybury, rushing from his table.

'You're forgetting your flat white.'

'It'll have to wait, Debbie.' He blew her a kiss and hurried away.

The wait for the lift was an agonizing one. But eventually, the doors opened and Maybury ran in. He pressed floor fourteen on the pad and waited for the lift to rumble into action. The doors closed and off it went, Maybury counting the floors as they ascended.

'Come on,' he said to himself through gritted teeth. He didn't understand quite how an inspector could haul him over the coals for being ordered by a commander to go to the canteen. Still, he needed trouble like a hole in the head. His last assessment had been less than inspiring.

The number fourteen appeared in red neon, and Maybury hurried from the lift down the corridor. Daley's room was on the right, away from the main wards, all in darkness, patients asleep. He passed a doctor in white Crocs, green overalls and a white coat. Maybury had learned that they wore a stethoscope round their necks like badges of office. Quite petty, he reasoned.

As soon as he turned into the short corridor in front of Daley's room, he sensed something was wrong. Daley was in an observation ward. Windows halfway to the floor afforded a view of his bed. And that bed was empty.

'Shit!' Maybury put the radio to his mouth and called in the problem with trembling hands.

Daley and the man he only knew as Tipton were in a service lift. Beattie had gone ahead to get their escape vehicle. This place was away from the white, antiseptic corridors of the hospital, walls rendered in a dull, brown paint that looked less than sterile. They shared the lift with an old janitor, who complained about the state of some of the nurses' stations he had to clean.

'They leave shit all over the place,' he said in his strong Caribbean accent. 'Chocolate wrappers, cigarette packets, empty drinks cans. It's disgusting. How can people get well when the place is filthy?'

Tipton nodded in agreement. 'Diabolical, mate. Taking right liberties, they are.' He looked every bit the part in his nurse's uniform and mask. They'd wrapped a bandage round Daley's head to make him look less conspicuous, though with his large frame in a small wheelchair, he didn't exactly fly under the radar.

Daley was in agony, and now the movement of the lift was making him feel nauseous. He wondered just how he was going to manage in a vehicle. Still, he trusted Beattie, and this resolution to his hopeless situation afforded the detective few options. The pain he felt in his broken body was nothing to the pain in his heart over Liz. Silently, Jim Daley wished he'd never joined the police force. Something he'd done in the course of his duty, somebody he'd brought to justice, clearly bore him such ill will, he or she was willing to kill his wife, just to destroy Daley's soul. He thought of his son back in Kinloch and wanted to scream.

The lift stopped. Tipton said goodbye to the cleaner and pushed Daley rapidly along the corridor towards a sign marked *Exit*. So far, so good.

'Hold your horses, Tipton,' said Daley. 'I'll end up really fucked up if we crash this bloody thing.' He was being pushed along at running pace down a long passage.

'We need to get out of here pronto, mate. The gaffer's out there. I'm not keeping him waiting.'

Daley felt his stomach churn as they turned a corner. Facing them was a shorter corridor, a fire door at its end.

'This is it,' said Daley's temporary porter.

'Hope you're right,' said Daley as he was pushed towards the fire door.

'I have to laugh,' said the big man. 'My name isn't Tipton. Fuck knows where he got that from.'

For no reason at all, this revelation unnerved Daley. Yes, not using someone's real name during a covert operation was nothing new. But it was something about the way Beattie had spoken it so deliberately that set off Daley's suspicious instincts.

'Right, on the other side of this door is your salvation, my friend.' Without hesitating, Tipton pushed open the fire doors.

The rush of cool air came as a shock to Daley's system, as he stared into the darkness. 'I can't see anything,' he said.

Tipton cursed under his breath. 'That, my friend, is because there's nothing to see. Where the fuck is he? If we don't get out of here sharpish, the whole place will come crashing round our ears.'

The pair stared into a dark yard, the only light coming from the moon as it flitted through the clouds high above.

Daley was first to hear raised voices. 'Do you hear that?'

Tipton nodded. 'Sounds like they're on that long corridor we came down. Shit!'

There was no doubt that the voices were getting louder. The men waiting by the fire door could now hear footsteps as well as shouts.

'Just go!' said Daley. 'It's not worth getting brought down by this mess. I'll just shrug my shoulders and say I thought you were porters.'

'Not that simple, mate.'

A door slammed and a voice called out, 'They must be down here!'

'Go, man!' Daley roared.

Just as he did, he heard the screech of brakes. A black Transit van appeared round a corner, lights flashing, making an unholy racket. Daley spotted that a metal ramp had been thrust out from the open back doors of the vehicle. Sparks flashed on the tarmac as the metal ramp scraped across the yard, and the Transit's doors swung free, almost bouncing off their hinges.

'Now!' yelled Tipton.

Before Daley could reply, his minder had pushed the wheelchair out into the night. They bumped across the yard, Daley hanging on desperately. The van's brakes howled as it was forced to a dead stop by Beattie at the wheel. Tipton took a run at the ramp, just managing to push the wheelchair and Daley's not inconsiderable bulk into the back of the vehicle. With the back doors still open and the ramp fully extended, they took off, Daley having to grab on to the frame of the Transit to stop himself flying backwards on to the yard. He yelled as pain flashed through his broken body.

'You OK in there?' shouted Beattie from the driver's seat.

'Yes, but you need to get the ramp up and shut the fucking doors!' shouted Tipton.

Then they heard the shrill wail of sirens.

51

Brian Scott had just arrived at the hospital when he heard an ear-splitting noise. It reminded him of the farmers dotted about Kinloch as they scraped the dung from their concrete yards with implements attached to the back of tractors. But this was louder, a grating metallic squeal.

As he desperately tried to work out what was going on, a vehicle appeared at the end of the street that passed the hospital entrance. A dark-coloured Transit van, its true shade hidden by the orange glow of streetlights, was approaching at speed. Behind it, a chequer-plate ramp bounced on the road, sending up sparks and flashes like a mini-firework display.

The van flashed by, going far too fast for the road conditions. As Scott stood open-mouthed, he could hear the familiar sound of a police siren. Sure enough, in moments, two units sped past, clearly in pursuit of the van.

'Somebody trying to spring oor Jimmy,' he said to himself with a smile. The very idea was ludicrous.

Scott carried on into the hospital foyer through a pair of sliding doors. Though he'd agonized about the call to Unwin, he was sure he'd done the right thing. Despite all the years he'd known Eddie Beattie, the long time he'd spent in London must have surely changed the man. The happy tales of all their yesterdays were fine. In all honesty, though, what did it really mean? Scott had no idea how the Met worked – he wasn't really interested. He just wanted justice for his friend.

As Scott made his way to the long front desk, he heard his name being called from further back near the entrance.

'Brian!' Jill Unwin was hurrying towards him.

'I'm sorry about all this, Jill. Just had a bad feeling, you know what I mean?'

Unwin was out of breath. 'You were right,' she spat out, still trying to compose herself.

'Eh? What are you on about?'

'They've taken Daley.' She leaned against him, still breathing hard. 'We nearly got them, but it was just too late.'

Scott looked behind her to the front entrance. 'Do you mean he was in that Transit van I just saw – the one making all that racket?'

'Yeah, he was. We have two units with eyes-on.'

'Kind of hard to miss since they're dragging a pyro show behind them, no? Reminded me o' the last time Rangers won the league!'

'We'll get them. Don't worry.'

Just as Unwin was regaining her composure, her Airwave radio burst into life.

'Unwin. Go ahead, Sergeant.'

'They've lost them, ma'am, over.'

'What!? How on earth did they manage that, over?'

'I just know they lost visual contact with the vehicle, ma'am. Stand by, over.'

'Is it time for me to start worrying now?' said Scott. 'I mean, if you lot cannae keep track o' an eighty-miles-per-hour firework display, what's the chances?' He shrugged.

'Do you have them on street cameras, at least?' said Unwin.

There was silence for a few seconds, then, 'That's a negative, ma'am.'

'Bastard!' Unwin stamped her foot like a toddler. 'I hate this fucking job sometimes.'

'No' as much as Jimmy hates it right now, I'll wager.'

'You should have told me long before you did what Daley had passed on!' Unwin thrust an admonishing finger into Scott's chest.

'You shouldn't have bent cops all over the fucking place!' said Scott by way of a curt reply.

'I can't believe Daley fell for it. Can you, Brian?'

'He's full o' painkillers, morphine. Likely thinks he can fly oot o' there. Cousin o' mine jumped off the roof o' a multistorey in Glasgow.'

'Drugs?'

'Aye. Mind you, he'd tied some pieces o' carpet to his arms. Witnesses said he was flapping right to the last.'

'Nasty.' Jill Unwin didn't really know what to say following this revelation. It was the matter-of-fact way Scott had related the short tale. Was this type of thing par for the course in Glasgow? In any case, she had more to worry about than this.

'Listen, if you were in Jimmy's shoes,' Scott blew out his cheeks, staring up at the ceiling, 'how well would your rational mind be working?'

Unwin shook her head. 'I don't know. We just really need to find them, and quick!'

Daley could see nothing now, apart from a stationary red light, fixed high behind the van. Beattie appeared with a torch directed on the ramp, which was now twisted and broken.

'Right, Jimmy, we need to get you out of this thing. The ramp isn't looking good, but we can try.'

'What then?' said Daley. 'You've got half of the Met looking for us now.'

'Not all, though.' Beattie directed the torch on to his watch. 'But we have to be quick. It'll soon dawn on them we've taken cover near by, and the whole area will be sealed off. Let's get going, Tipton!'

Much more gently this time, Daley's wheelchair was pushed back on to the ramp. Daley realized they were in a large, empty space, perhaps a warehouse, maybe even a disused car park. He couldn't be sure. Distantly, he heard water dripping, and their voices echoed in this cavernous space.

The ramp protested with a loud crack as soon as the wheelchair was pushed on to it.

'You sure about this, boss?' said Tipton.

'It's been knocked about, but it should hold,' said Beattie.

'OK, I believe you.' It was plain that Tipton didn't share his boss's confidence.

With four wheels on the ramp now, the whole process became most precarious. With a clatter, one side of the ramp attached to the van broke free and sagged alarmingly, almost sending Tipton and Daley on to the concrete floor. Only the policeman's sheer strength was enough to keep the chair from toppling over.

'This is madness!' shouted Daley, the pain he was already feeling sent through the roof.

'Give it a break, Jimmy. You'll have coppers all round coming down on us. Can you still push it, Tipton?'

'I can try, sir.' With no little effort, Daley was pushed at an angle down the remainder of the ramp, as it creaked and clanged.

319

Daley was mightily relieved when they were back on an even keel.

Beattie flashed his torch to the right of where Daley sat. Parked a few yards away was a black Mercedes SUV.

'You expect me to get in that?' said Daley.

'It's the only thing we can do, buddy. Plus, you'll have to lie on the back seat until we get out of the city, at least.'

'I don't think I can do it, Eddie.'

'Well, it's either this or back to the hospital. That way, you'll have a nasty fall, or maybe a doctor will make a mistake with your medication. Happens every day. Long and the short is, you'll be dead before lights out tomorrow.'

'Bit dramatic, no?'

'You think? They killed one of their own – someone working with them. They won't hesitate to kill you.'

'Bright, you mean?'

'Aye, Bright. He's had his nose in the trough for years. He could only do that with help from the top. That's why he was appointed SIO on your wife's case.'

Daley took a deep breath. *Your wife's case* sounded so cold, so clinical. 'Why did they kill him then, Eddie?'

'Look at the state you're in, Jimmy. That came from Bright, nobody else. It spoiled their plans. He paid the price for being a prick.'

'Why not just let me end up in court? With all this fabricated evidence, it would have been a no-brainer. I'd have been away for a full-life term for certain, with me in the job.'

Beattie swallowed hard. 'I don't think that's what they want.'

'Who are *they*, by the way?'

'Whoever set this all up. And it's been so carefully planned over many months. Even down to Liz and her—' Beattie stopped mid-sentence.

'Just say it, Eddie. My wife's affair!'

'Aye, that's it. And no matter how painful this all is, it's happened. And somewhere, the person or persons responsible had a great deal of help. I need to find them, Jimmy. But I need time, space without worrying about you getting topped. We take you to a safe house in the country. I have a team working on everything. They will find the answer, though it will take time. Fuck, I wish Brian wasn't floating about.'

'What problem can Brian be by himself?' As soon as Daley had spoken the words, he remembered many occasions where Brian had utterly changed the course of events all on his own. Despite the pain in his body and heart, he smiled.

'Apart from your son, who do you have left in your life who is closer to you than Brian, eh?'

Suddenly, Daley got the point. 'You mean, they'll go after Brian to get to me?'

'I do. But I can get a message to him safely. He needs to disappear for his own good. He needs to leave this to me. He wasn't up for it when we last spoke. I'm surprised they managed to turn his head about me so easily.'

'I can persuade him that you're one of the good guys, Eddie. I'll need to talk to his wife. She can call him directly with no suspicion.'

'And if I can find out who sowed that seed of doubt in his head, I'll be halfway to finding out who hates you enough not only to see you ruined but tortured to death into the bargain.'

'Charming.'

'Right, Tipton. Push him to the door, then we'll have to drag you in, Jimmy. It won't be pleasant. But the alternative is much worse. Trust me.'

There followed a process of wheeling Daley to the back door of the SUV. From there, Tipton manhandled him out of the chair, almost throwing the Scottish detective headlong on to the back seat. Now at the other side of the car, Beattie pulled Daley further towards the other door, then laid the big man's head on a small pillow.

'We'll get a blanket over you, Jimmy. Then we go.'

Jim Daley was almost in too much pain to talk. 'I get it,' he said through gritted teeth.

'Jimmy, I'm sorry for this, I really am,' said Beattie. 'But I can't see another way.' He turned to his colleague. 'OK, do the business.'

Daley managed to turn his head to face Tipton on the other side of the car. He was advancing in on top of Daley, with something in his hand.

A moment of sheer panic overtook Jim Daley. He wanted to move, but a mix of fractured bones, sheer agony and the fact Beattie was pushing him down on to the seat made it impossible.

Tipton pulled the sleeve of Daley's hospital gown up, revealing his forearm. Using a syringe, the policeman roughly inserted its needle into a muscle and squeezed the brown liquid from the syringe into Daley's bloodstream.

'You bastard!' Daley said, feeling a rush of tiredness engulf his body. What strength he had left melted away like snow in the rain.

'This way, it's easier, Jimmy. I'm sorry,' said Beattie, just as Daley's eyes closed tight shut, and his body became limp on the back seat of the Mercedes SUV.

52

Brian Scott was sitting opposite Jill Unwin now. The sun rising over London filled her east-facing office, despite the blinds being only partially drawn. The silhouetted London's East End skyline reminded him of ruined teeth, the various heights and shapes of buildings looking ugly, out of place. He listened absently to one side of a telephone conversation Unwin was having with someone he didn't know.

Unwin slammed the phone down.

'Still nothing?'

'It was toxicology. Ashley Winston is the boss of the department. She's been working on Liz's bloods. Been at it all night, she has. Workaholic, that's her problem. Plus, she owes me a favour or two.'

'Ah, right,' said Scott sheepishly.

'Not right, as it happens.'

'What do you mean?'

'Elizabeth Daley was badly beaten – we've all seen that. But it's not what killed her.'

'I don't understand.'

'She'd enough ketamine inside her to floor an elephant.'

'I suppose you think big Jimmy did that, too.'

'I think it was administered not long before that CCTV footage was taken.'

'That's no' Jimmy on there, Jill. My man in Kinloch can almost prove it.'

'Almost?'

'Give him time! Anyway, *your* guys should be working on this, no' mine.'

'I have a theory, Brian.'

'Which is?'

'Say that isn't your pal on the footage. Let's just think that for a moment.'

'I'm up for that.'

'So, when you saw Liz half-dragged into that alleyway, she was already dying.'

Scott lowered his head.

'She'd never have survived that dose.'

'So why did that big bastard – no' Jimmy, before you say it – kick the shit out of her? What was the point?'

'I hope you don't mind me saying this, but it was a good show. You're left in no doubt as to what's happening. And look, it's your mate what's doing the dirty deed. We all saw it, right?'

Scott shook his head in disbelief.

'Think about it. However the ketamine was administered, it's not dramatic, is it? The beating was done to frame Daley. It's all I can think of.'

'This just gets more disturbing by the minute. Who does this kind of shit?'

'A person who has spent years and years storing up hatred for somebody, that's who.'

Scott stroked his chin. 'I should tell you something.'

'What now?'

'You might know this. A few weeks ago, this guy cut his own throat in Jimmy and Liz's bedroom.'

'Yeah, I know.' Jill Unwin looked disgusted.

'They were in the room at the time.'

'Not nice.'

'It's a long story.' Scott told her Lambie's tragic tale.

'OK. I take it you've checked his family, friends, and so on, for somebody still bearing a grudge?'

'Aye, still looking. But it's no' one o' the family. One o' the kids is respectable, lives down south. The other is a lassie, recovering user. She doesn't have the wherewithal for anything like this. No resources, plus it's a day-after-day struggle to stay straight, never mind become a master criminal.'

Unwin eyed Scott. She suspected he'd experienced a similar struggle. 'The wife, maybe? She lost her husband, after all.'

'Nah, solid citizen. Left oor boy when he went off the rails. Saw little of him after that. Remarried, and her second husband died not long ago. She's no' had much success in that direction.'

'You still think it's connected to him, this cop?'

'I don't know.' Scott yawned. 'Could be nothing to do with that case. What are the chances of your mob finding Jimmy?'

'Hard to say right now. We're not sure what kind of team your old pal has.'

'Eddie?'

'Yeah, Eddie.'

'What a mess.'

'I want everything you know about the deceased driver, Brian. And I mean everything, right?'

'Aye, sure. I'll get it to you this morning. Of course, the fact the guy cut his throat in the big man's bedroom doesn't mean the answer lies with him. May be just coincidence.'

'It's a start.' It was Unwin's turn to yawn. 'I don't know about you, but I'm done in. I need a kip for a couple of hours. You get back to your hotel. We'll pick you up when things start moving. I'll call as soon as we have anything, I promise.'

'Eddie wanted me to go back up the road.'

'Out the way, you mean?'

'Aye, I suppose so – now, anyway.'

'Get me everything on the cop that killed himself. Then I'll get somebody to take you back to the hotel, OK?'

Scott nodded. 'Right, I'm on it.'

'The office next door is free. Get in there and do what you have to do, mate. Just give me a shout when you're ready.'

Scott did as he was asked. He sat in the empty office next to Unwin's. He wasn't going to use the desktop computer, flashing the Met's logo in a never-ending screensaver as he gazed at it, seemingly transfixed, deep in thought. He was going to use his phone. Scott dialled Duff's mobile.

'The number you're dialling isn't available. Please call later or leave a message.'

'Typical, just when you need something.' Scott dialled again, without success.

Following his third attempt and wondering how on earth anyone could spend so much time on the one call, Scott decided to ring the CID suite at Kinloch. Surely somebody could get a hold of Duff.

'Good morning. DC Cooper, Kinloch CID. Can I help you?'

Scott recognized Dianne Cooper's friendly tones. 'How are you doing, Dianne? Listen, it's me, Brian. I need to speak to young Duff. Where is he?'

'Gaffer, he's not here.'

'What do you mean?'

'They put him on nights with me. He didn't appear.'

'I spoke to him yesterday.'

'Well, he wasn't here when you did.'

'Why is life so shit, eh?'

'Another thing, gaffer. The place is packed with brass. After – you know.'

'It's half-six in the morning!'

'I know. Plane arrived at Machrie just after five.'

'What's going on?'

'All the goings on. You know what I mean.' Dianne Cooper lowered her voice. 'I need to go. I've got company.'

'Boss?'

'Aye, a big one. Anyway, I'm glad Mrs Scott and young James are safe. That must be a weight off your mind. Need to go!' Cooper ended the call.

'What!?'

Scott was pleased to hear that Ella and James were safe. But safe from what? He dialled Kinloch police office again.

'Police Scotland, Kinloch.' The reply was curt, officious.

'I need to speak to DC Cooper, please,' said Scott.

'On the contrary, you need to speak to me, DI Scott.'

'Who are you?'

'ACC Laing. I want to know what you've done with DC Duff.'

'How should I know where he is? I'm in London!'

'Wherever you are, stay there.'

'Why?'

'Because you're about to be arrested.'

'Wait, what for? I've done nothing.'

'That is most certainly true, DI Scott.'

'I want to know about Ella. What happened.'

'Your wife is safe, DI Scott. As is young James Daley. I want to know where you are, this minute!'

'Fuck off!' Brian Scott ended the call with a flourish.

He was trying to work out what to do when the door to his temporary office swung open. 'Jill, you got something?'

She looked at the floor. 'I'm sorry about this, Brian, I really am.' Unwin stepped aside, revealing two tall uniformed constables behind her.

'What the fuck?' Scott got to his feet.

'Brian, you know the drill. We've been asked to question you by Police Scotland. I don't have a choice. DPS are on the way.'

'Is that your internal investigators?'

'Yes.'

'How can they investigate me, then? I'm no' internal tae you!'

'Just do me a favour. It's just the usual bullshit, Brian. Play the game, eh?'

'I'm no' the one playing games. But I'd like to know who is.'

53

The day had dawned overcast over much of the west coast of Scotland. Hills that for the last week had described every shade of green under the bright gaze of the summer sun now looked grey, leached of life.

The same went for the sea. Out in the sound, the clear, almost Caribbean blue had been replaced by steel grey. It was almost as though a giant hand had cast a pall over the water overnight, changing its character from welcoming to forbidding.

As John Graham and his son Alex stared into those waters, they could see no reason why their nets had snagged, but snagged they most certainly were.

'Get that bloody net hooked to the main winch, Alex!' shouted John to his son. 'We'll have to pull it free by sheer force.'

'Another net ruined,' Alex replied.

'It's either that or we'll be stuck here all day. Is that what you want?'

'No, it certainly isn't.' Alex hauled over a massive hook attached to a wire hawser. The rest of its length was wound to a large winch. It was only used when an especially heavy haul of fish was trapped in their nets. That happened less and less these days, and they normally made do with the small winch nestled under the gunwale.

'When I was young, we mended nets. Now – well, it's like everything else. You don't mend it, you throw it away and buy new. Nae wonder the world is in such a bloody state.'

'Maybe we've snagged something expensive?' said Alex, a man whose cup was more likely to be half full than half empty like his father's.

'Aye, and maybe it's a torpedo from the war. You didna think o' that, did you now? Haul her up as carefully as you can, I'm no' wanting blown to kingdom come.'

Alex, who hadn't thought of the torpedo scenario, hooked the winch on to part of the semi-submerged net and engaged the big winch at low revs, pulling at whatever was caught on the seabed. The task had to be done most carefully, lest things took a turn for the worse. It wouldn't be the first item of ordnance found in the sound, a regular passage for naval vessels during the Second World War.

The winch's diesel motor thudded and sputtered as it did its job. Suddenly, there was a snap, and the winch roared free as its burden was lightened.

'Right, Alex, steady. Bring her up, just so.'

More of the net was pulled from the sea, dripping wet, disgorging some of its catch. Smaller fish wriggled free of its clutches, along with seaweed and other marine detritus.

'What's that, Faither?' shouted Alex, as he spotted a length of straight polished wood amongst the silver flashing fish and assorted green and brown hues of weed.

'Haul her in on the boom, we'll get it in the hold. Whatever it is hasn't been in the water long, by the look o' it.'

The boom swung the bulging net from the waters of the sound to just above the fishing boat's hatch.

'Let her go, son!' shouted John.

The net opened and poured its contents into the hold.

'What on earth?' said Alex, staring down into the hold.

'Here, let me take a look.' John grabbed a large lantern, hooked to the side of the wheelhouse, and dangled it down. He took a step back when he realized just what they'd snagged in their net.

'What's up, Faither? You're like a ghost. It's no' a torpedo, is it?'

'Take a look for yourself while I set a course back for Kinloch.' John Graham handed the lantern to his son, before hurrying back to the wheelhouse.

Alex took a tentative look. He caught his breath when the lantern's light caught the sheen from the polished wood of a coffin, sitting proud on the rest of the catch that now looked like an improvised pyre.

'We better call the harbour master at Kinloch! Some poor soul consigned to the depths to rest, and now we've disturbed them.'

John Graham wandered back down to the hold. 'There is another way, son.'

'Which is?'

'Well, as you say, we've trawled up a resting soul – though whoever sent the coffin into waters this shallow was asking for problems. Anyhow, we could simply put the coffin back where it belongs.' He stroked his chin thoughtfully.

Alex eyed his father with something approaching distaste. 'Why did you bother sending me to the nautical college, if you were determined to cut corners, Faither?'

'Ach, you've no idea the bloody hoops we'll have to jump through before this coffin finds its way back to the bottom of the sea. And that's where it will end up, you mark my words.'

'Shut up a minute, will you?'

'Indeed, I will not. This is still my boat, remember. You'll have your hands on her soon enough.'

'Listen!'

John Graham cocked his head to one side. 'Is that your mobile phone, Alex?'

'No. It's coming from the hold – from the coffin!'

'Right, you call the harbour master, I'll get her moving. This gives me the creeps!'

54

Daley awoke on a long couch, covered in a rough blanket. His head was pounding, but it had been since the day he awoke on the park bench near Canary Wharf. Rude awakenings, it seemed, were part and parcel of his world now.

It was odd, really. For the first few seconds of wakefulness, his mind was almost at rest. In moments, however, that changed, and the biting sorrow of Liz's death hit home again, as though newly learned. Yet again, Daley felt as though he was sinking into the abyss.

'You're awake, Jimmy?' Eddie Beattie was standing above him.

Daley could now feel his pain levels rising and rising. 'We made it then?'

'We did. I'm sorry we had to knock you out. You wouldn't have been able to take it.'

'You should have let me try.'

'Don't worry. I have a fine selection of painkillers here. Tramadol, liquid morphine? Take your pick – take both.'

'I'll have a drop of morphine, please.' Daley was frightened to move. This was the first time since the attack that his pain hadn't been managed by very strong pain relief.

'Help me get him up, Tipton.'

Before Daley could protest, he was being hauled into a seated position by Beattie and Tipton. Despite himself, he bellowed in agony.

'Just as well our nearest neighbour is about three miles away,' said Tipton.

Beattie approached him with a small syringe. 'Don't worry, we're not going to stick you again. Open wide.'

The morphine was sickly sweet. Beattie had given him a reasonable dose. Daley swallowed it back in the hope it would work its magic, and soon.

Beattie held a cup of water at Daley's mouth and the big man gulped the medicine.

'Where are we?' he said weakly.

'Somewhere they can't find you. It's one of our safe houses. In the middle of nowhere,' said Tipton.

Daley looked about, to the extent he could move his head. It was a tidy room from another time. The wallpaper looked as though it was straight from a Habitat catalogue in the eighties. The suite reminded him of something he and Liz had owned in their first flat together. A few paintings adorned the walls, cheap prints of rural themes in cheaper frames. Through a picture window, he could see trees in full leaf, before rolling hills.

'The home counties, Jimmy. Beats where we grew up, anyway.'

'I don't know. I've seen better,' replied Daley.

'You hankering for Kinloch, or whatever it's called?' said Tipton.

'I'm *hankering* for my dead wife.'

'Sorry, mate. That was insensitive.'

'Go and make a pot of tea by way of a punishment,' said Beattie. 'NATO standard, Jimmy?'

'Yes, milk and two.' Daley took a moment to reflect on the nation's tea obsession. He'd just been sprung from custody. A murder suspect, freed by a senior Met officer. And yet, everything still stopped for tea. 'What's the plan?'

'I have people working on things. My best people, in fact. I couldn't leave you to rot. You were going down, one way or the other.'

'I know. Come on, who would go to the trouble of doing all this out of hatred for me? Why didn't they just shoot me?'

'Too easy. You have to suffer. It's the name of the game for this one: suffering.'

'Our chances? After all, you're in it big time too, now.'

'They're good. I've had my eye on a few bad pennies for a while. This promises to be a bumper harvest.'

'I hope you're right. I really do. I need to get home and bury my wife, hold my son.'

'On that point, I need to have a word.'

Daley felt the bottom fall from his world. He'd been so wrapped up in Liz, he'd hardly had time to consider James.

Beattie went on to explain the attack on Hamish's house, where Ella and James had been staying. Fire, a chase, a hill cave – he could barely take it all in, as Beattie related fact after fact.

'But they're safe now, that's the main thing.'

'OK. I want to surrender, Eddie. It's bad enough Liz has gone, without my son being even more fucked up by this. Leave me somewhere for people to find. I'll take whatever it is they throw at me.'

Beattie knelt before the stricken detective. 'The boy needs his father more than ever now. Don't be stupid.'

Tipton arrived with the tea on a tray. 'Found these biscuits, guv.'

'There we go, tea and biscuits. What more could you ask for?' said Beattie.

Daley sat on the couch, still in agony. He needed much more than tea and sympathy. But what was the point asking for it?

55

Seven men stood round the coffin in the Kinloch harbour master's spacious outer office. It was more of an eclectic store, really, where all kinds of nautical bits and pieces found a home. Everything from old fishing nets and seaboots to radar parts and oilskins hung from hooks or were packed on to shelves.

One side of the coffin had been stained slightly by the sea, otherwise it looked brand new. The only thing that seemed unusual about the casket was its weight. After being winched on to the pier, it had taken seven men to load it on to a stout gurney and take it to the office. On the gurney it sat, still.

'Go ahead, please,' said Superintendent Cowie. He was a tall, cadaverous man, who looked very much as though, had his career as a police officer failed, he would have made an excellent undertaker.

MacSporran the joiner looked at him with his eyes half shut, assessing the task in hand.

'I'm just wondering what could be inside this damned thing – apart fae the obvious, that is. I mean, look at the heft o' it. It's no' been in the sea for long, I can tell you that. We could all go up in flames – could be a bomb. My arse might end up on the other side o' the toon.'

'There are no signs of explosives. Our dogs would have picked that up. Please, let's get on with this,' said Cowie impatiently. 'The most likely item to be found in that coffin is a dead body. My goodness, you Kinloch people are so dramatic.'

Two forensic officers stood in long rubber capes and masks. The taller of the two muttered something about preservation of the cadaver, which appeared to be roundly ignored by the superintendent.

'Here, I've no' agreed a price yet,' said MacSporran.

'You'll be very well remunerated if you do this *small* job for us. If you're unwilling, we'll get someone else. Now, please do as you are asked!' It was Cowie's turn to narrow his eyes at the joiner.

'OK, I'll dae it. But surely you can get me a bumper before I start. I mean, fuck knows what horrors I'll come across. Aye, and I'm no' a professional ghoul like yous lot.'

'Get him a drink, Constable,' said Superintendent Cowie.

'Where from?' said Anderson, a local constable. 'The off-licence is up the top of Main Street, sir. It'll take me a while.'

'Do you know, I've never come across anything like this in all my life.' Cowie glared at the constable. 'Use some bloody initiative, man!'

'I've a bottle here,' said the harbour master, delving into a drawer. 'For emergencies, you understand.'

'Of course, we all need a whisky in an emergency,' said Cowie with more than a hint of sarcasm.

'Here, Simon. It'll need to be a mug, for I've no glasses.' He handed MacSporran the bottle of malt whisky.

'I widna bother too much about that, Malky.' In a fluid motion worthy of a dancer, the joiner whipped the cork from the bottle with one hand, while the other placed the spirit to his mouth. He glugged down more than a good measure and licked his lips. 'Man, that's a better dram than I thought it would be. Here's me thinking Islay whisky was poison all these years. Maybe it's just force o' circumstance.' He wiped his mouth dry with the sleeve of his filthy tweed jacket.

Malky Morrans, the harbour master, grabbed the bottle from the man he knew so well, before he had the chance to take another bountiful swig. 'Bugger me, you've polished off near quarter o' a bottle! I'll be looking for compensation, Superintendent.'

'You people have no decorum. Why my SOCO officers weren't able to remove the lid of this coffin, I'll never understand!'

'Because they've no' got the right equipment, that's how. And I'm no' letting rank amateurs near the tools o' my trade. I've had these since I was an apprentice.' To emphasize his point, MacSporran passed wind magnificently.

'Just do it!' Cowie roared.

'Hey, I'm no' one o' your underlings. Please alter your tone, Superintendent. I'm about to pop the bloody thing presently.'

'Please substitute presently for immediately, Mr MacSporran.'

The joiner removed his bunnet, revealing a bald head as pale as milk. From a canvas tool satchel, he removed a small metal bar, hooked at one end. 'This is a job for the wee jemmy,' he said, as he inserted the hooked end under the coffin lid. He pushed down with both hands, his face turning a ruddy hue with the effort. 'She's a tough one, right enough,' said MacSporran, redoubling his efforts.

'I'm sure,' said Cowie with a raise of his eyes.

There was a crack, a loud snap, and part of the coffin lid was at last released.

'I'll need to go round and do the rest,' said the joiner. He repeated the task five more times and stood back. 'I'll leave your men to do the honours, Superintendent. No idea why they used nails rather than screws.'

The two SOCO officers took their places, one at the head, the other at the foot of the casket.

'Go ahead, men,' said Cowie.

Gently, after a count of three, the coffin lid was removed, and a collective gasp filled the space. Inside was a sealed box, constructed from Perspex, clearly watertight. Within, the body of a man lay, his eyes appearing wide in terror, lips blue, arms folded over a laptop. The box was filled with water, giving it the look of an oversized, hideous snow globe.

'Good grief!' said Cowie, his mouth hanging open with surprise.

'Sir,' said Constable Anderson, his expression one of sad distaste. 'That's DC Duff, from our CID.'

'You mean this man is a police officer?' spluttered Cowie.

'I'm afraid so, sir.'

'Nae wonder she was so heavy,' said MacSporran, placing his bunnet back on his bald head. 'What a horrible thing. I'm glad I had that dram.'

'Mr Morrans.' Cowie turned to the harbour master. 'Did I hear the fishermen say that the location of this coffin meant it would have almost inevitably been washed ashore?'

Morrans scratched his chin. 'It's hard to say, Superintendent. There's nothing inevitable about the sea, and that's a fact. But the air in the coffin would have given it buoyancy, despite the weight o' the thing. Take into consideration the tide, and currents in that part of the sound, and the fact it was in such shallow water, then it's the most likely outcome.'

Cowie looked blankly at the body inside the casket. 'Constable Anderson, get back to the office. Tell DC Duff's colleagues I want his desk searched with a fine-tooth comb. And tell them to use gloves and be quick about it. I'll stay here and discuss with SOCO what must be done.' He looked on as Anderson left the building. 'There are some really sick people in the world, it has to be. A young life destroyed.'

Those remaining gathered round the coffin, staring at the desperate face in the water-filled Perspex box. The eyes of the deceased appeared to follow them round the room in one last cry of desperation.

At Kinloch police office, DC Dianne Cooper had been retained on duty. She was tired after a long nightshift, disturbed by all that was going on. As if what had happened to DCI Daley and his wife wasn't bad enough, the place was awash with strange faces, senior officers and forensic specialists.

Constable Anderson appeared in the CID suite, his face flushed.

'Robbie, what was in the coffin?' said DC MacDonald. 'Buried treasure?' He laughed.

'It's Duff . . . he's dead,' spluttered Anderson, his eyes filling with tears.

'Aye, good one, Robbie. If you fancy acting, you should apply to the Conservatoire in Glasgow.'

In a flash, Anderson, a tall, well-built young man, rushed across the floor and grabbed MacDonald by the collar of his shirt. 'I'm sick of your shit, right! He was a decent guy, clever with it. You weren't there to see what they did to him. Just fuck off!' Anderson pushed MacDonald roughly back into his chair.

'Steady, big man.' MacDonald fixed his collar. 'I thought you were at the wind-up!'

'Is it only you two here?' said Anderson.

'Yes,' said Cooper, her voice small, shock spread across her face.

'Right, you've to go through Duff's desk. Aye, and wear gloves. Cowie wants it done now – and carefully, too.'

'We're on it,' said MacDonald. He was feeling rather sheepish now he'd discovered that Anderson had been serious about the death of a colleague they all knew.

'I'll do it,' said Dianne Cooper. 'I didn't know him that well, but I liked him.'

MacDonald nodded.

Cooper proceeded to go about her business methodically and thoroughly. Truth be told, there wasn't much to be found in the drawers of the unfortunate DC's desk. Cooper unearthed a phone charger, a pair of leather gloves, a book by a crime writer she'd never heard of with an image of a castle on the cover, a set of tiny screwdrivers, an unopened packet of microfibre cloths, a tin of mints, a jotter, a collection of pens and an empty mobile phone case.

'Check the side panels. They could be hollow. He might have made a concealed hiding place,' said MacDonald, who had been looking over his colleague's shoulder throughout.

'Aye, right, Sherlock. I know what I'm doing,' she replied waspishly. She pulled clear of the desk. 'You can check that. It looks fine to me.'

'Not much to show for your life, eh? Few odds and sods,' said MacDonald.

'It's the drawers of his work desk, not his worldly goods, Kenny.' Cooper was so annoyed she dropped the tin of mints, which landed on the carpet with a clatter. The detective had to kneel on the floor and reach under the desk to retrieve it. Something attached to the leg of the desk caught her eye. 'What the fuck?'

'What is it?'

'Hang on, will you?' Dianne Cooper pulled at the tape that was binding the small flash drive to the desk leg. 'Here, look at this,' she said, brandishing it in front of MacDonald.

'It's a flash drive, so what?' MacDonald shrugged.

'Why's it taped to the leg of his desk, you tit?'

'Right enough. I never thought of that.'

'Somebody'll have to search his flat, too.'

'Listen, we'll wait for Cowie. I'm not charging ahead with this, Dianne. Dead copper? This is big time.'

Cooper shook her head. She sat back on her chair and plugged the flash drive into her own desktop.

'What the fuck are you doing?'

'I'm a detective. I'm detecting.' She looked on as the drive booted up on her screen. It was video content. She waited until whatever it was had downloaded on to her machine then pressed *play*.

The now familiar scene in the London alleyway played out before her eyes.

'I can't watch this again,' said MacDonald. 'I still can't believe he did it – Daley, I mean. What a bastard!'

'Give your gums a rest, will you?' Cooper watched the video over again. She closed her eyes as Liz Daley was pushed into the doorway and kicked mercilessly. The whole thing made her feel sick. But as the video ended, and DCI Daley looked up at the camera, something happened. The screen froze; layer by layer of Daley's face peeled off until the man staring at the camera looked completely different.

'That's not the boss,' said MacDonald.

'Take a fucking gold star, Kenny. Get Cowie, now!'

56

Scott sat in front of two inexperienced DCs. The questions were telegraphed, hardly probing, tedious. They centred around his relationship with DC Duff, a relatively new appointee to the CID staff at Kinloch. It appeared that he was missing, with no explanation as to his whereabouts. Someone – likely from Police Scotland, Scott reckoned – thought Scott would know something about it. Who knew, the way things were going with Daley, perhaps they suspected him.

'Is Detective Constable Duff in London, sir?' asked the uninspiring DC. 'Is he helping you in your quest to try and prove Daley innocent?'

'No. Where do you get this stuff? Aye, I've spoken to the lad since I've been doon here. Yes, we've communicated by phone, email and that. But I'm his boss. Is that so unusual?'

'You say *stuff*, DI Scott. 'What is this *stuff*, if you don't mind me asking?' This, from DC Wheelan, a young woman who had cast her male colleague disapproving glances when he'd asked particularly vapid questions.

'Listen, you seem switched on, dear. The *stuff* I mean is messages, you know, texts. I thought you younger folk would be all over this. I hate to tell you, I'm no computer expert but you're welcome to check my phone and laptop. Anything of interest he's sent me, I've told your inspector about.' Scott sat back, his arms folded. This was just a waste of time.

'OK, we'll follow that up with DI Unwin.'

'Aye, you do that.' Scott yawned. 'Listen, son. Any chance o' a mug o' tea? I'm parched.'

The door to the interview room swung open. Jill Unwin entered, her face flushed.

'You pair, give us the room, please.'

Scott watched the young detectives leave. 'Hard tae think I was ever like that.'

'You probably weren't. Young Mandy's got a future, but her pal is bloody useless. He won't last. Recruitment standards slipping across the Met, Brian.'

'Huh, same up the road, don't worry. They're after graduates now. You know, they can instantly calculate the cubic capacity o' a pickle jar but cannae get the lid off.'

'Talking of young detectives, tell me how well you knew this Duff in Kinlock, then?'

Scott smiled at her pronunciation of the town he was surprised to be missing so much. 'New lad, clever – right into tech. That's the future, you know. He fixed my kettle in jig time. In ten years, folk like us won't have to get off oor arses. There'll be drone cops to do the dirty work. Good luck tae them, I say.'

'Duff's dead.'

'What?'

'They found him in a coffin, sealed into a Perspex case filled with water.'

'Eh?' Scott looked incredulous.

'That's it.' Unwin shrugged. 'Poor boy.'

'And you lot think I've got something to do with this? Aye, stroll on.'

'They found this too. Comes from a flash drive they picked up hidden in his desk.' Unwin held out her phone.

Scott squinted at the screen. 'Ach, no' this again. I cannae dae it again. It's sickening.'

'Wait until the end.'

Scott did as he was asked, shifting uncomfortably in his chair as the now familiar footage played out. But his mouth gaped open when he saw layers peel from Daley's face and reveal an altogether different individual. 'He did it!' Scott roared. 'Young Duff did it! I told you he was a tech expert.'

'Paid a heavy price,' said Unwin.

'Aye, he did.' Scott tempered his enthusiasm, before another thought struck him. 'Wait, did you no' tell me that the witness – you know, the one you got killed. Did he no' describe the guy who dumped Liz's body as being o' Slavic appearance? Well, take a close look at that. Bloke looks like Vlad the Impaler.'

'Yes, he did. Pity we lost him.'

'Pity? It's a bit stronger than that, is it no'? Still, you've got his statement.'

'That's true. I'll make sure the comparison is underlined.' Unwin cleared her throat. 'So, back to your boy in Kinlock. Any ideas?'

'The lad was sealed in a Perspex case full of water?'

'Yeah, so it seems.'

'He drowned, I take it?'

'They don't have a PM result yet. But that's what's being said, yeah. Looks like drowning.'

'It's simple then.'

'It is?'

'Our man died trapped in his car on the day Jimmy and that Lambie weirdo were chasing him. It's too much of a coincidence.'

'Thought his car blew up?'

'It did. But he drowned first, I'm sure. Find anyone close to him and we have it! It's never been about Lambie.'

'That simple, eh?'

'Aye, why not? We've been obsessed with Lambie, and somebody wanting to punish Jimmy for what happened to him – what he went through after the incident. It's all been a diversion. We should have been looking at the BMW driver all along. Or is that just stupid?'

Jill Unwin's phone buzzed with a message.

'What's up?'

'You've to go back home on the first available flight, pal.'

'You being serious? Jimmy's still fuck knows where. I want him found before I go back home.'

'You've no choice.'

'OK. I resign. They can't tell me to do anything.' Scott jutted out his chin.

'You're a suspect, Brian. They want to talk to you.'

'They think I sealed poor Duff in a box and drowned him, while all the time I've been here. Aye, that's a good trick.'

'Let's be honest, mate. Somebody wants you out of the way. Either down here or up there, I don't know. But I have my orders. You're to be taken to the hotel to get your things, and then it's Heathrow.' She shrugged. 'Nothing I can do, Brian. I'm sorry.'

Scott flung his head back in the chair to contemplate the ceiling. Poor Duff. He knew that he was in part to blame for his death. Another ghost to follow him about. His gaze returned to Unwin. 'I've had enough of it all, you know. All the cruelty, death. I'm finished with this shit. But promise me you'll find Jimmy. There's enough to clear him now, surely?'

'Might be, I dunno. I'm not all over this the way I'd like to be. I'll do my best, mate. We've got to find him first.'

'That'll do me, Jill. Find my buddy, please. See whoever did this to Lizzie gets it, right?'

Unwin's phone buzzed again. Her expression darkened. 'I'll need to get this. The lads who'll take you back to the hotel are outside. See you later, mate. It's been a pleasure. Take care.' She put the phone to her ear, answered the call and hurried out of the room.

All Scott could do now was follow her. With Jim Daley who knew where, at least things looked brighter for him legally. It was only then that the fear of what might be happening to his old friend dawned on him. He pictured Daley's dead eyes staring from a plastic box full of water.

'Shit!' he whispered to himself.

Unwin listened carefully as details were passed on to her. 'Right, got it. Ping me the satnav details, will you?' She ended the call and hurried to her office. As she walked, she dialled. 'They have him. Safe house in Kent.' Unwin listened intently. 'I know how delicate it is, believe me. I'll take a few lads from here I can trust. The last thing I want is the Tactical Firearms Unit all over this. It'll just make things more difficult for us, won't it.' She listened again. 'Right, consider it done. I'll update you as we go.'

Jill Unwin had just made the biggest call of her life. She had no choice now other than to go through with it. She clicked on a video she'd been sent on her phone. The image was sharp for CCTV, a couple arguing on a London street. The woman was wagging her finger in the man's face. She pushed him, turned on her heel and stormed off.

'Sorry, Jim Daley,' Unwin muttered to herself as she deleted the video.

57

Scott gazed from the police car as they meandered through the London traffic. He tried to imagine himself having to cope with this endless stream of humanity every day of his life, and simply couldn't.

'I'll be away back on tomorrow's flight at this rate, lads,' he said to the police officers in the front seats.

'Just the way it is, mate. You get used to it. We'll be there in plenty of time, don't worry,' said the driver. He hit the car's horn and made a gesture of bewilderment to a pedestrian who'd just walked out in front of them. 'Like lemmings, these bastards.' He and his colleague laughed heartily, though Scott's thoughts returned to Duff's demise. How many young men and women he'd seen dead before they'd really begun life, he couldn't say. Too many, was the inevitable answer.

Eventually, they made it to his hotel.

'Big spenders, your Police Scotland, eh? I wouldn't put me worst enemy in a place like this. What's wrong with a Travelodge, then?' said the police officer in the passenger seat.

'I paid for it myself,' said Scott.

'Tightarse,' his interlocutor replied.

'What's the score here?' Scott asked.

'We go in, you pack your bags, then we get to Heathrow. Simples, mate.'

They made their way up the front steps and into the hotel lobby. Waiting for them was Suraj, smiling from ear to ear.

'Good morning, good morning, officers. How nice it is to have the constabulary in my humble premises, oh yes.'

'What's that smell?' said the driver.

'I've been cooking. A lamb methi gosht, a favourite of my guests. I learned to cook it at my mother's knee. The best in London. You are welcome to some if you'd wish. It's always a pleasure to help police. My honour. The spinach keeps you healthy!'

'Can we trust you to go up there and pack your bags, sir?' The driver was clearly spokesman for Scott's police minders.

'I think I can manage to get packed by myself. It's been a while, mind you.' Though Scott said this with great confidence, he was a relative stranger to packing, Ella having done the job for so long.

'No! Surely you don't leave us so soon, Scotland?' said Suraj.

'Aye, that's me off. I'll come back wae my wife and see you next time, wee man.' Scott had taken to the fearless little hotelier. No, it wasn't the Ritz but who cared?

'Gentlemen.' Suraj turned to the uniformed policemen. 'Please, take a seat in the dining room. I will have your curries damned quick, and no mistake.'

Scott looked on as Suraj ushered his minders away. He took the stairs to his room, opened the door and began the process of packing. He was just about to place his dirty washing in a plastic bag – a trick Ella had shown him – when there was a gentle tap at the door.

'Who is it?' Scott shouted.

'It is me, Suraj,' came the reply in a loud whisper.

'The door's open, pal.'

The diminutive figure of the hotelier appeared in the room. He looked about, a furtive expression on his face. 'I have a message for you, Scotland.'

'Who fae?'

'From Eddie, of course. He needs you to join him. Yes, very quickly indeed.'

'Join him? Does he think I'm stupid?'

'He says to tell you that, at this very moment, there are people trying to kill your friend. Oh yes, tragedy indeed.'

'Listen, Suraj. He's the one who's in the wrong. Bad man, get it?'

'No, no.' He pulled a very old mobile phone from his pocket. 'Message, you listen.' He handed the phone to Scott, just in time for him to hear Beattie's familiar tones.

'*Brian, you need to listen. I don't know what you've been told, old pal. I have Jimmy here. He's sore but safe. You can't trust anyone, got it? We heard about the DC up in Kinloch. My people are here to keep the big man safe. Here, talk to your man.*'

Scott heard the phone being handed over, some mumbling in the background.

'*Brian, it's me. You need to do what Eddie says. No, I'm not under duress. But they're after me. We know about Duff and his footage. Poor guy. Suraj knows what to do.*'

The message ended as quickly as it had begun, leaving Scott in a quandary of indecision.

'You must listen to them, Scotland. It's the only way to save your friend. Eddie is a good man. You know this.'

Brian Scott chewed his lip. 'OK, say he is in the right. I've two big cops downstairs. How will I get to Eddie? For a start, I've no idea where he is!'

Suraj walked over to the sash window. After a push or two, accompanied by a grunt and some words Scott didn't understand, the window opened with a squeal.

'The fucking painters I hire do a crap job. Paint windows shut. I have to go round each one with a knife. Arseholes!'

'You expect me to go out there on the roof?'

'Very easy. I have done this many times myself. Out on to the roof, walk to where that chimney is. Beside it is a fire-escape ladder. It take you down to back of hotel. You go to main road. One of Eddie's men waiting for you in a Nissan SUV.' Suraj smiled, happy that he'd passed on Eddie's instructions to the letter. 'The other police, they eat curry. Happy men.'

Scott peered through the opened window. The roof was gently peaked, slates with a lead flashing ridgeline. 'Is it safe?'

'What you mean, Scotland?'

'I mean, will I fall through the bloody thing? It's no' as though this is the best-maintained building in the city, is it?'

Suraj looked downcast. 'I don't know how you can say this. My hotel could last through earthquake.'

These words were no sooner out of his mouth than the sash window fell shut with a clatter.

'This is minor problem only.' With another grunt or two, Suraj forced the window open again.

Scott grimaced. 'I better be doing the right thing here.' He pulled the chair under the window, stepped on it and ducked out on to the roof.

'No, you must take this. Eddie says you must.' From the waistband of his trousers, Suraj produced a pistol, dark, sleek and recently oiled, by the look of it. 'These too.' From the pocket of his joggers, he handed Scott two replacement clips.

'I'm no' keen on guns, Suraj. I've been shot twice, you know.'

'Then this is not problem. Just don't shoot yourself – easy!' He looked up at Scott through the open window. 'You go now. I say you must have shower. I bring you new towels, as excuse. I will give them second helpings. Police never turn down second helpings.' He shooed Scott away with both hands. 'Quickly! And remember, ladder beside chimney. You go!'

Scott turned to look at his route to the chimney. He jumped when Suraj slammed the sash window shut behind him. When he looked back, the little man was gone.

Carefully, Brian Scott began his passage towards the chimney at the gable end of the roof. He wasn't keen on heights but had learned through the process of tough experience never to look down. He'd the pistol and the spare clips in the inside pocket of his jacket, which made him uneasy.

Scott was in the middle of his journey when, without warning, a loose slate slipped from under his foot. He was off balance, one leg outstretched down one side of the roof, the other holding him upright across the ridgeline. For a sickening moment, his body teetered, Scott fearing he'd lost his balance completely. He readied himself for the fall, aware he'd have to try to catch something, anything, to arrest his descent. Miraculously, though, he regained his equilibrium and was able to carry on his walk to the chimney.

Scott spotted the ladder and then the drop. 'Fuck this,' he said to himself. 'I'd be better on a boat.' He gazed across his horizon, grey rooftops, towering buildings, the rabble of the city sounding all around. He heard the distinctive wail of a police siren, then plucked up the courage to man-oeuvre himself on to the ladder.

Scott reached down tentatively with one leg. When he felt his foot on a rung, he swung his body out and over. The sensation was troubling. Momentarily, it felt as though he was floating in mid-air, untethered, without support. Soon, though, he gained the ladder properly and carefully took one downward step at a time. While the ladder itself seemed sound enough, rust had taken deep bites from its frame. Regardless, he carried on.

By the time he reached the bottom, the relief of having just one foot on solid ground was more than welcome. Scott composed himself for a second, then made for the main road to his right. He stopped and looked both ways. Across the road sat a blue Nissan SUV. Its lights flashed.

Watchfully, he waited for the short window of time between traffic-light changes and hurried across the road.

'You going my way, son?' Scott said to the driver.

'Looks like it, boss. Jump in. I'm Samuels.'

Yet again, Scott was looking from a car window at the serried ranks of London's traffic, as it moved at a snail's pace.

'Where now, buddy?' he asked his new driver.

'Ever been to Kent?'

'No' that I can remember.'

'Well, now's your lucky day, mate.'

The lights changed to green, and they moved slowly off again through the traffic.

Samuels handed him an envelope as they stopped at another set of lights. 'You know this guy?'

Scott removed a black-and-white photograph. His jaw dropped. 'Aye, son, I know who that is.'

'The boss said to tell you that his old man was driving the Beamer. Does that make sense to you?'

Scott nodded sadly. 'Aye, it certainly does, pal.'

58

Jim Daley noticed that both Beattie and Tipton suddenly looked tense. Beattie was busy sending messages on his phone, cursing when he pressed the wrong character, while Tipton had his hoodie up over his head and was biting his nails, frequently checking the view from the lounge window.

'Shit! They have us,' said Beattie.

'Who do?' Daley asked.

'The so-called *good* guys.'

'Who's coming then?' said Tipton.

'Luckily, it's Unwin. We've won a watch there, at least.'

'Not the TFU, that's good from everyone's point of view, trust me!' said Tipton.

'He's right,' said Beattie, peering through the net curtains. 'We'll see them coming, at least. That driveway must be half a mile long.'

'Unless they come over the fields, boss,' said Tipton.

'Nah, too many fences. There's a coppice of trees that runs behind us. I didn't choose this place because it looked pretty, you know.'

Daley had been given a vial of liquid morphine, strong enough to ease his pain and make him drowsy, but not enough to send him to sleep. 'What next then?'

'We wait. At least I can talk to Jill. If not, we have a plan B.'

'Which is?'

'Let's see how plan A goes first, yes?'

'At least tell me what the current plan is.' Daley felt a twinge of pain from his broken ribs and winced accordingly.

'Unwin's a good cop, sound, old-fashioned – like us.'

'OK, keep talking.'

'We know that your lad up in Kintyre bought it. Clearly, neither you nor Brian caused that. He also managed to change the footage back to the original. Yes, they'll argue about it, but I'm told it would be too difficult to fake – changing back to the original, like that. The poor copper has done you proud, Jim.'

'Engelbert,' said Daley absently.

'Sorry?'

'It's what Brian called him.'

'You mean the same Brian that's been on the wrong side?'

'The very one.'

'He's on his way with one of my guys.' Beattie knelt in front of Daley. 'The main thing for us to do is keep it straight. Sure, we spirited you away from the hospital, Jimmy. But with evidence turning things in your favour, I hope they'll overlook that. You're an innocent man, after all.'

'With no wife.' Daley's voice was flat.

'You still have a son. Keep that to the forefront of your thoughts.'

'Sir, movement on the drive,' said Tipton.

Beattie got back to his feet and walked to the window. 'Two squad cars and two SUVs. Jill's not come empty handed, after all.'

'But not the TFU,' said Tipton.

'Who knows? Could be the Bulgarian Army in those Range Rovers, for all we know.'

'They've stopped, boss.'

'So I see. Wonder why . . .' The small convoy had stopped about halfway down the drive. 'What do you think, Tipton?'

'Loading up?'

'Are you serious?' Daley asked.

'Standard procedure down here, Jim. Never travel tooled up unless you're on protection.'

'You're surely not expecting a shoot-out, Eddie?'

'If it was the TFU, we would be,' said Tipton.

Beattie's phone buzzed in his hand. 'Hello?' He clicked the call on to loudspeaker.

'It's Jill, Eddie. You know the score, give Daley up.'

'I want assurances. This new evidence is there for all to see, Jill. The lad killed in Kinloch – one of our own – proved that beyond doubt. Not to mention your dead witness statement.'

'Statement?'

Beattie looked puzzled. 'The street guy. Don't mess about, Jill. He's gone but his words live on, right?'

'I don't know anything about that, sir.'

'What the actual fuck are you on about, Jill?'

Unwin's voice gained an urgent edge. 'You need to hand over Daley *now*, Eddie. They're not messing about, trust me.'

'You're OIC, right?'

'Give him up, sir. Really, I mean it.'

'Bit melodramatic, Jill. After all, I'm still your superior. We can stop a miscarriage of justice here. You know that, yes?'

'Do as I say, *sir*.' To those assembled in the safe house, it sounded as though Jill Unwin was speaking through grit-ted teeth.

'Fuck off! You come in and we can talk.' He listened for a reply that didn't come. 'Jill, you there?' Beattie dashed back to the window. 'What's this now?'

As he looked on, the two marked cars to the rear of the convoy on the drive, one after the other, began to reverse. 'What the fuck is this?' Beattie squinted at his mobile and dialled Jill Unwin's number, again placing the call on loudspeaker.

'*The number you have dialled is busy. Please leave a mes-sage or send a text.*'

Still, the police cars reversed back up the drive, soon out of sight of the safe house. Ominously, the SUVs pulled slowly forward, their blacked-out windows making them seem even more threatening.

'What is going on?' Beattie turned to Tipton.

Daley didn't know if it was the morphine dulling his brain, making him slow. Quickly, though, he realized what was about to happen. 'No!' he called at full volume.

Tipton pulled a pistol out from the waistband of his jacket, and at close range all but blew Eddie Beattie's head off, sending the rest of his body flying backwards and hit-ting the wall.

'Goodbye, sir,' said Tipton, entirely unaffected by his murderous actions.

'You bastard!' Daley swore at the top of his voice, while trying desperately to force his way off the sofa.

Tipton kicked him back, making the injured man yelp.

'Why? I don't understand,' said Daley, his voice wheez-ing in his throat.

'Because, that's why. It's what my old mum would say to us when we was kids. That was her standard answer when we wanted something we couldn't get. It's the same principle here.' He walked over to the windowsill and recovered a small, black leather bag, no bigger than a purse.

Again, Daley tried to get up to his feet but it was hopeless. Tipton just kicked him back again, this time with greater force.

'Time for you to nod off for a while again, Jimbo.' He produced a syringe from the leather bag; its needle flashed in the sunlight flooding into the room. He swung at Daley, sending the needle deep into the Kinloch man's upper arm.

Jim Daley wanted to shout, to hit back. But in seconds, he felt an overwhelming tiredness overtake him. He fell back on the sofa, eyes too heavy to keep open. In the few seconds it took for him to slip into unconsciousness, his brain registered new voices in the room. Only one of them was familiar.

59

'How long?' Brian Scott was anxious to get where he was going. The Kent countryside seemed to go on for ever, with its green hedgerows, fields and villages repeating themselves over and over. 'By the way, is that Taylor Swift you've got on?'

'Yeah, it is. Great, isn't she?'

'Nah, it's a racket. Give me Willie Nelson any time.'

'Who?'

'Never mind.' Scott folded his arms. 'How long until we get there?'

'Another ten minutes, mate.' The driver kept his eyes on the winding road in front of him.

'Can you no' go a bit faster?'

'I'm hitting seventy. We are police officers, remember?'

'Aye, in hot pursuit, no' just wandering aboot at oor leisure. My mate's up here somewhere. I want him back in one piece – well, sort of.' Scott recalled Daley's battered body.

Suddenly, the driver leaned forward in his seat and squinted through the windshield. 'Pull down your visor, now!'

'Eh?'

'Just do it!'

The command was so firm that Scott didn't object further and quickly did what he was told.

Two marked police cars passed by at speed, their occupants looking straight ahead, unconcerned by the Nissan SUV.

'Why the cloak and dagger, son?' said Scott.

'River motors, both of them. Jill Unwin was in the passenger seat of the first.'

'Aren't they going the wrong way?' Scott looked mystified.

'I need to call the boss.' The driver hit the screen of his phone, suspended on the dashboard in a plastic holder. It rang out, eventually ending on the answer machine. 'I'll try again,' he said. The same thing happened.

'Nae luck?'

'It's worse than that.' Without warning, the driver swerved up a farm road. He pulled the car to a halt on a tiny passing place. He dialled a number. 'Frances, do you have the boss's other mobile number? He must have run out of battery.'

'We can't get either of them.' The woman's voice was clear and concise.

'Not even Tipton?'

'That's a negative.'

'What should I do? I've got the passenger, as arranged.'

'There is backup, but they're as much as an hour out, at least.'

'Suggestions?'

'Be more helpful,' said Scott, unable to resist.

'Get to the farm but don't use the drive. We might have been compromised.'

'Just brilliant,' said Scott.

'Compromised by whom?' said Samuels.

'If I knew that, I'd have told you. Just observe for the

moment. And don't get caught. If you find out all is well, you call me immediately, right?'

'What will I do if it's turned to shit?'

'Keep it to yourself.'

Samuels ended the call.

'Fuck me, you have some right officious radio operators, cheeky bastards. I'd just be letting her know where to stick it,' said Scott.

'She's a superintendent.'

'And you're calling her Frances? Different world down here, right enough.'

'We're not like other groups. It's a job within a job. We're not just here to catch the bad guys. It's all about stopping them before they get the chance to carry through what they're up to. Prevention is better than cure.'

'Right, like saving Jimmy from a good kicking? You're doing a grand job at the prevention.'

'Listen, your friend was unlucky. We'd been on DI Bright's tail for over a year.' Samuels started the engine and pulled off.

'Now you're going to his funeral. So, who killed him?'

'The one night he managed to give our obs team the slip.'

'Unlucky for him.'

'Beattie, he runs a tight ship, you know. He's a friend of yours, right? You talk like him, no holds barred, and all that.'

'We were boys together.' Scott gazed from the window again. 'I just hope he's no' in bother. This whole thing has been like your worst nightmare.'

They drove on for about a mile on a road that was little more than a lane, stopping only once to let a muddy blue tractor pass. Once they reached a patch of trees, Samuels pulled up on the verge. 'You ready? It's cross-country from here.'

'Aye, and me wae my good brogues on, tae. Thirty quid in Primark.'

Scott followed the younger man out of the car and across a fence. Soon, they were on a narrow path between trees. Birds sang and insects buzzed all around. Scott saw the flash of a bobbing white tail as a rabbit scurried through the tall grass under the dappling leaves of trees. Despite his apparent nonchalance, his heart thudded in his chest. Ever since things had gone awry for the Daleys in London, it had seemed like a procession of false dawns. Just when he'd thought they were getting somewhere, another problem knocked them back. He wondered why Unwin was heading in the opposite direction to where Daley was located. A thought crossed his mind. 'Jill Unwin, you know her, aye?'

'Yeah, old-fashioned copper. Straight as a die but no grass, I'd say. She's part of the problem, I suppose.'

'Problem, how?'

'You know the type of thing. She knows something's up but doesn't want anything to do with it. That's the way it was when she joined. See all, say fuck all, when it comes to corruption.'

Scott trudged on. He looked back on his own service. All too often, he'd known about some bad apples and stayed quiet. It was the way things were – it was the job. One big family you accepted, good or bad. It was where he and Daley differed. The big man had no blind eye to turn; he faced everything head on. It had made Daley unpopular in some quarters; he had collected enemies by the dozen.

'Right, here we are,' said Samuels. They'd reached the treeline. Ahead was a well-appointed farmhouse and some outbuildings beyond. Honey-coloured stone almost shone in the reflected sunshine. The roof was terracotta, lending the place an almost Mediterranean aspect. It was a warm day. A heat haze shimmered over the cornfield that lay between the trees and the dwelling. High above, a bird of prey – Scott was unsure exactly what it was – circled in the sun, only to dive into the tall stalks then soar back into the sky in one swift motion, a struggling rodent held fast in its talons.

For a moment, Scott knew the panic the tiny creature must be feeling. Was he waiting for some horror to swoop down and carry him off?

Samuels' phone buzzed.

'Yeah, I'm here. No sign of anything. Nothing moving at all, in fact.' He produced a tiny pair of binoculars from his pocket. 'I can see right into the lounge. Nobody visible, no movement. What do you want me to do?'

Samuels listened intently before pocketing the mobile and the binoculars. 'I've to take a closer look, see what's happening.'

'I'm no' standing here in the trees like Richard Attenborough, by the way,' said Scott.

'David.'

'No, Brian. You must have a memory like a sieve, son.'

'No! It's *David* Attenborough.'

Scott screwed up his face. 'Who's fucking bothered!? It could be Gemma Attenborough, for all I care!'

'You want to come with?'

'Sorry?'

'*Come with*, as in come with me.'

'Is that the fashion now, no' finishing your sentences? Well, here's one for you. Get yourself tae—'

'OK, I get it, point taken. I'm carrying, by the way. We should be OK. But stay low and don't make a noise.'

'Listen, son, my first rodeo was long before you were

born. Come on!' Scott was first to slope into the cornfield, Samuels behind him. He'd decided to keep the fact he too was armed secret, just in case. It was clearly hard to tell friend from foe in this world, and the Scottish detective wanted a modicum of insurance, at least.

They huddled on.

60

The cornfield ended at a fence, on the other side of which was a neatly mown lawn surrounded by tall trees. Samuels signalled that they stop. Again, he produced the tiny binoculars.

'Nothing,' he whispered.

'Could be upstairs having a kip. Did that no' cross your mind?'

'No, staying in the lounge was pivotal to the plan. We've got recording equipment in there. If anyone from the Met was to arrive, all Beattie had to do was click an app on his phone. Instant evidence, mate.'

'Hold on. Are you telling me you were using Jimmy as a lure, bait for some of the oddballs the Met chose to give a uniform?'

'No. But we take an opportunity if it presents itself.' He shrugged.

'There you are then. That's your *opportunity* buggered. What now?'

'I want to listen for a bit. We'll be exposed on the grass.'

'Don't worry, I've exposed myself more times than I care to mention.'

'I bet. Right, let's go!'

It was quickly over the small fence and a dash across the

ten or so yards of garden. Both men crouched below the lounge window. Scott, unable to resist, was first to put his head above the parapet. He shaded his eyes as he stared through the double-glazing.

'Fuck, let's get in there!' Scott was off, Samuels trailing behind. He rushed to the front door of the building he'd seen from the trees. It was open. Scott ran through.

It took him a moment or two to orient himself with the layout of the place but he was soon in the lounge, where Daley and his so-called rescuers were supposed to be.

'Fuck no!' he shouted, spotting the blood spatter across the back windows, curtains and part of the wall. As he edged closer, he could smell fresh cordite in the air.

Scott's breath stopped in his throat when he saw the body slumped in the corner. Blood had pooled underneath it; hair, scalp and brain matter slathered across one wall.

'Is it Daley?' called Samuels.

'No, son, it isn't.'

Scott knelt over Eddie Beattie's corpse. One blue eye stared out of the ruined head, a large part of which was missing, spread round the room in a ghastly display of brutality. 'Fuck's sake, old pal. We never knew it would end like this when we were winching lassies doon at the youth club, eh?'

Samuels had drawn his weapon. He hushed Scott. 'We'll have to do this room by room. It's going to be tough with only one firearm.'

Scott produced the pistol given to him by Suraj, via the man now lying dead beside them. 'It came fae Eddie, so don't worry.'

'Bit late for worrying, I think.'

The police officers crept from the lounge, using only silent signals to intimate their intentions. The search was on.

61

Even though Jim Daley had regained consciousness, his eyelids were so heavy he kept them shut. As his senses gradually returned, he realized that it was likely a pungent smell that had helped him come to.

Still forcing himself awake, he tried to move his arm in order to scratch his nose. Nothing happened. His eyes shot open, taking in his situation. He was bound tight to the chair, and appeared to be perched above a mouldering, stinking mass of brown, mottled liquid. For a few seconds, Daley couldn't fathom what was going on. He cried out.

'I know you're a city boy, Daley. So, you might not be fully aware of what you're looking at.'

Everything came flooding back. He played out the moment Eddie Beattie was shot at point-blank range, his face blown off in an instant. He felt the sharp prick of the needle. He remembered the voice he'd heard before blacking out. 'It's a slurry pit, sir.'

'Sir? My goodness, your attention to etiquette does you credit, Daley.' ACC Sam Jordan walked towards the slurry tank, just within Daley's eyeline. His dark hair and piercing blue eyes were familiar, but his expression wasn't.

'I can think up many more names if you like, you murdering cunt!' Daley's teeth were clenched, every muscle tensed. Here was the man who'd killed Liz, ordered it, at least.

'Careful, my men aren't used to such bad language. Are you, lads?'

Daley listened as voices called out a muffled, unenthusiastic reply. Daley counted four of them.

'I do hope you're comfortable, Jim.' Jordan smiled up at the bound man. 'Do you know, I think the anticipation of something truly terrible happening is almost worse than the reality.' He turned to gaze at the slurry tank for a few moments. 'Though, in this case, maybe not.'

'Don't worry, you killed me the night you murdered Liz.' Daley spat out the sentence.

'Oh, not quite. Though I did rather enjoy that. Certainly, after the years of misery I've suffered at your saintly hand. Do you have any idea how sickening it is looking on as the *man who wouldn't bend*, the incorruptible James Daley, carries on the fight against the forces of darkness?'

'Better than being part of it!'

'That's where you're mistaken. I've never committed a crime in my entire life. Well, not until I took the life of your airhead wife, that is.'

'You helped Gordon Lambie to escape, remember?'

'Oh yes, poor Gordon. One of life's unfortunates. I had high hopes for him. He blamed you for the way his life spiralled downwards, you know. Ultimately, I knew he'd never be able to carry it through. Too weak, you see; rather cut his own throat in a grand gesture than get his revenge on the man who'd taken his family, his liberty, his respect. Odd, isn't it? But I wanted the pleasure of looking on as you suffered.'

'I was doing my job.'

'Good grief, *doing your job* seems to consist of a high

number of dead bodies, Jim. But I'm sure you console yourself with the misguided notion that you're a force for good, defender of justice.' Jordan walked towards Daley. 'Killing someone, taking their life, is not your prerogative, no matter how much you'd like it to be.'

'But it's OK for you. She was my wife!' Daley's voice echoed round the large open space so much that two pigeons flew from the barn's rafters.

'You've worked it all out, I take it.'

'You're his son. The dealer who was killing off kids all over Glasgow with the shit he was selling them to shoot up their arms. He was a murderer, or have you neatly forgotten that?'

Jordan's only reaction to this was the narrowing of his eyes.

'I was eleven when my father died at your hands. My mother had buggered off years before. I barely remember her. But he looked after me as though I was a prince. He took me to football, on holiday, we walked all over the mountains, we camped, we laughed. You killed that – all of it! I ended up in a home for a year before I was adopted. All down to you!'

'Your father dealt in death, every day. Ask the parents of all the kids he killed for money.' A relative calm had come over Daley now. His only regret was leaving his son. Though, as he had no means of escape, he comforted himself in the knowledge that Brian and Ella would look after the boy, probably better than he could by himself.

'My father owed bad people money. In exchange for wiping the debt, saving his own life, he ran their business for them. Those who died were junkies, nothing more. Who cared?'

'I did, their families did. That was enough!'

Jordan snorted his derision. 'My father died in the Clyde. It wasn't like it is now. It was a cesspool. So, like him, you'll find out exactly how it feels.' Jordan was directly underneath Daley now, looking up at him, his eyes pitiless. 'I understand that you're not as flexible as you'd like. Here's my set-up. Not bad at short notice, I think.' He held up his mobile for Daley to see.

The image had been taken when Daley was still unconscious. He saw that he was tied to a chair on a wooden platform, supported at one end by a forklift. At the other end, the rancid slurry pit showed many shades of brown, making his eyes sting. His fate was obvious. Daley realized that Liz had been killed to make him suffer. The attack on their home, her brutal death, his incarceration, all part of a plan designed to torture and torment him before he too died.

'Do your worst, you prick.'

'I fully intend to enjoy every minute.'

Daley watched Jordan disappear from sight. Then he heard the thud of a diesel engine firing up. The engine of the forklift that would tip him to his end.

62

Scott and Samuels were upstairs in the farmhouse now. It was clear the place had been abandoned for some time. In the bedrooms, sheets were damp, mildew crept up the walls and it smelled dank, unlived in.

When they checked the last room, they were satisfied that whoever had killed Beattie was gone. Samuels phoned in the findings.

Distantly, Scott heard a noise, the roar of an engine. He walked to the window and cracked it open. 'Do you hear that?'

Samuels ended his call and joined him.

'Coming from that barn, mate.'

Scott stared at the outbuilding for a moment.

'I'll call it in. Stand back from the window. Our support team should be here shortly.'

Scott bit his lip. 'Nae chance!' He took off out of the room, pistol in one hand.

'Brian, Inspector Scott! We have to wait!' Samuels heard Scott bounding down the stairs. 'Oh, shit!' He ran after him, cursing the Scotsman.

Daley felt a strange sense of calm wash over him. He was at the end of a wooden ramp, from which he'd soon be tipped into a putrid tank of slurry. He calculated that his passage to death would be a short but unpleasant one. Judging by his streaming eyes and difficulty breathing, though, this interval should be a brief one.

Liz was gone. His thoughts returned to it constantly. Life was over; he didn't care.

Jordan appeared again underneath him, Tipton at his side.

'We don't want the great detective's end to pass unmarked, do we?' said Jordan with a grin. 'I hope you die with more dignity than your wife.'

'You're as bad as him, Tipton. A murderer. You happy with that?'

'Piss off, you wanker. I know all about you, and it's not pretty.'

Daley looked on as a tripod was set up, ready to film his immersion into the slurry. 'You're a sick bastard, Jordan. Just get on with it!'

'I intend to. You know, my foster mother told me how he died over and over again. It was a punishment I had to suffer. I hated her, but that was my home at the time.' He had to shout, such was the noise made by the idling putter of the forklift.

Then Daley heard other sounds. A yell, the sharp crack of a gunshot. He tried to turn in his chair but pain, and the fact his chair almost tipped over, stopped him. He recognized a familiar voice in the din, though.

'There you are, you bastard!'

It was Brian Scott. He'd spotted ACC Jordan.

Scott walked in on the oddest sight he'd ever seen. Daley tied to a chair on top of a length of wood, a forklift ready to tip him over into a tank, from which emanated the foulest of stenches. He ducked instinctively, as the passage of a bullet swept not far from his face.

To his side sat a rusting plough. He dived behind it, shocked when someone scurried in beside him.

'What the actual fuck, Brian?' shouted Samuels.

'You need to cover me while I disable the forklift!'

Another bullet rebounded from a ploughshare with a spark of metal on metal. Men – four of them, Scott counted – came crouching towards them. Scott picked out a space and fired two rapid shots, making them scatter for cover.

'I'm going for it now, Samuels! I'll count to three, OK?'

'No, you'll never make it. They can hit you from too many angles!'

'Just fire about a bit. They'll never know where the shots are aimed. Are you ready?'

'OK. You are one mad bastard!'

'It's been said, son. One, two, three!' Scott broke from his cover. Samuels stood and aimed shot after shot roughly at the places he'd seen their adversaries hide.

Scott sprinted across the floor of the barn. He rolled behind a stack of plastic boxes, neatly avoiding another bullet that squealed overhead. From the corner of his eye, he saw someone moving but not in his direction. He had to take cover again, as Samuels exchanged fire with Jordan's accomplices.

'Fuck you, Jim Daley!'

Scott heard these words as, from his covered position, he saw feet running towards the forklift. Brian Scott took two deep breaths and stood, making himself a target for all those he opposed, and with his pistol gripped firmly between both hands, he closed one eye, took aim and fired. He heard a scream and threw himself to the ground, just in time to see a man fall to the floor.

All was silent now, apart from the thudding of the diesel engine. But Scott heard another noise, like an electric window of a car being wound up, from this distance. He slithered across the dirty floor like a snake. When he looked up, to his horror, the forks were pushing up towards the wooden board upon which Daley was perched.

More yelling and gunfire. It was now or never. Scott took another deep breath and bolted from behind the boxes. The arms of the forklift were now directly under the wooden platform. He vaulted over Jordan, who was struggling on the ground, his blood seeping into filthy straw.

The forks were almost engaged with the platform now.

Scott stumbled into the forklift's cab just as there was a crash. He looked to his right to see a black SUV force its way through one wall. Men in dark steel helmets and black suits, carrying automatic weapons, jumped out of the vehicle. More followed, fanning out into the barn. The acrid stench of cordite filled the air, along with the sounds of gunfire, screams, yells, shots, cries, chaos.

Scott looked at the levers desperately, as the ramp before him began to rise. His eye alighted on the ignition button, red on the muddy dashboard. He pressed it hard with one finger and felt the machine shudder to a silent stop.

Scott looked up in horror. To his relief, Daley was still on his chair at the end of the ramp. He made to dash out of the cab, but something caught his ankle. Jordan snarled up at him, his eyes mad, staring, blood slathered across his face. Scott picked up the pistol at his side, and with one neat shot, hit the twisted senior officer in the forehead. He looked on as Jordan fell back on to the straw-strewn floor then lay motionless. 'That's for Liz and Eddie, you prick!' said Scott through gritted teeth.

'Help!' Brian Scott shouted as he jumped from the cabin.

Two Tactical Firearms officers joined him. He looked up at Daley. The barn was quieter now, chaos subsiding as the TFU took control.

'You OK, sir?' said one of the helmeted officers. 'We had your description, so we knew not to hit you.'

'Fuck, that's good.' Scott looked up. 'You OK, Jimmy? Close thing, eh?'

When he turned there was no sign of his friend. The wooden board had tipped him into the slurry pit.

'Bastard!' Scott called out in panic.

The two Tactical officers were on it in seconds. They leapt on to the side of the tank, just as the chair legs were disappearing under slurry. Together, they pulled chair and man out of the pit. Soon, joined by colleagues, they dragged the stricken man away from the tank.

They untied Daley and laid him out on the floor of the barn. He was still, his chest not moving.

'No way!' Brian Scott slapped his old friend in the face, as another officer wiped the slurry from his nose and mouth. Scott looked round those gathered beside Daley. 'Someone's going to have to try CPR. Fuck it, I'll do it!'

Scott gripped Daley's mouth with one hand, puckering his lips. He bent forward, ready to administer the kiss of life.

Daley's body twitched, his eyes opened, their whites in contrast to his filthy face. 'Don't you think I've been through enough, Brian? Piss off!' He wheezed then coughed up putrid slurry.

63

Brian Scott paced about the CID suite in Kinloch. Jordan's guilt, despite his death, had been acknowledged by the Met in London. It was now official.

Alistair Shaw joined him. Today, he had ditched his uniform in favour of a sombre dark suit, white shirt and black tie, making him almost identical to Scott. *Almost*, in that Scott was trying to find the black tie he was sure he'd brought with him earlier that day.

'Hold on, Al,' he said as he dialled Ella.

'Before you say anything, I've got your tie here. You left it on the kitchen counter,' said Ella without preamble.

'Eh! How did you no' phone me and let me know?'

'*I do everything for a reason*, is what you said, I believe. Who am I to try and ponder the workings of such a great mind?'

'Aye, right. When you coming down?'

'Ten minutes or so. Any sign o' Jimmy?'

'He phoned. He's getting to the church under his own steam.'

'What about the wee man?'

'Maybe wae his granny? I don't know.'

'Thought she wisnae gracing us wae her presence?'

'Changed her mind when the solicitor produced the will. She wanted to be buried here, Ella. Simple as that.'

'It'll be hard, Brian. I'll see you in a wee while.'

Scott ended the call and turned his attention to Shaw. 'What's up, Al?'

'New orders for next week, gaffer.' He handed Scott a printed email.

'He's back next week. Decided not to go up the road for the new job.'

'Did you know?'

'Nope. I've hardly seen him since we came back three months ago. Ella went up, but it was all one-word answers,' said Scott. He shook his head. 'He was like this when his mother died. Didnae speak for months. You cannae blame him. He was only officially informed that he was no longer a suspect last week.'

'It's a sin, so it is.' Shaw looked crestfallen.

'You cannae bargain for nutters like Jordan. Blamed Jimmy for everything that went wrong in his life. Joined up, made contacts and waited for his chance.'

'Seven years before he got it.'

'True. But what a seven years, eh? Joins the Accelerated Promotion scheme. In no time he's a super. And all the while working away with the lowest of the low from the Met. Poor Eddie was right, God bless him,' said Scott absently.

'University high-flyers, that's what they're after now. We'd never get in if we applied these days.'

'Fuck that. I wouldnae join up these days.' He took a seat behind Daley's large desk in the glass box.

'What would you do?'

'Podcasts. My boy got me intae them. Money for old

rope. These guys are walking away wae a fortune for sitting chatting tae their mates. Nae guns, fights, shite, paperwork. You better believe it, I'd be behind the microphone in jig time.' He stared into space for a moment.

'Penny for them,' said Shaw.

'I was just thinking o' the lassie Unwin. An inspector down there. Twenty-eight years wae a squeaky-clean record. Two years tae go and she decided to take a back-hander.'

'Folk are strange, Brian. We all know that.'

'Huh, so much for her holiday home in Spain now. They reckon she might get as much as eighteen years.'

'What can you say?'

'There but for the grace of God. That's what I can say.'

They drank cups of machine coffee together. Ella arrived with Brian's tie, and it was time to go to Long Road Church for Liz's funeral.

The church was packed. Family from both sides gazed on as young James clung to his father's leg, his head buried in his father's trousers. The residents had come to say goodbye, too. Kinloch was a fine place to be interred, as was often said.

It was unseasonably cold for September. The wind from the sound blew its way past the island, over the loch, and tugged at the hats, ties, jackets and thinning hair of some who came to see the deceased pass into another realm.

Hamish stood beside Scott, waiting for the cords to be called. His attire was sombre, a hunting tartan of dark colours, above neat socks and well-polished shoes.

'They're looking after you at the home, right enough,' said Scott.

'Aye. You want to see the faces every morning when

they come in to give me what passes for tea. Just waiting for me to be doon here, and free up another bed. But it's warm enough. And they let me bring Hamish the cat. He's getting on now, too. No' so keen to be out and about in the cold at night. Brought in a huge rat the other day and handed it to one o' the gaolers, mind you.'

'Gaolers, listen to you. You've never had it so good, Hamish.'

'What about himself?' Hamish nodded over to Daley, his face pale as snow but his back ramrod straight. He was talking to the undertaker.

'He just needs time.'

'Aye, that's what we all need.' Hamish sighed. 'No' a bad wee place to face eternity, right enough. I often think that in my quieter moments.'

'Cold, Hamish, too bloody cold. I hate cemeteries.'

They ended their whispered discourse as, clearly and solemnly, the undertaker began reading the cord numbers, and those designated to lower Liz into the afterlife, including Scott and Hamish, gathered round the slim, black casket.

ACKNOWLEDGEMENTS

I've been writing books for around fourteen years at this point, and every time I stop and think about it, I still marvel at the whole thing.

One constant in all that time has been my lovely wife, Fiona. She's been there for me at every turn, to encourage, support – and yes, dear readers, to tell me to shut up when required. Profound thanks. I love you.

My move to Transworld and Penguin Random House has been nothing less than a joy. My editor Finn Cotton is an absolute rock, willing to go out on a limb to make things I thought impossible work seamlessly. Thank you, my friend. Also, on this book, thanks are due to line editor Tamsin Shelton, who has done such an exacting job so well.

Thanks, too, to the rest of the team – and it is a team. I'm so grateful to Emma, Melissa, Kate, Marianne, Anna, Catherine, and everyone else who has made the process so easy. Nothing is overlooked, and professionalism is taken as read. Fabulous stuff!

To Jo Bell, my dear agent. There's nothing Jo can't improve. She's a listening ear, a tough and effective nego-tiator, efficient, supportive, and a friend. She keeps the Meyrick train on the tracks, a task well beyond Casey Jones, let me tell you. I'm in her debt.

To all my friends and family, who are spread across the globe now. They share my happiest and saddest days. As I write, we've just lost a dear old pal, Margaret Dow, who was one of the very best. That's the thing about getting older: people you thought would be there for ever begin another journey, leaving one sad, empty and bereft. It happens to us all, and it's never easy. God bless you all.

To every bookseller, wherever you are. I owe you all so much. I urge everyone to go to your local bookshop and tap into their knowledge and enthusiasm. You won't regret it.

And lastly, to you, my readers. Without you – well, without you it means nothing. I appreciate and value each and every one of you. More great books to come, I promise.

DAM
Loch Lomond
February 2025

EDITOR'S NOTE

It is with great sadness that we announced the passing of the brilliant novelist Denzil Meyrick in February 2025. I had the honour of being his editor and working with him on four of his most recent books. We spent a lot of time talking over the phone – me in London, him at his house beside Loch Lomond – and we became firm friends.

This novel was the final manuscript that I worked on with Denzil, and as you will have realized by now, a lot of this book is about grief, about dying, and about losing the things and the people we love. Perhaps as he was writing, Denzil knew this would be his last DCI Daley novel – I think he had his suspicions. Re-reading it now with the knowledge that much of it must have been shaped by his declining health is a bittersweet experience, and I hope you have been as moved by it as I have been.

We have decided to honour Denzil's wishes – and the wishes of his widow – by publishing this novel as he intended, with the title and the cover that he wanted to use. We feel that to do otherwise would be a disservice. After all, it's strangely fitting that the final book in the DCI Daley series should be called *Last Orders*, while the first, his debut and the title that launched his writing career, is *Whisky from Small Glasses*.

As much as it pains me to say goodbye to Daley and Scott, two of the great characters in crime fiction, I know Denzil wouldn't want us to be sad. He was proud of his stiff upper lip, which he said came from his family, some of whom hailed from Yorkshire. As he wrote in one of the final emails I ever received from him:

'Now then, lad. Can't have you blubbering all over the place. You're a Yorkshireman, remember. Pull thee sen together.'

Denzil leaves behind a wonderful catalogue of stories to enjoy, places to turn to for solace and comfort in tough times. I know I'll be returning there often.

Finn Cotton
Editorial Director
Transworld Publishers
May 2025

Denzil Meyrick was from Campbeltown on the Kintyre Peninsula in Argyll. After studying politics, he enjoyed a varied career as a police officer, distillery manager, a director of several companies and an executive producer of a major TV adaptation of his books. Regarded as 'One of Scotland's finest writers' (*SWH*), he was the no. 1 best-selling author of the DCI Daley series and the Detective Frank Grasby mysteries, including Waterstones Thriller of the Month pick *Murder at Holly House*.

Denzil died peacefully at his home beside Loch Lomond in Scotland in February 2025. For more information about his books, visit his website: www.denzilmeyrick.com